FAIRY TALE

Sarah J. Pepper, Tish Thawer, M. Clarke, Amy Daws, L.P. Dover, Elizabeth Montgomery, Shannon Morton, Brynn Myers, Wendy Owens, Cameo Renae, Kellie Sheridan, Jessica Sorensen, Kristen Strassel, K.R. Wilburn.

www.amberleafpublishing.com

For inquiries contact: information@amberlfeafpublishing.com

Cover by Emma Michaels
ISBN: 978-0692539224

Sara _____

Tish Thawer

_____

Brynn Myers

_____

Wendy Owens

K. Sheria

Shannon Morton

Amy Daws

Jessica _____

L. P. Dover

M. Clarke

Elizabeth Montgomery
xoxo

_____

FAIRY TALE CONFESSIONS

Fourteen bestselling authors twist up your favorite tales.
Will *yours* have a happily-ever-after?

Get ready to meet some sexy, not-so-valiant princes, punk-rock princesses, villains turned heroes, and truly vile monsters wreaking havoc within our favorite tales.

Read about Dancing Princesses getting their groove on in a disco club, a seriously sexy Rumpelstiltskin, and one alluring Puss-in-Boots, plus many, many more captivating characters in these fourteen all new short-stories.

(This collection and its authors are being featured at RT 2016 at the Fairy Tale Costume Party in Vegas, hosted by
Sarah J. Pepper and Tish Thawer.)

Due to the graphic nature of some content, this collection is recommended for mature readers.

Most dearest reader,

For most of us, our love for the written word began with *Once Upon a Time...* Many associate happily-ever-after with prince charming, glass slippers, and that anticipated kiss at midnight. To be fair—who doesn't love a charismatic lover, fashionable kicks, and staying out late? Whether it's the villainous stepmother or the alluring huntsman, folklore and fantasy have been at the root of our imaginations for centuries.

But like roots of the world tree, fairy tales have grown, twisted, and turned into something that connects us all. From the Brothers Grimm and Hans Christian Andersen's originals, to Disney's ground-breaking remakes, fairy tales hold a special place in our hearts, now and then. But let's face it...in this day and age we're edgier and therefore we need our fairy tales to be, too.

We hope you enjoy our twisted, reimagined, and modern takes on these age-old tales. The stories you'll find within are all new content and range from a romantic ode to the original, to a dark flipped-on-its-head horror story, providing a little something for everyone.

~ Sarah J. Pepper & Tish Thawer

FAIRY TALE

UNCLOAKED
A Reimagining of Little Red Riding Hood
by Wendy Owens

Today is my twenty-second birthday, and I've been dead for exactly twelve months. Technically, Grams calls me reborn, but let's be real, no heartbeat equals dead in most people's books. My best friend from my living days was given a car by her dad on her twenty-first birthday. Mine... nothing nearly as cool. No, my old man abandoned me when I was little, and then, in case that wasn't bad enough, he left me with the hunter's curse.

Reborn? Please.

Being reborn would imply that I have a life, there's nothing about my new existence that resembles any life I've ever imagined wanting to live. While my friends have been spending the last year partying at the Alpha Chi Omega sorority house, or getting their drinks paid for by hunky college guys at the local bars, I've been training. It's not like I had high expectations of college life, even campus slut would have been better that what I got stuck with. Just as campus hottie, Kane Weathers took notice of me, I got the surprise of a lifetime. I found out I'm a hunter. Now getting too close to humans means an uncontrollable thirst to drink them dry. Draining your boyfriend of all his blood isn't the best way to find a lasting relationship.

Day in and day out, it's the same thing. A balanced diet of type A, B negative, or even the occasional treat of RH negative blood. I'm awake by early afternoon, though truth be told, most mornings I have trouble even falling asleep. Until the sun is down, it's studying the history of the hunters with Grams: who we are, who our enemies are, and what makes us the chosen ones. As far as I can tell, all we've been chosen for is a miserable existence.

These so-called wolves we've been supposedly chosen to defend the world against seem to be nothing more than a long forgotten fairytale. I've never seen one except for in the books I'm forced to stare at for hours.

I guess it's not all bad. At least that's what Grams keeps telling me. Hunters can be in the sunlight for limited periods of time. The exposure is like a bitch of a sunburn for us. If you're unfortunate

1

enough to be bitten into the Society of Red Hoods, more commonly known as Vampires, as opposed to joining by birthright, UV rays are an instant ticket to ash city. I think if I were bitten in, I would have already offed myself permanently.

I run my fingers over the worn spine of the book in front of me. "Grams?" I call out to the empty cabin. There's no answer. Some days I don't see her at all. She'll just leave a stack of books for me on the table. Today appears to be one of those days, not that I'm complaining. She can be a bit intense sometimes. We've never been close. I still wonder how I let my mom convince me to head out to the Big Wood and check in on her on my twenty-first birthday. Grams greeted me with a smile that day before locking me in a windowless room. She told me it would all make sense in the morning.

I'm still a little pissed about it all. Hell, I haven't seen mom since, well, since I died. It's not all by choice, though. Grams seems to think the safest place is under her thumb. All that changes today; today I get my first break. I get a small taste of freedom in the form of a visit to my mother. After a year, I've got control over my blood lust, not that mom wouldn't deserve a good bite after conspiring to seclude me out here with Grams.

There's at least one highlight to my day. He's six feet, four inches tall, a jawline that could cut glass, and his name is Flint Huntsman. Not only is he my combat trainer, but he might well be the sexiest creature on the face of the earth. Of course, he's a by the book kind of guy, so there's never any funny business, but it's still fun to watch him work up a sweat.

I jump when I hear a knock at the door. Pulling it open, I mentally prepare my taunts to Grams for forgetting her keys yet again. The door opens, my mouth opens, but the words never leave my throat.

Flint's absinthe green eyes are staring back at me, that same intensity in them he always has and that I'm pretty sure I'll never get used to. There's only quiet between us. If I didn't know Flint so well I would think those eyes were telling me he wanted to kiss me. I know better, even if my eyes are screaming for him to 'take me already.'

Grabbing his arm, I pull him inside, pushing the door closed. I notice the skin on his arms turns white where I just touched him, a red glow surrounding each fingerprint. "Jesus, Flint," I huff before rushing towards the sink. Dampening a cloth with cool water, I ask, "How long were you out there?"

He doesn't answer me. "Where is she?"

"Who?" I inquire, placing the damp towel gently across his skin. "Grams?"

He nods, pulling uncomfortably away from my touch.

I shake my head, shrugging my shoulders. "Hell if I know. She's probably avoiding me."

"Why would she be avoiding you?" Flint has never seemed to grasp the complicated relationship Grams and I have.

"Oh, I don't know, maybe because I'm supposed to leave to see mom tonight."

His tongue clicks against the roof of his mouth. The sound tells me he disapproves of me leaving as well. "She only wants to keep you safe," he reminds me.

I toss the towel into his firm chest, flopping back into the high back dining room chair. "Yeah, everyone seems to know what's best for me, except for me."

"She's been at—" he starts, but his eyes lock onto my glare, stopping him short.

"I don't know where she is," I say again.

"You think you're ready for the smell?" he asks, and though I refuse to look into those piercing eyes, I can still feel them on me.

"I'm not going to eat my mom's throat out if that's what you're worried about," I growl.

"Fear's in the air those mouth breathers suck in day after day. It can be intoxicating for someone like us." He sees I'm only half listening. "I'm serious Ruby. The human world can be just as dangerous as the wolves."

"What wolves?" I quickly snap. "And in case you didn't notice, I'm still human." A truth I've insisted on since I took my last breath. I may have grown an entirely new respiratory system, have no heartbeat, and can smell blood up to a mile away, but I was born a human. I'll continue to identify myself as such until I cease to exist, even if they insist otherwise.

Flint shakes his head as if he's trying to clear away what I just said, "Can we please not get into a debate today? I need to be in control of my senses if you plan to go through with this insanity."

"Not you too," I groan.

With swiftness I almost don't see, he pulls a nearby wooden chair up to where I'm sitting. He's close, so close I can feel the heat from his sunburn. He scoops my hand up into his and pulls it against his chest, then up to his lips. He doesn't kiss it, only lets it hover in front of his lips. "I care about you."

Ugh— talk about mixed messages, this guy is the king of them.

I swallow hard, take a deep breath and with the most bite I can muster, ask, "And?"

His guarded eyes lower, then lift again to meet mine. "I don't know what I would do if something ever happened to you."

Damn it! Do you want me or not?

"I'd never forgive myself. I'm responsible for you," he continues.

And there it is. All duty, no feelings. I pull my hand from him, crossing my arms over my chest. "Well, let me ease your conscious; I'm the only one responsible for me."

"Fair enough," he nearly whispers, but I can tell that's not what he's thinking.

My face is hot, still embarrassed by the inappropriate secret thoughts that have been rushing through my mind about him. I shake a finger in his face. "I hope you don't think for one second that you're coming with me."

"We've already decided this." He stands, obviously panicked.

"You and Grams may have decided that, but I never agreed." I remind him.

"It's not the same as you remember—" he continues.

"It has only been a year, I doubt that much has changed," I snap back.

"I'm not talking about the world; you're the one that's changed."

I want to throw my fists into his chest and beat him wildly. I want to scream at the top of my lungs that I'm not a monster. I'm not going to lose control and kill everyone just because I've become a hunter. I want to scream that I'm not some freak, a bloodsucking vampire rearing to kill everyone, but I don't because… because I know he's right. Most of the time I toss and turn kept awake by the pangs of hunger. I don't tell anyone about it, but I know they know.

"Forget it!" I shout.

"Calm down," he pleads, reaching for me.

I pull away, "Stop! You can tell Grams she got her way, all right? I'm not going."

"Ruby, please." His fingertips graze my skin. A barely there touch, but I feel it to the tips of my toes.

I shake my head, my eyes narrowing, "Don't!"

Before he can attempt another word, I dart into my small bedroom, closing the wooden door, clicking the lock to the right. He's Flint Huntsman, if he wants to get through the door, a silly little lock won't stop him, but I know he won't try. It's not him. It's not who he is. He is who he is and, well, no matter how painful it is to admit, I am who I am. Maybe Grams and Flint are right, perhaps it's time for me to start acting like the hunter I am and forget about my old life.

"Ruby! Hey Ruby, please can you open the door?" Flint's voice cuts through the silent images racing through my mind, the memories of a life that seems so foreign now. My fingers curl into white knuckled fists at Flint's persistent banging on the door. I leap up from the bed with a heavy and irritated sigh, rushing over to give him a piece of my mind.

Ripping open the door with such strength, surprising even myself, I bite my tongue as I narrow my gaze on his face. He stares back at me. My nose wrinkles involuntarily at him when I see the despair in his eyes. This isn't about me being pissed; something else has him concerned. He rubs his hands over his face, his fingers dancing across the stubble on his chin. He looks like he never left last night. Flint is always freshly shaven. Grams would never have…

My thought trails off as I finally find my words. "Where's Grams?" I ask.

He doesn't answer me. I lift an eyebrow, curious what's happened when I see him glance over his shoulder. I follow his eyes across the room, my breath catching in my throat when they settle on two unfamiliar faces. A petite redhead, with pale skin and a smattering of freckles, is standing in front of the door. My eyes travel over her quickly, though, as the other stranger's presence is much more notable.

Her hair is as white as snow, contrasted by her full and bright red lips, but what is most mesmerizing is the subtle hints of flames flickering all around her, like an aura. I move past Flint, unable to look away from the creature in front of me. She watches me just as intensely. Snow White's here to see me, I realize before wondering, why?

My body feels like it's being bathed in ice, and I have to concentrate on just standing. Looking at the woman feels as if in one moment I'm cocooned in the comfort of my mother's womb and the next as if I'm staring death in the face. My training runs through my mind. A hunter is always alert. A hunter is patient. A hunter observes, always searching for the upper hand.

She watches me as a hunter would, and suddenly I understand what it's like to be the prey.

"Who are you?" My voice is shaking, damn it, I hate that. My throat tightens, the angst inside me squeezing the oxygen from my lungs. Sometimes I still forget I don't need that air inside me. While breathing occurs, it's not necessary anymore.

"Are you Ruby?" The red head asks, taking a couple steps forward.

"Who's asking?" I press, annoyed.

"When's the last time you saw your grandmother?" The red haired girl asks, again ignoring my question.

Flint is standing next to me now, but Snow White's eyes don't shift from me.

"I already told you, she left yesterday, and we haven't heard from her since," he offers.

His response doesn't seem to have any impact on the glowing stranger. Her eyes narrow further. I blink long and hard, assuming I must be losing my mind as I see a flicker of red dance around her irises. My skin, no longer icy, suddenly feels hot under the intense scrutiny of her gaze. Her skin is so pale it looks like porcelain. Her jaw is clenched so hard you can almost hear her teeth grinding, but there is no sign of life in her body. Not even a blink or the twitch of a random muscle. Inside my head, I can hear my voice screaming, demanding she stop her burning glare.

My knees are weak, and my legs wobble as if they're turning to ash beneath me. I can't speak or scream. A thumping sounds in my ears, but I know it can't be my heartbeat, I don't have one. Pressure mounts all around my head, crushing pain, pushing inwards. Why won't you look away? A witch! You must be a witch!

I need to make the pain stop. There's no thought in my mind except to make this moment end. I lunge forward my hand raised. Snow White may have chosen to remain silent to my multiple requests for her identity, but she won't be able to ignore me as my hand swipes across her cheek. Will it burn? I wonder just before my hand makes contact with her skin.

My hand jerks back sharply, my wrist aches from the tight fingers wrapped around it. Snow White, she's fast.

"Ruby!" Flint exclaims from behind me. You'd think he wouldn't be surprised after a year of my impetuousness. Apparently that's not the case.

The witch's eyes are still locked on mine as I feel my body thrust backward. Floor. Pain. Ouch. A fog hangs around my head for a moment, before I see a hand in front of me. Following the long and lean limb up to the trunk it's attached to, my eyes lock onto the redhead. Reluctantly, I take her hand and stand.

"You're lucky she's in a good mood." The girl laughs. "I'm sorry, I just assumed you'd understand who she was when you saw her."

"What?" I shake my head in confusion. "What are you talking about?"

The red head with freckles cocks her head; I do my best to focus on her and not at the creature I just failed to attack. "You can see her in her form, can't you?" She seems concerned now.

"What the hell are you saying?" I shout, not shielding my frustration.

Freckles looks to Flint, "I thought you said she was a hunter."

He nods. "She is, but she doesn't understand how the rest of the Fae world works."

"Don't talk about me like I'm not here," I warn.

"Ruby, can you see her glow?" Flint asks, motioning with his brow in Snow White's direction.

"You mean that weird freaky fire around her? Yeah, I'm not blind. What is she? A witch or something?" They all laugh, only serving to make me angry. "What's so funny?"

"I'm the witch," Freckles offers. "My name's Piper."

"She's been training for the past year, but she hasn't ever actually encountered any other Fae." It feels like Flint is apologizing for me. He shouldn't apologize for me, it's just pissing me off.

I step away from him, crossing my arms. "Maybe if you and Grams weren't so damn protective I'd understand what the hell is going on."

"Look, we don't exactly have a lot of time," Snow White speaks at last. Her voice is normal, not that I'm even sure what that means anymore. "Do you have any idea where your Grams is?"

Stay calm. Breathe. Don't get worked up again. Don't let her see you're afraid. "I'm not telling you anything until you explain what this is all about." A bead of sweat gathers on my upper lip. I contemplate wiping it away, but don't want to bring attention to my obvious discomfort.

She turns and sits in the high back chair at the end of the room, positioning her arms behind her head and crossing her ankles as she props them up on the dining table.

"Comfortable?" Flint snarls.

She grins. "Very, thanks." Her eyes move back to me. "Name's Tynder Crown. I'm what the Fae call a Magistrate. I investigate crimes committed against any of the Fae kind."

"Are hunters Fae?" I ask hesitantly, wishing I had asked Grams more questions.

"Ding. Ding. Ding. I think she's putting it together." Tynder says sarcastically.

She's asking about Grams. She investigates crimes against Fae. "Is Grams okay?" I ask, glancing down at my feet, making sure gravity is still doing its job.

"That's why we need your help. Her superior reported that he received a dispatch from her yesterday. Apparently she's seen some suspicious pack behavior in the area."

I shake my head wildly, "No, that can't be right. The wolves are long gone."

Tynder looks at Piper and laughs, "You're new to this hunter game, aren't you."

"They're all dead!" I insist.

"Look, sweetie," Tynder's voice shifts from one filled with humor to one that is pointed. "Try to pay attention, the wolves are far from dead. They're hungry, and they're growing in number. If your Grams is on the trail of the monsters we're looking for, she's most likely already dead. If you can help us, maybe we can prevent a lot more deaths."

My body jerks, and I stiffen upright. Adrenaline. *Do I create adrenaline anymore?* I wonder. I turn towards the door, but as I move my feet forward, I can feel that I'm not moving. I turn and see Flint has me anchored in place with his large beastly hands wrapped around my deceivingly delicate looking wrists.

"Let go," I demand coolly and firmly. "I need to find her."

"What exactly do you plan to do?" Tynder scoffs in my direction.

I pull my arm free of Flint's grasp, then rush up to the wooden table and slam my fists hard onto the surface. Staring directly into Tynder's gaze that is now burning with the intensity of the sun, I reply, "More than you apparently."

She glowers at me, pulling her lips tight. As she moves forward and stands I notice her moves are each measured and calculated, like a cat on the hunt. "No, I'll tell you what you're doing. If there's any chance your Grams is alive, you're going to get her killed."

Anger washes over me. "She's likely already dead, right?"

The fireplace spills a soft and glowing yellow light, similar to that which illuminates Tynder. *What is she? Can I even trust her?*

"We want to help her," Piper interjects.

"Oh yeah? How's that exactly?" I bite.

"Ruby, let them explain," Flint pleads with me.

"We think your Grams is mixed up in something that she doesn't fully understand," Piper continues.

"See all these books?" I snap, shoving a stack of them in Tynder's direction, watching as they scatter haphazardly across the tabletop. "Grams knows more than anyone I've met. I seriously doubt there's anything that would surprise her."

Tynder's tone softens, "These aren't like any wolves she could have ever experienced."

I shake my head, rolling my eyes, "I've been out here for a year, and I've never even seen a trace of a wolf. They're fairytales. There are no wolves."

Tynder moves in closer, "Are you and your Grams close?"

"What?" I gasp, surprised by her question. *Close?* Close probably isn't the right word to explain my relationship with the woman who helped steal my entire existence. It was her son, her genes that handed me this hunter's curse.

"I'm just wondering if things were strained between you two," she adds.

I shrug. "What if they were?"

"I'm just trying to figure out if she even made it out of this house." Tynder growls at me tauntingly.

"Go to hell," I shout. Wishing I could connect my hand with her face, just once, but I've already seen how that turns out.

"I've been there, I don't recommend it," she laughs. "It's rather hot and untidy."

"Tynder," Piper whines in a pleading voice.

"Oh come on, I'm just having a little fun with her," Tynder huffs in response.

I stall, my jaw dropping as I look at her in disbelief. *Cruel. Bitch.* So many words race through my mind to describe her.

"Suck it up, Buttercup," Tynder chides me. "I'm just messing with you."

"I'm glad while my Grams is out there with God knows what, you can still manage to entertain yourself," I snap. My eyes are fixed on her now. I'm no longer afraid, the anger has drowned it away. She shifts and the coolness has seems to fade briefly. For a moment I think I might see a glimmer of empathy. She glides across the room, standing directly next to me. I freeze, my jaw clenches as I see her hand move swiftly towards me. This time, when her hand connects with my skin, I feel a rush of calm, followed by an empty aching inside my chest. It's unlike anything I've ever experienced. An undertow is taking me under, my limbs lose their ability to fight against it, and it's leading me where it wants. Delivering emotions the current wants me to feel. I'm helpless against the force of her touch.

"If she's out there, we'll find her," she says.

"If?" I choke out the word, moving my arm out of reach, trying to regain control of my senses.

"What she means is we're going to find her," Piper interjects. "All we're asking is if you know anything that might help us track where she was headed, please tell us. She was vague in her last report. We thought maybe—"

"Well, sorry," I interrupt, shrugging and waving my hands in the air. "Grams would have never shared anything like that with me. I doubt she would have thought I was ready or that I could even handle that kind of information."

Piper's eyes scan to Flint. "What about you?"

I turn my head sharply, glaring at him. Unsure if he even knows anything to keep secret, I warn him with my eyes to reveal nothing.

He looks at me, then to Piper. "If she was tracking a pack, she sure didn't tell me about it."

"I don't think you understand what you're dealing with here. These aren't your random run of the mill Lycan Wolves. If that pack your Grams was onto were the same ones we've been hunting, her only chance is if we find her and fast," Tynder warns.

"What's so bad about this pack? I mean, a werewolf is a werewolf, right?" Flint inquires as I stand and listen silently, biting my unruly tongue.

Tynder laughs under her breath, rolling her eyes at our naiveté.

"They were made under a Blood Moon," Piper explains.

Flint gasps, shaking his head. "That's impossible, it's against Fae law."

"Since when does a mad man respect Fae law?" Tynder asks in an almost whisper, her arms crossed tightly across her body.

"You've seen proof?" Flint asks doubtingly.

I don't even see her move, then Tynder is standing in front of Flint, her face inches from his. "We've seen them— their victims too."

"She killed the man responsible." Piper boasts proudly.

"What? Who would—" The words slip from Flint's lips before he trails off with his mouth hanging wide open. She enamors him like a child enthralled with a street performer.

I listen for Tynder to answer him, but there's only silence. Turning my head to look in their direction my stomach twists sharply when my eyes lock onto hers. This time there's no mistaking the flickering colors of orange and red in them. Her nostrils flare. Locking my knees tight, I stare back defiantly.

"Don't even think about it," she directs me in a low growl.

"Think about what?" I ask, lifting my shoulders innocently, but I can tell she knows exactly what I'm thinking.

She squints, "The last victim of a blood moon wolf had to be carried away from the crime scene in dozens of zip lock baggies."

"Tynder!" Piper exclaims, before reminding her, "Her Grandmother."

"Exactly," she continues defiantly. "These animals will smell you coming, and if your Grams is still alive, they won't hesitate to end her. So let me do my job, got it?"

"If you're trying to scare me it's not going to work," I lie.

She licks her lips, comes in close to my ear and whispers, "Then you're even more stupid than I thought." She waits for me to react, and when I give her nothing, she moves with that same cool quickness to the front door. Pulling it open, she offers over her shoulder, "Whatever you do, stay out of my way."

Piper glances back at us apologetically as she scurries out the door after Tynder.

I shut the door, securing the lock, and immediately turn, walking to the cabinet on the far wall that sits between the bedroom doors. Pulling open the door, I remove the mother of all knives and strap it to my long, slender thigh using a leather holster.

"What do you think you're doing?" Flint asks, over my shoulder.

"Did you know?" My question is simple.

"The magistrate will find her," he assures me, avoiding my question.

I pause, turn my head, sharpening my focus on him, "She's out there, all alone. She'd never leave one of us out there." I turn back to the cabinet, pulling out the rounds of silver dipped bullets and feed them, one after the next into a clip.

"She would want me to keep you safe."

"Then come with me," I suggest.

"Where?" he asks.

Slamming the full clip into the base of the gun, I ensure the safety is on before tucking the weapon into the waistband of my skinny-fit jeans. My eyes lock onto his. "You tell me."

"How would I know?" I knew from the moment I met Flint he was one of the good guys. Though it was a particular talent of mine to sniff out a liar, he never could tell a decent lie.

I shove a pointed finger firmly into his shoulder, "Because I know the old bat wouldn't have gone anywhere without telling you first."

"That's not true."

"And because your ass has been planted here for the last day waiting for her. You knew she was gone, and the only way you could have known that is if she told you ahead of time."

Flustered, he huffs. "Damn it, Ruby! It's my head she'll have if anything happens to you."

I run my fingers into his thick hair on the back of his head, my mouth moving in close to his. I feel him stiffen underneath my touch and think this is probably the most reaction I've ever seen from him. But no matter how fun they might be, I'm not here to play games. I need answers, and fast. Tightening my grasp on his hair, I tilt his head back with a firm tug and warn, "Just imagine what I'll do to you if something happens to her."

His neck strains showing the corded muscles there, and his face pales. I know he can escape my grasp, but he doesn't. He goes limp, and his eyes tell me he's about to tell me exactly what I want to know.

"Krocker's Bar," he offers finally.

I pull away and look at him incredulously. "What? That dive off Route 42?"

He nods. "She heard about some disappearances over the last week. Something about it wasn't sitting right with her."

"And you let her go out there on her own?"

"She's been at this longer than any of us Ruby, she can handle herself."

"Obviously not." I don't wait for the conversation to continue. I have nothing left to say to Flint and a bar I need to go crash.

I hated Saturdays as a kid. Mom would take on an extra shift at the local bar to help make ends meet. Tips for an attractive female bartender on a weekend night could rival what she worked all week long to make. But just as I could rely on her leaving every Saturday evening for her shift, I could also count on being awakened by a raging argument between my parents when she got home. Mom used to tell me that Dad yelled because he loved her so much. God, I hated Saturdays. Oh yeah, and my dad died on a Saturday. Of course, that was after he bailed on my mom and me.

Luckily, today's Friday. Nothing bad can happen on a Friday. I shiver as I cross the gravel parking lot. Krocker's Bar has had two different owners in the year I've lived with Grams and at least a dozen more in the ten years before that. The interior rarely changes, down to the partially burnt-out neon in the window. Rumor has it, the last change of hands was due to a lost bet.

A cool breeze sweeps across the ground, licking at my ankles before I enter the establishment. If I believed all the ghost stories I've been fed over the past year, I might have taken it as some ominous warning, telling me to turn around and go home. It felt like I just walked over someone's grave, but everyone who knows me knows that despite being a blood sucking vampire, I don't believe in all these paranormal fairytales. Perhaps Tynder is right, and I am an idiot.

I shift my knee-length leather jacket, ensuring my concealed weapons remain that way, then let the door shut behind me. I look towards the bar. What the hell am I looking for? Did I expect to walk in and see Grams sitting there with a disapproving glare staring back at me?

The smell of burnt chicken wings fills my nostrils, and I make a mental note to avoid anything that comes out of the kitchen. Based on the slob in the corner pawing all over the forty-something in the way too short mini skirt, I doubt many of the patrons are here for the food.

I lean across the bar, motioning for the short man dressed in what looks like a women's leisure suit to make his way down to me.

"What can I pour you?" he asks in a low crackly voice.

I pause. *Blend in.* "Vodka with club soda." He stares at me for a moment, then begins to pour the mix. Discretely I pull out a photo of Grams and me from my pocket. As the bartender places the drink on the counter, I flash him the picture. "Have you seen her?"

He furrows his brow, glancing up at me, "I'm looking at her."

I sigh, feigning a smile at his attempt at humor, or perhaps it is just stupidity. "The other one. She's my Grandma; sometimes she gets a little… confused and wanders off."

He tilts his head, examining the image one more time. Pulling his lips tight he shakes his head, "Sorry, can't help you."

I notice the man to my left is staring at me now; I flip the image in his direction, assuming he's been listening. He shakes his head as well. I continue, making my way around the bar, repeating the feeble minded Grandmother story to anyone that will listen. The last thing I need to do is attract unwanted attention.

I catch sight of a young man across the room. Immediately, I notice he's far too handsome to be keeping company with anyone who is a regular in this establishment. Feeling his eyes on me I shift uncomfortable and move my gaze to the ground, hoping it isn't obvious I was staring. From the corner of my eye I see him moving towards me and a stirring occurs deep in the pit of my stomach. He has a slight limp, dragging his left leg ever so slightly behind him. To most, I think, the awkwardness of his gait would go unnoticed.

I should leave. The thought shoots into my mind when I realize he's headed straight for me. *Be strong, stick to the story.* I remind myself that I'm no longer a weak or fragile creature. No matter how many times I make other people call me human, I can't deny one simple fact, I'm a hunter and hunters are far from weak. My body stiffens; I lift my chin upright, locking eyes with the stranger. He's standing in front of me now, no longer moving and I wonder if my face tells the story of the myriad of emotions coursing through me.

Opening my mouth, I'm prepared to deliver the feeble Grandmother speech once again when my eyes catch something surprising. Peeking out from beneath the stranger's shirt cuffs, I spy a glimpse of multiple scars. They aren't the kind that one gets from a weekend's recreational bike accident. There's a story behind those scars, and I'm left wondering what secrets those dark brown eyes might be hiding. His gaze follows where I'm looking, and my face flushes red when I watch him as he uncomfortably yanks on the fabric to conceal his past.

Before I can stammer an apology, I feel the same scrutiny in his gaze. He looks to my fingers, then to my feet, observing me from the base of my body all the way up to my blue eyes. If most men had looked at me the way he just did, I probably would have delivered a swift knee directly to their nether region. But the way he looked at me… examined me… it's like he was trying to figure something out. Perhaps he too is curious as to what I'm hiding. I've wanted to tell someone for the past year. Anyone. *Secrets are dangerous*, I remind myself. Never let yourself be uncloaked.

"I think your Grandmother might have you fooled," he says at last, leaning in close to my ear.

My head jerks, my fists tighten into two balls, one crumpling the photo of Grams. "You better tell me where she is."

He shakes his head, never losing his cool for even a second. "I don't know, but my guess is, wherever she is, she doesn't want you to know."

"Excuse me?" I gasp.

He's watching me. Waiting to see if I'm going to react physically. I loosen my fists. *Stay calm*, I keep reminding myself. He moves in even closer, uncomfortably close, but I don't move an inch. I stay completely still as he lifts my hand and unclasps my fingers to reveal Gram's picture. He takes it between two fingers, lifting it up to examine it, looking back at me, then at the picture once more. "I don't see the resemblance."

"There's more than you could ever imagine," I answer.

"I overheard you asking around about her," he continues. "But the woman I met wasn't feeble minded."

My body involuntarily jerks as I snatch the picture from his hand. "So you've seen her?"

He nods with a half smile; he's enjoying this. "Last night."

I wait for more, but he's not the type to say too much. I can't decide if this is infuriating me or turning me on. "And?"

"She was in here, but not for long," he offers.

"So you're in here a lot?" I probe. *You're not here to find out about him! Find out what he knows about Grams.*

"I stop in occasionally…" he says in a near-growl, slowly licking his lips. "To quench my thirst."

15

Grams! "Did she happen to say where she was going?"

He tilts his head, strokes the five o'clock shadow on his face, as though he's deeply pondering my question. Shrugging his shoulder, he presses his tongue against the roof of his mouth, creating a clicking noise, and adds, "Sorry, I don't remember."

He's hiding something, but what? Why?

His jaw steels. I can see him looking at something over my shoulder. Suddenly I feel a firm grasp on my arm as I'm turned around with a jarring jolt. The room flashes past me until my eyes collide with Flint's stern glare.

"What are you doing here?" I ask in irritated disbelief.

"What am I doing here?" He sounds just as surprised. "Ruby, I told you it's not safe."

I jerk free from his grasp. "I'm fine. Leave me alone."

I move to turn my back on Flint, but he doesn't let me, gripping my shoulders now. "You're not fine. We need to get out of here."

"Hey," the brown-eyed stranger steps into the conversation. "The lady says she's fine."

Flint doesn't hesitate, taking a fistful of the handsome man's shirt he pulls him close. "Walk away," he warns in a harsh tone.

I fight the smirk that's trying to tear across my face, hidden pleasure aching with glee inside of me. The man I've wanted to notice me for a year seems like he might be jealous.

Grams! You're here to find Grams!

Thrusting my arms between the two delicious men I shout, "That's enough!"

Make it convincing. He'll never leave if you're not convincing.

I turn and face Flint, furrowing my brows. "You go home. That's not my home anymore. I never wanted to be there. I never wanted that life. And now that Grams is gone, nobody's going to keep me there."

His expression of shock causes a pang of pain in my gut, but I won't show it. I can't. It's all lies, but this guy, he's not going to let me get close enough to get answers unless I'm alone.

Flint stumbles back a few surprised steps. "You're just upset," he insists. "Let's go back to the cabin, I'm sure we'll hear from Grams soon."

"You're not hearing me," I snap. "I hope she's dead." The lie is the most painful words ever to leave my lips.

"I'll... I—" Flint stammers in incredulity.

"You heard her, now beat it," the handsome man adds from behind me where he's hidden safely.

Flint growls, but I lean in, breaking his concentration, motioning with my head and eyes in the direction of the door.

"You can't mean this stuff," he says, wounded.

I bite my lip, knowing I shouldn't waver in my sternness I compromise "Look, I need a night off, okay? How about you go home and wait to see if Grams shows up?" I don't wait for an answer, turning and placing a palm on the chest of the handsome man, "And how about you buy me another drink?"

We walk back over to the bar, and I can feel Flint's eyes burning a hole into my back.

Just leave damn it. Go home Flint.

The man next to me continues babbling on about things that don't interest me. I should be asking questions about Grams, but all I can do is think about how mean I was to the only friend I have in this world. *Is he standing behind me like a hurt puppy?* The bartender places a fresh drink in front of me, I smile and nod my thanks. The handsome man tells me his name is Brett. I knew a guy in college named Brett. He was a tool. It seems only appropriate it's this guy's namesake.

Is he still there? Watching me, waiting for me to tell him I'm sorry.

I can't take not knowing if he stayed, I have to look. No matter how many times I tell myself not to turn around, I need to see if he's still there.

I spin on the bar stool, expecting to see Flint glowering at me from across the room, but he's not. He's nowhere. He left. He left me here.

Isn't that what you wanted?

I feel sad, relieved and pissed off all at the same time.

I shift back around slowly, my jaw hanging open in disbelief. He left. Brett isn't talking, I suddenly realize. I glance over at him and notice he's staring at me. Oh hell, did he ask something? "I'm sorry, what?"

"Is there something wrong with your drink?" he inquires.

Grams! Don't forget why you're here.

I wrap my hand around the glass and take a big gulp before slamming it down on the bar and staring at Brett defiantly. "So, my grandmother," I continue.

"Who knows, maybe you got lucky, and somebody murdered the old hag," he snickers.

As if by instinct my fingers release the glass in my hand and wrap themselves around his throat. "She's my Grams, only I can say—" My words catch in my throat as my vision blurs. I squint, loosening my grip when I see the veins bulging in Brett's forehead.

"I don't feel right," I mumble, unsure if the words are even understandable, my arms falling to my side.

Motherfu— Brett is grinning a hazy and devious toothy smile at me. *Why are his teeth so big?* The question stumbles through my thoughts.

"Looks like you need a ride home sweetheart," he announces loudly.

"What did you put in my—" the room fades away as I feel his arm wrap around my hips.

Damn it.

And just like that, everything goes silent and dark.

I sit upright, opening my eyes. I'm alone. My hands and feet are free, even though I half expected them to be bound. I'm still dressed, again a surprise based on my last memory. I pat my side pocket. Damn, phone's gone. It couldn't be that easy, could it? I lick the roof of my dry mouth, trying to remember when I last fed. I touch the back of my hand to my forehead; I'm cold … wait, I'm always cold.

I spring into action, taking in my surroundings, just as all the training I've received has taught me. There is a door, heavy, with a small 4-inch window in it that's currently shut. I pull on the handle. It's locked, of course. My eyes dart to the left, there's a fireplace that appears to have been bricked over years ago. The walls are covered in a peeling floral wallpaper. On the far side of the room, I see the curtains and cross over to them hastily, ripping them open, only to reveal that the window has been bricked over as well. I slam my fists against the center to check for stability; they're meant to keep whoever is in here right where they are, supernatural strength or not. My knuckles tingle and I can feel the panic creep in. I stretch out my fingers and shake them wildly. *You've got this. Calm down. You know what to do. Think.* Quickly I search the room for anything I can use as a weapon. A couch, two throw pillows, and a blanket. Nothing else. *Think. Think.* Who the hell is this guy? Grams. He has to know where she is.

Suddenly a pain splits down the middle of my forehead. What the hell? I haven't had a headache since I became a Hunter, now whatever this creep gave me has me waking up with the mother of all headaches.

The small window inside the door opens. I turn cautiously, staring into the eyes looking back at me. Dark hazelnut, there's no mistaking who they belong to.

"Brett," I groan.

"Good morning, beautiful," he says. "I've got a treat for you."

Oh, have I got a treat for you too, you piece of—I glare at him, backing up slowly.

"If you could just sit down, I can unlock the door," he adds.

"I'm all the way over here," I protest.

"And like any other Hunter, it would only take you a few seconds to make your way to the door."

Pfft. As if me sitting would slow me down. I'm unable to hide my smirk as I slide down the wall. *Lucky for you, I need answers first.*

I listen as the key slides into the lock and clicks, the tumblers falling into place. As he said, any good Hunter has a set of skills, and one of those is lock pick. You'll never know when that craft will come in handy. I'm suddenly glad Gram insisted I continue to practice.

He moves into the room with a tray and secures the door behind him. He doesn't seem to be working with anyone on the immediate other side of the door. Either he's alone, or his accomplices are in another part of the building.

He places the tray on the couch and motions me over. "I know what you want, but I just can't have you regaining your strength, so I'm afraid a strong cup of coffee will have to do."

"What I want?" I innocently ask as I stand and make my way to the arm of the couch.

"Blood," he answers coolly.

He knows exactly what I am. "Who are you?" I ask.

"We'll get to that," he answers, then his voice twists. It's now full of hate and his brows narrow as he commands me, "Now sit, drink, it's rude not to partake of something your host offers you."

"So you can drug me like you did at the bar? No thanks."

"Fine," he snaps, standing and leaving the tray with the single mug where it sits. "I'll leave it with you then. Drink or don't, it makes no difference to me." This guy seems to have more personalities than I have pairs of underwear.

"Maybe I'll just get what I need to drink from you," I suggest.

He laughs mockingly and looks back at me. "Oh please, try." He offers me his neck. Normally, this would be the part where I cross the room, using my super-speed skills and sink my teeth into his throat, but my lack of feeding has left me far too weak for such theatrics.

I stand and glide casually to him. "Don't tempt me." He doesn't move as I close in on his location.

"Go ahead, I won't stop you." He taunts me, the corners of his mouth curling into a smile.

This is far too easy. It has to be a trap. Why would he— "Of course. You're a Lycan."

He tilts his head upright, "You are quick, just like your Grams said."

I bite my lip, resisting the urge to snap his neck. I might need him to find her, and I'm in no condition to take on a werewolf. *Damn it! How did I miss he's a wolf?* Because he doesn't act like most wolves, that's why. I run through the list of things that indicate what a wolf 'looks like' in my mind…

1.) Unibrow. Apparently the longer a man has been a werewolf, the closer the brows grow together. I look closer at him. No, not even a hint of poor grooming. Perhaps he's newly bitten, or maybe I happened upon one of the Lycans into manscaping. *Jesus.* I can't believe this is my life now.

2.) It's a well-known fact that any person who has a ring finger longer than their middle finger is likely a werewolf. That happens as a result of the first shifting.

I run my fingers across his chest flirtatiously, unsure if he will buy the routine. He allows my digits to dance their way down to his hand. I run my fingers over the tips of his. *Bingo!*

3.) Aggressive behavior. Hmm … he did get into it with Flint at the bar, but he backed down. It's my first encounter with an actual wolf, I wouldn't call myself an expert, but they never back away from a fight. Unless maybe— perhaps their objective was bigger than a bar fight. *Me.* I was his objective.

4.) Excessive body hair. I saw the scars, no telling what else he's hiding under that suit.

5.) A heightened sense of smell and hearing. He did say he heard me telling someone at the bar about Grams, but I don't remember seeing him before that first time. *Could he hear me from across the room?* Of course he could, filthy Lycan.

"Your mood shifted quickly," he notes.

I tilt my head, still running my fingertips along the flesh of his hand. He doesn't stop me. "Any friend of Grams is a friend of mine."

He laughs, "Oh, I never said we were friends."

I feel a knot in my stomach. It tightens as it shifts up my throat. "Oh no?" *Control yourself. Don't let him see he's rattling you.*

"No, in fact, I was sent here to kill the two of you," he states casually.

I stumble back a couple steps, looking into his eyes for a glint of humor; there's nothing but coolness in them. "Kill us?"

He nods as if the information he's just imparted to me is nothing more than the simplicities of a grocery list. "Yeah, but—" he hesitates.

Hesitation is a weakness.

"But what?" My tone is soft and sweet, my eyes are wide. I can even lie well with my face.

He swallows hard, "When I saw you in the woods I knew I had to see more."

"Saw me in the woods?" I ask. I need more information.

"I've been following you for almost a month now," he admits with a lopsided grin.

"Why?" The question slips out before I can think about it.

"Because my master told me you were the last of your kind, and you were a danger to us."

"Last of my kind?" I whisper to myself, confused.

"Oh yeah, and trust me, you were not easy to find."

That's why Grams has always been so psycho about me not going out alone. "I bet." I bite at my tongue for the uncontrolled sarcasm.

"But then I saw you, and I knew I had to get to know you."

"Is that why you approached me at the bar? Do you know where Grams is?"

He places a hand on his chest and feigns an expression of discomfort, "I'm deeply disappointed that you think I would make such a shallow attempt at getting to know you. Oh no Ruby, I know everything about you. I know that you like to take baths that are nearly boiling because you miss the heat on your skin. I know that you like to drink your nightly blood rations in a wine glass because you want to pretend you're not a monster."

I can tell he has more to share, but I need him to stop. "How?"

"I've been living alongside you for this past month. Looking through the window of your bathroom. Outside the wall of your bedroom. I can smell you in whatever room you're in, I've even crept into your bedroom to read your journals."

"You what?"

He looks confused, "I knew you'd want me to know everything about you."

He's flipping crazy!

"But that, of course, was how your grandmother caught my scent. I shouldn't have gotten greedy. I should have known she would smell me."

"Where is she?" I ask again.

"Don't worry, she won't be keeping us apart anymore." I want to read hope into his statement. I want to think that he has her locked up somewhere. He'll let her out if I beg him, but I know the truth. Not only is he a Lycan, he's also mad. Pure crazy-town.

Grams is dead.

Think. Think. You have to get out of here.

"When's the last time you kissed someone?" I ask boldly. He can't be this stupid.

"What?"

"You know, sucked face, made-out, frenched, tongue wrestled. Perhaps had a bit of snogging?"

He flushes red. *Wow, he's stupid.* Of course, sex or anything resembling getting to sex always makes people stupid. Especially crazy irrational people who think they're in love.

"I don't know, why?" his voice cracks. There's that weakness again.

"Because I want to kiss you for finally ridding me of the old bat."

He closes his eyes and presses out a set of pouty lips. *Jesus.* It would be so easy right now to kick his ass, but I can't take the risk. It's been at least 24-hours since I last fed. I need to feed if I'm going to have any chance of killing him. I can't feed on him; Lycan blood is toxic to Vampires.

I swallow the sour bile that has risen in my throat and taken up residence inside my mouth from the site of his pouted lips. He'll want to save you, I think. Men always want to save the damsel. Leaning in I let my lips just barely graze his, then fake a fainting spell, falling to the floor with a thud.

He's on his knees next to me in a moment, scooping me up into his arms. I keep my eyes closed. Three more seconds. Don't open your eyes yet. You have to make him worry. One. Two. Three.

"Ruby!" He gasps. The sound of his genuine concern alarms me, like he's certifiably a psychopath. I don't respond. He shakes me gently. "Are you okay? Damn it. Damn it. Damn it," he mutters under his breath.

I gasp for air I don't even need, and then wilt away into a helpless and fragile heap, coughing as I repeatedly wince in pain.

"What's wrong?" he asks.

"I haven't eaten in days," I moan. "But I'll be okay as long as I'm with you." I don't open my eyes. I'm afraid if I do he'll see the truth. I know I'm good, but not sure if I'm this good.

"Isn't that dangerous?"

"I'm sure I'll be fine, can you just help me to the couch?" The entire time his hands are on me I have to fight the urge to rip his throat out.

He carries me to the worn and weathered sofa, securing a blanket around me. His caring and sensitivity might have scored points with me if I didn't know he was a murderer.

"Wait here," he commands tenderly.

Minutes pass. I hear scuffling in the hall. The door opens, and a terrified young woman who appears to be injured by the amount of blood on her, enters the room, followed by my handsome monster. Then the door shuts.

What the hell is this? He better not even think I'm up for a threesome. *Creep!*

He's pleased with himself. It's obvious from his expression that this moment is bringing him close to ecstasy. I understand now. My darling creeper has just brought me dinner.

"Can you see it?" he asks me. "Her whole world crumbling. Can you hear her lungs heaving, burning with panic? She wants to run, but there's nowhere to go. She's unsure, but pretty certain being here means she's going to die."

"Please," the woman pleads, falling to her knees, bits of spit spraying out from her bloodied lips.

"Why the blindfold?" I ask.

His dark, cold glare tells me the answer before his words, "It's all part of the game. The dark is a scary thing for most."

My mind runs through the kaleidoscope of options I have at this moment. I need strength. I need him to trust me. I need to eat. I lick my lips, my eyes fixated on the offering crying in front of me. "Do you mind if I eat alone?"

23

His eyes fix themselves on me, studying me, a glaze of mistrust clouding his pupils. There's a moment of stillness. *You're losing him.* "I don't want you to think of me differently," I add.

I look at my captor. He's still watching me, and I'm unsure, but it appears the mistrust may be fading. He motions for me to move in closer. *Make him trust you.* I glide over to his side, doing my best to shield my face from revealing the loathing and disgust in my gut. He ignores the weeping blindfolded woman, now cowering in the fetal position on the floor and instead wraps an arm around my waist and pulls me in against his body. He's aroused. "Don't you see, I love you because of the monster inside, not despite it."

I feel the air shift around me, and then his breath on my neck. *Grams. He took Grams from you. If he knows how much you loathe him, he'll take your life from you too.* I remind myself. Leaning into his grasp, I close my eyes, touching my lips to his, slowly and gently, counting in my head the seconds that pass. Not too quick or he'll know. Not too slow or he'll know. I feel him shake beneath me. *Perfect.* I pull back and open my eyes slowly.

"I've never been with anyone so romantic," I choke out.

"You deserve it," he breaths. I can feel the acid of hate churning in my stomach.

I swallow hard and look away bashfully.

"What's wrong?" he asks.

So easily manipulated.

"Nothing," I whisper.

"Please, tell me," he begs. The whimpering of the wounded women starts to fade as she has found something to occupy her thoughts.

"It's just—" I shift my eyes around anxiously. "I haven't eaten in so long. I'm afraid I might—never mind." I shake my head and blink heavily.

"No, please tell me," he grips my wrists and tries to get me to look into his eyes.

"I'm afraid I might get sick, you know— throw up or something. It's important to me that you don't see me like that."

"You're stubborn," he says firmly, before tracing the lines of my cheek with his fingertips. "And so beautiful."

Without another word, he turns and leaves the room. I wait and listen for the click of the lock. But there's nothing. I smile. *Last mistake you'll ever make asshole.*

The facts of the situation haven't changed. I'm still far too weak to fight him in hand-to-hand combat. I need to eat. My eyes move to the whimpering creature on the floor. But unlike what I led him to believe, I won't get sick. I'll only get stronger. I'm on my knees, running my hand across the woman's oily hair. She convulses, pulling away from me until her back is against the wall.

"Please, no," she whimpers.

"Don't worry," I whisper. "We're going to get you out of here."

"What?" And there, in her voice, as she speaks to the darkness, I hear a hint of hope.

Hope, what a silly human emotion. There's survival, and then there's darkness. The grayness in between disappeared with my heartbeat. "I just need to eat first," I tell her. She'll understand. Eventually.

A motionless body lies on the floor across from me. I feel a slight and vague sense of remorse over what I've done, but nothing significant. Not like the first time I fed on a human. Perhaps this is normal. I can expect to lose a little more of my humanity each and every time I sink my teeth into the soft and supple flesh of a human. *Aren't you still human?* I stare at the body. *Aren't you still human?* I ask myself again, more unsure of the answer than ever before.

I miss the nagging phone calls from my mother. Was I keeping up with my laundry? Because you know, you never want to be in an accident while wearing dirty underwear. I laugh softly to myself, wiping at a drop of dried blood that settled in the corner of my mouth. She always worried about the most insane things.

I miss the way I used to agonize over that latte because of the calories. I miss that mindless joy I got from shopping trips with my friends. I bite my lip to remind myself that though I am dead, I still exist. *No, you're not human. You haven't been human for a long time.*

My thoughts shift to Flint. *Will I see him again? Does he know how I feel about him? Does he know I couldn't have made it through this past year without him?* He has this ability to tap into my brain, and hone in with great precision on how I'm feeling.

I look at my arms where earlier the flesh had been littered with random slashes and bandages on my wrists from my struggle during the abduction. The feeding is already doing its work. Only small pale white veining remains as a reminder.

"You'll heal quickly now," Grams had explained to me when my transformation into Hunter first happened.

Grams. I spent so much time hating her and blaming her for what I'd become, I didn't realize how much I needed her. And now… now I may never get the chance to tell her that. There's so much more she'll never have the chance to teach me. *Damn it!* I hate Brett. I'm going to kill him.

"What are you?" A voice cracks from the corner. The woman is stirring. Her hand slips to the puncture wounds on her neck.

"Today, I'm your savior," I answer, standing up and dusting the dirt from my bottom. Her eyes widen, fear dancing in them. "Do you want to live?"

She hesitates, then nods.

"Lay completely still, play dead."

"What?" She gasps.

I cross the room, place a hand on the door handle. "If you want to live do as I say. Whatever you hear outside of this room, don't move."

I don't wait for her to respond. She has no idea how lucky she is that I stopped feeding on her before I consumed her life as well. If she listens to me, she might have a chance. If she doesn't, her blood will be on her hands, not mine.

The door is still unlocked, I pause, surprised by the trust Brett has so easily given over to me. *Does he trust you? Maybe it's a trap.* As I walk cautiously down the long and narrow hallway, I unwrap a bandage from my wrist. I assume it's the remnants of a deeper wound from the abduction. Brett wouldn't have bandaged me if he really just wanted me dead, would he? It can't be an act. He doesn't strike me as that clever.

The cut that was once on my arm has healed significantly, just as all the other scrapes have. I move into another room, a main room of the house. There's another fireplace, but this one has small flames flickering from within it. A couch and chairs are positioned in front, I lean forward onto my toes to ensure the seats are empty. Behind the couch is a desk, littered with papers and debris. The edges of the room are covered in trash and show the disrepair of the building, but this small concentrated area appears to be used regularly. My eyes dart around the space.

The far end of the room opens up into what appears to be the entryway. Just beyond that is a large wooden door. An exit. A way out of my captivity. *It has to be locked*, I think. But what if it's not? I need a plan. Clenching my fists and stretching my muscles outright, I roll my head in a circular motion. Listening to the popping sound of my bones I take stock of my condition. I can feel the feeding coursing through me, waking the beast inside, suffocating the weakness that was starting to emerge.

Can you take him on? Are you strong enough? Maybe you should get Flint and return.

I move towards the door, pausing next to the desk, my eyes catching a glimpse of a bright red piece of fabric from inside a black sack that's been tossed among the items on the weathered surface. Instinctively my hand glides to the familiar color. My fingers wrap around it, pulling it slowly from the hiding place. I swallow a vile and putrid regurgitation of blood climbing my throat. It's a hooded cape from our clan. I bite my lip as I flip the hood back, knowing full well what to expect. Stitched in the lining are Grams initials, just as mine are stitched into my cloak back at the cabin.

"I thought you'd like to have it," Brett's cool voice announces from behind me.

I'm starting to shake. Everything that has been hovering just below the surface begins to rise inside of me. A desperate desire to relieve his body of his head is overwhelming me.

I've got this.

I turn to face him, holding Grams' hood in my hands. His eyes settle on me, then he quickly looks back down the hall.

"I saw what was left of your dinner. Feeling better?" He's smiling like an eager dog, wanting praise from his owner for offering them a dead bird. I force a smile, there are so many other things I want to say, but I want to rip out his throat more than I want to unload the sarcastic snippets racing through my mind.

"Much, thank you," I answer.

"I wish you would have let me watch," he growls.

"What?" I ask.

"Mmm… To hold life in your hands, wrapping your fingers around the heart as it takes its last few beats—" he begins, clearly excited. "Nobody else can understand that feeling of euphoria, you know?"

He thinks I killed her. He thinks I'm like him. He has no idea I'm about to kill him. He's nuts.

"Where's Grams?" I ask, unsure if he'll lead me to a corpse, a shallow grave, or worse. Pain and loss are shredding their way through my insides, but I hide the daunting grief with a tight-lipped grin.

His nose is sharp, just like his jawline. His jaw tenses, his eyes squint causing his black lashes to twitch in front of his dark eyes. "She doesn't matter anymore. She can't control you now."

He thinks he knows me. He knows nothing.

I force a smile, and swaying my hips from side to side I move with as much swagger as I can muster, gliding up to him. I am no longer thinking of running out that door to Flint for his help. No. Brett's mine. He's right about one thing, I was excited about holding a life in the palm of my hands… his.

Eagerly, he places a hand around my waist, pulling me close, pressing the evidence of his desire for me against my thigh. I twist my body, our hips grinding against one another. He smells of the outdoors and wild animal. He buries his face in my neck, kissing it repeatedly, while his fingers entangle in my hair, "I knew when I was watching you all those nights that we would have this connection."

I let him snuggle against me, whispering his sweet nothings, building that trust while looking forward to ripping it away from him soon enough.

I need to know. I have to know if she's dead or if she's wasting away in a cell somewhere.

I untangle myself from his grasp, pulling a fistful of his hair in return. He looks shocked at first, then grins before lunging forward and sealing his lips around mine. A groan of ecstasy slips from his mouth, and I can feel how eager he is. Tugging on his hair sharply, I pull him into a submissive position while making certain it still feels playful.

"I want to see her body," I say.

He bites his lip, a twinkle in his eye, and I think he might explode in anticipation in front of me.

"You're more twisted than I thought," he starts. "I knew we were a match made in heaven."

"I need to see her body before I can move past this—before we can have some fun."

He laughs.

"What?"

He shakes his head, "It's just funny how well I know you."
I can't wait to kill him.
"What do you mean by that?" I ask.
"I had a feeling you might want the final blow."
She's alive. Thank God, she's alive. "She's alive?" I gasp, his eyes reveal there was too much hope in my voice. I lace my arm around his back and hug him close, leaning in and nibbling on the tip of his ear. I growl, "You do know me, don't you."

He kisses me again, his mouth tastes of death and I wonder if the most recent kill on his breath is animal. From the lingering hints of iron, I recognize the distinct flavor of human. When our lips part, I see foam has gathered around the corners of his mouth. His excitement has worked him into a frenzy, and I can see glimpses of the beast lurking within him.

"Will you take me to her?" I ask.
"In time," he grins deviously. "I have other plans first."
I shake my head, I can handle a little touching, the occasional kiss, but I'm not sure how much longer I can pretend. How much longer I can stop myself from ripping his heart from his chest.

"I hope she didn't give you too much of a challenge."
At that he laughs, "No offense, but I don't understand why my master is so worried about your kind." He looks disbelievingly in my direction.

A knot forms in my stomach, an invisible hand gripping my throat, tightening with every breath he took. I need to kill him. I need to end him in a way like I've never felt. I feel like at this moment I'm strong enough to rip his head clean off of his smug shoulders with my bare hands.

"I know, seems silly to me." Better he thinks we're weak. "So what did you do with her?"

He looks at me, his eyes widening, "She's in the belly of the beast."

I shake my head. "What?"

He grins. "She's locked in the cellar. Between the cocktail I injected her with and lack of feedings, she's a mess." He's laughing. No. Cackling. I take a step back from him. He doesn't seem to notice, his head is tilted towards the ceiling, as he's still delighting in his cunningness.

The time's come. This nightmare needs to end.

I glance around the room. No silver. Without silver, beheading is the only way.

I'm smiling now. This is going to be fun.

Suddenly he falls quiet, he's staring at me, and it's at this moment that I realize it's impossible to know truly what a psychopath is thinking. His eyes tell me he wants to cut me open and surround himself with the warmth of my blood and body parts, while the bulge in his pants tells me he wants to ravish me in a completely different way.

Whomp. A thudding crash pounds down the door behind us. We're both frozen where we stand as we watch.

I spin around and see Flint, standing in the doorway. There's a golden light from the porch that's framing his body, and damn does he look good. He has on a pair of dark denim jeans that hug him perfectly in every place I always admire. He's wearing a gray V-neck T-shirt, with a black leather jacket, and for a moment I feel like the floor might fall away from under me.

Brett! I have a job, a mission.

"Ruby, are you okay?" Flint asks. Behind him, in walks Tynder and the witch, Piper. At Tynder's side is a long silver sword. I close my eyes. I can't let her take this from me. He's mine.

"No. Stop!" I shout, raising my hands up waving them wildly.

I feel an arm across my chest, pulling me back. "Get behind me, darling."

Even now he thinks I'm his.

My eyes dart to Flint, the confusion reflecting in his stare causes a pang in my chest. "Ruby?" This time his voice is almost a whisper. I disappear behind Brett. "Let her go," Flint adds in a more demanding voice.

Brett laughs, "I'm not keeping her idiot. She loves me."

I say nothing, none of this can be easily explained. I don't need to explain, I need vengeance. All that matters now is ending Brett and freeing Grams. I tighten my fists into two balls.

I am not a paper doll. I am not fragile. I don't need to be rescued. *Damn it, Flint, I just wanted you to want me, not to try and be my knight.*

"Your master's already dead." I hear Tynder shout from across the room.

Brett's eyes shift to me anxiously, then back to Tynder. "You're lying!"

Piper steps forward, shaking her head. "She's not lying. All of the Blood Moon wolves are being hunted down, but if you surrender now, maybe we can—"

"You can what? Work out a deal where I live out my days in a cage!" Brett shouts.

Flint's eyes are still fixed on me. *Stop staring at me, damn it.*

Slit his throat? With what? Will my hand be able to rip through his chest? I'm stronger than humans, but Lycans have a harder than average skeletal structure. What about a bash to the head? Could I knock him unconscious? Then I could steal that sword from Tynder and—

"How about we calmly talk about the options?" Piper asks in a squeaky voice.

Brett glances back at me. I wonder if he can see the plotting in my eyes. I doubt it based on his gaze. He looks back to the three visitors, "How about I kill you all and we be done with this?"

A grinding and clicking noise begins to grow from deep within the bastard I was just contemplating on how best to kill. My jaw drops as I watch motionless. He outstretches his arms, his back arches, the vertebrae spiking upward out of his flesh and his head pops. His jaw gruesomely dislocates, tearing and distorting into a large, long muzzle. His knees unhinge, clicking into a position that makes no sense for a human. It's as if his bones simply dissolved, falling apart, and something completely new and terrifying sprouted up in their place. His razor sharp claws emerge from where his hands were, and now paws exist. As his massive form takes its bone-crunching shape, I watch his now ill-fitting clothes fall away to reveal the thick, coarse hair that is now covering what used to be bare skin.

I've seen the Lycans in books, but none of it could have prepared me for seeing it in person. I can hear Tynder and Flint shouting something, but it's muffled in my ears. Brett lets out an ear-bursting shout, and where the psychopath who loves me once stood, there is now a predator. He turns to me; the small dark pools have disappeared, replaced by narrowed and viscous animal eyes. Much to my surprise, I still see the desire reflecting in them. Brett's still in there. The man I need to kill is there.

His head snaps, he's glaring at the intruders, ready to pounce and tear them limb from limb.

Tynder moves forward, lifts the sword and shouts, "Stay behind me, in his current form only this silver can penetrate his flesh."

He pats his foot along the old and dusty wooden floor. I've waited too long, I think. I've missed my opportunity. He leans in low, his teeth bared.

I don't think, I only react. Leaping onto the beast's back, I wrap my legs around his ribs and squeeze as firmly as I can. He stumbles, falling onto his side and with both hands I grip his chin, pulling up with a blood ravenous scream, "Now!" Tynder crosses the room swiftly, and with a quick sweep, slides the silver blade across the wolf's throat. A dark warm bath of red washes over me as the body beneath me falls limp.

Shoving the corpse aside, I look up at Tynder and motion towards the sword. Without a word she hands me the blade and I free the animal the rest of the way from its head. Kicking it swiftly in the chin, I send it across the room.

"Love's a bitch!" I snarl, spitting on the body at my feet.

"Ruby, are you okay?" Flint asks.

I'm coated in blood, it can easily be assumed I'm in the most disgusting state I've ever been. I look up into his eyes and there, reflecting in them is a truth I've never been able to see before. My heartache. He wants to be my knight, not because he thinks I'm weak, but because he loves me, even if he doesn't realize it yet. He's hovering just above my lips, I close my eyes, thinking he might kiss me. But he doesn't. Of course not.

"I will be as soon as we free Grams," I answer at last, opening my eyes again.

His eyes widen as he asks in disbelief, "She's alive?"

I nod and smile. "She's in the cellar."

"How about you two go and set her free while we clean up the mess?" Piper suggests.

"Um, yeah, I'm not touching that," Tynder snarls pointing at the bloody corpse.

Flint and I laugh at the disgusted look on Tynder's face, then turn towards the hall.

"Wait," I hear Tynder's voice behind me. "That was smart work."

"What was?" I ask.

"Gaining his trust like you did," she explains. "We should talk more. I could use someone like you on my team."

I turn to continue towards the cellar, careful not to reveal her comment has flattered me. Right now, at this moment I just want to reconnect my dysfunctional and completely perfect family. We can talk about killing wolves later.

Release Grams first.

Flint's fingers grasp my shoulder as he pulls me to a stop.

"What is it? Do you see how to get to the cellar?" I ask, eyes wide.

He shakes his head as he loosens his grip, concern creasing his brow.

"What's wrong?" I ask, clutching his arm.

"Ruby, I thought—" he starts, while grazing my skin with his thumb. The tenderness is new. I like it.

I smile and nod. "I'm fine." I can see his concern wrinkling his nose. His eyes move to my neck, then up to my chin, and linger on my lips. I part them, waiting with fullness and longing, but as quickly as his gaze settled on my pout, it darted away and bonded to the floor.

"Flint," I whisper. His chin slowly lifts as he bends towards me. I've waited long enough, I think. Pressing upward onto my toes, my mouth brushes his. His lips are soft at first and as they touch mine it's like a tender caress. The kiss is sweet, and nothing like I'd imagined it over the past year.

Just as I'm about to relent and slip away from him, he pulls me back with a possessive grasp that sends a chill up my spine. The kiss changes to something deep now, his fingers entangling into my hair, gripping me firmly as he explores me. His lips leave my mouth, but not my body, burning a trail down my neck and resting in the crease on my shoulder.

He disconnects, the desire still burning in his eyes. I steady myself against him and grin. Maybe being immortal isn't going to be as bad as I'd thought.

The End

Wendy Owens was born in the small college town, Oxford Ohio. After attending Miami University, Wendy went onto a career in the visual arts. After several years of creating and selling her own artwork she gave her first love, writing, a try. She has released the YA fantasy series, The Sacred Guardians. She also has a NA Romance series, The Stubborn Love Series.

When she's not writing, this dog lover can be found spending time with her tech geek husband, their three amazing kids, and two pups. She loves to cook and is a film fanatic.

*If you enjoyed this fairytale retelling, be sure to check out more fae inspired tales in the serial series, The Tynder Crown Chronicles, by Wendy Owens. To learn more, visit: http://wendyowens.com/

BLAYZE & ASH
A retelling of Beauty & The Beast
by Jessica Sorensen

I've always thought my name was odd, but I'm kind of a strange girl. It's Friday night and while most of my friends are hanging out at parties, I'm chilling with my dad, reminiscing about my mom and how I got my beautifully strange name.

"It's why we named you Blayze, because we knew you were going to blaze through the world like a wildfire and do great things." A faraway look crosses his expression as he stares at the flames hissing in the fireplace. "Your mother wanted to name you Wildfire, but thankfully, I talked her out of it."

I'm not sure if I agree with him. Sometimes kids at my school make fun of me because of it. I wouldn't change it for the world, though.

I hug my legs to my chest. "Why'd you guys give me the middle name Beauty?"

My father tears his attention away from the fire. "Because the name's so fitting. You truly are a beautiful girl, Blayze." He smiles, but pain floods his eyes. "That you get from your mother."

It's been over four months since my mother died of cancer, and my chest still constricts whenever she's mentioned. It's hard to think that I only had eighteen years with her, but I'm grateful that I got them.

"What's wrong?" my father asks, noting my sullen expression.

I shake my head, suck back the approaching tears, and force a smile, not wanting to burden him with my problems. "Nothing. I'm just tired."

"You haven't been sleeping well?"

"It's finals week at school."

He nods distractedly and stares at the fire again.

My dad used to be a healthy looking man, but lately, he's been paler, lost weight, and permanent bags reside under his eyes. I know something's been troubling him, but every time I ask about it, he just tells me not to worry.

He abruptly rises to his feet. "I'm going to go to my study and get some work done. If you need anything at all, please come talk to me

1

Blayze. And don't stay up too late studying. I love that you love to get good grades, but I don't like you wearing yourself out so much." When I nod, he hurries for the door. "Oh, and if your sister shows up, tell her I want to talk to her."

"All right, I will," I reply, even though it won't do any good to pass along the message to my older sister.

Ivy never listens to anything anyone says and throws a fit whenever she doesn't get her way. The only person she kind of listened to was my mom and occasionally Max, my older brother. But he's traveling around the world right now. With his absence and my mom's death, Ivy's inability to follow the rules has gotten even worse.

I spend the next half an hour watching the fire fizzle out, allowing myself a few moments to cry in the privacy of the living room. Then I collect myself and head for my room.

Right as I'm crossing through the foyer, the double front doors swing open and in Ivy strolls.

She's only a year older than me, but we look like total opposites. Ivy is short, blond, and curvaceous while I'm tall with long, wavy brown hair, and a body type that some call modelesque. Me, I think of it more as gangly.

"Oh my God, I had the worst night ever," she whines, dropping handfuls of shopping bags onto the floor.

All the bags have designer logos on them and probably contain jewelry, shoes, or clothing. Ivy loves pricey... Well, everything. Thankfully, my father is one of the wealthiest men in the city.

"Is everything all right?" I ask her as she kicks the door shut.

"No, Blayze, everything isn't all right." She dramatically huffs as she shucks off her jacket. "You know I've been wanting to go out on a date with Leo Brallmin, right?"

I nod, sinking down on the bottom step of the marble stairway, knowing this conversation has the potential to carry on for a freakin' long ass time. Any conversation about Leo Brallmin usually does. Leo's dad, Lyle, is *the* wealthiest man in the city—maybe even in the country—which makes him the target of Ivy's dire need to marry a rich man. My dad actually works for Lyle, too, and it's how Ivy met Leo.

"He totally blew me off." She kicks one of the bags and shakes her head. "We were supposed to go to his dad's club tonight, but he didn't show up and left me standing in line all by myself. When I finally made it to the front, the bouncer wouldn't let me in. It was so humiliating."

"I'm sorry you had a bad night," I say as she sulks toward the sitting room and flops into a sofa, melodramatically draping her arm over her head.

"A bad night? Blayze, this was more than just a bad night. I was humiliated. Do you even know how that feels?" Without giving me a chance to respond, she snaps her fingers at me, beckoning me to come to her.

Sighing, I push from the stairs and take a seat in the sofa across from her. For the next hour, I listen to her go on and on about how Leo is a jerk. When she finally pauses, waiting for me to say something, I've almost dozed off.

I clear my throat and try to console her. "I'm sorry he was so rude to you, but maybe this finally means you can be free."

Her brows knit. "Free?"

"Yeah, you know, from this crush you've had on Leo." I kick my bare feet up onto the coffee table. "I mean, you've had a crush on him for practically forever. Maybe it's time to move onto someone who'll treat you better."

She gapes at me like I've suddenly sprouted a unicorn horn between my eyes. "I'm not just going to dump Leo because he ditched me one night." She continues to stare at me like I'm some sort of foreign creature she doesn't understand. "Do you know how wealthy his family is?"

"Money isn't everything. There are plenty of happy people who don't have everything."

"You're so naïve sometimes. I could never be poor *and* happy."

"You don't have to be poor, but don't you want to be with someone you love and who loves you?"

"We're not living in a fairytale, Blayze. Love's not going to make you happy."

I feel so sorry for her at that moment. "Mom and Dad were happy even back when they were poor."

"If you really believe that then you're more naïve than I thought." She gets to her feet, smoothing the wrinkles out of her green fitted dress. "If they were so happy then why'd Dad end up taking his job, huh?" When I don't respond, she grins. "He's not a saint and you know it. He does bad things for a lot of money—he pretty much sold his soul for wealth."

I don't agree with her. While my dad may do some questionable things for work, it doesn't mean I believe he's a bad person. Leo

Brallmin's father on the other hand… that dude is seriously scary. I've heard so many rumors about what he does to people who piss him off; burning off their skin, cutting off their tongues, just to name a few.

But instead of arguing with Ivy, I pass along his message to her. "Dad wants to talk to you. He's up in his office."

She just laughs. "I'm sure he does."

After the depressing conversation with my sister, I go up to my room, crank up some music, and lounge in my bed. Music has always helped me relax and even though I don't possess any musical talent, I hope to one day pursue a career in music by opening up my own vintage record store. I spend a lot of time now, browsing around at the local shop, working on my collection. I'm even taking a few business classes come fall, when I officially start college. My dad and Max love the idea, but Ivy thinks it's silly. She keeps telling me it's a pointless dream to chase and that I should just find someone rich to marry, like she's been trying to do. Ever since she graduated a year ago, she's done nothing but chase Leo around, waiting for a ring to be put on her finger. Unlike me, her whole world centers on guys. I've been out on a total of two dates, one of which my friends set me up on and the other was with a son of one of my dad's business acquaintances. Both were a disaster. Despite the fact that the guys were attracted to me, something they both told me toward the end of the date, they just didn't click with me, which is basically code for I'm too much of a weirdo.

How do I know this?

Because it's the story of my life.

So beautiful, I've been called, many, many times.

But so different, has always echoed the compliment.

Different, because I don't love designer clothes, fixate on my looks, spend all my time trying to impress guys. So nice, so polite, so caring and compassionate. Like those are bad things. They're not. At least, my mom always said so. She used to tell me all the time that it was better to have a big heart and compassion to share with the world than to have beauty and wealth to share with yourself. That one day I was going to find a guy to share my big heart with, that I'd come to love him so much I'd do anything for him, even when he challenges me and pisses me off. That I'd love him so wholly, I'd love him more than myself.

The kind of love my parents had.

Something, I got to see every day back when she was alive.

Bang! Bang! Bang!

"What the hell was that!" I bolt upright in my bed, my pulse soaring. Holy shit, was that a gun shot? No, there's no way—

Bang! Bang! Bang!

Right as I jump to my feet, my bedroom door swings open.

My dad barges into my room, red faced, sweat beading his skin, and his fingers are wrapped around the silver handle of a gun. "We need to go. Now."

I round the bed toward him. "Dad, what's going on?"

He's breathing so heavily I'm worried he's going to pass out. "I messed up," he says, pushing me out the door.

"Messed up how?" I ask as we rush for the stairway.

Without looking at me, he utters, "I'm so sorry, Blayze, for ruining everything."

His words feel so ominous. I can feel it, in the pit of my stomach, that nothing will be the same again. It's the same feeling I got when my mom told me she had stage four cancer.

Seconds later, I realize my feeling is correct. Because at the bottom of the stairway, lying in a pool of blood, is Lyle Brallmin.

***

The next few weeks rush by in a stream of chaos as we travel out of the country to a small town in Scotland that I'm now supposed to call my home.

Turns out, my dad's extra stress was stemming from the fact that he was going to testify against Lyle Brallmin to help the police put him behind bars. My father, Ivy, and myself were supposed to be going into witness protection because more than likely Lyle Brallmin would have a hit put on him. It wasn't supposed to happen for a little while, though, but apparently Lyle found out what my dad was up to. He was planning to kill my dad when he confronted him that night, but my dad killed him instead. The police still put us in witness protection because they worry the people that work with Lyle will come after him. Thankfully, Max is everywhere and anywhere, constantly on the move, so he's safe from all the chaos.

For the most part, I've been handling the change okay. I mean, it's difficult getting used to my new last name and the thousand square foot cottage we now call home. But I'd honestly be okay with the cramped living quarters if I didn't have to listen to Ivy cry and complain twenty-four-seven.

"God, this place smells," she gripes every morning at breakfast. "I miss our old house and my old bedroom and my old clothes." Tears spring from her eyes and stream down into her cheeks into her oatmeal. "I should've gone to college. Then I wouldn't be stuck living in this shithole."

After almost three weeks of crying, I'm starting to grow a bit concerned for her. She didn't even cry this much after my mom died.

"Hey, Ivy." I put my bowl in the sink. "I'm going to walk around town. You know, get some fresh air and check out all the sights. I was wondering if you wanted to come with me."

"What sights? There's nothing here but crappy a little house and a stupid store that sells secondhand clothes. Second hand!" She begins to cry even harder. "How am I supposed to wear clothes someone else has already worn? And getting stuff shipped out here is practically impossible without paying a fortune, and since Dad can't get ahold of most of his money, we can't afford it!"

"Maybe there's more stores than what we saw driving in," I say, trying to entice her to go with me. "It wouldn't hurt to look, right?"

She gapes at me like I'm a raving lunatic. "How can you be so happy about all of this? Our lives are ruined, Blayze. No more money, no more designer, no more Leo Brallmin."

No more house that carries memories of my mom, I think to myself.

Tears pool in my eyes, but I suck them back. "Things'll get better."

"No, they won't." She pushes back from the table. "But I'll go to town with you. Anything's better than staying here with *Dad*."

She says Dad's name so venomously. She's been hard on our dad about what happened and tells him every day how much she blames him. I hate that she's treating him so poorly. Yes, it's because of my dad that our world got turned upside down, but he was trying to do a good thing by testifying. It just kind of backfired on him.

I say goodbye to Dad, who's been spending a ton of time online looking for a new job in town.

"Be careful," he warns, looking exhausted, pallid, and way too thin. "And keep your phone on you at all times."

Nodding, I slip on my leather jacket, bulky black boots and wave goodbye. Then I head on foot to town with Ivy. She managed to bring a few pairs of glittery four-inch stilettos with her when we took off to

Scotland. She's wearing a pair now, along with a tight dress and a fur coat. Back in the city, she fit right in, but here, she stands out like a disco ball in a Goth club.

"God dammit, my heel keeps getting caught in the cobblestone," she complains as we wander up and down the streets lined with shops, cafes, and ancient looking churches and museums.

"I don't even see any clothing stores around." Ivy wiggles her heel free. "Face it, Blayze, from now on our lives are over…" She trails off, her gaze drifting toward the corner of the street. A grin curls at her lips. "Okay, I take that back. Maybe this place isn't so bad."

I track her gaze and find her staring at a tall, lean guy, with hair as black as ink and golden eyes as fierce as the sun, staring in the window of a store. He shoves up the sleeves of his jacket, seeming deeply engrossed in whatever's inside the store. I hate to admit it, because it makes me feel so shallow, but I think he just might be the most gorgeous guy I've ever seen.

"I wonder where he buys his clothes," Ivy mutters from beside me. "They look designer. Oh! I bet he's rich!"

I don't really know how she can tell, since all he's wearing is a jacket, a pair of dark blue jeans, and boots.

As I'm standing there, openly gawking at him, he turns his head and looks at me. His gaze sweeps me up and down, making me feel exposed. When our gazes meet again, his lips quirk to a cocky smile then he turns away and steps inside the store.

Ivy snatches my hand and strides down the sidewalk with determination burning in her eyes.

"Where are we going?" I ask as I stumble behind her.

"I'm going to ask him where he shops." She stops in front of the store and adjusts her boobs before marching inside.

Sighing, I trudge after her.

My mood instantly lifts as I take in the music posters and memorabilia on the walls and the rows and rows of records lining the aisles.

"It's a record store!" I exclaim loudly.

A few customers and the cashier stare at me with confusion, but I hardly notice because I'm in a record store again!

"See, this is why you never go on second dates," Ivy hisses from under her breath.

I shrug her off and hum along with the song playing from the store stereo as I wander toward the aisles.

"It smells gross in here," Ivy remarks. "Like old, smelly stuff."

"Well, records are old," I tell her as I begin flipping through Section L.

"Whatever. I just need to find that sexy eye candy so I can ask him where to shop and slip him my number. Then I'm so going home." She pauses, glancing around the store. "Wait? Where'd he go?"

I shrug. "How would I know?"

"Um, because you were totally staring at him. Seriously, Blayze, I think a little bit of drool came out of your mouth."

I pretend not hear her and focus on Section O. She heads off to God knows where to do God knows what after that. I spend my time scrolling through the selections and even chat it up for a bit with the cashier guy named Zeke, who yeah, seems a little obsessed with tarot cards and smells like he rolled around in an array of spices, but who's really sweet and has a genuine smile.

By the time Ivy returns, I've made it all the way to Section V and have at least ten records in my hand. I can't afford to buy them but at the back of the store are listening stations, and I plan on camping out there until either the store closes or the owner kicks me out.

"Hey, when you head back, can you tell Dad that I'm here and that I might be a little late? I'll text him but you know how he is about checking his messages," I say to Ivy as I flip through more records. "And tell him I'll bring dinner with me too. I don't want him trying to cook again. I love the man to death, but seriously, do you know how much effort it took for him to burn that soup and sandwiches he tried to make the other day."

I hear someone chuckle from beside me, a chuckle that's way too deep and masculine to belong to Ivy. I glance up and to my horror, it's not Ivy, but the guy I was gawking at earlier.

"As much as I'd love to pass along the message, I'm not sure I'd be the best person for the job," he says with a trace of an accent. "Considering I have no idea who you are, who your father is, or where you live."

"Sorry, I thought you were someone else." My cheeks warm with embarrassment.

"I figured as much." Then he just stares at me, as if waiting for something.

"Did you need something?" I ask after the silence turns awkward.

"Yeah, for you to move," he says.

I step back. "Sorry."

"It's fine." He moves forward and begins sifting through the section of records I was just searching through.

I stare at him for a drumbeat or two longer, wondering what his deal is, before I drift across the aisle to Section E. I find two albums from one of my favorite bands and add them to my ever-growing stack.

"I heard they're good." The guy with fierce gold eyes startles me as he steps up beside me.

"Yeah, they're pretty good." I fix my attention on Section I when his hand appears in my line of vision.

"I'm Ashford, by the way."

I shake his hand, even though the dude is confusing the crap out of me. One minute he's as chilly as leftover ash in a fire pit and now he's trying to act warm like a soft lull of fire.

"It's nice to meet you, Ashford. I'm Blayze."

"Blayze?" He ponders the name for a moment. "Are you new to town?"

"Yeah, my family just moved here a few weeks ago from the States." I bite down on my tongue. *Shit.* That was way too much information.

"How do you like it here so far?" he asks, seeming pretty uninterested in where I'm from.

"It's not too bad. A little colder and cloudier than what I'm used to, but I'm not really a sunny, beach sort of girl."

He eyes me over. "Yeah, you don't really look like it."

"My sister is, though. She really misses our old home."

His brow arches. "Is your sister that blonde girl you walked in with early?"

I nod, my gaze skimming the store. "Yeah, she wandered off a bit ago… looking for you actually."

"Really?" He seems smug about this.

I resist an eye roll. "Don't get too excited. She just wants to ask where you bought your clothes."

"Everywhere and anywhere," he says with a hint of arrogance. "I honestly couldn't tell her where, since I don't shop for myself."

"Who does it for you, then? Your parents?" It seems odd considering he looks at least as old as me.

A cocky half-grin tugs at his lips. "No, my servants do."

"You have servants… How old are you?"

"Eighteen. But I'm an overachiever." His arrogance grows. "I owned my first business when I was fifteen. By the time I was seventeen, I bought my first house. You probably know the one. It's up on the hill at the end of town."

I do know the house. Ivy's been yammering about it ever since we got here. Very castle-esque. Very fancy. Very big.

"Do you live there all alone?" I ask, tucking a strand of my hair behind my ear.

"Of course. Well, except for my countless servants. But they're under strict orders to not be seen or heard."

"You never see your servants and you live there all alone... Doesn't that get a little lonely in such a big house?"

He gives me the same look Ivy does whenever she thinks I'm being naïve. "I'm not alone. I have parties all the time." He shoots me a charming grin as he crosses his arms. "In fact, I'm having one the weekend from next. You should come."

I offer him a forced smile. "Thanks, but I'm not really a party type of girl."

"Are you sure? It'll be a great party. I only invite those that are rich and beautiful. I promise." He nods in the direction of the front counter. "No guys like Zeke will be there." When I don't remark, he adds, "I saw him bothering you early."

"He wasn't bothering me. We were actually having a really nice conversation about bands I need to see live."

He looks at me like I'm the silliest girl in the world. "Guys that look like Zeke are always bothering anyone when they speak to them. You just might be too nice to admit that."

W.O.W. This guy could give my sister a run for her vanity title. "I'm not just being nice. Zeke is a nice guy, at least he was to me, and I'm planning on talking to him again and maybe even spending time with him."

"So, you're saying that you'd rather hang out with Zeke than go to my party?" A mixture of amusement and bafflement dances in his eyes.

"Yes, that's exactly what I'm saying." I back towards the stations. "You should ask my sister to go, though. She loves parties, and she hasn't been to one since we moved here. Plus, she seems more like your type." I wave bye at him, hating that I feel so flustered over our conversation. "It was nice meeting you, Ashford." I turn around and jog up the steps to the station area.

After I get settled in a booth, I close the glass door, put the headphones on and place the record on the player. A symphony of music floods my eardrums and lulls me into a state of calm as I relax back in the comfy chair. I tap my feet to the rhythm and thrum my fingers against my legs as I sing along with the lyrics. The longer I listen to music, the more relaxed I get as thoughts of Ashford and his arrogance drift away. I shut my eyes. Get lost. Float away to another life where I used to spend time with my mother, doing the exact same thing.

Like me, my mother loved music. She had some talent though, could sing and play the guitar. The first time I ever went to a record store, I was with her.

God, I miss her so much.

A few stray tears escape my eyes. With no one around, I allow more to pour out.

I'm unsure how long I would've remained in that booth crying if someone didn't touch my ankle.

Startled by the unexpected touch, my eyelids snap open. The door to the booth is open and Ashford is sitting near my feet with a quizzical look on his face.

His lips move to say something, but I can't tell what he's saying. I hesitate for a moment or two, debating whether to take off the headphones and listen to him.

My inner kindness wins and I slip off the headphones. "I'm sorry, but I couldn't hear you. What did you say?"

He momentarily stares at my tears before elevating his gaze to mine. "I wanted to tell you that I invited Zeke to my party."

"Okay…"

He adds, "So, now you have to come."

"I already told you that I'm not really the partying type."

"But I invited Zeke for you."

"You invited Zeke to your party just so I'd come?"

"Obviously." He says it like I shouldn't have known that to begin with it. "So, you'll come, right?"

I really don't want to go, but I don't want to just reject his invitation. "I'll come, just as long as my father says it's okay."

"All right, I guess I can accept that answer," he says, sounding the slightest bit irked.

A tiny bit of anger simmers under my skin. "And what if I would've said no?"

"Then I wouldn't have accepted the answer," he replies simply as he rises to his feet. "The party is on Saturday, the eighth, at nine. It's the biggest house in town that will be filled with the most beautiful people, so you can't miss it."

He throws me another, what I'm sure he thinks is a bedazzling, panty dropping smirk, before he saunters away.

I return to my music until Ivy pulls me out of the booth, looking more excited than she's been in weeks. "You'll never believe what just happened?"

"A super hot guy named Ashford asked you to go to his party," I say as I return the records to the correct sections.

"Who the hell's Ashford?"

"That guy with the nice clothes. The main reason you dragged me into the store."

It registers who I'm talking about, and she quickly waves me off. "He's so old news, Blayze. I met someone much better than him."

"Really?" It's really hard to buy considering Ashford seems like Ivy's type.

"Yes, really. I met his father who's like ten times richer than him."

"*What?* His *father?*"

"Yes, his father." She rolls his eyes. "Aldman was outside of the store when I wandered out, pulling up in a limo, actually, looking for his son… that Ashford guy that you were gawking at early in the street. He rolled down his window. Told me I was hot. One thing led to another and well, he asked me to fly to Paris with him this weekend."

"Dad's never going to let you go."

She places her hands on her hips and narrows her eyes at me. "I'm almost nineteen years old. Dad can't tell me what to do."

"He just wants you to be safe, Ivy. So do I."

"I'll be safe with Aldman. He's a grown man for God's sake."

"How old is he even? Like forty?"

"I don't care how old he is. The only number that's important to me is how much he has in his bank account." She flips her hair off her shoulder, reels around, and marches for the door.

I know where she's going. Back home to tell our dad she's going. In the end, she'll get her way and use this Aldman guy for his money. I just wish she could see things for how they really were for once, or see how wrong she is.

Until she does, she'll never be happy.

Like I predicted, Ivy spends the weekend in Paris with Aldman. When Monday rolls around, Ivy returns home with bags full of clothes and shoes and gushing about what a wonderful time she had and all the stuff Aldman bought for her.

Tuesday morning, I leave the house and go for a walk, needing some fresh, Ivy gushing free air. No surprise my legs take me directly to the record store, excited to see if they got anything new in over the weekend.

"We usually only get new stuff in once a month, but if you give me your number, I can text you when we do," Zeke tells me when I ask him.

I ask him for his number and text him mine. "Thanks. I really appreciate this."

"No problem." He fiddles with his eyebrow piercing while chewing on his lip ring, appearing as though he wants to say more.

Zeke is a unique looking person with hair as blue as the ocean, tattoos inking his arms, hands, and neck. Metal piercings cover his face along with a massive, thick scar that traces his jawline. Some people in the store seem afraid of him, but I think he's beautiful to look at, like a painting full of so many various colors and intricate details and shapes that somehow fit together perfectly.

"Hey, you wanna see something really cool," he finally says to me.

"Sure."

He looks as giddy as me listening to a new record as he steps out from behind the counter and motions me to follow him to one of the booths.

"Is it okay that you're back here?" I ask, casting a worried glance at the few people wandering in the store.

"Yeah, people tend to spend hours browsing before they buy." He takes my hand in his.

"I totally get that." I stare down at our interlaced fingers, wondering what he's doing.

"I'm going to read you your fortune," he explains, like he read my mind.

"You know how to do that?"

"I'm the best in town. Well, besides my mom."

I grin. "All right, let's hear what you got."

"Let me see." He muses something over as he studies the lines on my hand. "You'll live a long, healthy, rich life."

"Really?" I sound mildly disappointed.

"Yeah, but rich doesn't necessarily mean wealthy. It could mean that you live a life rich with happiness and love where you marry the love of your life and have a happily ever after."

"Aw, it sounds like I'm going to live a sappy romantic movie."

"You could, but… It's not going to be easy, though. You'll have to make sacrifices, ones that'll change you, but if you can see the bigger picture, then it'll be worth it. If you make the sacrifice, then you'll blaze through the world like a wildfire and do great things."

My heart stops in my chest and shock laces my tone. "My dad says the same thing. He told me that's why I was named Blayze."

Zeke looks up at me with a huge smile on my face. "See, I told you I was one of the best in town."

I smile, but on the inside I'm creeped out. I've never really believed in palm reading, tarot cards, psychics, witches, and stuff kissed with magic, but the fact that he said the exact same words my father said to me on the night we had to move sends a chill up my spine.

"Creepy cool, right?" Zeke asks.

"Definitely creepy cool, Zeke."

"Good, I'll take that as another satisfied customer." He frowns when he notes Ashford, standing in one of the aisles, sorting through records. "I really wish he didn't come in here every day."

"He comes in here every day? Really?"

"Yep. For the last two years, pretty much since his mom died. She actually died here. Had a heart attack near section S."

I feel a ping of sympathy for Ashford. Even if he's a little arrogant, I know first hand how difficult it is to lose your mom.

Zeke sighs, turning his attention back to me. "I hate hating people but the guy's a total jerk. Although, he did invite me to one of his infamous parties. I don't get why, though. He's never invited me before."

"I think that might've had something to do with me," I say. "Sorry, but I told him I didn't like parties and for some reason he thought I'd go to his if he invited you… I don't get why he wants me to go so badly. He doesn't even know me."

"Probably because you're gorgeous," he says with a shrug.

My cheeks warm at the compliment. "But still, he doesn't even know me."

"That doesn't matter to guys like Ashford. All he sees is looks. Which is why he's never invited me to a party before. Or half the town for that matter."

"Zeke, you're not ugly. In fact, I think you're really beautiful."

He stares at me with astonishment but then shakes his head. "You're a little odd, Blayze, but in the best way possible." His gaze darts to the register. "Shit, I got go take care of this dude."

He leaves me in the booth alone with the door wide open.

The noise from in the store drifts inside, and I pick up a record sitting beside the player, turn it over, and read the list of songs on the back. My gaze travels to the booth across from mine when Ashford steps inside it and shuts the door. He doesn't seem to notice me watching him as he loads the record player with a record, slips on the headphones, and sits back with his legs stretched out across the booth.

His lips move and his fingers tap to the rhythm as pain and sadness radiates from his eyes. I can't help but think of what Zeke told me about his mom and how he comes here every day. I suddenly find myself leaving my booth and knocking on his.

His gaze lifts from the record sleeve he's holding, and a haughty smile spreads across his face. He leans forward and pulls open the door. "I was wondering when you were going to stop admiring the view from afar."

"I actually wasn't admiring from afar. I just noticed you look kind of sad and wanted to see if you were okay."

His grin falters for a fleeting second, but he promptly collects himself. "Of course I'm okay. I have the perfect life."

"That might be true, but sometimes people just say that because they don't want anyone knowing what's really going on. Like my dad. He's always telling me he's okay, but with everything going on, I know that can't be true. And he looks worn out and forgets half the stuff he's supposed to do…" I trail off, realizing I'm rambling.

Ashford seems mildly amused as he reclines back and tucks his hands behind his head. "You know, last week, you seemed so offish toward me that I actually started to question myself. At first, I wonder if maybe you were blind and couldn't see how gorgeous of a guy you were talking to, but then I thought maybe I'd lost my charm. I'm not going to lie, I lost a little bit of sleep over the idea. But now I get it."

My brows dip. "Get what?"

"That I make you nervous."

I shoot him a dirty look. "You so do not."

His stupid smirk takes over his entire face. "Just admit it. I make you nervous because you've probably never had a guy as hot as me hit on you. I'm not saying you're ugly or anything—you're beautiful—but you've got that slightly shy, quirky, oblivious to your looks way about you that probably scares a lot of guys off. Lucky for you, I don't scare easily."

"Lucky for me? Yeah, I'm so lucky that the cocky, arrogant asshole isn't too scared to talk to the quirky, shy girl." I start to leave, fuming mad, but swing back around. "And FYI, I came over here to see if you were okay because I heard about your mom. You looked sad, and I know how hard it is to lose your mom. So, I hope you're okay." I walk away, waving bye to Zeke, before I push out the doors.

"Blayze, wait up!"

"You have got to be kidding me," I mutter under my breath, but stop at the corner and turn around.

Ashford jogs up to me, a little out of breath. When he reaches me, he doesn't say anything, simply staring at me with those crazy intense eyes of his.

I'm about to leave when he sputters, "I'm sorry." He massages the back of his neck, seeming baffled. "Huh, I've never said that to anyone before… It's definitely… interesting."

I zip up my jacket. "Well, you should definitely try it more often. It can be very therapeutic, and I hear if you say it enough, it can turn you into a nicer person."

His lips quirk. "I'll give it some thought."

"Thank you for apologizing." I start to walk away, but he catches my arm.

I glance over my shoulder at him, frowning at his hand on my arm, even though the touch makes my stomach go all butterfly crazy.

He slips his hand down my arm and threads his fingers through mine. "Come have a cup of coffee with me."

I should tell him no, but I catch the slightest glimpse of vulnerability in his eyes and find myself wanting to have a cup of coffee with him, if only to hear his story. "Only if you say please."

He presses his lips together. "Please, Blayze, will you have a cup of coffee with me."

"Okay, Ashford, I'll have a cup of coffee with you."

"Call me Ash… *please.*" The corners of his lips teaser upward as we start up the sidewalk, holding hands. "You know I've never said please before, either," he says, strengthening his grip on my hand as I try to pull away.

"I'm not really that surprised," I tell him as we stop in front of a quaint café.

He opens the door and steps aside for me to walk in first.

Slightly shocked by his gentlemanly manners, I step inside.

"Quit looking at me like that," he says. "I might be a cocky asshole, but my mom taught me to always be a gentleman, even if the girl is being mean to you."

"I'm not being mean."

"You're being challenging."

"No, I'm just being real."

He misses a beat.

I take a moment to assess the choices of coffee on the marque. "Your mom sounds like a nice, caring person, though."

"She is... Was..." He grows silent beside me.

When I look at him, I find him watching me in puzzlement.

"Why are you looking at me like that?" I ask.

"You're just so... different from most of the people I've met. Usually people are so fake and agree with everything I say..." He shrugs, facing the cashier as she asks him what she can get him. "It's kind of refreshing yet frustrating at the same time."

"It can be *just* refreshing if you let it."

He tries not to smile but as he orders his cappuccino, he's practically grinning from ear to ear. For some silly reason, it makes me smile too.

After I order my drink, he pays for them despite my protests, then we take a seat at the corner table near the window.

"You said you moved from the States?" he says, fiddling with the sugar tray. "Why did you decided to move here of all places?"

Nodding, I stare out the window.

"Okay, we don't have to talk about it if you don't want to," he says.

I look at him. "It's not that I don't want to. I just can't."

He moves on. "So, you're obsessed with music." It's not a question. Just a simple statement.

"Yeah. I mean, I can't sing or play anything, but I find music comforting, you know. Like it turns everything off. All that worry and pain and whatever's bothering you and it's just you and a song, helping you get through whatever you need to feel."

"I've never really thought about it that way, but I can see your point."

"Are you a big music fan?"

He lifts a shoulder, giving a half shrug. "I guess you could say that. Although, if you ask anyone else, they'd probably tell you I have an unhealthy obsession with the record store. You've heard my story, though, so I'm guessing you've probably heard that I spend every day there."

"I *heard* a story about you." I fold my arms on top of the table. "But it doesn't mean it *is* your story. Anyone can say anything about anyone. It doesn't mean it's true. The only stories I truly believe are the one's that I've heard from the people who've actually lived them."

"You're the most fascinating person I know, Blayze," he says, sounding genuine.

"Thanks. I think I'll take that as a compliment."

"Do, please. I rarely hand out any kind of compliments, so when I do, it's always genuine."

"You should try it more often. People might be less fake around you if you did."

He leans back in his chair as the waitress brings us our drinks. "I'll give it some thought."

I move my arms so she can set down my cup. "You should try genuinely smiling too. It might make you come off as less of a cocky asshole."

"I'll try, but no promises." He dumps sugar into his coffee and stirs. "You want to hear my story, I'm guessing."

I gather the mug in my hand and take a sip. "Only if you want to share it with me... After my mom died, people tried to force me to talk about her death because they thought it'd make me feel better. But whenever I tried, they'd always tell me something like 'I'm so sorry you're going through this' or 'it'll get easier' and it never made me feel better. In fact, it made me feel worse because it never got easier... But it's not really their fault. I mean, half of them had never lost someone so close to them."

"How long ago did she die? If you don't mind me asking, that is."

"Almost five months ago."

"I'm not sure if this is going to make you feel better or not, but those people are kind of right. It does kind of get easier, day by day you'll start to not think about her death so much. Does it get easier not to miss her? Probably not. But it does get easier to deal with getting through the day, not feeling like you're going to lose it every second of every hour."

I set my mug down. "Is that how it was for you?"

He nods and adds some creamer to his coffee. "I was with her when she had the heart attack in the store. I held her hand while the ambulance was coming… she died before they got there."

Oh my God, he saw her die! How awful. "I'm so sorry, Ash. That had to be hard, just losing her so suddenly."

He wavers to say anything, as if he's afraid to open up to me. "Death is death. Losing anyone in any way is always hard." He stares inside his mug. "How'd your mom die?"

"Cancer. By the time they found it, it was so bad she only lived for a few more months and those months were really hard, watching her fade away like that… by the time she died, she was in so much pain, just a skeleton of herself…" I swallow hard as a lump wells in my throat. "My dad took it really hard. I think a part of him faded away with her."

"That's sad, but I guess it's kind of a good thing too."

"How do you figure?"

He meets my gaze. "My father didn't even come to my mom's funeral. They weren't divorced yet, but I found out he'd been seeing a young woman and was planning to divorce my mom. When I confronted him about it, he told me I shouldn't be surprised. That my mom was well beyond her prime and he should've divorced her years ago, before she started to age."

"You dad sounds like an asshole," I say, then add, "Sorry."

He shrugs me off. "No, you don't need to be sorry. He's an asshole, and everyone knows it. Even him."

I scrunch up my nose. "I think he might be dating my sister right now."

"Yeah, sorry about that."

"Hey, that's two sorry's in a day. See, you're already getting the hang of it."

He rolls his eyes but grins. "Don't get used to it. I'm sure by tomorrow I'll return to my asshole ways."

I wonder if tomorrow we'll even speak to each other. If we'll have as good of a conversation as we just had. It felt so nice to talk about my mom without worrying about stressing out my father.

We spend the next hour talking about lighter things. I find out he goes to the record store because he actually does like music. He even plays the guitar and the piano.

"I can teach you how to play sometime," he offers as he walks me up the hillside toward my home.

"I might just take you up on that offer." I stare up at the stars. "Although, I should warn you that my mom tried to teach me how to play the piano once and she got so frustrated with how musically incompetent I am that she had to leave the room and have a mini meltdown."

"At least she left the room instead of yelling at you like my father would've done." He takes my hand. "Besides, with my talent, you're sure to succeed."

"You know talent isn't contagious, right?"

"Of course, but with as beautiful as a you are, you must have some hidden talent."

I sigh. He has some misconstrued logic. "You know, just because someone is beautiful, doesn't make them perfect. Everyone has flaws. It's what makes us human—what makes us real."

"Perhaps." He doesn't sound too convinced.

I sigh again as I catch him eyeballing my tiny, rundown house with disgust. I wait for him to say something about it, but he remains quiet.

"Thanks for walking me home." I start to slip my fingers from his, but he tightens his hold.

"If I were to kiss you now, how would you react?"

"Well, considering I never kiss on a first date—if that's even what this is—then I'm guessing I'd probably reject you. Normally, I'd feel bad about doing it and maybe let you steal a pity cheek kiss, but I'm guessing your ego can't take the ding."

"You're very blunt."

"Funny, since you called me shy only hours ago."

"Yeah, I know I did." He stares at my mouth momentarily with his lips pressed together. For a moment, I think he's going to try to kiss me anyway. But then he steps back and releases my hand. Surprisingly, I'm disappointed.

"I'll see you at the store tomorrow?" he asks then leaves without waiting for my response.

What a strange, strange day, full of unexpected events. It makes me wonder what's going to happen tomorrow.

I spend the rest of the week cooking and cleaning while my dad buries himself in his new job as a craftsman. My sister is beyond gone in Lavish Land, spending every waking hour with Aldman who showers her with gifts.

When I'm at the record store, I hang out a lot with Zeke, getting tarot cards read and listening to stories of his family, his past, particularly high school. He was teased a lot by Ash and his friends and part of me wants to stay away from Ash because of it. But I believe that sometimes people deserve a second chance.

So, when I'm not chilling with Zeke, I spend time sorting through records with Ash, and getting to know him.

I learn in front of Section B, that when his mom died he cried for three days straight, then never cried again.

"My father caught me and chewed me out for being so weak," he explains. "Please don't ever tell anyone I cried."

"Your secret's safe with me." I nudge him in the shoulder. "And thanks for saying please."

He actually laughs at that, and it makes me happy for some crazy reason.

It's in front of Section E that I discover he does in fact get lonely in his big house.

"I'll admit," he says, like I'm pulling teeth. "That sometimes I wish I had someone there to share the space with."

"You could always get a dog," I tease. "Or a cat. You kind of seem like a cat person."

He narrows his eyes at me. "Only if it's a badass and flashy cat like a tiger."

I roll my eyes at him, but laugh when he playfully pinches my side.

I laugh a lot when I'm with him and realize that I haven't laughed very much since my mom died.

"I really miss her," I admit one day in front of Section A. "I even cry sometimes, but only when I'm not around my dad; otherwise he'll fall apart."

"Is that why you were crying in the booth that day?" he asks, wandering toward Section U with his hands stuffed in the pockets of his jeans.

I nod, trailing after him. "Listening to music helps me let it out."

"I'm sorry you were hurting that day." He reaches out and brushes his finger across my cheek before focusing on the records. "When I cried for those three days, I blasted music so loudly the neighbors called the police. Told them I was disturbing them."

My cheek scalds where he touched me. "Did they know you were mourning your mom?"

"Sure, but they didn't care. It's not like I'm a nice guy that everyone cares about."

"You could be, though. You have potential, anyway. If you could get past your ego."

"That'll never happen."

"You never know. The sky could fall. Hell could freeze over. Ash could become a caring, compassionate person."

"You're caring and compassionate enough for the both of us," he says, like we're a couple.

I'm unsure how I feel about that. At least that's what I tell myself, but the insane butterflies come alive inside my stomach again.

It's toward the end of the week, when we're sitting in front of Section T with a stack of records surrounding us, I realize that I might really, *really* like him. I'm noticing more and more that there's more to Ash than I first thought. It just takes a lot to break through the surface.

"Do you want to get something to eat after we're done hanging out here?" he asks as he skims the list of songs on the sleeve of a record he plucked from Section I. "You can ask your dad to come, too. I know you hate him eating alone."

"He won't eat at one of those fancy restaurants you like, though," I tell him.

"That's okay," he says. I open my mouth to protest, but he cuts me off, placing a hand over my mouth, causing an adrenaline rush to go all mad, mad kinds of crazy inside my body. "We can eat wherever he wants. And you're letting me pay. No arguing this time."

I shut my mouth and decide to let him win this one, even though I hate letting people buy me things.

It's on Saturday, the morning before the party that his generosity gets a bit out of hand.

"Close your eyes and stick out your hand," he says to me as I'm standing in front of Section F.

"Why?" I ask, switching over to Section U.

"Just do it, Blayze," he says with a drop of annoyance.

"Fine, if you're gonna have a tantrum about it..." I shut my eyes and put my hands out in front of me.

Seconds later, a cold metal object lands in my palms. I start to crack open my eyelids open when soft lips touch mine. I gasp as a tongue enters my mouth and teeth graze my lips. I groan, clutching onto him when my knees just about give out from under me.

The kiss is brief but intense and leaves me breathless.

When he pulls away, I open my eyes then gasp again at the sight of the necklace in my hand; a silver chain that winds around a large black stone trimmed by tiny diamonds.

"It was my mom's," he explains.

I urge him to take it back. "Ash, I can't accept this."

"Of course you can." He backs away from me, one side of his mouth tugging to a proud grin. "Wear it to the party tonight, okay?"

Before I can say anything, he kisses me again then leaves the store with a skip in his walk. I stare blankly at Section L, unsure what the hell to do with the necklace.

"It's like he's branding you," Zeke says as he strolls up beside me.

"He's just being nice."

"Ash is never nice unless he gets something out of it."

"He's nicer than you think he is. You just don't know him like I do."

"Is that so?" He deliberates something. "Because I'm betting tonight, at the party, when he's surrounded by his friends, you'll get to see the Ash I know—the one who thinks everyone is beneath him. Who mocks people who are poor or that look different."

"That's not who he is anymore. The Ash you told me about, the one that picks on you, he's nice to you now."

"You really believe that?" he asks and I nod. "Well, then, I guess I won't have to do anything tonight."

I'm not sure what he means by that, but I leave the store with that same ominous feeling in my stomach that I've gotten two times in my life.

* * *

I try to shove my worries of Zeke aside as an older woman greets me at the front door. The moment I step inside, I realize I'm way underdressed in the flowery dress, leather jacket, and boots I'm wearing. Almost every girl here is wearing a prom-worthy dress, and the guys are wearing ties.

"Don't worry, you look beautiful," the woman assures me. "And with how much Ash talks about you, I'm sure he'll think so too."

"He talks about me to you?" I ask loudly enough that she can hear me over the music.

"All the time." She motions me to follow her as she heads for the wide stairway. "For the last couple of weeks, everything that's come out of that boys mouth has been Blayze this Blayze that. I gotta tell you, I didn't think the boy had it in him to talk about anything other than himself. Sure proves me wrong."

"That's always good to hear," I say as we stop in front of a door on the second floor. "It's so much quieter up here."

"That's because Ash has strict rules about anyone being near his room."

"But I'm here."

"But you're not anyone, are you?"

"Apparently not. Or so I've been told." I suddenly grow nervous. This is Ash's room, and no one is around. We'll be all alone. Wait, is he even here? Why did she bring me up here?

"Don't be nervous," she says. "I'm Elladonna, by the way, but you can call me Donna since I'm sure we'll be seeing a lot of each other."

My worries soon settle as Ash opens the door.

He's dressed up like the rest of the people downstairs, but his tie is loose around his neck. He looks tired, like he was about to fall asleep. But the tiredness vanishes when he sees me.

But he tries to contain his excitement. "I was worried you weren't going to show."

"Yeah, sorry I was a little late. I had to make dinner for my dad otherwise he'd probably burn the house."

A smile spreads across his face when he notices the necklace around my neck. He steps back and holds the door open, gesturing for me to come in.

I step inside the dark room, telling myself to chill out. But then the door shuts and the room is smothered in darkness.

I can hear the soft lull of music playing from inside the room and smile to myself. "You're playing the first song we listened to in the booth together."

"It's a good song," he murmurs. "It reminds me of you."

My lips curve to a smile, but the smile swiftly falters. "Ash, why are none of the lights on?" I ask with my hands out in front of me. "And why are you sitting up here by yourself?"

"I thought you weren't going to show tonight, and I was about to fall asleep... I hardly ever hang out at parties."

"Then why do you have them?"

"Because it's what I'm supposed to do," he utters quietly.

My fingertips brush across his hard stomach and I clutch onto the bottom of his shirt. "Can we turn the lights on now that I'm here?"

"I'm kinda of liking the dark even more now." Then his lips brush mine and I nearly stop breathing.

Out tongues tangle as he backs me into the room. I clutch onto him for dear life, gasping against his lips as my fingers drift up the bottom of his shirt.

"Your skin's so soft," I murmur against his mouth.

He slips off my jacket and traces his fingertips up and down my arms. "So's yours."

My eyes drift shut as his hands continue to search my body. Before I know it, my boots and dress are on the floor along with Ash's shirt. I'm about to undo the button of his jeans, when the backs of my legs bump into something solid. I fall backward and land on a mattress with a bounce. With a soft growl, Ash climbs onto the bed with me, covers his body with mine, and continues to kiss the air from my lungs. He kisses me until I'm so breathless I can't breathe. Until my heart is racing so violently I swear it's going to flee out of my chest.

"Your heart is racing so fast," he whispers with his hand resting on my chest. "Are you nervous?"

"A little bit," I admit.

"It's okay... We don't have to do anything you don't want to."

I wish I could see him because I can feel him staring down at me.

He brushes my hair out of my eyes then his hands wander down my side, tracing my ribs, before residing on my hip. "You're so beautiful."

"You can't even see me right now."

"I don't care. I still know you're beautiful. You always are no matter what."

He kisses me again, almost painfully slow as his fingers brush across my thigh and slip inside me. Minutes tick by. Hours. I get so lost, consumed by everything he's doing to me, that I almost forget where I am.

By the time he pulls away and helps me get dressed, I wonder if this night has the potential to turn out perfectly.

I should've known better, though.

"Let's get a drink," Ash says when we head downstairs to the party.

I let him lead me to the bar area but start to notice right away a change in Ash's demeanor. That smug smile has returned to his face, and he keeps snubbing some people who try to talk to him yet chats and hi-fives others. He even pushes a guy out of his way, muttering, "Who the hell invited him?"

"Are you okay?" I ask as he pours me a drink.

He shrugs indifferently. "Yeah, why wouldn't I be?"

My mood deflates. I hate to think it, but perhaps Zeke was right. Maybe Ash is different around other people.

"Hey, you look… disheveled," Zeke says, suddenly appearing by my side.

I look down at my wrinkled dress. "I was just…"

"Getting it on with the rich douche," Zeke says.

"He's not a douche," I argue. "Ash, is just—"

"Why the fuck are you here?" Ash's voice cuts through the air.

Zeke gives me an I-told-you-so look before turning to Ash. "Because you invited me."

"No, I didn't," Ash smirks. "Trust me. I'd never invite a loser like you to one of my parties."

A bulky guy sneers behind Ash and fist bumps the guy beside him.

Ash leans over the counter, his eyes darkening. "Why don't you do everyone in this room a favor, and get your pasty face out of this room. Spare us the pain of looking at the hideous thing."

Instead of growing angry, Zeke gets a pleased glimmer in his eyes. "I've been waiting a long time for this."

Ash's forehead creases, but then he shakes his head. "Get the fuck out before I make you get out."

"Gladly, but only after." Zeke sticks his hand out, palm up. "You think so highly of yourself, Ashford, but I wonder if that arrogance would remain if you became hideous yourself. I have an idea." His eyes darken. "How about we find out?" His lips move as he chants under his breath.

The room grows so quiet you can hear a pin drop. Even the music has stopped playing.

Then it happens.

26

Ash screams out in pain, collapsing to the floor, at the same time the lights in the house flicker on and off. Everyone panics and stampedes for the door. I try to run to Ash, but I get jostled out of the house with the crowd.

Once the mob has cleared out, I make my way back to the front door and knock. No one answers so I try the handle. It's locked and none of the lights are on.

"Ash!" I bang on the door. "Open up! Please!"

Crickets chirping are my only answer.

I try to text him.

Silence.

So much silence.

It makes me think too much.

About Ash and that scream he let out before all hell broke loose.

<hr />

The next few months pass by slowly yet quickly at the same time. Before I know it, summer has ended and fall has kissed the land with pinks and golds. I enroll in online classes while my father continues to work in the shop downtown, building furniture from scratch. He seems happier than he did before we moved, now that he has something to keep him busy.

"I feel like I got a fresh start," he says to me the morning after Ivy informed us that she's no longer dating Aldman.

Nope, she's moved on to bigger and better things. The bigger and better thing being a fifty something billionaire who she met in Paris when she was on a trip with Aldman. She tried to convince us that she was in love with this guy, that he bought an eight-carat diamond and her own condo, so how can she not be in love with him? She'll never truly love someone, though, until she starts seeing past the money, which I tried to tell her.

She hung up on me after that.

"I'm still sorry you had to change your life for me, Blayze," my dad says to me. "You've given up so much."

"Not really. I still have all the same plans and I still have you. That's all that really matters." I give him a hug. "I love you, Dad."

"I love you too," he says, wrapping his arms around me.

After we pull away, I leave the house and head for the record store because today is when they should be getting their new shipment. Zeke doesn't work there anymore. In fact, I haven't seen Zeke since the night of the party.

When I've picked out my records, I go to Ash's, like I do every day. Donna lets me in and leads me up to his room.

"How's he doing today?" I ask as I slip off my jacket.

She takes my coat and hangs it up. "The same. He stays in his room. Won't come out, only to grab his food that I leave by his door."

"He's eating, though, right?" I ask as we head upstairs.

"He is."

"Has he… do you know what's wrong with him yet? Why he won't see anyone?"

She pauses at the top of the stairway. "I do, but I can't tell you."

"Why not?"

"Because it's not my story to tell."

She's right. I should be getting the truth from Ash.

When I reach his doorway, she leaves me there alone. When I knock, I have to wait a couple of minutes for Ash to come talk to me. He never actually opens the door, only speaking to me from the other side. Sometimes we'll talk for hours and other times he'll only talk to me for minutes, depending on his mood. Still, I've opened up to him more than anyone, even trusting him enough to tell him why my family really left the States.

"Hey," he finally says from the other side of the closed door.

I lower myself to the floor and recline against the door. "Hey, it's me… Blayze."

"I know… you're the only one who visits me anymore… The only person I want to visit me."

"Ash." I sigh. "I wish you'd tell me what happened to you."

"I can't." His voice is so soft, breakable, like glass.

"You have to be getting lonely by now."

"I'm not *that* lonely… I have you."

I stretch out my legs. "But we only ever talk through this door. That isn't much."

"Of course it is. I love our talks. And the sound of your voice… You have such a lovely voice," he says. "I do miss seeing your beautiful face, though."

"Then open the door and you can see it," I say, crossing my fingers he will.

"I already told you I can't do that." His voice sounds strained. "Please, Blayze, I need to talk about something else."

Sighing, I give up on getting answers from him today and change the subject. "Your father and my sister broke up... did you know that?"

"No. I haven't spoken to my father in forever." Pain mixed with anger fills his tone. "I'm not surprised they broke up, though. At this point, my father's usually moved on to someone he thinks is better looking."

"She actually broke up with him."

"That might be a good thing. His ego needs the bruise, just like mine did. I just wish it wasn't such a horrible, permanent, hideous bruise... But I know I deserve what happened to me."

The sound of his voice breaks my heart.

I turn around and press my hand to the door. "Oh Ash, please open the door. I want to see you. Want to hug you better. Whatever's happened, we can fix it together."

Quietness is my only answer.

"Ash?"

Still nothing.

I sigh and get to my feet, knowing our visit is over for the day.

I spend the entire night trying to figure out what Ash could possibly be hiding from me. The next day, I find out on my own, though.

When I make my daily visit and go to knock on his bed door, it creaks open on its own. I shouldn't walk in. Ash has made it clear that whatever's going on with him, he wants to keep it to himself.

I start to step back when Ash exits his closet, wearing nothing but a pair of jeans. Instead of the smooth skin I traced my fingers along that night at the party, his skin is covered in rough, jagged scars that go up and down his chest, wind over his shoulders, and drag up his jawline.

I gasp escapes my lips and I quickly slap my hand over my mouth.

Ash startles back, his eyes meeting mine. At first he appears horrified, but the horror rapidly shifts to anger.

"What are you doing in here?" He strides for the door. "I told you to never open this door." He moves to slam the door, but I stick out my hand, stopping him.

"The door opened on its own." My voice trembles.

"Well... Good. Maybe you'll stop coming here now that you've seen me." He tries to close the door again, but I squeeze inside the room.

He sighs in frustration, slumping against the door. "Blayze, why are you here?"

"Because I want to talk to you."

"I know that but..." He rakes his fingers through his hair, growing more frustrated. "You have to be getting tired of all of this."

I step toward him. "Tired of all what?"

His hand falls to his side. "Having a boyfriend that you can only talk to through a door. You haven't seen me in months... since the party..."

"I know that... And I've missed you..." I gently place a hand on his chest, ignoring the strangled noise that leaves his throat. "Ash, what happened to you?"

"I can't..." He chokes up as my hand wanders toward his jawline, smoothing across a scar there. "Do you believe in magic, Blayze?"

"I didn't always, but there were times... When I was talking to Zeke... He knew things there was no way he could've known."

"I think he put a curse on me," he whispers. "He showed up the day after the party, saying all these things about how I deserved this for all those years I treated him like shit. He said I was cursed and that the only way to break the curse was if someone loved me enough to bare it themselves... At first I didn't believe him but, then I had doctors look at the scars and tried laser treatment to fade them, but they only got worse."

I think of what Zeke said to me in the store the morning of the party: *Well, then, I guess I won't have to do anything tonight.*

"Have you seen Zeke since then?" Anger boils under my skin. Yes, Ash was rude to him at the party, but punishing him this way was wrong.

Ash shakes his head, causing strands of his hair to fall in his eyes. "I think he left town."

I have an idea of how to find him, but it means risking calling someone from my old life. Before I take such a risk, I need to know...

"Ash, why did you so act so different at the party?" I ask, sweeping strands of his hair out of his eyes. "You were always so nice to me when we were hanging out and you seemed cool with Zeke whenever we were at the store, but you were so different... so cruel. Saying all that stuff to him in front of everyone."

"I know I was. And I regret it now—regretted it then. I hated that you saw me like that." His shoulders slump as he lowers his head. "I've been so used to not caring. All of my life, that's how I was taught to act. Then you come along and made me care, but that night... I got scared. I felt so... I don't know, like everyone could see the real me, and I panicked. It's no excuse—I never should have been that person. I get it now."

"Get what?"

"That looks and wealth aren't important. That there's so much more to life than that." His eyes blaze fiercely. I think he might kiss me but then he presses his back against the door, as if he's afraid of me. "How can you stand looking at me when I look like this? I'm hideous."

"Looks have never been important to me, Ash. You should know that. And you're still you, the same guy who sat in the café with me and listened to me talk about my mom. Who made me feel better when no one else did. Who I've been talking with for months now, through a door. Who understands my crazy love for music."

His lips quirk to a ghost smile. "I never did teach you how to play the guitar."

"We still have tons of time." I stand on my tiptoes and kiss him with everything I'm feeling inside, hoping he can feel it too.

By the time I pull away, I'm panting and want nothing more than to stay with him. But I need to do something first.

"I have to go somewhere, but I'll be back soon," I promise him, kissing him once more.

"Where are you going?" he asks as I hurry out of the room.

"To go find Zeke."

He shouts a protest after me, says I don't need to do this. But I run out the front door and down the road.

My father always said I'd do great things with my life.

It's time I started living up to my name.

***

It takes a few days for my friend to track down Zeke, but she finally manages to get a location. Turns out, Zeke is in town, living in a friend's basement where he makes money telling people their fortunes.

He has a client when I burst in without knocking.

"It took you long enough to find me," he says after the client leaves the room. "But I guess I shouldn't be surprised. With a guy like Ash, I'm surprised you're even here at all."

I sink down in the chair across from him. "Tell me how to break the curse, Zeke."

"I think you already know the answer to that." He leans forward, resting his elbows on his knees. "I think the real question is whether or not you want to make the sacrifice."

I suck in a breath and slowly let it out. "If I wanted to make the sacrifice, then what exactly would happen?"

"You've seen the scars, right? All of those would be put on your body."

"And he would go back to how he was before?"

He nods, observing me with a curious look. "So, I guess now the question is whether or not you love him that much. I mean, I know you liked him when he was hot... But now he's just ugly guy with an ugly personality."

"He's not ugly and neither is his personality... never has been... He was just raised to act that way. When he's not around his friends... He was nice."

"I don't care how he was raised. He should've never treated people like he did."

"I know that... But that's not all there was to him. He was a good person sometimes...." I shake my head in frustration. "There was potential there to be a kind person all the time."

His brow arches. "Are you saying you could've changed him?"

I stare down at my hands, "Maybe... If we'd gotten to spend more time together."

"You have too much confidence in him. Always have." He shoves up the sleeves of his shirt. "I still like my way better. Makes things more interesting, but if you must save him, then I'll remove the curse, but only if you're willing to bear it for him. So, tell me, Blayze, do you love him that much?"

Do I love him that much?

Love.

Is that what this is?

"Yes," I say, answering both Zeke and myself.

I do love Ash. Enough that I want to take his inner pain away.

"Fine. Take all my fun away." He sighs disappointedly. "Come on. Let's get this over with."

"Now what do we do?" I ask as he starts to get to his feet.

He sticks out his hand. "Now we shake on it and seal the deal."

It seems oddly simple, but I shake his hand away.

"Now, we go to Ash," Zeke announces.

We leave his house and drive up to the hillside to Ash's three story home. We find Ash in the living room, sitting in the window seat. When he spots me with Zeke, he jumps to his feet, fuming mad.

"No, I won't let you do this," he says, storming across the room toward me.

"It's too late." Zeke grins. "She already made the deal. There's no going back."

Ash throws a tantrum, breaking furniture and punching holes into the walls as he curses.

"I take back everything," Zeke says, looking pleased. "I think watching you deal with this might be even more entertaining."

Ash strides toward Zeke. "She doesn't deserve this."

"I know she doesn't," Zeke says. "But a deal's a deal."

"You have the power to break it," Ash growls.

Zeke considers this and a thoughtful look rises on his face. "I'll tell you what, since you seem to care so much about her, something I thought would never happen, I'll be kind enough to make you another deal. You both carry the scars. Half on you. Half on her."

"No, only me," Ash snaps.

"Last chance. All her or both of you," Zeke says. "It's your choice. But I'm starting to wonder though if you're really not taking the deal because you want to be free from the curse yourself."

Ash looks at me with wide eyes and for the briefest moment I question if that's what's really going on. But then I grow angry with myself for seeing Ash like Zeke sees him.

"Do it," Ash whispers, carrying my gaze. "Either keep them all on me or put them on us both, but I won't let her carry the curse herself."

A smile curls at Zeke's lips. "Look at you, being all noble. See, the curse did work."

Ash glares at him. "Just do it and get out."

"Fine." Zeke rolls his eyes then mutters something under his breath.

I shut my eyes, too afraid to see, but I feel the scars slowly crawling across my body. By the time I open my eyes, Zeke is gone and Ash is kneeling on the floor, crying.

"I'm so sorry," he says as tears stream down his cheeks. Half of his scars have faded and smoothed out, and he looks more like the Ash I first met. At least his physical appearance does. The raw emotions emitting from him are definitely something he didn't show me when I first ran into him at the record store. "I'm sorry for bringing you into this mess. You didn't deserve this... I wish I could go back. Do things over... You're too nice... doing this for me."

I walk up to a mirror and take a good look at myself. A few faint scars line my cheeks and run across my arms, but strangely, it's not as bad as I thought it would be. When Ash walks up to my side, it seems even less bad.

"Please say something," he begs, grasping my hand.

"I forgive you," I say because it seems like it's what he needs to hear. "But Ash, I didn't do this because I'm nice. I did it because I love you."

He sucks in a sharp, surprised breath and then his lips are devouring mine. He kisses me so passionately that I'm sure I'll have a bruise. I don't care, though. It's worth it. All of this is worth it, just as long as he's happy.

"I'm going to make you so happy," he says when he comes up for air. "I promise I will."

I rest my forehead against his. "I'll be happy just as long as you are too. No hiding behind closed doors anymore."

"I promise," he assures me then kisses me again.

Over the next years we spend together, he makes good on his promise. I fall in love with him more and more each day, despite his flaws just like my mom said I would. Sometimes, when he has dark moments of regret, he questions how I can possibly love him.

The answer is quite simple.

I loved him before the scars, and I love him after. How could I not? The scars are just marks on his flesh, and each one tells a story of how we got here. A beautiful, real, raw, less than perfect story. But it's our story. And that's all that really matters in...

The End

Jessica Sorensen is a New York Times and USA Today bestselling author from the snowy mountains of Wyoming. When she's not writing, she spends her time reading and hanging out with her family. To learn more, visit: http://jessicasorensen.com/

THE LITTLE MERMAID

Retold
by K.R. Wilburn

I am in agony.

My lungs scream for water, but my gills aren't working. In a last ditch effort I part my lips and attempt to drag the seawater in through my mouth but nothing comes, just a flash of intense heat. The taste reminds me vaguely of something I've not felt since I was a fingerling. Despite my growing panic, my mind seizes on the word.

Dry.

A repetitive keening noise bounces around my head. A rough choking sound fills my ears and I realize with a start it is coming from me. My gills are bound. My hands claw at my neck, desperate to free those three vertical openings on either side. I cry out when they close around the unfamiliar, scratchy coverings smothering me instead.

Black spots dance along the edges of my vision and my voice sounds guttural as I choke on the foreign air, my windpipe paralyzed in the scalding heat. I grasp at the bindings, wailing plaintively as I try to pull them free I claw and tear at the tender skin in my haste. But I don't care. I'm desperate now for water, knowing if I don't get oxygen I'll die.

"Calm down and breathe baby! Come on, breathe for me! Don't you quit on me now dammit!"

A firm hand grasps my wrists and tugs them from my throat, pinning them to my chest. My eyes fly open and the sweetest, darkest eyes I've ever seen on a merman are gazing into mine, commanding me to be still. His other arm slips around me so I'm leaning into him, trapped in his gaze. His other hand moves in comforting circles on my back and my heart flutters.

I forget for a second that my gills aren't working.

I forget that I'm dry and the air scorches, and I don't know where I am.

I forget everything but him and something pulls at the back of my mind, a shadow of a memory dancing in the depths of my head.

I try to ask him a question, but a rush of hot air flows over my throat and my lungs expand reflexively. Relief fills me to my fins and my body knows what to do, taking over the business of breathing, my chest rising and falling like the waves. The feeling is new, but it's better than suffocating from a lack of oxygen.

"That's it, baby girl." He smiles at me and I am dazed, the corner of my mouth tugging up to mimic the gesture. His teeth are like the whitest pearl, bright against the darkness of the unfamiliarly short hair, or the golden skin. He is beautiful.

The keening sound grows louder and more insistent and more voices fill the space.

"Lieutenant Prince, if you can't stay out of my way I'm going to have to ask you to leave."

My eyes swing to a gentle face next to him. Her complexion is dark and beautiful, and her face is stern but kind and she glares at him without sincerity. I frown and whimper a little when he pulls away from me, his grin rueful. My skin cries out for the contact again.

"She woke up and panicked Linda, she was ripping off her bandages. I can tell you next time I'll sit by the wall and let her bleed out if you want me to, but we both know I'd be lying."

The Merwoman's dark eyes focus on me, and the need to defend myself swells in my chest.

"Aaaaahhhhh..." the breathy sound rushes over my tongue, an unfamiliar sensation I cannot master and I'm lost in the hopelessness of the moment. I clutch my neck. Water is pouring from both my eyes and cascading down my cheeks. It's as if the sadness of my heart is overflowing my body and escaping.

"Don't fret, Miss" the woman soothes. "You've had some injuries to your throat. Your vocal cords aren't working as they should yet, but they'll heal up with time. That sometimes happens with wounds like yours. Do you remember what happened?"

"It's okay, sweetheart. Whoever hurt you won't get the chance to do it again. They'll have to go through me first."

Lieutenant Prince moves around to my other side, but his movements are strange, slow and lacking grace. My head aches again. I turn and follow his advance, noticing my surroundings for the first time. Bright white barriers surround me, and an opening in one reveals pale yellow light beaming in. A soft blue sky dotted with puffy white clouds lies beyond and horror washes over me with recognition. I've only seen the sky once in my life on my sixteenth birthday so many years before.

I'm on land.

"I'll go get the doctor," Linda says as I start to shake. The dry heat is replaced by fear as cold as the Northern Kingdoms.

"I'll keep her company," he replies and she chuckles in response, as if it's a forgone conclusion. I force myself to lift my eyes and look at his fins, dreading what I'll find. When I see long robust limbs instead of shining scales my heart cracks in my chest.

Lieutenant Prince is a human.

"I know you're probably wondering who I am." His smile betrays his nerves. He runs his hands through his short bristle of hair and pulls a shiny object to my side to sit on. "I'm Sean. I'm the guy who found you."

I tilt my head in confusion. I stare at the door pointedly and back at him.

"Oh, why is she calling me Prince? I guess the Lieutenant part didn't ring any bells for you. I'm an officer in the Navy. A SEAL actually." His chest puffs out with pride.

I cocked an eyebrow at him. I'm not a fry. I know the difference between a seal and a human. Although perhaps he's delusional. My heart starts thrumming again but this time fear sets the pace.

The repetitive keening speeds up and Sean grins at me. "All the ladies hearts speed up around a SEAL. It's part of the recruiting pitch."

I roll my eyes and throw back the covering over my body, ready to drag myself away from the human by any means necessary before he tried to harm me in some way.

The staccato beat erupted into a single, high-pitched note that echoed through my ears. My gaze drops to where my beautiful shimmering green fins should be and found instead two long legs complete with ten wiggling toes.

My mouth opens in shock and whatever held back my memories pops like a bubble, sending pain rippling through my head.

I'm hiding from my father. My godmother, the Sea-Goddess Amphitrite promised to hide me where he will never find me, where I will never be subjected to his plays for power again. If I stayed, I would be married off to a barbarian of a King to shore up his own reach, like he had all six of my sisters. I am the youngest.

I had borne witness as each one before me had been cast out like bait to appease the predators, watched as they wasted away and died a little more inside each day. When it was my turn, I went to Amphitrite for help.

I wiggle my new toes and bury my face in my hands as the truth broke over me like a wave. I can never go home again.

I am in exile.

I am a fugitive.

I am a human.

I'm lucky. That's what Sean tells me as the days pass. He found me washed up on the shore unconscious, naked, with slashes in my throat and assumed someone tried to kill me and left me for dead. So he brought me to the hospital, stayed with me while they operated on my wounds and stitched up the cuts so deep I should've died.

He's a hero, and a hottie. That's what the nurses tell me. I don't know what a hottie is, but the heat that curls low in my stomach whenever he flashes his smile at me gives me a hint.

He has duty, but he always comes to visit me afterward, when they bring me my evening meal. He is there the first time they served me a dead fish on a plate. My heart shatters, and I glare at the orderly, flinging the dishes from the tray and whatever else is in reach until the man flees from the room.

He thinks I'm something called a vegan, but he promised he would make sure nobody serves me meat again, and then he holds me in the circle of his arms while I wept. A few tears for the fish, but more tears for myself. As much comfort as I find in his embrace, I don't belong here. This isn't my home.

I no longer have a home.

I still cannot find my voice. I realize my Godmother's magic allows me to understand their speech would likely allow me to communicate with them as well, except I still can't figure out how to coax the air over my throat. Occasional noise is the best I can do. Sometimes they sound like words, which is how I got my name.

Ana.

I try to tell him my true name, but the breathy moans didn't accurately translate and Ana is what he heard. It sounds nice. It seems human.

"Ana!"

I glance up from the strange thing they call paper they handed me, and the long colored stick for marking on it and smiled. Sean crossed the room and pressed his lips to my cheek in greeting. He's familiar in his address, more familiar even than the other humans with all their unfamiliar hugging and hand patting rituals. I don't mind. His touch brings comfort, and other new feelings I cannot name.

"No luck with the writing, huh?"

I shake my head emphatically. Try as I might, I can't write, but I like tracing patterns.

"Well, that presents a problem for you, but I think I've got a solution if you're open to it."

I squint at him, and push the hospital table away from me, patting the bedside where he likes to sit whenever Linda or the other nurses aren't around to chase him off.

He takes my hands in his and gazes intently at me. "Your bandages come off today," he says, releasing one hand to trail his fingers over the scars of my surgically sealed gills. A shudder rips up my spine. I flash hot and cold. My lips part and I inhale raggedly.

"Sorry," he apologizes, pulling away and I shake my head, grasping his hand and squeezing. "There's no reason to keep you here anymore. I guess you haven't remembered who you are or where your family is?"

I move my head from side to side, lying in gesture if not word. I remember all right, not that it does any good. I no longer have family.

"The police haven't had any luck running your prints either, so you're not a felon." He laughs a little at his joke, and I smile too even though I don't get it. "But I don't want to see you on the streets. My roommate is at sea for another few months so if you want, you can stay with me. It's not much, but if you'd let me, I'd like to be your friend."

I don't even have to think about it. I nod happily, pressing a kiss to his cheek. I hadn't even considered what would come after this place, but being exposed to the elements for sure wasn't part of the plan. I could stay with Sean until I learned how to be a human.

"Yes," I say breathily, surprised when the word falls from my lips. Such a small syllable, and the sound barely registering to my ears, but he hears it.

"Yes?" His dark eyes gleam happily. I grin and it slips from my mouth again, trying to put more force on it without much success. His hands cup my face and he presses his lips against mine joyfully and pulls back, stunned.

My mouth rounds in a perfect circle and heat climbs my neck and settles in my cheeks.

"I shouldn't have done that Ana, I apologize. If you've changed your mind I would understand," he murmurs.

But I'm not offended, and I haven't. I stifle the urge to sift through the sensations he stirred in me and mimic his gesture, cupping his face between my hands and pressing my lips to his.

He stills under my touch in a moment stretching out for an eternity, before it slams back into place with a force that knocks my newly found breath from my body. Hands slide around my waist and tug me closer until his chest flush with mine. His mouth slants over mine, nipping at the tender flesh until I gasp, giving him the opening he seeks. His tongue delves into my mouth, stroking me, turning my bones to water in his grasp.

My hands glide from his cheeks to the nape of his neck, skimming down to rest on his shoulders as he breaks away from my mouth. He leans his forehead against mine and drags in a ragged breath that turns into a chuckle.

"I guess that means you haven't changed your mind?"

I smile at him and press a kiss to his cheek in response.

"Ahem." Linda coughs loudly from the doorway and glares pointedly at Sean.

Her displeased expression is belied by the twinkling of her eye as he untangles himself from my arms and steps away from the bed. My cheeks flush crimson, and I want to hide behind my tangle of hair. I want to capture this moment and analyze it a thousand ways. My hands are shaking, and I fold them on my lap so nobody sees.

Linda makes a show of checking my 'vitals' as she calls them and talking to Sean about my pending release. He winks at me over her shoulder.

I think I might like being human after all.

⁘

The skies are dark when we reach his apartment. It's near the beach and after he shows me around, I stare out the window at the violently rolling waves. Thunder rumbles, making the floor vibrate beneath my feet. My pulse quickens.

It's my father. I can feel his anger reaching out from the salty water like tentacles, searching desperately for me. He can't secure his seat of power without the loyalty of his allies and he knows of no other way besides sacrificing his own blood, no matter the cost. He terrifies me, but I inhale the warm, humid, air and remind myself I am beyond his reach.

"Would you like some coffee or soda? I think my roomate left some wine in the back too if that's more your style..." Sean is in the kitchen, leaning over the cold box and moving things around. I know about coffee (horrible bitter stuff) from the hospital, but the others are unfamiliar.

"Yes," I breathe. It's still the only word I can say, but it's enough to make him stand and look at me. The corner of his mouth turns up ruefully as if remembering I can't tell him my preference.

"Soda sound okay?"

I nod, and he pulls out a metallic cylinder and hands it to me. My palm opens reflexively against the chill, and he catches it before it drops to the floor.

"Here, let's put that in a glass for you. I guess the aluminum can be cold." I watch carefully as he pops a little tab until a pop of air sounds and pours the dark liquid into a tall glass where it fizzes. I take a small sip. My eyes fly open as the bubbles dance enticingly over my tongue, exploding in a sweetness that envelopes my senses. A happy moan escapes my throat, and I lift my gaze to Sean, happy to share my discovery with him.

His pupils sharpen as he watches me, and his jaw flexes. He reminds me of a coiled eel, all tense muscle under tight control. I notice for the first time today he's not in his multicolored uniform. The dark blue of his pants obscures his legs, but it's the pale gray shirt that captures my attention. The soft fabric stretches over his shoulders and torso, leaving his well-muscled arms bare. Dark green bands, the color of old seaweed, wrap around each bicep, curling in on themselves in intricate patterns and unfamiliar designs.

The soda drink is long forgotten, and I place it on the counter. His stare is predatory as I lean towards him and avidly look at his arm. A sharp intake of breath draws my attention back up to Sean's face, the only indication he's aware of my perusal. He gives a small nod and the corners of my mouth turn up with a smile.

I step closer, ready to inspect further when he reaches for the bottom of his shirt. He tugs it over his head, revealing an expanse of golden copper skin with more of the green markings.

"Look at the tattoo on my back. She's my pride and joy."

His muscles bunch under my touch as I move around him to his back and flatten both my palms against his shoulder blades, feeling as though the breath was stolen from my lungs. Covering his back is a large depiction of a mermaid on a rock, her fin tucked under her torso as she gazes into a clamshell and its pearl. Her face is obscured by her dark, billowing hair and unlike the other tattoos, her fins are colored in pale shades of purple, teal, coral and green.

Like mine used to be.

"She's beautiful isn't she?" He turns his head and glances at me over his shoulder.

"Yes."

Emotion suffuses the word now. Longing. Desperation. Desolation. Isolation. So many feelings wrapped up in such a short breath that flows over my vocal cords and past my lips, feelings I couldn't begin to tell him even if I knew how.

"I've always loved the sea," he tells me, turning towards me and pointing at another marking on his chest. This one I recognize, many of them are scattered about the bottom of the ocean floor, giant metal hooks with rotting ropes coiled around them. "It's why I joined the Navy. Can't really call yourself a sailor without an anchor tattoo right?"

I force the image of the mermaid from my mind and focus on the anchor. I lean towards him and trace the design with my fingers, his flesh hot against my fingers. His hands move to cover mine, pressing them against the smooth skin and holding them captive.

I glance up at him, startled at the intense expression on his face and smile, trying to calm my wildly fluttering heart. He leans closer, his breath grazing my cheeks and ghosting over my mouth. My eyes flutter close as he brushes a kiss over my lips, once, twice, thrice. I shiver weakly as he moves back and captures my gaze with his own.

"You know you can stay here no matter what right? That this, between us, whatever it is, that's not why I invited you to live here."

I nod, and press myself against him, eager for a return of the sensations his kiss had brought in the hospital. I wanted to explore and delight in this aspect of being a human, so different from the cold, perfunctory interactions of merfolk.

"Thank God." He cups his fingers around my face and takes possession of my mouth again.

I melt into him, awash with new sensation as he presses me into the countertop. The hand on my face wanders into my hair and the slope of my neck. My own fingers flex and dig into the warmth of his chest and that simmering heat that is becoming my constant companion in his presence flares to life and consumes me.

I'm burning from the inside out. I'm lost in his touch and fairly vibrating with desire although I can't pin down what my body is crying out for. He breaks away from my mouth and skims his across my cheek, his moist breath dancing on my sensitive skin as he explores my neck. I moan, and follow his example, wanting to leave him full of the same feelings. My lips move over his jaw, sucking and nipping lightly. The saltiness of his skin makes my pulse race with familiarity. My fingers drift over his chest of their own accord, tracing the lines of his muscles, absorbing the heat seeping from him. It is as if he is my own personal sun.

His hands slip down my back and under my legs, pulling me up so I have to wrap them around his waist and cling to him rather than fall. I take the opportunity to nuzzle his ear, exploring the shell with my tongue. Unfamiliar words pour from his lips as he carries me to one of the sleeping chambers.

He falls with me to the bed, pinning me with his weight and continuing his assault with his kisses. Something firm and rigid presses at the core between my legs and my eyes fly open in amazement. I rock against him, suddenly understanding whatever my body is yearning for. It has something to do with this.

Sean moans my name and his hands skim under the shirt they gave me at the hospital, pushing it up my body and exposing my stomach. He peppers kisses across the flesh. I melt into a seething mass of touch and emotion. He moves up my body, taking the garment with him, blazing a fiery trail of wet, hot kisses across my sensitive skin. When his mouth closes over one of my breasts, stars explode behind my eyes.

"Yes." I moan, clenching my thighs around his body. His hands move of their own volition, skimming down my legs, catching in the waistband of the soft hospital scrubs. He breaks away long enough to tug them from my body, and remove his pants as well.

When he claims me for his own, I am neither human nor mermaid. I cease to be anything but his. Sensation floods me, washing away everything but this moment.

"Sean." The word flows over my throat like a wave breaking on the sand as the thunder violently rumbles overhead.

"Ana," he cries in return.

With a sudden clarity, I can see everything. Past, present, future.

I'm no longer adrift, tossed about in the storm.

I'm safe.

I'm home.

⚜

"It's another hurricane." Sean wraps his arms around me and pulls me into his chest, lending me his warmth against the chill as he points out the swells and breaks of the water. "This one might hit us so we need to stock up and board the windows. I wish I had somewhere to evacuate you to." He buries his face in my hair as I stare over the roiling waters.

I'm standing on Sean's balcony staring out over the tempest, my hands clutching the iron railing until my knuckles turn white. For the last two months, I've watched the darkness growing in the distance. The skies grow ever darker, each day the storm breaking stronger and more violent.

"Are you sure you can't leave?" I beg.

The words still only come bidden with effort, the fruit of long hours of practice with Sean. I disdain their use as much as possible.

They all taste like lies.

"That's a no-go. The commander wants the SEAL teams on standby for possible rescue efforts should they become necessary."

My heart sinks like a stone. I take a steadying breath and focus on the horizon.

Every day Father searches for me. But since he cannot find me, he grows more murderous. I've tried to hide away in the haven of Sean's arms, but the reality stares me in the face whenever he turns on the news. Father's rage is devastating the human world.

The Navy Sean works for has had to put all their ships to dock, huge lumbering ships of steel and magic for all I know, helpless before the might of a Sea King. Sean has had to work late most days, preparing the base should disaster strike here as it has elsewhere.

Yesterday a Tsunami spread across the breadth of the ocean and devastated a small island nation. Tens of thousands of lives lost, all because of my rebellion. In the circle of Sean's arms, we watched the news reports together on the box he called a television. It shared images of the devastation triggered by an undersea earthquake.

An earthquake I know originated in Atlantia.

My selfish heart demands I stay with Sean. How can I bear to be parted from him now? Now that I've tasted real love, real emotion? How can I ever consent to return to my Father's control and sold to the highest bidder?

I know not how to do it, only that it must be done. The guilt eats me alive.

"When?"

"Tomorrow night at the earliest."

I know then I will never spend another night in Sean's arms. My heart cracks in my chest, missing a beat, giving it to the void.

I spin in his arms and cling to him, burying my face in his neck, the sad water leaving my eyes and slipping down my cheeks.

"What's this?" he asks, clutching me to him as I tremble. "It'll be okay baby. I'll be here with you through the storm. They won't recall me until afterward for any cleanup."

I lift my face and kiss him, letting my desperation and sorrow spill over into my touch. His passion ignites. Soon we're fumbling for our clothes and falling on the couch together.

When we become one this time, there's no relief for me, no feeling of homecoming and peace. I look away from him. There's dampness on my cheeks as I silently bid him goodbye.

He is my home, but I love him too much now. I would give all to keep him from harm.

Even when all means him.

His chest rises and falls at an even pace. We labored all day preparing his apartment for the onslaught. Windows have been boarded, supplies purchased and hoarded. His military gear is packed and readied for rapid recall. The work was wearying, but I kept a cheerful face all day long for him.

He knows me too well though. He's aware when my smiles don't reach my eyes, but has attributed it to the coming storm. He's been extra careful with me today in his touches and his holds. He thinks I fear the sea after my 'attack'. He thinks I fear the water breaching the lower floors of his complex.

He's right. I do fear the sea, but not for the reasons he thinks.

When I'm sure, he's asleep I slip from between the sheets and tiptoe to the bedroom that was to be mine, with the bed I've never slept in. In the darkness, I slip on the clothing I hid there earlier in the day. Sean bought them for me when all I had were scrubs. I'm distressed they'll be left behind, but I only need them long enough to get to the water.

Once I'm in the sea, the spell will be broken. I will no longer be a human. What use has a mermaid for human clothing?

Once I'm dressed, I move stealthily towards the front door and ease it open. The hinges creak and I freeze, listening for any sign Sean has been awakened. When all remains quiet, I slip out the door.

The stone stairs are uncomfortable under my bare feet, but then everything is uncomfortable under my feet. Every step has been an agony, my fins having made for rather delicate skin that feels every grain of sand, every blade of grass, and now every cold hard inch of slab concrete.

I'm sobbing before I reach the beach. The cries rip from my throat. The pain of the sand on my bare feet is nothing to the agony of my heart breaking. My resolve falters. I pause, ready to turn back and bury myself in Sean's arms, consequences be damned.

Static electricity dances over my skin and lightning flashes, striking the sand a few hundred feet away. I scream and jump reflexively. I slam my hands over my mouth to stifle the sound, but it's too late. It echoes through the night. I know Sean will hear it and wake.

I'm running out of time.

I make a mad dash for the shore, stumbling as I pull the clothes from my body and cast them aside. I'm nearly there when I stumble, nude, into the sand and crawl towards the water. The waves beat on the sand, reaching for me, stretching to grasp me and drag me back to Father when his voice rings out.

"Ana!"

"Stay back Sean," I sob, holding my hand up like a ward.

He ignores me, moving steadily towards me, confused. "I'm all for night swims babe, but this isn't the time. You need to come inside before you get hurt."

The thunder rumbles in the distance as if punctuating his words.

"I love you, Sean."

I move backward towards the water, the ache subsiding as the surf rushes over my toes, swirling around my calves.

"I love you too, Ana. Come on, let's go back to bed." He's pleading with me now, knowing something is wrong. There's an edge to his voice, but as the next wave sweeps over me, my skin begins to glow brightly as the moon.

"Ana!" Sean dives for me, unsure of his eyes but desperate for my safety.

It's too late, the water is up to my waist now, and the magic is taking hold. I scream out in pain as the bones in my leg melt away in molten agony. The skin fuses together and the white hot pain sears through my whole body, ripping through my neck as my gills re-open. Stars burst behind my eyelids, darkening everything in its wake.

I feel Sean dragging me from the water, but it's too late.

Where once I had legs, now existed six feet of golden green glimmering scales. Blood trickles down my neck in rivulets where the skin broke open and I gasp, grateful my lungs will still pull oxygen from the air.

"Oh my God, Ana." Sean's voice is high pitched and he repeats the words over and again as he falls back in the sand, his arms still locked around me. "Oh my God!"

The advancing tide reaches us again, bathing us in the sea water. Thunder booms and lightning flashes wildly, striking the sand all around us. The sea looks as though it's boiling and I recoil knowing it can mean only one thing.

He's coming.

"Sean!" I gasp his name, finding the words harder to speak with my gills working. "Sean run! Please!" I beg him, salty tears slipping down my cheeks. He blinks as if he's reached a decision.

"You're a mermaid." It's not a question.

"Yes, and you need to leave, now!" Desperation and frustration overwhelm me. Can't he see he's in danger?

"How does this work? Is it like Splash? Do you have legs on land and a tail in the ocean? Obviously it's not all water." He blushes, remembering my introduction to his shower, most likely.

The waves churn and the wind screams in my ears telling me we're almost out of time, However, I know Sean won't leave without an answer.

"I was hiding Sean. But I can't hide from my fate anymore." I gesture at the growing storm. "Too many people are dying. You're going to die too if you don't leave now. Please, Sean, he's almost here. You're running out of time."

That catches his attention. The alpha male in him kicks into overdrive, determined to protect me.

"You don't have to be afraid of anyone, Ana. I'll never let anyone hurt you."

He gathers me into his arms and captures my mouth in a searing kiss that he means to be reassuring. It brings only pain with the promise that he'll stand by my side.

A roar fills the air and the ground shakes beneath us. I cling to Sean for stability, but I know it's futile. I can feel my father's presence behind me, radiating power like the heat from the sun. I bury my face in Sean's shoulder, holding on for one moment longer than I should. One moment more where our hearts beat in time. One moment more than I deserve for all the damage I've caused.

"So this is where Poseidon's whore hid you away Amphinome. Come, daughter, what say you? Will you submit? Or will I be forced to kill you now?"

"I submit," I say. Sean tightens his grip on my hand and tugs me towards him but it's too late. Father pushes the water out towards me until it's deep enough for me to swim.

"Ana, no!" he argues, trying to keep me at his side, his eyes pleading. "You don't have to go with him. I can protect you. I'll keep you safe. We'll figure this out, but please don't go."

"I have to." I caress his face reassuringly. "It'll be okay. If I do as he asks, I'll be fine. I won't let anyone hurt you either."

"You wouldn't have run if you weren't afraid!" he insists.

I swallow thickly. The water hovers around his chest now and continues to swell. Father is toying with him, I need to go.

"Enough of this Amphinome. Your foolish choices have already put our treaty with the Northern Kingdoms at risk. I've covered your absence and put off your marriage as long as I was willing but no more."

Sean looks as though he's been struck. "Marriage?"

"Not my choice," I insist and Father's patience has snapped. He commands the current to pull me back to him.

"Not your choice," he seethes. "As if the sealing of a mermaid is a choice. You wed at my command!"

His grasp is painful, and he leers at me menacingly. "If I let you live after this stunt. I may just make an example out of you. If you can convince the Northern Kingdoms to still take you, you may live. If not, you'll find use showing my people what happens to those who disobey me."

A whistling noise sounds in the air. Father waves his hand and the air around us shimmers. A blade, the one Sean calls his last line of defense, hovers in the air for a moment before falling helplessly into the deep.

"Let Ana go, now." Sean's voice is deadly serious as he treads water.

He's moving towards me with a purpose, refusing to admit defeat. I cry out his name. Father curls his lip and a bolt of lightning flies from the heavens. I scream his name and struggle against my father as I try to reach his rapidly sinking body.

"You killed him!" I sob brokenly.

"Enough," he commands and drags me below the water in the dark depths but my eyes are locked onto Sean's body as the sea swallows my handsome sailor, embracing him in her bosom.

* * *

Anguish and anger simmer in my stomach until I feel sick with it.

I can't close my eyes without seeing the bolt of lightning striking Sean and stealing the life force that animated him. I see him everywhere, his sparkling eyes, his gentle smile. Even my own fins betray me, bringing the image of his sun-kissed skin to mind.

My sealing has been declared, but will be taking place here now. The Northern Kingdom is willing to send for me as initially agreed, but my Father does not feel I have been punished enough. Keeping me here allows him more time to watch me suffer. More likely he sees the darkness he created in my heart and fears it.

He should fear it. The fear should stalk him across the vast expanses of his kingdoms. It should lurk in his dreams because one day I will avenge Sean.

It's the only thing I have left.

Amphinome, come.

I curl my lip in disgust but obey the summons anyway. I know that as much as it pains me, I have to behave like the contrite daughter until the moment presents itself.

The throne room is empty, except for Father. I keep my head bowed the same. He sees fealty and fear, but I know that if I meet his gaze, he'll see the hate simmering for him there.

You summoned me, Father?

The advance party for the Northern Kingdoms arrives today. You will remain at my side during the proceedings. You will not speak or you will be punished severely. Tell me you understand.

I understand.

His voice echoes through my head. I move to my place below him and behind him, a position of subservience. I keep my eyes on the sea floor and watch the sea grass moving in the current. As painful as human speech had been, I long to taste words in my mouth again, if only to know that Sean was alive to hear them.

Sonar whistles burst through the water, heralding the arrival of the advance. I grip my hands tightly in front of me. The water shifts as they move into position near us.

Welcome, Father bids them and holds his hand out imperiously, waiting for the emissary to show deference. *You look familiar to me, but you are not Reinhardt's usual delegate.*

It's not a question, it's a statement. I glance up and find my eyes caught in dark gleaming eyes. My heart lurches in my chest. My gills fail to take in water.

Sean.

How is this possible? How is he alive? How is he a Merman?

His gaze shifts from mine back to my Father's. He smiles wickedly. *I am not. But I have come with his tribute nonetheless, a symbol of his fealty.*

Father strokes his flowing beard and indicates that he is happy to accept whenever someone wishes to pay him tribute.

Sean motions the merman behind him who comes bearing a large clam shell. Sean opens it and removes a gleaming dagger from the shell and holds it out, the grip and the blade each resting in his open palms.

Father smiles sharply. He moves as if to take it from him.

Poseidon's blade, Father says reverently. *Where did he find this?*

He didn't. It was given to me specifically for you, but he is happy to claim credit nonetheless.

Father glances up, his expression troubled once again as he tries to place where he's seen Sean before. As he studies him, Sean's hand closes over the grip and with a strike faster than the lightning that had robbed me of him, plunges it into Father's heart.

16

The effect is instantaneous. Father's body glows bright blue and turns to ash, floating to the sea floor below us.

Sean! I rush to him and fling my arms around him, hugging him close to me. When I feel his heart beating against mine I melt against him, relief covering me. If mermaids could weep, I would weep for joy.

How? I ask.

Your Godmother. Because I died in the sea, she claimed my soul for her own and brought me back in a new form. She loves you as much as I do.

But Father? How?

That was Poseidon himself. Turns out he's also real and really sick of your Dad's bullshit. Threatening his wife must have been the straw that broke the camel's back.

What is a camel? And a straw?

He shakes his head, and his chest vibrates with laughter. *It doesn't matter. All that matters is with all the other crazy things that I've found out are real, mermaids and gods and goddesses, as long as I have you, Happily Ever After isn't a stretch.*

His lips curl into a smile before he dips his head down and captures my mouth with his own.

The End

KR Wilburn has traveled the world with her family but currently calls Graham Texas home. When she isn't writing about the creatures that intrigued her Irish ancestors, she is busy studying nutrition science and reading everything she can get her hands on. She's a fan of Supernatural and Gone with the Wind, Jennifer Armentrout, Amy A. Bartol and Tara Brown and makes a mean omelette.

She is the mother of six crazy, creative and hilarious children and married to her childhood best friend and hero Ben. When she isn't busy with her dogs Trouble and Denali, you're likely to find her in a corner with her nose buried in the latest Deadpool and Red Sonja comic books and counting down the moments until she can find inspiration capturing the perfect Aurora through the lens of her camera. To learn more, visit: http://krwilburnbooks.com/

DANCE WITH ME
A retelling of The Twelve Dancing Princesses
by Tish Thawer

"Father, stop! Please," Gwen begged, reaching for her sister. The crack of the belt on Adele's back matched her torturous cries.

"Why do you force me to do this every morning?" Richard demanded, like it was *our* fault that he beat us.

Gwen straightened and wiped her cheeks. "We don't force you to do shit, it's your choice to beat us instead of love us."

Richard snarled and spun to face his eldest daughter. "Do not speak to me of love. If you loved me, you and your sisters wouldn't defy me night after night." He threw the belt onto the floor with a loud clank, then ran his fingers through his hair.

Jana, the middle daughter, leapt from her bed and moved to comfort their younger sister, Adele. She pulled her t-shirt down over the red angry welts.

"Maybe we wouldn't *defy* you if you'd let us out of this God-forsaken-house once in awhile. Why do you insist on keeping us locked up like some sick, twisted king?" Gwen pleaded.

"Because!" He turned to walk away.

"That's it? That's all you have to say?" she exclaimed.

"You wouldn't understand, and it's not your burden to bear."

Gwen laid a hand on Adele's shoulder. "You make it our burden to bear." Richard gasped, and Gwen hoped her words had finally reached him. "Maybe we'd be honest with you if you did the same."

They stood there, staring at one another. Hope blossomed in Gwen's chest that he'd finally open up and tell them why their lives were now filled with secrets and lies. But instead, he walked to the door, tight lipped and nostrils flaring. "I'm your father and owe you no explanation."

"Fine, then don't expect an explanation from us either," Gwen screamed, slamming the door in his face.

1

"Adele, I'm so sorry. I was sure he'd pick me again." Gwen shifted Adele's long, blonde hair to the side, then lifted her shirt and blotted a wet cloth along her back.

"It's okay. It probably looks worse than it feels."

"I doubt it." Gwen replied with a trembling chin.

"I don't understand why he's like this. We've always done exactly what he's wanted: minded our manners, studied hard with our tutors, pretended to be the perfect little family at all his stupid events. Why is he such an evil bastard when it comes to us going out and having a little fun?" Jana threw herself onto her bed, casting her long red locks over the white feather duvet.

"I don't know, but we're old enough to not have to deal with this shit anymore. I say we head out again tonight, but only if you're up to it, Adele," Gwen amended.

"Of course. I always feel better once I'm out of this place," Adele stated. She looked around their lavish prison and sighed. The oversized room contained three large beds, antique dressers, modern electronics, and glistening chandeliers. It was palatial, just like the rest of the mansion. But as with every other room, all they wanted to do was escape. "What a messed up life we lead," she added.

Gwen pulled her long raven hair into a pony tail and gave an understanding nod. "I know, honey. Despite the fact we're all in our twenties, he treats us like imprisoned children, and I simply can't take it anymore. Let's get some rest and we'll start getting ready after dinner, as usual," Gwen concluded as she finished bandaging Adele's back.

Both her sisters nodded, excited at the prospect of another night out.

* * *

"Claymore, it's Richard. As we've discussed I'm in need of your services. My daughters continue to escape their room every night, but I am unsure of exactly how. I need you to start your investigation tonight. Are you available?" Richard asked into the phone. "Okay, good. Thank you, young man. Please be here at 6:00p.m."

* * *

"Girls, this is Claymore Sheeran. He'll be residing in the house for a few days. Please make him feel welcome."

Claymore stood and reached out to shake each of their hands, lingering a little too long as his fingers glided over Gwen's. "It's nice to meet you all."

"Likewise," Gwen lied.

Claymore's touch set her on edge, but his handsome features, deep brown eyes, and dark short hair left her wondering what possible business he could have with her father, as he was much younger than his usual associates.

The sisters ate in an amicable silence, contributing to the conversation only when spoken to. But when the last course was being cleared, Jana cut to the chase. "Exactly what kind of business do you have here, Claymore?"

"Jana!" Richard slammed his hands on the table. "His business here is of no concern to you. Now please, have some manners and show our guest to his room."

Jana pushed back her chair with a sickeningly sweet grin plastered on her face. "Apologies, Claymore. Please follow me." She grabbed a glass and the decanter of wine on her way out the door.

"May we be excused?" Gwen asked, eager to follow Jana.

"Of course," her father replied, almost too kindly.

Gwen and Adele tiptoed to where Jana was depositing Claymore. The guest rooms resided on the same floor as theirs, but at the opposite end of the hall. Jana was just closing the door when they came around the corner.

"All done." Jana smirked, swirling the contents of the glass container.

"How long will he be out?" Adele asked.

"Once he takes his first drink...all night long. We're good to go." She winked.

The sisters rushed into their room, laughing and giddy at the prospect of another night out. Jana poured the rest of the laced wine down the drain in their bathroom then crawled into bed, sharing a knowing look with her sisters. They awaited their father to officially "tuck them in."

"Good night, girls. As always you are not allowed to leave this room until morning. Sleep well," Richard stated flatly then locked the door from the outside.

Jumping from their beds, they each placed an ear to the door, waiting until their father's footfalls could no longer be heard. With the coast clear, Gwen fished out their party clothes from a box hidden in the back of their expansive closet. Black leather, fishnets, and stiletto heels weren't exactly proper attire for the elite Von Brandt ladies.

Oh well...

⁂

By 9p.m., eyeliner was thick, hair was big, and clothes were tight. The sisters looked stunning and were ready to hit the clubs. With one final check on the door, it was time to leave.

"Stand back," Gwen instructed.

Reaching down to the bottom spindle of her four poster bed, she twisted the leg then quickly moved aside. The familiar sound was eerie, but the excitement was undeniable as the floor beneath her bed opened onto a set of stone stairs.

It had only been a couple months ago that they discovered the hidden entrance. A bump under the floor and a whisper of adventure prompted them to break their father's rules and start exploring as if they were feature characters staring in *The Secret Garden*.

"Let's go."

The click of their heels against the stone echoed through the thick air as they descended the stairs. The large slab door automatically sealed back into place as they raced forward into the underground tunnel.

At its end, they opened an elaborately carved wooden door and walked out onto a street lined with three massive buildings. One made of shining silver, one of glimmering gold, and the third of sparkling diamonds.

"So, which will it be tonight, ladies?" a voice rang out from behind them.

They all squealed and turned to face three hot guys walking in their direction.

"You're here!" Jana exclaimed.

"Of course. My brothers and I will be here every night now that we've met you," said the blonde hunk.

Jana bit her lip as he grabbed her by the hand and pulled her close. The other two brothers reached for her sisters, following suit.

"Let's check out the golden one tonight," Adele suggested.

"Whatever you want, baby," crooned the handsome brunette with the deadly smile. Adele giggled and snuggled close.

"You okay with this," asked the older, black-haired brother as he stared into Gwen's eyes. She became lost in his gaze for a few seconds before answering.

"Absolutely!" She snapped out of it.

The couples radiated pure joy as they entered the golden club. Music bumped and people swarmed the dance floor. The girls and their dates wasted no time joining the frivolity. They danced all night, just as they had for the past month, practically wearing the heels of their shoes down to nubs. At the night's end, each sister received a single kiss from their dates and reentered the tunnel that would return them home. Once again at the base of the stairs, they listened and heard their father rooting around their room, throwing his usual fit. He'd knock things off their dressers, throw pillows, and toss their blankets onto the floor. They waited patiently until he left, slamming and locking the door again. Entering their room, they hid their worn shoes and party clothes in the closet, then crawled into bed, giggling and sharing stories with each other about their night.

"Colin is so amazing. He trains horses," Adele boasted.

"Frederick is an artist and says he wants to paint me," Jana giggled.

"Liam is a musician and says he's going to write a song about me," Gwen added.

As their heads hit their feather pillows, they gave a collective sigh and drifted to sleep.

* * *

"Wake up, you fool!" Richard bellowed as he shook Claymore by the shoulders. "The girls are gone, again!"

Claymore woke slowly, rubbing the back of his neck and shaking his head to clear his thoughts. Being pulled from an unplanned sleep, took some effort.

"They've disappeared again and I have no idea how. You have to find out where they are going. It's a matter of life and death."

Claymore mumbled his understanding and slipped on his shoes, following Richard down the hall to the girls' room. Richard turned the skeleton key in the lock, and they both crept inside. Claymore looked from bed to bed, seeing all three ladies sound asleep. Just as Richard reached for Gwen's blanket, Claymore grabbed his arm, stopping him from acting on his rage. Claymore shook his head and pulled him from the room.

"What are you doing? I want answers, and I want them now," Richard demanded.

"Terrorizing them won't get you answers. Let me do my job, sir."

"If you had been doing your job tonight instead of sleeping, I would already have the answers I seek," Richard spat.

"Getting to know my targets takes time, and trust me, I've learned a fare deal in just one night. Return to your room and act as if nothing is wrong in the morning," Claymore instructed.

Richard flipped the lock and stomped away, while Claymore returned to his room, taking a moment to throw the tainted glass Jana used to drug him with into the fireplace.

"Well played, ladies."

The girl's woke, surprised at the fact that their father wasn't standing at their door with his belt in hand. As usual, he knew they'd escaped again, and punishment was always dealt out first thing the next morning.

"Perhaps he doesn't want to show his guest what a monster he truly is," Jana surmised.

"Yes, that's probably right," Gwen agreed. "Still, let's do our best to not provoke him at breakfast. Be on your best behavior, understand?"

Jana and Adele nodded in agreement, then followed Gwen down to the dining room with their eyes downcast and their lips sealed. Dealing with their father lately had been a nightmare, but dealing with him when you had no idea what was coming was downright torturous.

"Good morning, Father, good morning, Claymore," Gwen greeted.

"Good morning, girls," Richard replied.

While Claymore offered nothing more than a cordial nod to Jana and Adele, his gaze was locked on Gwen, inquisitive and heated. "Good morning, Gwen."

Gwen scrunched her brow at his pointed attention as she claimed her usual seat at the table. There was something different about him this morning that Gwen couldn't put her finger on.

"What are your plans today?" their father asked.

Gwen shot a panicked glance at her sisters. Never before had their father showed an interest in how they spent their days. He was always too busy to care. Besides their morning chores, they were free to roam the estate until the sun went down. Dinner was served promptly at 6:30p.m. and that had been their curfew for as long as they could remember.

"Nothing specific, Father. Is there something you'd like us to do?" Jana piped up.

"No, no. I was just curious. I have a few business meetings this morning, but Claymore will be around. If you could be sure his needs are met while I'm out, I would appreciate it."

Gwen cringed at the smirk on Claymore's face, and realized the punishment they thought they'd escaped this morning had just taken a different form. It took everything she had in her to agree to her father's request.

"Of course," Gwen replied, sinking into her chair.

"Good. Then it's settled. Claymore, if there's anything you need, just ask the girls."

"Thank you, Richard. I'll do just that."

Gwen, Jana, and Adele all spent the rest of the meal in silence, eating their breakfast and contemplating what their father had up his sleeve. Jana actually cringed when he finally bid them farewell with a jovial wave.

"If you'll excuse us, we have to attend to our chores, but we'll be back shortly," Gwen stated flatly.

"Of course. Take your time," Claymore replied.

* * *

"What the hell? Why do we have to babysit this guy all day?" Adele plopped down on her bed.

"I think it's more about him babysitting us," Jana stated with a lifted brow.

7

"Whatever the reason, we need to be careful what we say," Gwen instructed. "Hopefully he'll just want to hang around the house, and honestly, there's really not much to do here so it should be fine."

Jana and Adele agreed, then each headed off to attend to their chores. Gwen made all the beds, while Jana scrubbed down the bathroom, leaving Adele to address the laundry. Once done, they all changed out of their work clothes and into casual sundresses and flats, returning to the dining room in under fifteen minutes.

"That was quick. You all look lovely." Claymore placed his napkin on the table and rose from his chair.

"Thank you," Gwen replied. "Is there anything you need at the moment?"

"I'm not sure. What do you have planned?"

Gwen looked at Adele and Jana, then quickly supplied an answer for them all. "We were just going to go read in the library."

"That sounds pleasant. Mind if I join you?" Claymore asked.

Gwen sighed. "Not at all."

Jana grabbed Adele by the hand and walked towards the library located at the end of the main hall. Gwen followed just a few steps behind with Claymore hovering close at her side.

"Do you all read every day?"

"That's an odd question." Gwen couldn't contain her building frustration.

Claymore laughed. "Why is it odd? I just wondered if you read because you *have* to, or if it's something you all enjoy doing."

Gwen relaxed slightly. "We enjoy it. Some of us more than others." A small smiled played at her lips as she thought about the long talks she and Liam had shared, discussing their favorite books and poems.

"Well, I for one, love to read," Claymore expressed. "What other way can you escape to a far away land and fight dragons or rescue a princess, than by losing yourself within the pages of a book?"

The sisters shared a knowing glance and giggled. *What other way, indeed?*

"Do you dream of fighting dragons and rescuing princesses often?" Jana laughed.

"But of course, it's my job." Claymore winked.

The strange statement caused goose bumps to break out over Gwen's skin as she entered the library. "Well, here you are. Take your pick of adventures, *dragon-slayer*," Gwen replied in an attempt to play along with his teasing.

The rich mahogany shelves and tall glass windows were impressive, but not nearly as much as the vast the selection of books rising from floor to ceiling. The classics were there of course, but in addition to Shakespeare, Dickens, and Leroux, there we more modern selections as well.

"Wow. This is fantastic," Claymore said as he glanced around, taking in all the room had to offer.

The sisters quickly grabbed their favorites and each took a seat upon one of the many settees. Adele chose *Alice in Wonderland*, while Jana grabbed her worn copy of Poe. Gwen's go-to book, however, was a modern title about three sister witches. Gwen didn't see the title Claymore finally chose after a lengthy perusal of the shelves, but what she did notice—after an hour of being stared at—was that Claymore didn't seem interested in reading anything at all. He just kept sneaking peeks at each of them, looking at their books, their clothes, their hair, and she simply couldn't take it anymore.

"Can I help you with something?" Gwen snapped.

"No. Why?" Claymore calmly replied.

"Because, you keep looking at us as if we're going to explode."

Claymore laughed. "That's an interesting choice of words, since I was just wondering what makes you all tick." Claymore rose and returned his book to the shelf then stood in front of them.

"It's obvious you have a flare for the dramatic." He gestured to Jana who huffed. "And you," he pointed to Adele, "are a lover of all things artistic." He turned to Gwen. "But you...I haven't quite figured out."

Gwen slammed her book shut and pushed to her feet. "Why exactly do you need to 'figure us out'?"

"I find it makes my business trips more pleasant if I get to know my hosts. Isn't there anything you want to know about me?" he asked.

"Yes, actually," Jana interrupted. "I asked you before and I'll ask you again...what business do you have here?"

Claymore straightened his shoulders. "Ask me anything else and I'll be happy to answer, but my business dealings with your father are not up for discussion."

"Then it looks like we won't be getting to know each other after all." Gwen gestured to her sisters then walked out the door, leaving Claymore behind with nothing but a smirk on his face.

* * *

The room shook as Jana slammed the door. "Damn that bastard! I want to know what Claymore is doing here," she cussed.

"I'm curious too, but you heard him, he won't be sharing. And you know Father's always been secretive about his business. Sometimes I wonder if we're the daughters of a German crime-boss." Adele threw herself across her bed.

"It doesn't matter," Gwen interjected as she flipped on the TV. "It's not like we ever leave this house anyway, so let's just continue to act normal and ignore him. If he wants to stare at us while we read, whatever...other than being totally creepy, what difference does it make? As long as we get to go back out at night, I couldn't care less what that man does during the day."

Jana and Adele agreed, then settled in to relax as their favorite show started to play on the flat screen. Gwen missed the opening credits and the first ten minutes, finding herself lost in thought, instead. Claymore was a conundrum. She meant what she said, she didn't care what he did while here, but one minute he seemed interested in her, then the next, he was giving Jana a rigid response to a simple question. He had Gwen confused, and the fact that he was attractive wasn't helping to clear her head.

* * *

Standing alone in the empty library, Claymore dialed his phone. "Madame Vizol, are the items I requested ready?"

"Yes."

"Fantastic! Please have them delivered to the Von Brandt house this afternoon. I'm in need of your expertise."

"Of course, my apprentice. But conceal the magic well, for the task at hand requires stealth and patience."

"Thanks for the advice. As always, I'm honored to be your student."

Gwen awoke to a soft knock.

"Is everything okay?" Claymore whispered from the other side of the door.

Gwen rose and opened the door, peeking through the crack. "Yes, everything is fine. My sister's fell asleep."

"I'm sorry to interrupt your afternoon respite, but I'm in need of some assistance. Would you mind helping me?"

Gwen felt a chill and rubbed her hands down her arms. "What exactly do you need?"

Claymore motioned for her to exit the room, placing a finger to his lips as if not wanting to wake her sisters. Gwen eased the door open and slipped into the hall, placing her back against the thick wood.

"How can I help you?" she offered.

"I have some clothes that need repair, but when I looked for someone to ask, I only found the kitchen staff, and they informed me there wasn't a tailor in town. Do you know of any good shops where I could replace my tattered items?"

Gwen cocked her head to the side and frowned.

"What's wrong?" Claymore asked.

"I'm just trying to figure out why you sound like you're from the 1600s."

Claymore laughed. "I'm sorry if my formality irritates you. I was raised with the old world manners of my mother, and it's simply a part of who I am." He gave a quirky little shrug.

A tiny spark of interest flared in Gwen's mind. Maybe Claymore wasn't as bad as they thought. "All we have is the kitchen staff to attend to our meals, and they're right, there isn't a tailor in town. But, if you'd like, I can help you do some online shopping later to get your things replaced."

"Thank you. That would be great."

"You're welcome. I'll meet you back in the library later." Gwen turned to open her bedroom door when Claymore grabbed her by the arm. Spinning to face him, her breath caught when she saw the look in his eyes.

"You asked me why I needed to 'figure you out' early today." He dropped his hand back to his side. "What I said was true. It does make my visits more pleasant. But with you...it's something more."

Gwen watched him walked away. Slowly, confidently, and in no way apologetic for the feelings he'd just shared. A blush spread across her cheeks, but she instantly felt remorse. Her heart tightened when she thought of Liam.

Gwen jumped as the door opened under her hand. Jana and Adele stood grinning from ear to ear. "That sounded...interesting," Jana teased.

Gwen pushed into the bedroom, shutting the door behind her. "Whatever. It was odd. He doesn't even know me."

"Sure sounds like he wants to, though," Adele added.

"Well, that's just too bad." Gwen plopped down onto her bed. "Because I've got a date tonight."

The sisters squealed in anticipation at meeting the guys again, quickly forgetting about Claymore, and their father's rules. A night of dancing in the arms of their boyfriends was exactly what they needed to unwind.

* * *

"Girls, how was your day?" Richard asked from across the dinner table.

"Fine," Gwen replied. "We did some reading in the library, watched some TV, and took a nap. Then this afternoon, I helped Claymore with some online shopping. We were lucky to find a local store that would deliver same day for free."

Richard glanced at Claymore—finding his gaze transfixed on Gwen—and nodded in approval. "Well, thank you for taking care of our guest while I was out."

Gwen, Jana, and Adele ducked their heads and, as usual, continued their meal in silence. All the while, pining for the evening to come to a close so their night could actually begin. Their father seemed pleased to excuse them early, most likely to discuss business with Claymore, but all to the girls' advantage. They raced back to their room and pulled out their hidden stash of clothes.

"I think I'll wear the stiletto boots tonight. They're sexy!" Adele bounced back into the closet.

"They would look great with that new skirt Gwen just got, though," Jana winked at her big sister.

Gwen couldn't contain herself and laughed. "What? Did you think I wasn't going to take him up on his offer of payment?" Gwen held up a fur-lined leather vest and a pair of killer high heels.

"Sure looks like you got the better end of the deal," Jana added.

"I definitely did. The only things he had me order for him were a pair of strange military pants made out of some weird material, and more button-down shirts."

"Military? Do you think he's some kind of soldier, then?" Adele asked. "I mean, he did make that comment in the library about rescuing princesses being part of his job."

"I don't know and I don't care." Gwen's tone was indifferent as she stuffed her newly purchased items back into the closet.

"Tuck in, ladies. Father will be here shortly."

They didn't have to wait long for their father to bid them goodnight, stating his nightly demand, and locking their door. Within seconds, they shot from their beds and pulled on their chosen outfits.

Gwen let Adele borrow her skirt, while she donned her new heels and a killer dress she'd been saving for Liam. Jana threw on her favorite pair of leather pants and paired it with a backless halter and a pair of wedges. With one twist of the bedpost, they descended into the tunnel that would lead them to their suitors.

Adele stopped short just after reaching the bottom of the stairs. "Hold on. I think I heard something."

Gwen and Jana froze, listening intently. "I don't hear anything," Jana stated. "Come on, let's go."

They continued forward, ignoring Adele's warning. The tunnel seemed longer tonight, which was most likely due to their eagerness to reach the end. Finally, they arrived at the door and stepped out into a cool evening breeze. "Good evening, ladies. You all look beautiful," Liam said as he took Gwen in his arms. The world fell away as he stared into her eyes, the intensity of his gaze setting her blood on fire.

"Which club do you want to visit tonight?" Colin asked Adele.

Still feeling on edge from the sound in the tunnel, she diverted, , "I don't care. Why don't you pick?"

Colin ran his hands up and down Adele's arms. "Okay, baby. How about we hit the silver one first, then if there's time, we'll visit the diamond club later?"

Everyone smiled, including Adele, but hers didn't quite reach her eyes. The three couples filed into the silver club and quickly found their way to the dance floor. The music here was more upbeat than that of the golden club. The grand space was dripping with chains, and balls of glittering silver hung from the ceiling, lending perfectly to the techno vibe.

"This is fun!" Frederick yelled as he and Jana gyrated to the music.

Adele quickly followed suit and forgot her worries as she and Colin moved to the beat.

* * *

The evening flew by, leaving no time to visit the diamond club. *There's always tomorrow night*, Adele thought. They bid farewell to the guys and descended back into the tunnel.

"Do you think we'll ever get to spend more time with them?" Jana asked. "Maybe we should just tell Father that we all have boyfriends and invite them to meet him."

"Are you crazy?" Gwen spat. "Father would not only have their heads, but ours too, once he learned how we met." She shook her head. "No. This has to remain our secret."

Jana sighed and glanced at Adele, who seemed agitated once again.

"What's wrong with you?" Jana asked her little sister.

"I don't know. I just keep getting the feeling like we're being watched."

"That's impossible and you know it," Jana snapped.

Adele frowned and continued up the stairs to their room, ready to bring this evening to a close. Gwen pushed through the opening and signaled that the coast was clear. The night had been fun, but there was a palpable tension in the air. The sisters disrobed, hiding their party clothes as usual, then crawled into bed, each struggling through a night of fitful dreams.

· ✧ ·

Earlier that same evening...

"Have you found anything yet?" Richard asked Claymore from across the empty dining room table.

"Not yet, but tonight I will have your answers. I'll just need the key to their room," Claymore requested.

Richard hesitated, not liking the idea of a man in his daughters' room after dark, but finally relented. After all, he was the one who hired the magical investigator. "Okay. I'll tuck them in as usual, then leave the key with you, but I want a report first thing in the morning."

"I'll be in your office by 8 a.m.," Claymore confirmed.

14

Richard nodded, then proceeded to the girls' room. "Good night. Sleep well, and of course, you're not allowed out of your room until morning." He locked the door, handed over the key, and retired to his room, anxious for this night to pass. These last few months had been the worst of his life. Even more so than when he lost his beloved wife. It was because of his promise to her that he'd become so vile and crazed with keeping their daughters safe. Crazed to the point that he was willing to hurt the ones he loved most in the world.

Claymore returned to his guest quarters and gathered his things: his noise-cancelling pants and knapsack, and the invisibility cloak Madame Vizol had delivered. Fully disguised and unseen by all, he crept down the hallway and listened at the girls' door.

The rustling of clothes and laughter filled his ears until a loud 'boom' sounded, and he knew it was time to move. At the first hint of clicking heels, Claymore twisted the key and silently entered the room. He rapidly scanned the scene and rushed down the open staircase with the stealth of a jaguar.

Claymore caught up to the ladies within seconds and was stunned by their appearance. Struggling to maintain his composure as he stared at Gwen leading the way, he stumbled and kicked a stone into the nearest wall, catching Adele's attention.

He froze and listened as the sisters dismissed her concern. Minutes later he followed them onto a street where they were met by three young men, all of whom seemed *very* acquainted with them.

Entering the silver club, his head throbbed at the intensity of the music, so as soon as he was certain they were staying put for the evening, he ventured back into the street. Closing his eyes he felt the tingle of magic roll across his skin. He needed to find out exactly where this "street" was.

Venturing north, past the diamond club, he reached a dead-end within minutes, the pavement butting up against a thick wall of trees. Turning around, he ran to the opposite end of the street only to find the same. However, at this end, he spotted a small path that led into the woods.

Pulling a potion from his knapsack, he threw it onto the path to determine its safety; red smoke would mean high danger, while blue or white meant safe travels. The smoke was pink. "Well, damn," Claymore cussed.

Pulling his cloak tight, he walked back to the silver club and found a seat inside. He needed to gauge the timetable of the girls' evening, before he went scrambling off into the unknown forest.

Three hours later, the couples kissed each other goodnight and Claymore followed the ladies back through the door and into the tunnel once more, returning to the safety of their bedroom. Hiding under his cloak, he tried to remain the gentleman he was raised to be as the sisters undressed. Despite all his efforts, however, he couldn't help but sneak a peek at Gwen's beautiful skin and deadly curves as she slid out of her dance clothes and into her bed. Shaking himself free of the torrid thoughts currently plaguing him, he slipped out the door, as soon as the girls were asleep.

* * *

"Your daughters are sneaking into a magical realm every night, dancing their evenings away with three young men," Claymore explained.

"You lie!" Richard slammed his fists on the desk.

"No. I do not. I will need more time to figure out where they are actually going, and who the young men are, though."

Richard shook his head as he paced his office. "I can't believe this. How in the hell did they gain access to a magical realm? I had this house fortified when their mother and I moved in."

"There's a tunnel that runs from underneath Gwen's bed."

"Dammit! You can have two more nights, but I want proof that what you say is true," Richard demanded.

"Fine. I'll bring you proof tonight."

The sisters woke feeling restless and didn't talk much on their way down to breakfast. Adele's concerns throughout the night apparently weighed on them more than they cared to admit. "Good morning, ladies," Claymore offered.

"Good morning," Jana and Adele mumbled in response, while Gwen remained silent. still unsure of her feelings towards this enigma of a man.

"Where's our father?" Jana asked, noticing the empty chair at the head of the table.

"When I left his office this morning, he said to start without him. Apparently, he had a few phone calls to make."

Gwen narrowed her eyes at Claymore who returned her gaze until the tension was broken when the first course was served. She gave a clipped nod to the staff, and with her eyes firmly downcast to avoid any further awkwardness, buttered her bread.

"Did you sleep well last night?" Claymore asked just as she took a bite of her toast.

Gwen coughed. "Yes. As well as any other night. Why do you ask?"

"I thought I heard you rustling around when I grabbed a glass of water before bed. From the sound of your dreams, it seemed you were upset about something."

"What makes you think it was me? It could have been Jana or Adele for all you know," Gwen replied.

"Very true, but I've grown accustomed to the rich timbre of your sexy voice, so I know it was you."

Toast went flying from Gwen's mouth as Jana and Adele gasped at Claymore's forward comment.

"What?" Claymore asked. "We're close enough in age, and you're very beautiful. Did you not think I'd find you attractive?"

Panicked, Gwen looked at her sisters for help but found none. "I'm sorry. I just don't know what to say," Gwen admitted.

Claymore lifted a shoulder in indifference but remained silent, continuing to enjoy the discomfort he was purposely causing. He needed them off their game if he was to bring this investigation to a close within two nights.

"Wait a minute!" Jana declared. "Is *this* your business here? Is our father trying to set the two of you up?"

Tears formed in Gwen's eyes when Claymore leaned back in his chair with a smirk on his face. Arranged marriages weren't unheard of in their culture, even in this day and age. How dare her father do this to her?

"Holy shit, Gwen. I'm so sorry," Jana stammered.

Gwen composed herself as quickly as possible, wiping away a small tear as it escaped onto her cheek. "Don't apologize, Jana. There's nothing to be concerned about. And I'm sorry Claymore, I'm not sure what arrangement you have with my father, but please know, it will not include me."

Gwen pushed away from the table and left the room without another word. Adele stared at Jana who just shook her head then filled her plate before following suit. Making their way upstairs, Jana and Adele found Gwen crying uncontrollably into her pillow.

"Oh Gwen, it'll be okay," Jana offered, setting her plate of food on the bed.

Gwen snapped upright, huffing and snarling her next words. "Oh, I know it'll be okay, because after tonight, Father or Claymore will never see me again."

"What? What are you talking about?" Adele pleaded.

"I'm saying, when we go to meet the guys tonight, I'm not coming home. I'm going to stay and make a life with Liam."

* * *

The entire day passed without any interruptions from Claymore or their father. Gwen worried, at first, what their combined absence could mean, but chose to spend her time focusing on her plan to run away with Liam, instead. Adele and Jana continued to offer support each in their own way. Jana pulled out and folded the clothes Gwen had indicated she wanted to pack, while Adele continued to brush through her big sister's long black hair. "I understand you're upset, Gwen, but if you leave with Liam to escape Father, that means we'll never see you either." Adele sniffled.

"That's not true. You can easily slip through the tunnel and visit me whenever you'd like, and besides, I'm sure Colin and Frederick will ask you to marry them soon as well."

"What?" Jana exclaimed. "I thought this was just you being upset, are you saying Liam actually asked you to marry him?"

Gwen nodded. "Yes. Just last night."

The sisters threw themselves onto Gwen's bed. "Oh my god...congratulations!" Adele exclaimed.

"I was planning to approach Father about an introduction today, but, well...that's obviously not going to happen now." Gwen's shoulders slumped.

They all picked at the remnants from their breakfast while Gwen told them everything. "While we were dancing, he leaned in close and whispered in my ear. *'I need to talk to you alone.'* So we headed to the end of the bar where we could hear a little better and he said, *'Gwen, I'm the eldest in my family, and it's time for me to choose my bride, and I choose you. Will you marry me?'* It was sweet and simple and I said yes."

"I can't believe this is happening," sobbed Adele.

"What's wrong?" Gwen hugged her sister. "I thought you'd be happy for me."

Adele pulled back and wiped away her tears. "I am happy for you, but everything is just happening so fast."

"I know, honey, but I feel something special with Liam. I can't exactly put my finger on it. It's like magic." She reached for Adele's hand. "I guess it's true what they say...when you know, you just know."

Adele's sad smile wavered as she tried to push past her feelings of jealousy. She wasn't jealous of Gwen's happiness, but of the freedom they all longed for.

"Can't we just come with you? I mean, even if they don't ask us to marry them too, can't we just stay with you and Liam so we can all be together?"

Gwen ran her hand down Adele's arm. "I'll ask Liam when I see him tonight, and if he agrees, the two of you can come back and get your things and return tomorrow for good."

Jana and Adele beamed at each other then jumped off the bed and disappeared into the abyss of their massive closet. They both returned with Louis Vuitton suitcases and started to pack, clearly excited for the prospect of their new lives.

<hr/>

Jana rushed back through the bedroom door with two huge plates in her hands. "Time for dinner!"

Gwen and Adele sat on the floor, digging into the stolen garb. It wasn't much: fruit, bread, and cheese, but it definitely hit the spot.

"Did you see Father?" Gwen asked, popping a grape into her mouth.

"Nope. I didn't see anyone. Actually, I don't even think the staff is here. No one made dinner, so I just grabbed all this stuff out of the fridge."

"I bet Father took him out so they could *seal their deal*," Adele frowned.

"Oh well, lucky for us." Jana interjected. "We can eat and get ready early. I can't wait to see the guys tonight and find out if we can join you, Gwen."

Gwen nodded and bite her bottom lip. She wanted to share in their excitement, but in reality, she was worried her plan would backfire. What if Liam said no? What if their family didn't allow pre-marital co-habitation? Her sisters would be devastated, not to mention, left at their father's mercy, which would no doubt become even crueler after he learned of her escape.

"I'm excited too." Gwen pushed for sincerity but wasn't sure if she managed it or not. She was hopeful, but the entire situation was edged with fear and necessity, and that made her uneasy.

Adele gasped, causing her sisters to flinch.

"What's wrong?" Jana asked.

"Something just touched my leg."

Gwen scurried off the floor, looking for a spider of bug of some sort. "Did it bite you?"

Adele jumped up. "No, not like a bug. Like something...bigger, touched me."

Gwen and Jana exchanged looks of concern. "It's probably just a muscle twitching from sitting on the floor for too long," Jana suggested.

"No! It wasn't." Adele ran into the bathroom, shutting the door behind her.

Gwen shook her head and called through the door, "Honey, let's just get dressed and head out of here. You'll feel better once you see Colin."

"Okay," Adele said shakily. "I'll be out in a few."

Gwen and Jana peeled off their day clothes and threw on their evening attire. Tonight was special, so they'd both chosen beautiful full-length gowns; Gwen's was lavender while Jana's was a deep forest green. Adele came out of the bathroom and walked straight over to Gwen.

"I want you to have this." Adele handed Gwen the diamond tiara their mother had left her.

Tears began to swell in Gwen's eyes as she shook her head. "No, Adele. I can't. Mama left that for you to wear on your wedding day."

"I know, but I want you to have it. That way, if we aren't able to come see you again, you'll have something to remember me by."

Adele fell into Gwen's arms, sobbing uncontrollably as her fear and worry finally broke free of the emotional damn she'd so carefully built. Dealing with her mother's death, and now with how cruel their father had become, the idea of losing her big sister was simply too much to bear. "Sweetie, don't cry. It'll be okay," Gwen comforted.

Adele pulled back, wiping her cheeks. "No, it won't. Even if Liam says we can come stay with you the following night, Father won't allow it. The second he sees you're not here, he'll beat us both and never let us out of his sight again."

Gwen looked up into Jana's shining eyes. It seemed they all shared the same fear.

"Then, that's it. We'll all leave tonight and never come back. If Liam doesn't allow you to stay with us, then we'll just find a place of our own."

Adele's brows lifted as hopefulness replaced despair. Jana handed her a tissue box after snagging a few for herself. "Then it's settled. Tonight, we'll finally be free."

* * *

Claymore huddled in the corner of the girls' bedroom as they ate their dinner, listening to all their plans from under his invisible cloak. It was Richard's idea to make them think the house was empty, so Claymore could follow them, unimpeded, and obtain as much information as possible. Unfortunately, hours of crouching in silence left Claymore uncomfortable and with no further information about where it was that the sisters actually went. The only thing he did gain was a colossal headache and the knowledge that his two-day time frame had just been shot to hell.

The girls were leaving, permanently, tonight, and it was all his fault. He hadn't expected Gwen to react so fiercely to the announcement that they were being set up. Yes, he used the information to spur them on so he could speed up the investigation, but if he was being honest with himself, her refusal was a blow to his pride.

Claymore stretched out his left leg, trying to ease the cramp that was currently forming in his calf. *Shit!* He'd accidentally grazed Adele. He remained still as they reacted, then was finally able to stand once Adele raced into the bathroom. Unfortunately, he was still trapped in the room with Gwen and Jana, leaving no way to warn Richard of their plan.

He looked away as Gwen and Jana began to undress, but couldn't deny himself another glimpse of Gwen as she slid into her beautiful lavender dress. He'd been intrigued when he received the offer from Richard, that if he were to solve the case so many others couldn't, that he'd be set-up with his eldest daughter. But never once did he imagine that he'd actually fall for her.

Bound and determined to bring this case to a close, Claymore waited patiently under his cloak then followed the sisters when they descended the stairs for what they thought would be the last time. They'd each packed a bag, taking clothes and mementos that carried specific meaning to them all. They were greeted immediately by the three boys Claymore had seen the night before. Paying close attention to their interaction, he listened while Gwen explained the situation.

"Liam, I've accepted your proposal, but can't live without my sisters. Will it be all right if they come to live with us now?"

All three young men broke into wide salacious grins. "Of course, they can."

The hair on Claymore's arms stood on end. Something about these guys was off, but he couldn't quite put his finger on it just yet.

"Let's skip the club tonight, and take them home to meet Father," Colin suggested.

"That would be great," Adele agreed, throwing herself into his arms.

Claymore followed the couples to the trail he'd observed before, pulling his knife from its sheath before stepping into the forest. The guys continued to make small talk as they guided the sisters deeper and deeper into the woods. About a half-mile in, they came upon a clearing which contained a beautiful white castle, sparkling in the distance. Even though it was after dark, Claymore could see bits of silver, gold, and diamonds worked throughout the structure, just like the disco clubs where they had all danced their nights away.

"This is spectacular!" Adele cried.

"Thank you. I can't wait to show you the ballroom," Colin stated. "We'll be able to dance together forever."

Claymore froze. He knew where they were and what he was up against. Madame Vizol had told him of the land of the Fae, and he was now certain that before him stood the three Unseelie Princes. Stories told that until a person *asked* to stay in their realm, the Fae had to allow them to return home, but once the request was made, they'd be prisoners forever, forced to dance until they died, their energy and pain feeding the Unseelie family.

The girls were walking straight towards their deaths, and it was all his fault. If he'd done a better job at understanding where they were, he would have never taunted Gwen like he had. He was the reason she'd run off tonight and brought her sisters with her.

Throwing off his cloak, he roared! "Stop...it's a trap!"

Everyone stopped and spun in his direction.

"What are you doing here?" Gwen yelled.

"I'm trying to save your lives!" Claymore exclaimed, brandishing his knife at the Princes. "Now get behind me!"

"Fuck you—We're never going..." Gwen's rebuttal was interrupted by loud growling and hissing. The sisters spun around and screamed as three beasts launched themselves at Claymore—beasts that used to be men.

Gwen, Jana, and Adele huddled together on the ground, crying and praying for a miracle. Flashes of fangs, rotted flesh, blood and fur were all Gwen could see from the cyclone of the fight. Puffs of black smoke filled the air that she could only assume was magic potions, each eliciting a pain-filled cry from one of the guys.

Minutes later, all was silent. Gwen eased her sisters to stand and raced towards Claymore. "What were they?" she asked, glancing at the deformed remains of the three brothers.

"Fae. Unseelie Fae to be precise. Now, come on. We have to get out of here." He reached to the ground and retrieved his cloak. Pushing the sisters to run as fast as they could back up the forest trail, they quickly reached the street that would lead them home.

"How did you know?" Jana panted through ragged breaths.

"Your father hired me to investigate where you disappeared to every night." He shook his cloak in the air, and then draped it across his chest to demonstrate its affect. "Obviously, I have a bit of magic at my disposal and was able to follow you here last night."

"See...I told you something was in the tunnel with us," Adele exclaimed, happy for the validation. When Claymore's eyes met Gwen's he shuddered. Her twitching jaw and heaving chest leveled him. He knew she'd be mad when she found out the truth—mad at him, mad at her father, but he hoped she could understand now knowing the danger.

"You were spying on us?" she screamed.

"Yes," he whispered. "It was my job."

Gwen stepped closer to him, ready to express her rage when Jana grabbed her by the arm.

"How did you know the guys weren't as they appeared?" Jana asked.

"I didn't at first. It wasn't until the one mentioned dancing that I put two and two together. I'm sorry I wasn't faster."

"You saved us in the nick of time, so I'd say you're fast enough," Jana stated.

"I wouldn't be so sure about that," a deep voice boomed.

Claymore pushed the sisters behind him as he faced the Unseelie King. He was well over seven feet tall, cloaked in furs and jewels, and radiated pure evil.

"You just killed my sons and now you will all pay with your lives."

The girls' screams pierced the air as Claymore raised his knife in defense. There was no way he'd defeat the king with such a measly weapon, but when a white light burst from the door behind them, all became irrelevant.

"You will not touch my daughters, nor my future son-in-law. For the rules of our lands remain intact."

Gwen turned to see her father towering over them all. He wore a white sparkling suit, while a jeweled crown rested upon his head.

"Do not speak to me of rules, you just broke the main one by stepping foot into my realm," the Unseelie King exclaimed.

"Only to claim what is mine, which according to our rules, you have no right to."

"They asked to stay, so the right is mine."

"Your sons pursued my family, and therefore broke the law."

"It's not my fault they didn't know who the females were."

"Enough!" Richard bellowed.

"I am the Seelie King and the law states you have no claim over any of my family or kin. Walk away now, or you *will* face my wrath."

Claymore and the sisters stood dumbfounded as the Unseelie King turned and stomped back down the path, returning to his castle.

"Girls. Are you all okay?" Richard asked.

They all nodded their heads slowly, too shocked and afraid to speak.

Richard smiled for the first time in years and extended his arm towards the door. "Let's go and I'll explain everything back home."

They followed their father through the tunnel, watching as he shrunk back to his normal size with each step he took. Emerging in their bedroom, he ushered them aside then threw some sort of magical substance onto the slab in the floor. The seams of the door glowed, then a loud crack split the air, and the entrance to their nightmare disappeared completely.

The sisters slowly lowered themselves onto their beds, while Claymore leaned against the wall with his arms crossed and jaw tight. They all stared at Richard in silence, waiting for the explanation he promised.

"I'm sorry I deceived you all," Richard started. "I knew somehow the girls had gained access to the Unseelie realm, but it's forbidden for me to enter unless the King or his family breaks the rules." He gestured to Claymore. "That's why I needed you. I had to have someone I could count on that would keep my daughters safe. Thank you for protecting them."

Claymore nodded and glanced at Gwen, trying to gauge her reaction to Richard's compliment. Unfortunately, she gave none.

Finally finding her voice, Gwen asked, "How could you keep something like this from us?"

"Because you're mother asked me to. She wanted you to have as normal a life as possible, but when she died, I'll admit it, I went crazy. I was so worried I'd lose you, my strict and vicious ways ended up being the reason you fled night after night. I'm so sorry, can you ever forgive me?"

The sisters all lowered their heads, not sure how to process everything that had happened.

Richard sighed and continued, "I'm the Seelie King and rule this land. It was made to resemble the human world, and is why we kept you under lock and key. You're mother didn't want you to discover the truth of your heritage, but to remain free and have the ability to grow up and choose your own path. But, when I realized magic had invaded our lives, I hired Claymore to find out where you were going and to protect you."

"Oh, and don't forget the payment you offered as well?" Gwen spat.

Richard lowered his head. "Yes. I did offer your hand as payment if Claymore were to succeed. But only because I knew your mother would approve. He's a strong man, Gwen, a caring man, and comes from a family your mother was very fond of."

"What are you talking about, Richard," Claymore asked, joining the conversation.

"Your mother was a dear friend of my wife's, and together, with the help of a Fae elder, they weaved the spell that concealed our world. They both agreed that they wanted their children to grow up knowing different lives, and not be tied down by the politics of the Fae community. You're royalty, Gwen, and therefore hold claim to the throne if you want it."

Claymore looked at Gwen, who for the first time, finally saw the man in front of her as something more than just a bother. Pushing from the bed, Gwen crossed the room.

"Thank you for saving us. I fled because I was mad at my father and annoyed by your arrogance, but I now understand you had a job to do."

Claymore stood stock still, not sure if Gwen was accepting or dismissing him.

"This is all a lot to process, but you seem to have a better handle on it than us," she gestured to her sisters. "You're familiar with magic and seem to be good at your job, so if you're willing to take it slow, I'd be happy for you to show us more of our true world."

Claymore's heart caught in his chest as he dipped his head. "It would be my true pleasure, but I'm no more familiar with the Fae world than you are. The only reason I've been successful as a magical investigator is because of my teacher, Madame Vizol."

Suddenly, an old woman appeared in the center of a room. Her weathered face and silver hair, however, faded away as she grew in height and stature. Though still seemingly mature in age, she was now taller and more elegant and carried herself with an air of importance.

"Madame Vizol, I presume," Gwen surmised.

"My lady." Richard bowed, confusing everyone.

Madame Vizol moved to Claymore. "You have fulfilled the prophecy by killing the Unseelie Princes." She winked at Gwen. "And if the Princess will have you, then you may take your place as the Seelie King, for its foretold only a great warrior will best the Princes and win the heart of the new Queen."

Gwen gasped, looking to her father for further explanation.

"How do you think I met your mother?" He grinned wide. "Madame Vizol is the Fae elder I told you about. She is also the Seelie oracle and has watched the prophecy be fulfilled time and time again throughout the centuries. The Unseelie King will have more sons and one day, far in the future, these events will replay themselves, providing the new successors to the throne, but for now, it's you two, if you're ready."

Madame Vizol reached for Gwen and Claymore's hands, joining them in front of her. "Everyone gather around."

Jana, Adele, and Richard linked hands, completing the circle. Gwen felt the steady pulse of magic flow through her and gasped as their world fell away and a new reality took its place.

Rolling green hills and flowering trees dotted the landscape, surrounding them with breathtaking beauty. But only after Madame Vizol snapped her fingers and transported them to the palatial palace, did Gwen feel the truth of her heritage seeping into her bones. She could feel her mother here; her presence oozed from the walls and calmed her heart.

A shadow passed over the castle and Jana and Adele ran to the nearest window and squealed. There, drinking from the river in the distance was a real-life dragon with a multitude of Fae children climbing on its back.

Gwen turned to Claymore. "It looks like your dragon-slaying services won't be needed here."

He took her hand. "I'm sure I can find other adventures to fill my time."

Gwen reached up and placed a light kiss on his lips. "Thank you for saving us."

Claymore thought of all the lonely nights he'd spent without family or friends and pulled her close, returning her kiss with one that spoke of loyalty and love. "Thank *you* for saving *me*."

The End

Award Winning Author, Tish Thawer, writes paranormal romances for all ages. Her magickal elements and detailed world-building are a welcome constant in every novel.

Before becoming a writer she worked as a computer consultant, a photographer and a graphic designer. She also operates a custom glass etching business, in addition to being a wife and the mother of three wonderful children.

She's been a fan of the paranormal for as long as she can remember. Anything to do with superpowers, myth and magic has always held a special place in her heart. From her first paranormal cartoon, Isis, to the phenomenon that is Twilight, this genre has always been a part of her life.

Tish is represented by Gandolfo, Helin, and Fountain Literary Management. To learn more, visit:
http://www.TishThawer.com

AWAKENED
A retelling of Sleeping Beauty
by Kristen Strassel

Darius

"This is all your fault!" The oldest of the women who'd congregated outside of Lani's hospital room shook her finger in the faces of the rest. They all looked somewhat like Lani, depending on the amount of plastic surgery they'd indulged in, and most casual onlookers would guess they were her aunts. But I knew better than that. They were witches. Curses and spells swirled thick in the air, disguising my brand of magic. "She could've used her talents to help people. She didn't have to be famous. It's a waste. I warned you all this would happen!"

A younger witch stood up, locking eyes with her accuser. "This is your fault," she growled. "You convinced her father that being a musician would bring her to the devil. She could've played for the symphony. But instead it became a self-fulfilling prophecy!"

"Because I was right!" The older woman shook with anger. "Look at that band she's in. They all look like they crawled out of Hell. I choke on the evil every time I hear them play."

The two women relaxed when they saw me, their eyes lighting up, their faces too stiff to show much emotion. "Hello, Doctor," the younger one purred.

I wasn't a fucking doctor. They saw what I wanted them to see.

And they were wrong. This was my fault.

They weren't wrong about everything; supernatural like me, they had a sense for things, especially evil ones. I may have crawled out of Hell. The last three hundred years certainly felt like it. Every part of the afterlife had been an atonement for my mortal sins, until I met Lani.

Now, I planned to finish what I started.

"Is Alannah's next of kin present?" I asked the gathering once they settled, every one of them more interested in getting into a doctor's pants, and more importantly his wallet, than whatever news I had for them about their niece.

"They'd love to be," one of them said too quickly, attempting a frown. *Bullshit.* I knew neither of Lani's parents had spoken to her since she joined my band, Wicked Intentions. "But it's the Cannes Film

1

Festival. They'd already committed. And Mr. DeAngeles is hoping this film revives his career. It's taken a hit since…" The entire room glared at her. She didn't need to continue. Everyone knew they'd taken a public beating since Lani had emerged as the gothic hellcat lead singer of a heavy metal band. "Oh. No, they're not. We're her aunts, and her parents are a phone call away."

"You might want to get them on the phone."

The ladies nodded. Lani's mother didn't bother to hide her irritation when they reached her. "Now what?" she said through the speaker.

"The doctor is asking for Alannah's next of kin." The woman with the phone peeked up at me, her red lips curling up in a half smile, like depending on what I had to say, she was hoping I'd take her out for a drink after.

"Oh." Her tone changed. "Has there been any improvement?"

"As you know, Alannah is suffering from a massive blood loss of an undetermined origin. Her body is rejecting transfused blood, causing an allergic reaction. We've tried using her blood type, as well as others. All cause the same trauma. It's slowed her organ function, and they're beginning to show signs of fatigue." I racked my brain, trying to remember what else I'd heard the night shift doctor tell the interns at the beginning of their shift. None of these women would remember any of this, but on the off chance it came back to them in bits and pieces, I wanted it to align with what the real doctors might have told them. I'd fucked up enough, landing Lani here. She was my first, my last, my everything, and I couldn't make any more mistakes. "The progress we were hoping to see has not manifested yet, and at this point, it's unlikely she'll be able to produce more blood. In fact, with the weakening of her organs, she will lose more."

"She's failing," her mother said. Some of the witches in front of me wept, but the witch on the phone showed no emotion.

"As of now, Alannah's in a holding pattern. We can keep supporting her organs artificially, or we can take her off the support, to see if she'll thrive with the use of medication."

"She can't die!" The old witch wailed. Several of the others encouraged her to calm down. She sat down, lowering her voice. "Alannah can never die. She's our future."

Her mother sighed. "This is too much to even consider right now." She didn't sound overwhelmed, more inconvenienced. "We can't do anything until Cannes is over. Our focus is here now. If we can keep her on the support, it can wait until we get back to the states."

* * *

Using this much glamour in one night drained me like I'd drained my precious Lani, but I didn't have any time to waste. I couldn't be here with her during the day to protect her from her family or the medical professionals who despite their best efforts, couldn't save her. I was the only one who could do it. The same poison I'd brought her under with would be the best medicine.

Lani was my future. If I lost her, I'd crawl into her grave and hold her until death came for me as well.

The witches had fallen into a deep sleep, so this part of the glamour was working. I still wore a doctor's clothes, but as I weakened in the early morning hours, my features bled through. My black spiky hair replaced the slicked back, receding hairline of my facade, my jawline strengthened, and a little bit of the eyeliner I'd left on after last night's show was still smudged under my eyes. I'd blame it on the night shift if anyone asked. Every night in ICU was hell, and they'd never believe anything different.

Like Lani's parents, Wicked Intentions had tried to go on without her, too. My band mates insisted we didn't need our frontwoman, that we'd pull in the fans no matter who sang. *Bullshit.* Like me, our fans held vigil outside the hospital, singing our songs and crying on each other's shoulders. I'd joined the crowds several times, their energy the only thing helping me survive without Lani. That was the closest I could get to her as Darius Blackburne. Immediate family only in the ICU.

Those women weren't her family, they were her blood. Tonight, I'd give her my blood and make her my family.

It took too long to shut down the machines. Concentrating hard to keep the department staff busy, I slowly unhooked Lani from her life support. She couldn't afford any more shocks to her system. This time, I wouldn't ask for help. Her body was as light and soft as a feather in my arms. Without waking, she sighed, lips turning up in the tiniest smile.

"You're safe now, my sleeping beauty," I whispered as I carried her through the halls of the hospital. No one saw us pass, but I didn't want to risk them hearing anything they shouldn't. I glamoured the entire hospital now. Only a few fans held vigil in the parking lot at this hour, uniformed in all black, earbuds in, listening to Wicked Intentions, scanning their phones for hopes of any update. The update passed through the crowd unnoticed. Lani Angel, as her admirers knew her and loved her, had been checked out of the hospital, against doctor's advice, and tonight I'd make her my queen.

Lani

I only remembered bits and pieces of what happened.

Nothing unusual. Wicked Intensions lived for the night. That's when we crawled out of our bus and kicked the ass of whoever didn't get out of our way. Blackouts were part of the party.

The fans fucking loved it. Every night I gave them my blood, sweat and tears, and they made sure not a drop was wasted. We'd been on the road for almost two years, and I was addicted to the feeling of stepping on stage. The roar of the crowd possessed me, controlled me. Alannah DeAngeles, America's Sweetheart, melted into the puddle of hypocrisy she was and Lani Angel took over, stomping through the ooze my alter ego left behind, on her way to the place she belonged.

I was born for this. My heart beat in time to the double bass drum, and my core pulsed with the vibration of the bassline. Throbbing, dripping, addicted to this. Craving its maestro. Darius Blackburne, the beautiful man manipulating the strings, turned my body inside out every night. His music cast a spell over me, sending me into a frenzy that I couldn't parallel.

All I'd wanted since Darius approached me to sing in his band was for him to make me feel the same way. Not for any audience. Those talented fingers strumming my body, not the tight strings of his bass. Making music only we could dance to. But he refused.

"You can't handle me," I'd tease. Every so often, I'd crawl into his lap, still sweaty and shaking from our performance. Fans would be everywhere, and when I was this high, I was too cocky to consider he'd reject me in front of a crowd.

"Not like this," he'd whisper in my ear, that English accent liquefying me as he eased me away his body. He'd always hesitate. I loved that. "But I will have you, my beauty. You don't have to beg for it, you already have me on my knees."

Like *that* would make me behave. Music wasn't the only thing that made Darius beautiful, nor was that accent, although he got serious bonus points for being born in the United Kingdom. All the guys in the band dyed their hair black, and I joked it was part of their contract. The rest of them wore it long, but Darius kept his short and spiky, and I had to sit on my hands sometimes not to pull it. Those eyes, the color of sea glass, always teased me. There was only so long he could expect me to hold out before I ravished him. And why, really? He'd named his band Wicked Intentions. He'd better have some.

His pale skin was wrapped in ink, telling a story I didn't know the ending to yet because it was obscured by his clothes. He'd punctuated it with metal, and last night on stage I'd run my tongue down the line of piercings on his sternum. It had been a risk, and the crowd went wild. Darius tasted like ice water and sin. I was instantly addicted to the taste, and I'd do anything to have more of it.

Instead of pushing me away after the show, Darius scraped his teeth against my neck. No matter what I did, I'd never forget that. The sensation electrified me. My back arched, my hair whipped back, and the little crowd lucky enough to witness our exchange backstage roared. The fans wanted Darius and me to hook up, even more than they wanted us for themselves. They said we'd make the perfect couple. Fuck, I'd been expected to be perfect all my life. I'd had enough of that shit. I wanted messy, dangerous, and most definitely orgasmic. Darius was all of those things, a broken puzzle I'd had yet to piece together. Tonight, it looked like I might finally get my wish. The room was stunned to silence when I crawled off his lap, holding my hand out to beckon him to follow. Always hesitating, my beautiful fallen angel. It broke my heart for so many reasons.

He followed me back to the hotel, thank God we didn't have to go back to the bus tonight. Darius and I deserved to be alone for the first time, to be totally consumed by one another without the threat of our asshole bandmates pulling back the curtain so they could watch.

I slammed him against the wall as soon as we returned to the hotel room, and went up on my tiptoes to try to kiss him. His whole body was hard with me pressed against him, wanting the same thing I did. I couldn't reach, even in my stilettos, instead I licked the piercings again, to make sure they were as delicious as last time. The second taste was even sweeter, like the first snow of the season. But the sharp bite of sin was still there, and that's what did me in.

Darius pulled my head away from his skin by my hair. I purred, licking my lips when I met his eyes. Something I'd never seen before swirled within them, a violent ocean storm. His bassline rumbled through me, even though we finished our show over an hour ago. "No." There was force behind that soft word. "We won't do this like you don't matter, Alannah."

"You know I hate that name," I groaned. I despised being reminded that I was Alannah. That bitch came with a set of expectations I had no intention of living up to. I'd run to the corners of the earth, but her prissy ass always followed me. And now Darius used my real name? And he still thought he was going to get me naked? *Oh, hell no.* If he'd changed his mind about this, all he had to do was say so. I'd fight him tooth and nail on it, but I'd probably let him have his way. Because it would make it hotter. "This is the place I can be who I want to be, and that's Lani."

"Lani is a character, a place for you to hide." Darius cupped my chin. I didn't know if he'd ever kiss me at this point, or if he wanted to keep me from mouthing off. "If I go inside of you, I want to know I'm really with you, not a façade you use to piss off your parents. I can have anyone's body. But I want your heart, your passion, and your soul. Can you give me that, Alannah?"

I fought the smile forming on my lips. If anyone else ever said that to me, I'd give them so much shit, and remind them that I'd forget their name in the morning. Leave this room without turning to see if the door latched. But when Darius said it, my knees buckled. Maybe it was the accent, but it was the most romantic thing I'd ever heard.

Okay, it was the only romantic thing I'd ever heard.

"I can try." It was the only honest answer.

He nodded, understanding. "Lay on the bed."

My legs were rubber noodles. I fell on the bed, pushing out my chest to still look sexy when I landed. I giggled, like I meant to do that, but Darius' smoldering expression remained constant. No man had ever looked at me like that before, like once he came inside me he never intended to leave. It made me feverish, not because he wanted me, but because I'd craved this for so long. Our fans, the string of nameless, faceless dudes I'd wasted too many nights with…they were great and all, but they left a gnawing in my belly that could never be satisfied. I craved someone's complete adoration. To be their whole world. Maybe that's why Darius tried to resist me for so long, because this was overwhelming.

I unhooked my corset. We'd still been backstage when this started, and I hadn't changed out of my stage clothes yet. My fingers trembled, and I couldn't see what I was doing past the swell of my breasts. They were aching to be free.

Darius moved like a whisper, I didn't know he was beside me until he covered my hands with his. "No." His touch sent goosebumps skittering over my skin.

I rolled my eyes, but he was melting my defenses. He always did. Darius was the only person who I felt comfortable showing little glimpses of the real me. The girl who used to be Alannah, the one who wore pink fuzzy things and liked to eat ice cream sundaes. Not the bad ass loudmouth the rest of the world had come to know and love. "Just because you're older than me doesn't mean you can boss me around."

"You have no idea what I intend to do with you. And I've been waiting a long time for this." His face hovered above mine, studying like he'd never seen me before. I trembled under his touch, his hand on my stomach. That was it. "I don't want to mess this up."

He should've said he didn't want *me* to mess this up. I wasn't willing to guarantee many things, but I could fuck them up like no one's business. Lost in his gaze, the initial flash of anger faded, and everything made sense. I'd been throwing myself at anyone who would take me, locking lips and much more in front of Darius ever since the tour started. I'd do anything to get his attention. Trying to get him to make his move. We'd shared so many scorching glances on stage, white lightning between us, but never more than a casual touch. "Fine. We'll play by your rules. This time."

"Every time, Alannah." His lips brushed across mine, feather soft. He pulled back before I had a chance to respond. "And you'll like it." The next kiss was like a tattoo on my soul. I'd never gotten one, they were too permanent for me. Forever was the only thing that scared me.

Darius' lips moved slowly and softly, like he played violin and not bass. The kiss had a haunting melody, and the lyrics broke my heart. It had been a long time since Darius had let anyone love him. He wanted that, more than anything. Then why did he keep pushing me away? I wouldn't ask him, since we were in such a fragile place and I didn't want him to change his mind about me. Together, we could be invisible.

He was shy, afraid to shed his sinister armor, and he needed an invitation to come inside. Parting my lips, he sucked on the bottom one with an intensity I'd never experienced, I was beginning to see things his way. I fought to get my hand out from under his, still on my ribcage with my heart begging for escape underneath, but he tightened his grip. Complete control with his lips and fingers. He was right, I did like it.

I followed his lead, our tongues tangling together, that ice water taste rushing inside me, flowing into my veins. With the weight of Darius' body on mine, I came to life. Writhing below him, I managed to get my hand free from his. His arms were like marble, hard and smooth. I couldn't budge them, even if I wanted to.

Darius' sharp teeth pierced my lip. I knew what he was, but surprise still sent a ripple of electric shock through me. Pushing him away with my tongue, I didn't taste any blood, just Darius. If I had, I'd never be able to push him away. We'd all been careful around him, which wasn't easy in a heavy metal band. When we said we bled on stage, often we meant it. Darius could pass for human on many levels, but when the red stuff was concerned, he was all vampire.

He moaned, catching my tongue and rolling it around his, so close to those teeth. I'd been so blind by my want of him, that I'd become blind to what he actually was. "I'll never hurt you, Lani." His words were little more than a breath. "I want to keep the demons away from you."

His lips moved to my neck, my throbbing artery teasing him, daring him to come inside. *There.* I chuckled. The demons weren't the drugs or the booze, or even the meaningless sex. My family had been a virus that had infected me from within, a hereditary disease passed down between generations. Twisted and warped, they created me in their own likeness, then rejected me when they didn't like what they saw. They expected me to be better than them. The problem was, I didn't want anything to do with them. Wicked Intentions had become my family, showing me more understanding and affection in the last few years than I'd seen in my lifetime.

"Good luck," I said, but Darius didn't hear me. His face was still buried in the crook of my neck. Licking, sucking, and nipping. Teasing. I couldn't breathe. I wasn't scared at all. I wanted this. That familiar fade to black feeling came over me, from top to bottom like it did many nights, and I floated into the oblivion as Darius sunk his teeth deep into my vein. Our lives intermingled, and suddenly, forever didn't scare me so much anymore.

Darius

I'd made a mistake, taking her from the hospital. Lani should've come back to life with my blood. I'd fed her so carefully, coaxing every drop down her throat. I was delirious, I'd given her every drop I could spare. And I was fucking drained of everything; blood, ideas, and hope. The hope part scared the shit out of me. It was the only thing that brought me to my beautiful Lani. Without it, I would've walked into the sunlight long ago.

All I had left to give her was my promise of following her to the grave. We both needed blood, but I couldn't leave her.

Wrapping my arms around her, I inhaled her scent. As gray and lifeless as she was, she smelled alive. Vibrant. Like dew on the grass at sunrise. My stomach rumbled, it was the closest I'd felt to human since I'd turned. I didn't remember much anymore about being human, but this feeling was unmistakable. Wanting things I couldn't have. Maybe it was Lani. So close to having her forever, and I was still losing her.

Planting a kiss on her cheek, I prayed for a reaction, any little movement. A fucking sign. Nothing. I pressed my fingers against her neck, checking her pulse. It was weak, but there.

She needed a reason to live.

Hunger and need consuming me, I sunk my teeth into her neck. I ignored the voice telling me I was selfish, taking the blood I gave to Lani, but I hadn't given her life. Without my strength, I had nothing for her. It was risky as hell, but I had to take a chance. Or else we'd both die.

Lani's eyes fluttered, but not for long. I was losing my mind. Nope, she tried again, only one eyelid peeling up this time. Then the other. It was like seeing the sunrise after so long without it. The deep blue flecked with green, I hadn't missed daylight until now. Lani stretched, wincing after being still for weeks. We'd been here for five days, and if this hadn't worked, I would've had to bring her back to the hospital.

I loved too much about her to harm her, even if it meant we could never be together.

"Darius," she rasped, a faint smile playing on her lips. "You spent the night with me."

"Something like that." I pushed her filthy hair away from her face. Caked with dried blood, she'd go back into her coma when she got a look at herself. Lani never let anyone see her without her game face, as she liked to call it. Too much makeup if you asked me. I'd been afraid to move her, the doctors had described her condition as grave, her organs compromised. Explanation first, bath later. "I've spent many nights with you."

She chuckled, but no sound came out. Shit, was I losing her again? This was the dumbest thing I'd ever done. But Lani had me under her thrall. She had ever since I laid eyes on her. I begged her to join my band, but promised myself I'd never touch her. That night backstage I couldn't stand the temptation another second. If I had a brain in my fucking head, I would've left the band, got as far away from this bewitching beauty as possible, and started a new life. Anything but this.

"You're so romantic," she said. Trying to move again, her eyes widening in agony. "Everything hurts."

"I know." I kissed her lips softly.

"What did we do last night?" she asked, picking up her arm and squeezing her eyes closed when the effort proved to be too much. "Did we have sex? I can't believe I have to ask you that. It's not that you weren't amazing, if we did it, but I guess I drank more than I thought I did? I don't remember, Darius." Her eyes watered, tears tinged with red. It was a good sign. It fucking worked. "I waited for you for so long, now I finally have you and I can't remember anything."

"Shh." I brushed my lips over hers. Even weak and filthy, Lani could tempt me to do the wicked things that got us into this mess in the first place. I pulled back quickly. She had nothing more to give.

Lani frowned in confusion. "I'm starving." She attempted to sit up, but abandoned that idea quickly. "Let's get room service. One of those big, gross breakfasts. We'll put it on my mom's credit card. She won't even notice."

Yes, she would. With all the reports of Alannah DeAngeles leaving the hospital then vanishing, any activity would cause a stir. I'd been afraid to turn on the TV, I'd rather stay in ignorant bliss than know how close I was to losing Alannah.

I'd made her aunt's wish come true; Lani would never die. But she was *my* future.

"We need to talk, my beauty." I kissed her quickly. If I didn't keep her busy, she'd see the hard, brown crust of dried blood on her sheets and gown, and the red, sticky residue left on her skin. "Things changed since we've been together."

Lani smiled against my lips. "So of course you were amazing." Her laugh was stronger now. "Darius, listen, I care about you a lot. And I want us to be together. But you know how I am. Just because we slept together doesn't mean that everything has to change for us. It was one night. Let's take one day at a time and see where things lead us."

"Alannah, come with me." I scooped her up in my arms, she should've been light but I was so weak.

"Put me down!" My beautiful girl didn't do anything without a fight. "Darius, I'm serious. You're hurting me."

That was all she had to say. I set her on her feet in front of the mirror. Lani's trembling body clung to mine.

"Turn around," I instructed. She shook her head, defiant in this life as she was the last. "You'll see exactly what I'm talking about."

"Fine." She rolled her eyes and turned to the mirror, screaming when she saw herself caked in blood. I followed her down to the ground. She beat her fists against my chest with all the strength she could muster as she sobbed. "You made me a fucking vampire?"

"Yes." I cupped her chin in my hand so she couldn't turn away. "You wanted to escape your life, Lani. No matter where you went, you were always Alannah. Your family, your reputation, and all those expectations from complete strangers would never disappear. You'd never be happy as a human. I wanted to take you away from all that."

Lani narrowed her eyes, her trademark pout was back. "You could've asked me first." She sighed. "That's the problem. No one ever asks me what I want. Apparently *that* will never change."

"Honest answer?" I asked. Lani wrinkled her nose in confusion. "I didn't mean to do it. But being so close to you, I couldn't resist. I had to know what your blood tasted like."

"So you fucked up?" She smirked. I nodded. "I guess we have that in common, two fucked up souls together for eternity."

"I'd never been with a human without drinking from them." I couldn't apologize for making someone a vampire against their will. I wanted her. Lani was a quick student, and she'd need to learn the first rule of the afterlife quickly: never show weakness. That was a lesson for another night.

She leaned in closer. "What do I taste like?"

"Sunshine."

Lani bit her lip, and I couldn't resist catching it with my own, pulling it away from her teeth. The warmth had faded from her already, she tasted like dusk. She wound her fingers through my hair, pulling me into her, our tongues dancing together. Everything was new for her. We separated with a sigh, and she ran her fingers over my face, tracing over my lips, and landing on my sharp canine teeth.

"I'm not mad at you," she said. So typical of Lani to make it that simple. She drove everyone nuts with her black and white view of the world, but I found it refreshing. There was something old-fashioned about it. Things were too complicated now. "What you did was really sweet. Fucked up, and not fixable, but really sweet. You've never given up on me, Darius. I could push anyone else away, but never you. You were always right there, watching me, making sure I didn't get myself in over my head."

"I did it because I love you." I had all of eternity to tell her how I felt, but I didn't want to waste another second of my time with her.

"I know you do." She ran her finger up and down the piercings on my chest, the sound lulling me into a trance. "I love you too. My aunt always said I was cursed. Did I ever tell you that story? My family thinks they have special powers. I think it's bullshit, but whatever. Every one of my aunts got a wish for me when I was a baby. Kind of like a christening, but for crazy people. Anyway, they all wished for me to have talents that made me famous. Except for one, who wanted me to use my talents to help people. She got totally pissed at the rest, and said I'd be damned forever, that being famous would ruin me. But she had it all wrong, because it led me to you."

We kissed again, I loved the way her lips felt when they moved against mine. Dry and chapped, I needed to feed her. Scraping my wrist down the line of my piercings I brought it to her mouth. Lani knew what to do. She brought the open wound to her mouth, licking the length of the vein before drinking my blood. Just like in life, Lani drank with greed and enthusiasm, making little cooing sounds as she didn't miss a drop.

She popped up with a gasp, running her fingers gingerly over her lips. Her eyes glowed and skin flushed from her first feed. I'd never been more aroused in my life. She stared at the red tipped finger in disbelief. "Darius!" She giggled as I lowered my lips on her finger, licking her clean.

"What?" I kissed her lips, still tinged with blood.

"Everything feels so different." She blinked rapidly, taking in the room, but always coming back to me. "So much more intense. Your skin is like velvet, and your eyes are like laser beams. I can't stop staring at you. How will I ever get anything done when all I want to do is you?"

I envied her enthusiasm. It pulsed against me like a heartbeat. And I mourned, for myself, my own heart that hadn't moved in centuries, until I met Lani. I may have ruined everything, and she hadn't figured it out yet. "The same way you do everything else. On your own terms."

"How do you do it, though? I was never afraid of you, but now that I'm like this, it's overwhelming. I'm scared. Everything different, and…"

"Concentrate really hard on something," I instructed. She turned to the mirror, grimacing when she got a good look at herself. Skin and bones, matted hair, dark smudges under bloodshot eyes. Blood everywhere. A sob caught in Lani's throat. I crawled behind her, not in much better shape. "Now make that thing you choose appear as you wish the world to see it."

Lani met my eyes in the mirror. "Just like that, huh?"

"Just like that." I kissed her shoulder, then met her eyes again. "I'll tell you when I see it."

"Hold my hands," she pleaded, then swallowed hard. "Here goes nothing."

She closed her eyes, energy rising from her wasted, filthy skin. The heat was like a roaring fire, drawing me closer, transfixing me. Already the blood was gone. Her skin plumped, and her hair flowed like a flowering vine. She opened her eyes and gasped, leaning toward the mirror. "Holy shit! We can do this anytime, to anything? " I nodded. She kept touching her reflection, now looking as if she'd had a team of professionals working on her all day. She'd always been gorgeous, even ruined and wasted, but now she was ready to rule the world. "I've never been so hot!"

Lani stood up, dangerous curves in shiny black leggings and a red corset. Knee high boots tied tight around her calves. She shook out her freshly curled hair, and those blood red lips turned up in the smile that would forever make me her slave. I laughed, rising to meet her, and catching those incredible lips in a long, hot kiss. "You've always been the most beautiful woman in the world."

Lani

This glamour thing was fucking amazing.

"I'm still mad at you," I teased Darius a couple weeks later. Everything was tangled around us—our limbs, the sheets, our lives. Or should I say, afterlives. Since Darius brought me into his world, we'd been absolutely inseparable. We hadn't left his apartment since I'd awakened. Now that he explained the circumstances under which I'd been made immortal, I understood. I'd been discharged from the ICU against doctor's advice. With two famous parents and a family full of wanna-be fame whores, Alannah DeAngeles' defiance didn't go unnoticed. There was no chance of stepping out of the door unless we were firing at a hundred percent. Paparazzi feasted off weakness like we did blood. "I can't believe you were glamouring me all along!"

"Not all the time." My senses spiraled, everything was so intense. I needed to have some control over myself before I handed it all over to the masses. I'd thought Darius was gorgeous before, now I was glad I didn't need to breathe, because he would've stolen it all away. I couldn't keep my hands off him. "We see each other a certain way because we're the same, but it's too much for the fans, or even the other guys in the band. Humans are limited, you know that."

"Tell me about it." I ran my tongue along his piercings. His whole body was a work of art, flowers, fairies, dragons, and flames. Darius said it was his journey through the afterlife, and now he had to add his Sleeping Beauty to the collection. He was going to ink *me* on his body. Forever. How hot was that? "So how are we doing this? Shouldn't we start with something small first? Let me get my feet wet?"

"We should." He groaned. I'd come to learn in the last couple of weeks exactly how Darius liked to be touched. In addition to the heightened senses, we both had an insane threshold for pain. When hardly anything can kill you, it makes you stronger. I didn't miss the outside world at all, but it was time to face it again, this time through different eyes. "We could have you practice glamouring into another person, but if you're able to do that, your thrall will be strong enough to convince your family you never left them."

This was terrifying. One moment of weakness and we were dead. Darius would be arrested for kidnapping, I'd be back in a hospital, and neither of us could survive daylight. "And the fans?"

"They won't remember anything you don't want them to." Darius smoothed my hair away from my face. "They love you so much, Alannah." It didn't bother me so much that he called me by my real name anymore. The way it rolled off his tongue with that accent sent little earthquakes rumbling through my body. "Every night, they held vigil outside the hospital. They made signs, sang our songs. It was beautiful. Sometimes I'd join them because your spirit was so strong with them."

I had yet to get my vampire emotions under control, and the littlest thing made me cry. Already I'd embraced my red tears, seeing them as a sign of strength rather than weakness. Darius didn't understand the concept of happy tears, and he'd do anything to make them go away. Anything. I fucking loved that about him. "I miss doing shows so much. I can't wait to get back up on stage. It will be incredible, the music, the emotion…how will I handle that?"

"You'll understand when you need to use your glamour." Darius crawled out of bed, motioning for me to follow him to the bathroom. Time to get ready for the battle. Not that anyone would be able to really *see* us, but we couldn't take any risks. "But to get there, you need to deal with your family."

* * *

Flowered sundress, check. Blonde, wavy hair back in a twist, check. Sandals and pink toenails, check. "They'll never believe this!" I insisted. This outfit was my worst nightmare. Good thing I couldn't puke as a vampire. "And you look crazy with no tattoos."

Darius wore a gray suit with a white shirt underneath to meet my parents and family. Film festival season was over, and they were home. No amount of glamour could alter them, just their perception of us. The tats and piercings hid under a veil of magic, and his hair was slicked back, still black. No matter how he wanted us to see him, he was a beautiful man. "Your powers will please you. Trust me."

"You better please me later. I'm already suffering from withdrawal," I muttered as our driver stopped at the end of the driveway of my parent's house.

Lani would've rang the doorbell, but Alannah walked right in. "Hey, everyone! We're home!" I called out, clutching Darius for dear life.

"Alannah's here!" My mom rushed down the stairs, wrapping me in a hug. Maybe my glamour *could* change her. She hadn't hugged me since I was old enough to call myself Lani. She believed my aunt's prophecy, that I was destined to be evil, the loose thread that would unravel my parents' lives. All it took was a little vampire magic to wipe away twenty years of disappointment and anger. Why didn't I think of this sooner? "I missed you so much."

A party was already in progress out at the pool. The sun was high in the sky, and that's how I knew this was all a dream. I'd never see the sun again.

My aunts were actually pretty again. They'd all had too much plastic surgery, and none of it made them happy. Or maybe they couldn't show it anymore. They surrounded me, hugging me, and asking, "Who's this handsome man?" Some things didn't change. No one in my family would bat an eyelash at stealing Darius from me.

I knew he'd never have any of them. Just me, for the rest of time. Talk about feeling invincible. That was it.

"This is Darius. I met him when I was traveling through Europe last summer. We were both at a museum in Paris, admiring an amazing postmodern piece, and we hit it off!" I giggled as they all swooned. They bought every bullshit line I fed them, insisting we simply must try some adorable little café on the left bank. If they had any idea what kind of bloodlust swirled below this illusion, and how mouth-wateringly sweet they smelled, they'd be screaming. I hadn't got my hunger under control yet, and that was Darius' biggest concern. That my flowery, giggling form would rip into the neck of one of my aunts and drain every last bit of life from them.

As far as they were concerned, the curse never existed. My aunts never wished for fame and fortune as a result of my talents. "When do you start school? Are you excited?" one of my aunts asked.

"Nervous," I admitted. It was the only truth I'd tell today. "I have ten students, all with different levels of learning disabilities. But music therapy has proven to help, especially this young, so I'm excited to see what we can accomplish."

Everyone gushed over us for the rest of the party. My aunts trailed Darius like a litter of lost puppies, rattling off ideas on how he should propose to me.

All of them beamed in approval when I put my knee between his legs on the chair. Usually, this looked slutty as hell, but cute little

16

Alannah looked adorable doing anything. "I can't take this anymore," I whispered in his ear. "Get me out of here."

Steadying himself with his hands around my waist, he stood. "I hate to cut this short, but we have a charity event tonight. Traffic is terrible in the valley."

We ran out of there, the thick blanket of night shielding us as the driver sped down the driveway. The pastel flowers melted away, leopard print and latex replacing them. It wasn't lip gloss dripping from my maroon lips, but Darius' blood. "That was amazing," I purred, sinking my fangs in for another sip.

"That was all you." Darius moaned under my firm hold. "Now let's get you where you belong. On stage."

The End

Kristen shares a birthday with Steven Tyler and Diana Ross. She spends each day striving to be half as fabulous as they are. She's worn many hats, none as flattering as her cowboy hat: banker, retail manager, fledgling web designer, world's worst cocktail waitress, panty slinger, now makeup artist and author. She loves sunshine, live music, the middle of nowhere, and finding new things to put in her house. To learn more, visit: http://www.KristenStrassel.com

PRICELESS
The True Story of Rumpelstiltskin
by Sarah J. Pepper

Prologue

A high-pitch ringing in Emilie's ears drowned out everything unimportant in this cruel world. Snow fluttered onto her lashes as she squeezed them shut. The ethereal promise that Trevis would never leave, haunted her every waking minute. His ghostly touch sent shivers through her. His phantom kiss awakened yet another memory of their short time together.

Upon opening her eyes, her gaze fell heavily onto Trevis Miller's tombstone. Tears burned her eyes. Her heart ached. Screaming into the soundless night, she collapsed alongside his grave. She clutched her chest, wishing death would find her.

"I'd give *anything* to get Trevis back," Emilie whispered.

"Anything?" A deep, raspy voice cut right through the ringing in her ears. The timbre in it was like catching wind of the devil's confession alone in the night.

Cloaked in the darkness, Declan Stilts blended impeccably into the night—like any talented demon. He stood a few feet away, watching her weep. Immune to the perils of aging, he looked as if he was in his late twenties, just like they *both* had when they first met years earlier. She aged. He hadn't. His immortality was as apparent as his vindictive manipulation.

Dressed in a black, tailor-made suit, the moon's light cast onto his pale skin. His black hair held hues of red that she once thought were alluring fell over his emerald eyes.

"You promised me riches I couldn't imagine," Emilie whimpered.

Kneeling beside her, Declan cocked his head to the side and stared like he could see her broken soul trickle out with her teardrops. Yet, he didn't utter a sympathetic word. That would be too humane.

"Say something you...you *monster!*" Emilie yelled.

"Stop acting like *I* screwed you. Everything I promised came true. Nothing more. Nothing less."

"But it cost me *everything*. You promised me a happily ever after but instead—"

1

"I promised you *riches*, not *happiness*. It is not my fault that you confuse them as one in the same," Declan said condescendingly. His focus drifted from the diamonds on her jewelry, to the high-end clothes, and to the golden highlights in her hair. But he zeroed in on the cosmetic work she had done to her nose, cheekbones, chin, and lips. "You were a poor, ugly girl when you came to me for help…The first time was to make you beautiful. So I paid for your facial reconstruction. In return, I only asked for your confidentiality to tell no one about *any* of our agreements."

"But Trevis didn't fall for me, even after I was beautiful!"

"So you came to me a second time, demanding that I get him to marry you," Declan said impassively. "And I invested your few measly hundred dollars—practically spinning them into gold—just so he would notice you. I made you rich beyond your wildest dreams, and you got the proposal you so desperately sought. Yet all I asked was for a small percentage of that income to be put into a trust for safe keeping."

Emilie glanced down at her wedding band. A tear slipped down her cheek. "But he left—"

"—with his new lover," Declan mocked, glancing at the inscription on the tombstone. His eye twitched. He could sense a life's essence as well as the vacancy of what once was. However, below his feet was just worms and dirt. The entire memorial was an elaborate façade. "You made a mockery of death by pretending to bury him."

"I'd be mortified if everyone found out that he really left me for a mistress!" Emilie sobbed, "We were in love before you cam—"

"*You* were in love with him before I intervened. *He* gave two flying shits about you. It was only after I made you so filthy rich that *anyone* knew who you were. He simply offered you a hand in marriage before someone else did. It wasn't *my* fault that you couldn't please your husband, so he sought the pleasure of other women!"

She backhanded him. He didn't flinch. She hated Declan almost as much as she hated herself for what she was about to ask, but there was another request she *had* to ask of him—one third wish.

"I'll give you *everything* I own if you get Trevis to return to me," Emilie pleaded.

Time slipped by while he glared at her with much calculation. Finally, when he spoke, his voice ripped through the stillness of the night. "No."

"Why?" she screamed.

2

"It seems that you've buried him already," Declan said sarcastically and stood to leave. "While I can siphon their essence, I cannot bring people back from the dead. Besides, people would notice if Trevis magically returned to the land of the living."

"I'll move—anywhere. We'll start over." Emilie grabbed his hand to stop him.

The glare he gave her could have left her for dead, but it was a rusty dagger that he'd snatched from behind his back and pressed it up against her throat that cemented her theory. Declan Stilts would kill her if it benefited him.

Emilie spoke slowly as not to send him into a rampage. "Surely there's something you want. I'll give you *anything*."

"Your soul?"

She hesitated. Everything she wanted would be all for none if she gave up her own freedom to Declan. "Not mine."

After further consideration, he released her from his grip. "Your first born child's?"

"You have a deal!"

For years, before Trevis left, he and Emilie were married with no children to call their own. Even if Declan somehow managed to make good on his end, it wasn't likely she'd had any children hereafter.

An evil smile spread across Declan's face when he placed his hand on her flat stomach. The look in his eyes was unnaturally possessive. "I was hoping you'd agree to my proposition, Emilie."

All the blood drained from her face when she realized what he was saying. She was with child? No. It couldn't be. It didn't feel real. She didn't feel another being inside of her. As impossible as it was...she *had* been with Trevis near the end of their marriage.

"You planned this all along!" Emilie gasped.

Not bothering to confirm her suspicious, he retrieved a flip phone from his pocket and dialed Trevis' number. Distantly, his voice came through the speaker. Emilie held her breath in anticipation. Could Declan really convince Trevis to return to her?

"One million will be transferred into your bank account if you return to Emilie. You have five seconds to decide." After a moment, he nodded his head and closed the phone.

"What did he say?" Emilie asked, not bothering to hide the desperation in her voice.

"We all have our price. Trevis' is a million." Declan tucked his phone back into his pocket. "Per our contractual agreements, you cannot tell a soul about our concessions nor can you cut me off from the already agreed upon percentage of money made."

"And the million? Who pays that?"

"I will, but shouldn't you be more concerned about the livelihood of your unborn child?" Declan clenched his jaw and waited for Emilie to contradict him. When she didn't, he sneered, "You're a worthless, greedy woman, Emilie. You really deserve Trevis. You two are perfect for each other. Neither of you care about anyone, as long as your needs are met."

Emilie said, "You're the one who gets off from stealing other's money…like a million of *mine*."

Declan laughed. "You are no different, Emilie."

"*You're* a monster!" she spat.

"*I'm* the monster? *You're* the one who gambled away an innocent life for a man who doesn't love you *without batting an eye*. You're more concerned about money rather than the life inside you! I've never met a more pathetic human being, Emilie, and I make it my business to introduce myself to them. *You're* the monster here, not me." Declan tossed the dagger down at Emilie's feet. "Consider this a *friendly* reminder of our third agreement. When the time is right, I will return to collect what is rightfully mine."

Piper Miller
(Twenty Some Years Later)

Pepper spray was the obvious choice of protection for most twenty-year-olds. However, I warded off douche bags with a rusty, old dagger. Yes, little 'ol me carried a freaking dagger. Why? Good question: After I got my first period, my mother had presented it to me like it was a usual memento for such an occasion—as if Tampax had liquidated their merchandise and this was the next best thing to give a leaking, hormonal girl.

Her words of "wisdom" echoed in my ears. *"It won't protect you from the most vile-of-men, but it will scare away the cowards."*

I was ruining panties after adorable panties, and she gave me a rusty knife. What was I to say? Thanks Mom? All the same, my curves came soon after that. Even I had to admit that Trusty Rusty worked wonders to discourage advancements from persistent dickheads who couldn't fathom why I didn't want to date 'em.

Nevertheless, I wasn't the only person with mommy issues. As much as I hated to admit it, I wished for a different life—one where I wasn't surrounded by constant manipulation. I bit my cheek to keep the tears from coming and looked out of the taxi's backseat window.

Casino lights lit up the night sky like it was midday instead of midnight. Vegas had a way of making nocturnal-living the acceptable way of life. It had a way of changing people as well, especially since tourists and businessmen alike all flocked here in hopes of making it big. And let's not forget the predatory hussies. Women could be as cut-throat as any arrogant man. It just so happened that I called one such woman Mom...or used to when we were still on speaking terms.

Thank goodness good people still lived here, like the cabby with the kind smile. "Warmin' up?" He glanced back at me through the rearview mirror.

I blew warm air through my fingers. "Yes, thank you."

I wished the rain would quit. It wasn't even trying hard. It was just spitting down, slowly drenching me for the past two days.

Whistling softly, I wondered how long the cab driver would chauffeur me around to let my clothes dry out. It'd been quite obvious I had nowhere to go when I had him circle the strip, pretending I was a lost tourist. He'd seen right through my act and stopped the meter but didn't ask me to leave.

"That's an intriguing tune," the cab driver commented. "Sounds like something I've heard before."

Everyone always said that. "I made it up myself actually."

"Well, it's beautiful."

It was funny how the kindness of strangers out-weighed family support. And by funny, I meant sad. Sometimes those who love you were the cruelest people in the world. That's what my parents taught me. People you loved would only use it to their advantage.

Case and point: Emilie Owen, a.k.a. "Mom-of-the-Year," took out an eleven figure life insurance policy on my old man when I was a few years old. Then he died tragically in a "freak fire accident" at a fleabag hotel with his mistress. It coincided with a few soured business adventures that should have left my family penniless. "Luckily" my father died and the insurance kept my mother comfortably in the élite one percent. I'd always suspected my mother to have some hand in my father's death, but the police didn't rule foul play, even though evidence was uncovered that Mom and Dad had changed their identities after—get this—my father died. To this day, I doubt he's six feet under. My bet was that he fled the country to get away from my vindictive mother. *Personally,* I'd pay a small fortune to get rid of her.

In the years to come, other shady business charges were brought up against Mom, but none were prosecuted. Why? They couldn't find enough evidence. She used to hide documentation in my lunch box that I was to shove in the trash can at school after lunch. She'd sew receipts into my dolls. And hide them in my flute case. Instead of music books, I'd draw in inventory spreadsheets. I suppose that was why I got to be so good with numbers, and then began connecting the dots of my mother's business practices. I'd kept the most damning documents, in case of a rainy day. I might not have a small fortune to get rid of her, but carbon-copy receipts worked well as blackmail to keep her out of my life.

The only dirty money not tied to my name was the trust fund set up *before* I was born. Even though I was a sole benefactor, I didn't get a dime of it until my twenty-first birthday. That made me the richest poor person in Vegas. Trusts were a bitch that way. I could barely scrap together two stolen credit cards, but I had a quarter of a million waiting for me. I just had live long enough to drink twenty-one birthday shots next month. In the mean time, a Kinko's cardboard box was home-sweet-ho—

The cabby slammed on the breaks. I would've face-planted into the back of the driver's seat had it not been for the seat belt. High-squealed screams came shortly after the series of fender-benders. But the shouts weren't solely due to the Vehicular Armageddon.

Outside was the most eligible bachelor in Sin City. Declan Stilts. He was definitely a show-stopper. Literally. Some driver must have noticed the humdinger exiting the MGM and slammed on their brakes to get a better glimpse. I couldn't fault anyone though. Declan was definitely worth a brake pump or two. The burgundy hues in his dark hair were accented by the red flashing lights of the casino. It cast over his dark eyes, giving him this mysterious stare that even compelled me not to look away. From what I'd seen in MMA magazines, his stomach was a freaking washboard. The photos captured his rippling muscles in mid-action. It was sexy-as-hell. Judging from the width of his shoulders, and broad chest, he definitely packed a punch. The visual of him knocking out his opponent had been a frequent go-to fantasy of many women lately. #declandaydreaming had been trending on Twitter for months.

The *only* fault in his otherwise perfect physique was the scar on his cheek. However, it hardly offset the *multitude* of moral faults. With a blonde on each arm, Declan flashed his million-dollar smile at the horde of paparazzi trailing him out of the casino. A rain drop dripped down his brow—and one of his dates licked it off of his cheek.

Gag me!

While most women saw the potential Mrs tagged to the front of their name, I saw him for what he truly was: a fraud—but a good one at that. As one of the youngest professional counting-card criminals Sin City has ever known, he'd made billions selling the tricks of his skill to casinos on this side of the Rockies.

If the millions he'd made weren't enough to keep him satisfied, he'd taken up fighting. He publically claimed it was to fend off boredom, but his professional fighting career debuted shortly after a series of bar fights that ended with court hearings. Personally, I thought he fought as a way to manage his impulsive rage.

I dug in my jacket pocket and pulled out a stick of gum, ten dollars and a handful of carbon-copied blackmail receipts.

Slipping out of the back seat, I bid the cabby good-night and offered him a handful of the crumpled dollars for letting me dry out in his car. He refused to take the money even though he'd been eyeing the damage done to his vehicle.

He said, "You need it more than me."

"Thank you." Sometimes those two words weren't justice but right now, it was all I could give.

After pocking my cash, I raced across the street and looked at my reflection in MGM's gold pillars. I was a disaster. My three-day-old makeup gave me the appearance of a blue-eyed raccoon road-kill. I dragged my fingers through my light brown hair. The rain left it looking greasy, but there wasn't much I could do. Having a plethora of hair product at my fingertips wasn't my reality any more.

In search of Mr. Right Now, I slipped through the crowd. He'd taken harbor under the entrance canopy while waiting for the valet to return his ride. There were enough distractions going on with the traffic jam and the people flocking over Declan's appearance that no one noticed me. When I got close enough to smell Declan's cologne, I "accidently" bumped into the blonde who'd licked the rain off of his face.

She fell to the wet ground. "My outfit is *ruined!*"

While Declan attended to his escort in the dirtied sequenced-cocktail dress, my hands were already tightly secured around the big thing in his pants. Score! I plucked a single card from his *wallet*, gave it the once over, and shoved it back. A photographic memory had its perks.

"Watch it!" Declan's glare was enough to stop me dead in my tracks, but he grabbed my jacket, turned it around his fist, pulled me against him and held me still.

In the swarm of chaos, neither he nor I moved. Time stood on end, waiting for one of us to react to the other. His body stiffened to the point where I wasn't sure if he was breathing anymore. Was I?

"Emilie?" The deepness of his voice cascaded through me like the tiny ripples in dark waters.

The fear of being pulled under black water by a supernal being was the kind of effect Declan had on me. Staring into his eyes was like being drowned by a demon—a demon who went by the name of Declan Stilts.

"You've got the wrong girl," I whispered, unsure if pointing out the mistaken identity was a good idea.

He cocked his head to the side. "I doubt that."

As he looked me over, his murderous expression was replaced with a blank stare. The maniacal thoughts passing through his eyes made me shiver. It was everything

I

could do to breathe when his gaze fell to my lips. His perilous stare left me without words. It was the very way a lover left you speechless with a passing glance. But Declan didn't just take a glimpse. He hardly blinked as he stepped closer, like he

wanted

all space between us eliminated. Simultaneously, I gravitated towards him and wanted to run away. Everything I thought I knew about love and hate was destroyed in a heartbeat. The two weren't opposing feelings; they were symbiotic. And it was all because of

him.

That excited me as much as terrorized me. I jerked my jacket out of his grip. He let me. There was no other way I'd be free of him so quickly. That was when it hit me: he was in complete control of the situation, and I was merely reacting to him. It bothered me, a lot. My fingers itched for my dagger that was tucked in my waistband, but too many people were around to use it. My face would surely be plastered in the newspapers if I gave him a matching scar on his other cheek. Whoever gave him the first one surely had to be dead. He wasn't the kind of person you wanted to piss off. As soon as that thought crossed my mind, he grinned.

Stop staring at his Goddamn smile and focus!

His expression softened to the point where he looked almost human. Almost. "If you're not Emilie then who are you?"

"A *nobody*," his date said, batting her fake eyelashes. When she couldn't gain his attention by pulling him close to her, she stepped between us.

I seized the opportunity and backed away. I bumped into several of the people circling us. Still, I didn't turn my back and run. Declan wasn't a person I trusted to take my eyes off, at least not until there was more sidewalk real-estate between us. As soon as I felt safe enough to run, I did. Pride be damned. As I high tail it outta there, I could still feel his eyes on my back. When I rounded the corner, I looked over my shoulder to take once last look. Our eyes locked. It was as if he knew that I was about to rob him blind.

⁃ ✕⁸⁞⁸⁃ ⁓

Declan Stilts

Power-hungry men and women who'd sell their soul to make a buck gravitated to Las Vegas. It was a feeding ground for others like me: An Incubus. I was a demon with a sweet-tooth for greed. A vampire of sorts who fed off of humans, but instead of drinking blood for substance, I consumed their life's essence. Their essence extended mine, resulting in my immortality, but it came at a steep price. Because I breathed in the vilest parts—greed, gluttony, covetousness—their moral faults became my own. I took their evilness, and in return it corrupted my soul. I hate who'd I'd become.

These moral imperfections became so engrained in me that I could smell it on them. What was worse than becoming a heinous Incubus was the hunger burning within my soul could never be fucking satisfied! I'd kill to be free of the curse! I couldn't rest with this festering appetite, especially with what still lay in my bed beside me…but they wouldn't survive me stealing any more of their essence.

In front of the master bedroom's windows, I pounded a suspended boxing bag and tried not to stare through the glass. I continued to find myself searching for the girl with the mesmerizing glare rather than taking out my aggression on the bag.

Frustrated, I slammed my fist into the bag. Piper was *so fucking close!* I could count the freckles dusted on her nose. My hands were literally on her, and yet I released her. I had to. There were too many people around, and her trust hadn't matured to its full capacity yet. It'd be further along if Trevis hadn't cleaned it out before skipping town. Again. He took a page from Emilie's book and faked his death—fleeing the country with his lover. Not that I blamed him. There wasn't enough money in the world to stay with Emilie, but it didn't matter. My agreement with Emilie clearly stated that he must simply return to her. She said nothing about him being a permanent fixture in her life. He simply had to return. And he took the million dollar bait to do so. So, at that moment, the offspring of the vilest women I knew was *mine*. But not even I could leave the girl penniless—not after I did what I intended to do. The final stages of my plan were nearly complete. I'd been patient this long. I could wait until she turned of age.

Glancing over my shoulder, I wiped the sweat from my brow. "One more…just one more damn hit, that's all I need."

My dates lay—barely breathing—on top of the bed sheets, covered with hundred dollar bills. Nothing could pacify the greed that consumed me, not even the two gold diggers. I was shamelessly addicted to them. On a daily basis, it was everything I could do to watch them pass by without touching, without taking their gluttonous essence, but these two…these two were begging to be taken, and I didn't have to remove a shred of clothing to do so.

Clutched between their hands were wads of cash. I brought them to the brink of death with smiles on their faces. They'd wake sometime tomorrow—well, one would at least. It wouldn't be long before the one who licked my face crossed over.

After peeling off the tape around my knuckles, I plucked my phone from the nightstand and dialed my right hand man. Jameson didn't bother keeping his disdain for me a secret, but I owned his ass, so his opinion of me didn't matter. Besides, I needed an errand boy.

The call started but he didn't bother with a greeting. "Captain Jameson, how are you doing this fine evening?"

"I swear if you're calling me to take care of another body—"

"Maybe two." One digger's chest still rose and fell without waver. The other? Not so much. Without thinking, I moved closer to them. Her breaths were hypnotizing. I could practically smell her scent. She would be strong enough to withstand another—

"Listen to me!" Jameson yelled. "Wherever you are, get the hell out. I'll send a unit to clean up your mess."

"Have them come to my usual room at the Mirage." I ended the call and backed away from the bed. I was still desperate for another…just one more voracious gold digger.

If I could find one at this hour in the morning, it'd be in this glorious city. Grabbing my room key and wallet, I left the room to go on the hunt. I made it as far as the elevator doors before I noticed one big, fucking problem.

My platinum card was out of place.

I turned back around and strode into the hotel bedroom. These two-bit whores were trying to play me—*me?* Several thousand dollars decorated the oversized bed, yet that wasn't enough for them! They wanted more. They wanted to clean me out. That sure as shit wasn't going to fly!

Pissed off, I grabbed a handful of blonde hair and pressed my lips against hers. I breathed in her greediness, I stole her life's essence. I didn't stop until I pried the cash out of her cold dead hands.

* * *

While Jameson's men bagged the lifeless bodies, I logged onto my online accounts. I had a pending charge from the Bellagio. I gave the card a sniff. It smelled like *her*. My rage erupted. Piper had stolen from me, not the no-dead gold diggers.

The body count wasn't over just yet.

Piper Miller

I'd died and gone to heaven—heaven being Room 901 at the Bellagio. The penthouse suite was Stilts usual; at least that was what the receptionist said when I checked in earlier that night. A stranger had loaned me their phone, and I booked a room using Declan's credit card information. Thirteen hundred square feet of luxury and all I cared about was a warm bed—*that* was my haven. I could care less about the chromed-out décor or the glam…although I had spent a fair amount of time taking a hot shower in the elaborate bathroom. I smelled like a freaking dumpster and was happy to rid myself of that stench.

After scrubbing off the grime from the city's streets, I slipped between the cool sheets of a king-size bed. I didn't bother to put on any clothes. I'd lived in those filthy clothes for months, and even though I'd had the hotel launder them, the softness of a made-bed wasn't a luxury I wanted to pass up. It'd been far too long since I could lay down, close my eyes and feel safe without having to arm myself with Trusty Rusty. I placed the dagger beside my pillow and cuddled up to Egyptian cotton instead of the cold metal.

The soft glow of the city shined through the hotel curtains, illuminating the bedroom. The noise from the traffic was barely audible. The subtle honks were a reminder that I was just a stolen credit card away from watching the sun rise through a crack in my card board penthouse instead of through floor-to-ceiling balcony windows. I lay awake in a bed that had to cost a small fortune; it was just another "thing" that could be snatched away in a heartbeat. Possessions. Property. They were just temporary. Nothing lasted forever.

Not even love.

Unconditional love was an urban legend, a myth, a freaking fairy tale. It was a notion that parents whispered to their children before they ran off with their mistresses because they couldn't stand to share a bed with the person they married. Such was life. I wasn't meant to have a fairy tale kind of love. To be fair, I wasn't a goodie-two-shoes princess either. So to expect prince-charming to rescue me from my jacked-up life was laughable. That's all I could do. Laugh. To feel sorry for myself would only throw me into a self-induced emotional pit of doom. Besides, those who played the pity card wouldn't last one night on the streets of Vegas. I wanted to live on my own terms, even if they only got me as far as the homeless shelter or a stolen hotel room.

After I finally nodded off for what felt like hours, the click of a door key jarred me awake. Panicking, I scrambled for the dagger that was hidden between the bed sheets. I cut my hand finding it. Tangled up in one-hundred percent Egyptian cotton, I leapt for my clothes on the dresser, but it was the announcement of the police that stopped me dead in my tracks.

Words completely escaped me when *he* strolled into the room. Declan Stilts, accompanied by Vegas' finest boys in blue. So I did the only thing I could think of—look death in the face and smile.

Declan Stilts

Her rapid-fire smirk was subtle—a brief grin that melted into a poker face—was the first thing I noticed about Piper. Most people would've taken note of her sheet for a dress, but it was her mouth that first caught my attention. Dimples. She had these perfect fucking dimples…Even as she stood, draped in a sheet, with the police busting down the door, she had the audacity to smirk!

This girl with dull brown hair, this girl who had the palest pink lips I'd ever seen—Piper was an idiot if she thought I was just another push-over businessman. She was about to get schooled. Then she flashed those dimples at me and all thought vanished. Absence of thought was un-fucking-usual.

I hesitated to enter the room. I *never* hesitated, especially when it came to women and money. Piper was no different, I reminded myself. She screwed me over and thought nothing of it! That fed into my anger, which actually made me feel more like myself. Even so, knowing I'd get the last laugh kept me focused. I showcased my rage with a cunning smile of my own.

And the little twit returned my grin with a raised brow.

She pointed the dagger at us. Defiant shit she was, even when the police tackled her to the ground for threatening them with a weapon.

I cocked my head to the side, calculating Piper's expression and body language, taking note of her hand injury—Goddamn it! Jameson's officers were carelessly tearing open her cut, damaging what was mine! I did my best to silence the rage brewing inside me and think straight. Con artists: I never cared about them with any importance. Piper was no exception, I reminded myself again. She had a *one* purpose—a means to an end. But after the police officers pinned her to the floor, she glared at me like

I

purposely interrupted her beauty sleep for no good reason. Her defiance was attractive on an ethereal level. Fuck, she was a knock-out when she pouted like she wanted me to do something about it. But the most damning thing was that she had what I

craved

more than anything in the world: Freedom. What was the point of immortality if you were a slave to your hunger? And she knew it. I could see it in her deep blue eyes. Damn, could they be any more vibrant? The intellect burning in them intrigued me. Her sassy defiance beckoned me closer to

her.

My heart jolted when she winced after an officer tore her gash open further. I fought the urge to rub my chest. Centuries had passed since any such feeling rattled my ribcage. Figurative and literally. Three hundred and forty eight years since my heart skipped a beat. My heart pounded against my ribs every time I kissed my beloved Sophia; and then she stabbed me in the chest with that forsaken dagger.

I hated Sophia for it.

Since then, I'd carried the Incubus curse just as I carried the dagger—well, that was until I gave it to Emilie as a "reminder" that I'd claim what was mine. The truth was that I didn't trust that woman farther than I could see her. Since I was tied to that metallic shard by the curse, I could sense who carried it. For years, I'd been secretly keeping tabs on Piper and her deadbeat of a mother.

The girl with a perfect set of dimples would be my freedom. I'd be damned if I let our obvious attraction for each other screw that up.

Piper Miller

I was so screwed.

Like upside-down, backwards, doggy-style screwed. To make matters worse, blood dripped down my hand, staining the expensive sheets with my liquid DNA. I was literally caught red-handed. The irony wasn't lost on me. I'd robbed a man who'd made a freaking living from cheating the system. I should have known it'd take him a hot second to find me. I was *so* going to jail.

At least that's what I deduced after the two officers charged me. I guess I looked dangerous enough to alarm the police. Body-slammed onto wood floors would've sucked less if I had clothes on.

Like any.

At least the sheet covered the important parts. But as I said earlier, I was still totally screwed—at least that was what it felt like. A bad one night stand that ended with handcuffs slapped around my wrists while some middle-aged guy straddled me; I wished it was a kinky hook-up.

Even so, the floor burn wasn't the worst of it. I could take the physical sting; it was the sick feeling in the pit of my stomach that unnerved me when I looked into Declan's emerald eyes. He hadn't moved from his position by the door. Combine his ominous stare and clenched jaw with his dark jeans and a long-sleeved grey shirt; he leaned against the wall like he was posing for a MMA photo shoot. He did imposing well. Very well.

The more time passed, the more I understood the inner rage he possessed. To say he was upset with me was the understatement of a lifetime. I'd never seen a man so furious, yet barely moved a muscle—barely breathed. His chest didn't rise or fall. Being in his presence undid me; I physically and mentally reacted to him. I wanted—needed—to know what he was thinking. I held my breath, waiting for him to react. When that didn't work, I did the most subtle thing I could think of: smirk.

His gaze dropped to my lips. His eyes narrowed. His knuckles turned white. Oh, I'd gotten under his skin, and I'd barely done anything. Well, other than steal his credit card digits. But if I had to guess, my smile ticked him off more.

One of the officers rattled off my rights while the other pulled me up, bringing the sheets up with me. I expected Declan's gaze to fall when the corner of the sheet slipped. I wasn't mistaken. But his gaze only dropped as far as my lips. Again. This time I grinned, but it wasn't because I was taunting him. It was…oh hell, I didn't know—I enjoyed seeing him on edge.

"Gentlemen, leave us," Declan commanded.

Neither moved. They were unsure who should be calling the shots. Declan slammed his fist against the wall. My jaw dropped. The sheer amount of force carried with that punch…I didn't want to be on the other side of that fist. The rage he carried was evident in his rigid posture.

"Leave. Us. Now," Declan ordered.

The deepness of his voice sent pin-pricks through my body. I trembled. The last thing I wanted was to be alone—practically naked—with him.

My preferred exit strategy was to be escorted out by these two men in blue. "I'm going with you two."

Declan tore his obsessive gaze off of me to give the officers a dose of his potent stare. "No, she's not. Tell Captain Jameson that I am not going to press charges...yet. I'm sure this simple misunderstanding between me and *this young lady* will sort itself out."

One officer placed my dagger on the night stand before leaving. That made me more nervous than anything. Leaving a weapon in the room meant they didn't trust Stilts any more than I did. My chances of walking out of the room alive plummeted when Declan locked the door behind them.

"I own the law," he whispered like I was his ex-lover—sexy with a hint of condescending undertones. His possessive gaze petrified me, but it was the curiosity brimming in his eyes that made it impossible to look away. "And I own you, Piper."

He knew my name?

I asked, "So acting like you didn't know me was—"

<hr />

Declan Stilts

"—a formality," I acknowledged blatantly. That I knew her name made Piper extremely uncomfortable. Good. "You seemed like you didn't want to be found, hiding on the streets when you come from money. Exposing you obviously wasn't what you wanted."

"So you respect my privacy, is that it, *Declan?*" She spoke my name like it was a *curse* word.

If she only knew how cursed I was.

"What do you want, Declan? Payback? Are you so strapped for cash that you personally investigate every thief?"

"I assure you that my concerns lie much deeper than a penthouse charge, Piper."

My confession stopped me cold. The cold-hard truth rarely slipped from my lips and in no time at all, this girl had coaxed it out of me. I rubbed my chest wishing that the burning sensation would suppress. The untamable desire that I usually associated with the Incubus curse hit me whenever I laid eyes on her.

Staring at me with much consideration, she whistled. It was six, short high-pitched sounds. The brief tune was incredibly alluring for being so brief; it was almost as captivating as those dimples.

"You like music," I said more than asked.

Who doesn't? "Stop with the creeper attitude already! You don't know me, and you don't scare me!" she sneered.

I could hear her heart beating out of control. Her fear blanketed her body like a scent meant to draw me near. I closed the gap between us so that there was little more than a thin sheet between us. It took all the control I could muster not to lay a finger on her. If I did, no matter how badly I wanted her, it wouldn't end well—not with this hunger festering in me.

"You are a liar, Piper."

"So what if I am?" she said as defiantly as one could in a pair of handcuffs. "You've already made your decision about what you're going to do with me, haven't you?"

"There are many things I want to do to you. And I will. I own your ass," I said more for my benefit—not hers. Her soul was mine; her mother offered it away. While I could steal other's lives and kill them, Piper was different. I could literally do what I wanted with her because I owned her soul.

"Yours? Ha! No one owns me! Not you. Not one freaking person. And as soon as I have access to the trust, I'm getting the hell out of Dodge. I'll be *free* of every manipulative person in my life." She mentioned freedom like it was an unattainable dream that only the privileged possessed.

My chest ached. I hated it. She wanted exactly what I was so desperate to attain—what she already had but didn't realize. *Fuck!* She wasn't plagued with the same unsatisfying hunger, yet she felt trapped. For the first time in decades, I hesitated.

Could I go through with my plan to pass this curse onto her and free myself of it?

I'd set Piper up with a trust after completing my second agreement with Emilie. *All I asked was for a small percentage of Emilie's income to be put into a trust for safe keeping.* Money should keep her semi-satisfied until she learned to control the greed corrupting her soul.

Guilt—that wasn't an emotion I'd felt in years. And yet, when I looked into her wild blue eyes, I was overwhelmed with it.

"You're free right now," I whispered. The words sounded detached even to me.

She clanged her handcuffs together. "Feels like it."

Pulling out a police issued key, I reached around her thin frame. A soft gasp fled from her lips. I relished in that beckoning noise! My demonic side wanted to coax it out of her over and over again. *She's no good to me if I fed on her.* Instead of giving into my demonic temptations, I slipped the key into the lock and freed her.

The cuffs dropped unceremoniously onto the floor. She wasted no time grabbing the dagger from the nightstand and pointed it at me. With much curiosity, I watched her struggle to hold up the sheets along with the dagger. *Amateur.*

"You have a pair," I said, half impressed.

"Get out," she demanded.

She crinkled her freckled nose in an extremely endearing manner. It was meant to be intimidating, but it came off as…adorable.

Crossing my arms, I raised my eyebrow and gave her the once over. Her adorableness was irrelevant. If I was going to be free of this curse, than I must stop staring at her Goddamn smile and focus!

"I'll leave when I damn well please, Piper. And I'm not done with you just yet. *You* stole from *me*. Remember? Or is that tiny detail insignificant to you?"

Piper Miller

We met people who inevitably changed our lives—even if they were seemingly insignificant. The random choices that brought us together were sometimes the ones that altered our destiny forever. Declan was one such person. I didn't care if we'd just met or that we'd barely held a conversation. I knew that there was more to him than his superficial reputation. That inalienable truth burned in my soul. I ran into Declan for a millisecond, and I knew my life would be forever changed—however long that may be.

Time slipped by. Seconds multiplied to minutes. Yet he didn't seem to be alarmed I was armed with the dagger. He circled me, like he was inspecting a piece of merchandise. He stomped down on the corner of the sheet. It exposed my bare back, but I clutched it tightly to keep from giving him a peep-show. I shot him a glare.

The fucker smiled.

"Nice dimples," his said, staring at the indentations in my cheeks even though he was talking about the ones south of the border.

Son-of-a-bit— The way his grin curled upward was infuriating, but what I hated more was the way it made the corner of *my* mouth tug upward when he smiled.

"So if you aren't going to leave, what are your intentions?" I asked.

He leaned against the wall casually and crossed his arms over his chest. "I'd like you to feel comfortable around me. I find your company to be quite…intriguing."

"Intriguing?"

I expected him to give me the once over, glance at my lips or make a snide remark. But instead, he gave me the full force of his calculating stare. His eyes locked with mine, and I couldn't remember how to breathe.

His voice came out rough. "*Quite* intriguing."

Tearing his attention off of me, Declan picked up my jacket that was on top of the dresser. He flipped it between his hands and gave it a sniff.

"You steal but have little interest in money." He looked quizzically at me for an explanation. "You're not instinctually greedy."

"Therein lies the essential difference between us, Declan."

"You are *no* different from me! I was exactly like you, before this blasted Incubus cur—"

—he shoved me against the wall and pinned my injured hand above my head. The speed at which he moved was incredible, as was his grip. No wonder he wasn't concerned about the dagger; his freaking body was a weapon! Clearly, he'd been toying with me.

I may not be very apt in knife-fights, but even I couldn't miss the gigantic vein in his neck. As he tightened his grip around my wrist, I brought the blade against his carotid artery.

"Get off of me!" I pressed the dagger against his neck.

In a flash, he ripped the dagger from my grasp and chucked it across the room with expert precision, like he'd thrown that dagger a thousand times before. Sparks flew from the blade when it slammed into the wall. It had to have struck an electrical outlet—there was no other logical explanation.

"My apologies." The words stumbled from his mouth like he'd never said them before. "My temper rules me, not the other way around."

Guilt showed in his eyes. It was like he wasn't sure if he wanted to be my enemy or my ~~friend.~~ No, scratch that. A friendship wasn't right. He was contemptible enough to be my enemy, but the connection between us was closer than a mere friendship. But to define it wasn't easy, especially when he was holding me so close.

He brought my injured hand to my chest and then hesitated. "You *must* be more careful, Piper."

He cared? Normally, I would have responded with a witty retort, but I couldn't remember how to speak as he slowly slipped his fingers over mine. His touch was so faint I could only focus on how he caressed my skin. This man—so cold and detached—had a gentle touch. It was so unexpected.

Without warning, he pushed away from me and retrieved his phone from his pocket. He didn't greet the person on the other line nor did he wait to hear what that person wanted to say. "Send a medic to Bellagio, room nine-o-one." There was a pause while he glanced back at my hand that was bleeding all over the sheets. "No, a body bag isn't necessary this time."

He ended the call. His indifference to the person on the phone had not gone unnoticed. People were disposable to him. Was I? If I was, wouldn't he have *done something already?* So it begged the question: What did he want with me? He was dangerous. Period. But there had to be a reason why he was so desperately manic. People weren't just this frantic for no good reason. What was his?

I swallowed the lump in my throat and decided to start with a reason why *I'd* become so desperate. Why had I chosen to live on the streets instead of a mansion; why I cherished the kindness of strangers over family; why I wanted a different life? It all boiled down to my mother. Emilie was septic. Her corruption spoiled absolute. Declan knew her—or at least of her. Maybe it would shed some light on to why he was the way he was.

"You whistle when you concentrate," Declan stated.

That took me by surprise. I hadn't even realized I did that. But I refused to get side-tracked. "You thought I was Emilie when we were outside of the MGM. What do you know about her?"

He jerked the dagger out of the wall. Again, sparks flew. That it hadn't caused an electrical fire was a small miracle. He stared at the dagger possessively. The longer he glared at it, the more I realized he was reliving a horrible painful moment. The dagger *had* to be significant to him, even though it had been in my family for years.

Nevertheless, nothing showed in his expression, which was his tell. When his face became vacant of emotion was when he was trying his hardest not to reveal his true self. Then, as if noticing that I was memorizing his every move, he became cold once more.

He casually tossed it onto the bed, like it meant nothing to him. That was a bluff. It meant *everything* to him—or was symbolic to him in some form or another. I'd bet my life on it.

Hatred seeped from his confession when he spoke. "I know that Emilie would sell her soul if the price was right."

I laughed. "No, she'd sell mine."

Declan Stilts
She'd sell mine.

Piper's comment resonated in my mind. How much did she know about the offer I'd made to Emilie? I watched demeanor to gage her knowledge about what she knew about the night I found Emilie sprawled out on Trevis faux tomb.

"Why do you think that?" I asked casually.

"I was merely a byproduct of a failed marriage," I said. "I was simply a gigantic expense to her. It cost to clothe me, feed me, and so anything that wasn't necessary to keep me physically alive was dismissed as unnecessary. I meant nothing to her and she'd give me up if it bettered her. And it was painfully obvious that Dad didn't love her, so after he mysteriously died, money was all that mattered to my mother."

"Money comes first to many people," I admitted. "You'll learn that cold-hard truth soon enough."

She narrowed her eyes. "What do you mean by that?"

"I mean that I wished your circumstances were different." *I wished our circumstances were different.*

"By circumstances…"

Unable to keep myself away—I pushed off of the wall. I strode closer to her, wanting her more and more with each step. Clenching my teeth, I tried to get a grip and focus. This girl—this prize I reaped from decades ago was unfurling my demeanor without even trying. She didn't miss a beat, telling me off about how our circumstances were nothing alike—damn it. I didn't care what she was saying. Her voice fucking called to me in a way that was both tempting and agitating. I just wanted to shut her up. Needed to. God, I'd do anything to make her speechless.

"Stop. Talking." I pried the dagger from her hand once again. I didn't remember grabbing it. I didn't remember taking her injured hand and clutching it safely against my chest. I didn't recall tucking her hair behind her ear so that it didn't take away from her gorgeous fucking eyes.

Of course she didn't stop talking. Why would she? She disobeyed my every order thus far.

She yelled, "Why will nothing be the same?"

Her heart pounded more rapidly when I traced my thumb over her bottom lip. Finally, she stopped talking but she was far from being soundless. A faint whimper slipped from her delicate throat.

"Because we finally met."

The animalistic desires that accompanied the Incubus curse were magnified the longer she allowed me to caress her. I thought I knew what Greed was. I thought I understood what it was like to be consumed by a single feeling. But I hadn't a clue until now. Until Piper.

A knock on the door interrupted my lust filled scrutiny. I was actually grateful for the interruption—grateful that I hadn't done something *stupid* like kiss her.

In a few steps, I made it to the entrance and opened it. Jameson, posing as a medic, was on the other side of the door. I let him in. As soon as he assured me that Piper would be fine I left. I couldn't stand to be in the room another second with her and not do something incredibly stupid.

Piper Miller

I couldn't stand to be in the room another second with him and not get through my thick head that Declan was sooo wrong for me! I was on edge. And excited. And scared. And…and lonely? That he'd stormed out of the room left a void I didn't know was empty.

And then there was the way he looked at me when I talked about freedom. It gave me the chills…in a good way. I'd finally met someone who understood what it meant to be trapped. How he was trapped—I hadn't a clue. But that connection between us was instantaneous.

"That's a lovely tune," the medic said, interrupting my thoughts as he secured the bandage around my hand.

Dang it! I was whistling again. I really needed to work on that "tell."

He commented, "You must be thinking about someone special."

"No one special," I said, the lie saturating my tongue. I glanced at his name tag. "Jameson."

"To Mr. Stilts you are. He rarely leaves survivors and when he does, it's just to use them, so watch your back around him, okay? He's a *genius* at manipulation, and what he can't get people to do willingly, he'll buy. With as much money as Stilts has, you'd think he was printing it. The way he invests is like watching someone spin straw into gold. He's got a talent when it comes to numbers. It's unreal to watch him work."

"Why are you telling me this?"

"He got me out of a few sticky situations, so I owe him, but that doesn't mean I like the guy. He has zero morality."

With his crew cut hair cut, tattooed-free skin, and clean cut style, he didn't look like he had been in many sticky situations. "Gambling problem?"

"Races," he admitted.

After Jameson left, I changed into my clean clothes and slipped on my jacket. Only then did I realize why Declan had taken his sweet time in fondling it.

My carbon-copies were gone! The only way I could ensure my mother would hand over my trust fund from my father, the only proof I had against her had disappeared. My ticket to freedom was gone!

Declan wasn't done with me. Not even close.

Declan Stilts

I wasn't done with Piper—not even close.

One of the first things a con artist learns was the slight-of-hand. Flipping Piper's jacket in my hands should have been a dead giveaway that I was stealing from her. That she hadn't noticed when I was taking one of her most prized possessions meant that she'd been quite distracted by me. I'd done due diligence in taking her mind off of things. That pleased me insanely.

Nevertheless, I had to hand it to Piper. It was genius to obtain evidence to use against Emilie. The woman was ruthless, and I wouldn't put it past her to try and lay claim to the trust I'd set Piper up with.

So why did I take the carbon-copies from Piper? I needed a reason to keep her around and make it appear like it was her decision to stay in Vegas, not mine. That was how to be successful in manipulating others to do what you wanted.

And I wanted to be free of the Incubus curse.

However, guilt struck me each time I thought about passing along the Incubus curse to her. But I couldn't do it anymore! Cursed for centuries was long enough. I *hated* that it had to be Piper. I wished it could have been *anyone* else, but I didn't own anyone else's soul. Everyone all had their price. People came to me, willing to wager all their property, their bank accounts, *any one thing* to get what they wished. But Emilie was different. I knew it as soon as I smelled her desperation, which was when I began planning my freedom. Emilie was the only person who'd ever taken me up on my offer to give away another person's life.

* * *

Weeks passed. Piper made no effort to contact me. Being in the public eye, the casino's golden boy, and up-and-coming MMA fighter, it wouldn't be difficult for her to get my contact information. But I didn't even hear so much of a peep from her on social media. I fought the urge to go to the Bellagio. I knew she was there from the credit card statement. However, it was quite irritating that she racked up the bill there. Pay-per-view, the massage service, extravagant shopping trips—I knew she didn't care about any of them. This was her way of sending a message: Give her back her receipts and she'd stop racking up the credit card bill. I understood that asking anything of me would be a sign of defeat, just like it would be if I turned my card off...but damn I hadn't expected her to be so cunning.

Every day, her purchases got more and more. I knew she was daring when I got a picture message from her when in front of MGM's gambling monitors, pointing out card counters to Captain Jameson. It was the first time she'd ever contacted me—apparently I'd gotten her a new cell phone last week. That was sure nice of me.

The image was a selfie. The adrenaline rush that accompanied any thought of Piper was unlike anything I'd felt in centuries. An enormous black diamond chocker encompassed Piper's neck. In the foreground was her fucking smirk. I could barely take my eyes off her dimples...when I was able to tear my gaze away from the picture, I logged onto my bank account. Ten grand!

"Damn it, Piper!" I chucked the phone across the room, smashing it into the wall, shattering it.

"Woman problems?" Jameson quipped.

I gripped the table and willed the persistent rage to calm. I fought the urge to smash in someone's fucking face in, which would just be a freaking delight to the captain who was just itching for a public excuse to lock me up. He may work for me, but I knew he loathed me. I could smell the stank on him. I wanted to end his life, siphon all the essence from his soul. But more than anything else, I wanted to kill *her*.

Piper Miller

Declan wanted my head on a platter. At least I figured he would want to kill me after I sent him the picture of my five-figure bling. Curled up on the hotel bed, I twirled the dagger in my hands wishing I knew why the weapon was so important to him. When I closed my eyes, I relived the moment when he pried it from my hands and looked down at me like it pained *him* to know I was hurt. The cut on my hand had long since healed, but his light touch was embedded to memory. He had a long-lasting affect on me.

After weeks of radio silence, I would be damned to admit out loud how much he affected me, much less *ask* him for my carbon-copies. He would give them back to me willingly. I'd make sure of it. This intense game we were playing—of pushing each other's buttons—made me feel more alive than I ever had before.

I probably should have just taken a cash advance on his card—after I reported that it'd been lost and they mailed a new one to the hotel—and skipped town. But I couldn't very well leave without my blackmail in tow. And the truth was, I wasn't done with Declan. I wanted, needed, to know more about him.

Even so, I wasn't expecting was the knock at the door after I sent him a selfie. A phone call would have sufficed. I got the impression

Declan preferred to make house calls instead of picking up a phone. The intimidation-factor was much higher when he could do his imposing stance. His voice may be sexy-as-hell, but it didn't have the same effect as being in his sheer presence.

Armed with the dagger, I cautiously approached the door. I wouldn't put it past Declan to send the police after me. I mean, he had so dramatically pointed out that he owned everyone in town—except me. I would *not* be putty in his hand like everyone else.

As I approached the door, my heart raced uncontrollably. I *small* part of me was excited to see him, just as I was freaking-out, scared, thrilled, pissed and overwhelmed by the biggest adrenaline rush that awakened my body knowing Declan was near.

I opened the door. No one was there. When I stepped out to look down the hallway, I tripped over a newspaper. A hotel staff person was delivering papers to each door like always. I grabbed the paper and slammed the door behind me.

Mother fuc—I'd kill to know what he was feeling right now!

Plopping back on the bed, I flipped open the paper. At least the front page news was interesting. Stilts *v. Jones* was the headliner article. I read the article for further details. Apparently Declan had instigated a bar fight the night I sent him the picture. They decided to settle it in the ring instead of a court house. The fight was scheduled for next Friday.

"I guess I'll have to find something modest to wear."

***

Declan Stilts

The most expensive seat in the house was reserved for Piper. I was so politely informed of her R.S.V.P via purchase alert. So I fully expected to see her smirk Friday night. But her seat was vacant! I swore to myself that if she didn't show I was going to her hotel tonight and end this one way or another.

Minutes before the match started Piper finally showed dressed to the nine's in a midnight blue dress that matched her eyes perfectly. From the rink's corner, I stood still, watching her make her decent to the front row. The noise drowned out to the drum of my heartbeat. The dress was lightweight, showcasing her trim frame—by no means was it a showstopper, skin-tight dress that demanded everyone's attention. But, she caught *my* interest. Her light brown hair cast over her dainty little shoulders that only made her appear breakable—not like the untamable women I'd berated in the hotel room. What sparked my irrational desire to tear off the designer dress and push her to the edge of her breaking point was when she smirked upon catching me drooling over her.

I slammed my fist into the corner post. *She* was the demon. *She* was the devil in disguise. *She* was the manipulative monster. But what truly set me off was that *she* was in control of this battle of the wills that we were fighting! I wasn't used to defeat. I wasn't used to fighting a valiant opponent like Piper.

If her grand entrance wasn't enough, Piper crossed her leg over the other, exposing much of her thigh that tempted me to take what was mine. Fanning herself with a piece of paper, she raised her eyebrow and whistled to herself. I swear she did it on purpose, pushing her lips at me like she wanted to do more than just whistle. Even through the screaming crowd, I swore I heard the faint melody, its sound enticing me. I narrowed my eyes. The rage boiling through me was going to make tonight's match end quickly with a KO. Fast money would be made on bets tonight. I just hoped it satisfied the agitation boiling inside me. Piper's presence wasn't helping calm me down. But she was seriously pushing me over the edge when she wiggled her little finger at me.

She did *not* just beckon me! *I* wasn't on her beck-and-call. *I* would not go to *her*.

I sat in the metal folding chair and stared at my opponent. My cheek still burned from the lucky punch he got in last week. That he was able to land a hit ticked me off about as much as that pointless necklace…that necklace that was tight against her skin. And just like that she had my attention again. She shrugged her shoulders and unfolded the paper. I immediately recognized it as a gambling ticket for tonight's fight.

Piper Miller
"Fifty thousand on Jones?"

Declan's chest heaved after he tore the ticket from my hands. His face deadpanned upon reading the details of the first bet I'd ever made.

Like I said, I wasn't a gambling girl. But to get back what was rightfully *mine*, I'd spend all of *his* money. Declan crumpled the ticket his in fist and threw it down at me. It landed by my heels. I didn't bother to pick it up, hoping he got the message that I didn't care about any of his money. I'd come here to get my hands on what was mine—my carbon-copies and then sit tight till my twenty-first birthday when the trust became mine. I only had a few days left until then anyways, and I wanted those carbon-copies back in case my mother tried to claim the funds as hers.

Standing up, I closed the gap between us. I could feel everyone's eyes on us as their camera's snapped our picture; their screams rang in my ears. With as much of a media presence we were getting, you'd think that *our fight* was tonight's highlight match.

I stepped close enough to feel heat radiating off of his body. Last time I stood this close to him, I stared death in the face and smiled. Tonight was no different. If he wanted to screw with me, I'd play the game.

"Your two-bit trust doesn't equate to this wager," he said.

"How do you know?"

"I did my homework on you Piper, I know everything about you," he sneered.

I laughed. "You. Know. Nothing. Not if you think any of this is about money."

He tightened his fists. "What's it about then?"

"Freedom."

He cocked his head to the side. His face was vacant, shielding his true feelings. "What if I don't want to be free of you?"

An official came up to him before I could reply. "It's time."

I grabbed Declan's arm. He flexed his arm like it was everything he could do not to fight me. That he respected me enough to hear me out meant a lot.

I said, "You have a decision to make. Win and lose a fortune, or lose and—"

"—Win you?"

"I'm not a prize to be claimed, Declan."

He turned his back away from me so I couldn't see the truth burning in his eyes, but I saw it all the same. I mattered to him. I mattered *greatly*. Declan ~~loved~~...well, cared for me anyways. Calling this attraction *love* was a little pre-mature, but the thought tugged at my

28

heart. What we had was unconventional. It was dangerous and unpredictable. But it was honest, and I loved that about us.

We didn't get to pick who we fell for. Sometimes they were Mr. Right's. Sometimes they were Prince-Charming's. And sometimes they were the vilest of men.

The official pulled Declan into the middle of the rink. In one swift movement, Declan removed his shirt. I forgot how to breathe as I took in the athletic splendor that was *him*. My jaw damn near hit the floor as I zeroed in on his chest—his chest that was the fantasy of so many women. I finally understood what it meant to #declandaydream. The magazines had not done him justice! Every core muscle flexed as he walked center-stage. His arm and shoulder bulged when he shook Jones' hand. His entire body moved in sync, like a machine. My mouth dried. The human body could be very stunning and magnificent in action, but after the announcer introduced the two fighters, Declan moved with angelic precision. Each hit, each kick, each hold was jaw-dropping…and I could tell he was holding back. I'd seen him move more swiftly in the hotel room. He was toying with his adversary.

Round One ended. As soon as the bell echoed, his gaze found mine. I'd thought I'd stared death in the face before. I was wrong. The hatred churning behind those eyes was immeasurable, but matched with that hate was undeniable passion. Declan hated me. And he desired me. I was right. He was toying with his adversary, I just didn't know if it was the other fighter or me.

Instead of plucking rose petals, playing *He-Loves-Me-Not* he used his fist to pound down his opponent; each time he let Jones land a punch, I knew Declan was fighting an inner turmoil. Lose a million and win.

In the third round, the crowd leaped from their seats when Declan gave the final blow, knocking out his opponent. As soon as Jones' body fell limply to the mat, Declan looked over at me. The referee grabbed Declan's wrist and raised it up in the air. His dark eyes narrowed as I stood and clapped politely for him. He had won, and it only cost him a cool mil. Ripping out his mouth piece, he approached his bag. He ripped an envelope from it and then strode over to me with determination. Even though he was covered in bruises and dripping with sweat, he moved with certainty. When he was just a few feet away, he cast the envelope to my shoes, slipped his hands on either side of my face and pulled me against his hot body.

He stole a kiss. He coaxed a moan from my throat. He silenced my non-verbal protests as his hot body moved against mine. When his lips collided with mine, passion between us erupted. Our kiss was a statement of our entire relationship. Dirty and addictive. I wanted him—craved him like he was a drug. He was dangerous, manipulative, and still the most striking man I'd ever set eyes on. He held me tight. It was like I was molded just for him to take. Moving his hand to the small of my back, he pressed me up against him. He moaned when I brought my hands up through his hair. His grasp tightened as he consumed my kiss.

When I tugged on his hair, pulling him closer against me, he suddenly released me. I knew it was the last thing he wanted to do, but his stare was apocalyptic and his stance was rigid. He was teetering on the edge of control.

He swore, "Whatever the cost, you'll be mine."

Without a second glance, he turned around and left me gasping for air. I watched him slowly disappear into the cheering crowd. I couldn't take my eyes off of him. Only then did I pick up the envelope and look inside. My father's death certificate—how and why Declan had given me that piece of material was unknown. Along with it were the carbon-copies from my mother's fraudulent business transactions.

<hr />

Declan Stilts

I chose Piper before she was born. I'd long since claimed her as mine. Even as the hunger erupted inside of me, I could still hear her faint whistling ringing in my ears. Raw desire churned in me; I wanted *her* just as much as I wanted all the money in the house. I was almost out of control; tonight would end with a body bag—that much I knew. I showered and changed as quickly as I could.

I couldn't fucking do it—not now. Not after I'd fallen for her. To pass this curse on to her, thus freeing myself of it, even I couldn't bear it. I may not be the man I was before I became an Incubus, but a shred of my old self still survived the corruption.

And Goddamn it, I'd just lost a small fortune by winning that fight—and I'd do it all over again, but it still didn't calm the demonic side of me. I needed to feed. The starvation in me was going to make me lose my mind.

Bad.

I stumbled onto the main floor of Mirage and found my way to the high-rollers table. I just needed to get a pair of dice in my hands and feed off of the greed around me.

My phone rang. Piper's number showed up on the screen. I silenced it. More than anything else in the world, I wanted to go to her—be with her, but it would end with a trip to the morgue if I didn't feed first. I wanted her uncontrollably; and I couldn't chance her. I'd never gamble away her affection. Never. I couldn't bear it.

I sat down at the first available roulette table when my phone rang again. "Dammit, Piper!"

I pulled it out and was immediately told that phones were not permitted on the grounds. I silenced the phone again, gripped the table, clenched my teeth, and then placed a grand on twelve red. I watched the little white ball roll around the wheel.

Of course my damn phone rang as soon as it fell on my number. I ripped the phone from my pocket. "What Piper?"

"Hello Declan. I believe you have something I want."

As soon as *her* shrill voice came over the speaker, I lost all connection with my human side. "It's been far too long, Emilie."

Piper Miller

As soon as I closed my hotel room door behind me, a barrel of a gun was pressed to my head. I turned around to find Jameson at the other end and my mother standing right next to him.

Effing Perfect

"What do you want?" I asked as calmly as anyone would with a red dot on their forehead.

My mother walked up to me. "You have something I need."

I clenched the envelope, anticipating her to snatch away the only proof I had on her. She'd do anything to try to screw me over from my trust fund. So when she went for my purse, I was confused. As much as it pained me to let her claw through my things, there was a gun pointed at me, so I had no choice. She dug out my phone along with the dagger.

Emilie said, "I figured the best way to keep tabs on Rumpelstiltskin would be to keep tabs on you. I wasn't wrong."

"What are you talking about?"

Ignoring my question, she turned her back to me and dialed the only number in the call list. "Hello Declan."

I took a step toward my mother when Jameson spoke up. "I'd think really carefully about what you plan to do and say next. Rumpelstiltskin isn't the man you think he is."

"And what is that? And why are you calling him that? "

"Rumpelstiltskin is his true name, and Incubus is his true nature." Jameson lowered his gun and exchanged a look with dear old Mom. "He feeds off of humans. Most end up in body bags. The lucky ones are left just exhausted. He fends off his own death by stealing our essence. He's probably fed off of you…"

Whatever lesson Jameson was set on giving me, I only heard half of it. This was all too messed up. I couldn't believe this to be true.

"…he's connected to the dagger somehow. It's the only way to kill him. And if he needs to keep track of someone, he offers it to them," my mother said. "It's cursed."

Dazed, I looked up at her. I didn't know how long she'd been talking. It didn't matter. "Wait. You gave *me* the dagger! You wanted him to find me?"

"He wants *you*, Piper. Not me. It's always been about you." My mother patted the seat on the edge of the bed beside her. "It's why I've always been so distant to you. I was afraid to love you. He's killed many people to hurt me, including your father."

Declan Stilts

It took every power in my being not to bust down the hotel door the moment I got to room 901. Instead, I did my best to reign in the brimming fury inside of me and wait. I had to know what they knew.

"Declan killed my father?"

Piper's voice cut through me like a knife. I couldn't stand to hear the hurt in her and not do anything, especially since it was a lie! I let myself into the room, ascertaining the potential threats: Emilie and Jameson. But all I truly cared for was the young woman standing in front of me. The look of betrayal was written all over her face. It killed me.

"Piper," I spoke her name as if it meant the millions of things that refused to leave my tongue.

"You lied," Piper said, inching closer to her vindictive mother who was sitting on the bed.

"Not to you," I replied.

Piper didn't look like she believed me. But now wasn't the time to convince her otherwise, not with all the damning evidence against me. A red dot tracked onto my chest. Out of the corner of my eye, I saw Jameson aim the gun at me.

I said, "You know that can't kill me."

"It'll slow you down," he sneered.

Not enough. I clenched my jaw to keep from admitting that little nugget of information. As difficult as it was to reign in my persistent urge to end that moron's life, I let him live. His life was irrelevant. I turned my attention back to the only person in the room that held any significance to me whatsoever. Piper was that person to me. When I was busy meddling with her fate, she'd changed my destiny forever.

I'd altered her life the second I knew of her existence. The choices that weren't random. She was seemingly insignificant at first. However, the cascading results from that one agreement I made with Emilie twenty years ago changed my life. I craved freedom—freedom from the curse that ruled me. I planned on finding freedom with Piper, but instead I became enslaved to my feelings for her. That inalienable truth tormented what was left of my soul. I was forever changed because of her.

"You're a monster," Piper whispered and waited for me to deny it. When I didn't, a tear fled her beautiful blue eye and glistened over the few freckles on her cheek.

I clenched my teeth together. I hadn't lied to her yet. I wasn't about to start now. "I'm not the only monster in his room, Piper. I assure that of you."

I'd give away all the money in the world to hold her in my arms, to taste her sweet kiss, for her to be truly *mine*… But if she taught me anything, it was that all the gold couldn't buy her love. Not after she stole my rotten heart.

"You're truly in love with her." Emilie stared at me like I'd just unveiled my darkest secret when I looked at Piper.

I yelled, "Stay out of this Emilie. I'm warning you!"

"You're a killer," Piper said, still in disbelief.

"Not your father's," I said. "He's very much alive and well."

"Enough." Emilie stood quickly and pressed the dagger against her daughter's throat.

My legs twitched. I couldn't stand her fucking hands so close to Piper's throat. It wouldn't take long for me to break her arms, but a mere flick of the wrist and she'd be dead. "Killing Piper solves *nothing* for you."

"Oh, that's where you're wrong. Killing her will bring me much satisfaction because it will *hurt you!*"

The thought of Piper dying…it was too much to bear. Even if she could never care for me the way I did her, I'd make a deal to spare her life in a heartbeat.

I asked Emilie, "Do you want Trevis back? Permanently?"

"I sold my daughter's soul if Trevis would return to me, even if it was brief. And you gave me that, nothing more, nothing less. And I held up my end of the bargain as well. Piper is *yours*. But that doesn't mean your time together is ever-lasting. She may be yours, but she can still die!"

"Declan?" Piper's plea came out in a whisper.

Enough of this shit. I charged Emilie. As soon as my foot left the ground, Jameson fired his gun. It hit my chest but didn't slow me. In one swift movement, I grabbed his head and snapped his neck. I spun around before his body hit the floor.

Piper! I caught her body and lowered her gently to the ground. Emilie had stabbed her in the chest. I stood and grabbed her mother by her throat. Unlike all the others, she didn't fight death. I breathed in deeply and relished watching the life in her face dwindle away. I'd *never* embraced a soul consummation more than I had with hers. She was a despicable person, and I was glad to rid the world of her. I should have killed her years ago, but the thought of Piper orphaned undid me. I thought growing up with at least one parent was better than none. I may have been wrong. When I finally released her, she dropped like the dead weight that it was.

Without a second glance, I turned my attention back to Piper. She lay, gasping for breath. I could already feel her life was slipping away. I could save her—give her the curse. However, the surreal memory of "my beloved" Sophia flashed before my eyes. I hated her for cursing me. I loved her and I thought she loved me back, but it was just a trick to get me to do what she wanted. And Sophia wanted freedom, just like I did now. But I couldn't stand the thought of Piper hating me or the thought of her soul rotting like mine. I couldn't turn her into…me.

"You'll find freedom in death," I whispered, wiping the tears from her freckled cheeks.

"I don't want to be free of you."

I tucked her hair so I could see her beautiful eyes before her soul left them. Before kissing her goodbye I whispered, "Forgive me."

And then I stabbed her in the heart with the Godforsaken dagger.

Piper Miller

As soon as Declan's lips collided with mine, he cursed me by stabbing me in the heart with the dagger. Sparks burst into flame around the blade. It felt a part of the dagger burning away pieces of me…the good pieces. Breathing in the essence of the greed, corruption and torment that'd he'd stolen over his lifetime; he shared a part that hunger with me. But he stopped halfway. I could sense him struggling to give me everything, even though I know he wanted to; he couldn't bring himself to give up everything. I felt a part of his soul residing in mine. The good part and the corruption. It was like he tore himself into two.

"I told you no matter the cost, you will be mine," he said, gazing at me like I was his everything.

And then Declan confessed everything. The good. The bad. The ugly. He claimed his soul was corrupt and his heart rotten, but I felt those parts of him burning inside me. And I knew he was everything he claimed, but he was so much more than just a demon. He was so much more than the evil that ruled him. He wasn't purely evil or he wouldn't have spared me from the full intensity of the curse; he wouldn't have kept half of it. I wouldn't be completely enslaved by the festering hunger, but instead I would share it with him—the demon loved me, saved me from death, but spared me from an immortal life of misery.

"You're whistling again," he said and then frowned when I stopped. He rolled his thumb over my bottom lip and glanced at the freckles on my nose. "Never stop. It's incredibly alluring, my pied Piper."

"Now what?" I asked, wondering where this left us.

"Wherever you want. Your story has just begun, Piper."

I fell in love with a monster. In doing so, I became one myself. But I never regretted the night I met Rumpelstiltskin.

Our passion consumed us. It ruled us. We were enslaved to it. And because we welcomed it, it freed us both. Our affection for each other was unconventional and all-consuming. But love was complicated for everyone, even in the sweetest of fairy tales.

The End?

I specialize in dark, paranormal romance – think "happy ever after" but with a twisted, dark chocolate center. Real-life romance isn't only filled with hugs, kisses, unicorns, and rainbows. True-love can be more thoroughly described in times of darkness and tribulation. It's in those harsh moments where you see what a person is truly capable of – both the good and bad. Sometimes prince-charming isn't always on time, and the glass slipper is a little snug. However, it doesn't mean Charming is not Mr. Right, and who says every shoe is the perfect fit?

"Warning: Addictive passion erupts from her mouthwatering descriptions" - recent review.

Sarah J. Pepper lives in South Dakota with her real-life prince charming. At a young age, she fell for paranormal books and now incorporates that genre with romance that thrives in the hearts of us all. When she's not storytelling, she's most likely biking, hoarding chocolate, or taking a bubble bath. To learn more, visit: http://www.sarahjpepper.com/

THE SNOW QUEEN
Retold
by Shannon Morton

Prologue

I see you. Yes, you. Sitting there reading your little collection of fairy tales. A feeble, love-struck creature desperately seeking a happily ever after. Or worse yet. Are you the predictable rebel? Rooting for the villain to kill them all and revel in their destruction?

Either way, you're pathetic. An emotional junkie devouring page after page to get your fix.

The worst part is you're too caught up in your voyeuristic escape to realize you've missed the whole point. Whether the heroine gets her prince and rides off into the sunset or the dragon burns them all to ashes is irrelevant.

These stories have blinded you to reality. You are slaves to the feelings evoked by words on a page. Just like the characters in these tales, you are too busy choking on your own emotions to actually live.

What a terrible thing to be ruled by your heart.

Fortunately, I don't have one.

But don't pity me. I'm not the one who's broken.

You are.

The Good Doctor

A rich mahogany desk, chocolate high-back leather chairs, and potted African Violets on a shelf in the corner make the room seem warm and inviting. Earth-toned landscapes adorn the walls instead of the shrine of diplomas and certificates one would expect to see. The sort of place designed to make you feel safe. Safe enough to divulge your most private thoughts. Your deepest secrets.

Only the sterile smell of the frosty air flowing through the vents gives any indication that this office is not cozy at all, but clinical. That the miserably ignorant people who come here are not clients or patients—as they are told. In reality, the small space is merely a laboratory; its visitors being dissected piece by piece.

The older woman sitting across the desk assesses me shrewdly with her steel-grey eyes. Though a few strands of her perfect chignon have faded from brunette to silver, little else about Dr. Emilia Parks has changed in the two years since I last saw her. I wonder if she thinks the same about me. It's true that I haven't changed much physically. My hair is still long and so blonde it's almost white. Eyes the same pale blue and skin just as fair as ever. Although I finally grew into my arms and legs I remain tall and willowy. So much the same as when I first walked into this office twelve years ago. But I'm not here to reminisce.

I wanted to come back to the place where it all started.

I've always known I was different from everyone else…better, really. Though not everyone was inclined to agree. After a few childhood pranks, I was shuttled from one doctor to the next. Some of them called me hyper. Others, defiant. A few had more creative names.

Dr. Parks didn't believe in labels. She told my parents that she worked with people, not problems. They were sold. So, barring illness or injury, I had spent two hours a week in one of these oversized chairs. One with my parents—a family session. The other with just the good doctor.

I probably could have gotten out of going altogether if I'd really tried. But I knew I would just be dragged to even more specialists. Given more useless drugs. She was the lesser of the evils, I had decided.

Dr. Parks, always perfectly polished in her tailored pantsuits, was different from the others in her profession. While they had gone to great lengths to make me feel things—love, remorse, empathy—she had instead appealed to my sense of logic. She asked endless questions about my thoughts and perceptions of others' emotions, but never forced me to admit that I lacked feelings of my own.

By the time I was eighteen, however, I had grown weary of her cognitive bullshit and informed everyone I no longer required her services. My parents seemed defeated but accepted my decision.

Dr. Parks had a different reaction. Instead of the lecture I expected, she sat like a stone in her chair. When I was finished listing off all the reasons I wouldn't be back, her mouth turned up just slightly at the corners. That ghost of a smile was the calm before the storm.

The words she spoke to me before I walked out of her office still echo in my mind.

"I hope you enjoy being a copy, Winter," she'd said matter-of-factly. "Because that is exactly what you are. Not an original but a mirror, only able to reflect the expressions of others. Capable only of mimicry, not truth." Her words tasted like battery acid and burned themselves into my brain, searing an image of myself I refused to accept. A girl forced to disguise her lack of emotion with a veil of learned expressions. Someone who was weak and malleable. A fake. I'd turned my back on her and walked out of the office that day with a single-minded determination.

I would make Dr. Emilia Parks eat her words.

I've been waiting for this day for a while now. In some ways I feel that my life didn't begin until I closed the door of her office that day, effectively putting my childhood to bed. That was the day I stopped taking my emotional cues from others. The day I decided I didn't want to be a copy. I wanted to make them.

* * *

Our unofficial staring contest continues for what seems like an eternity before she eventually clears her throat a bit and looks down at a legal pad filled with illegible scribbling on her desk. If breaking eye contact first really is a sign of weakness or submission of some sort, Dr. Parks seems unaware. Her haughty air remains perfectly intact.

"Winter," she finally addresses me with a formal tone and a face devoid of expression. "It's been awhile. How are…" she pauses slightly before finishing, "things?"

A montage of scenes from the last year runs through my mind before I answer.

"Things," I reply, emphasizing the word she'd carefully chosen, "couldn't be better."

"I'm glad to hear it," she inclines her head toward me in a small gesture of appreciation, though she seems almost…bored. This irritates me. I want her to be curious. More than curious. I want her clamoring; desperate to know what became of Winter Blake. After all, it's only fitting to have a proper build-up before the climax.

So, I bait her.

3

"I almost came to see you last year, but I decided with all the media coverage I should keep a low profile," I toss my hair back over my shoulder and relax into the chair.

"A low profile? She asks dubiously, raising an eyebrow. "That hardly seems like the Winter I remember."

"Seasons change," I shrug.

"Yes," she leans in, resting her elbows on her desk, hands folded except for her index fingers, which are pressed together. "But people do not."

I smile a little. She has taken the bait.

"What if you're wrong?" I ask, trying not to sound too smug. "What about turning points, epiphanies, and transformations?"

"Nice sentiments." It was her turn to shrug. "Are you trying to tell me you've changed?"

"Not exactly," I counter her doubtful expression with a small, sly half-smile.

"Well," she offers, sitting back into her chair, "why don't you tell me about the last two years and let me be the judge."

My smile widens in victory as I begin my story, reeling in Dr. Emilia Parks.

The Eagle Scout

I was less than eight minutes into a grueling three-day transfer orientation before I knew that Ryan Herrington was Boston College's "it" guy. The gaggle of girls pawing him, hanging on his every word, and giggling like morons was a dead giveaway. I was beginning to rethink college life altogether when he looked over at me and smiled.

A member of his fan club soon followed his gaze to me, and before I knew it, I had an audience. Wearing matching t-shirts and tanks drenched in maroon and gold, they glared in typical mean girl fashion, not yet realizing I'd written the book on the subject.

With what seemed like considerable effort, he untangled himself from the army of groupies attached to him and headed in my direction, his eyes never leaving mine. I had chosen a chair at the back of the auditorium near the exit. Away from crowd. Also, the best seat in the house for sizing up a new situation.

"This seat taken?" he asked with the confidence of a guy who had never heard the word no. His voice low and smooth.

"It is now," I decided to play along. With his wavy honey-blond hair and surfer-blue eyes he was practically a Ken doll begging to sit next to Barbie.

"I'm Ryan," he extended his hand as though I might actually shake it.

"Winter Blake," I replied, my amusement at his offer bleeding from my eyes into a slow side smile. He finally ran his outstretched hand through his hair and dropped it to his side.

"So, you're a transfer?" he asked, clearly trying to spark any type of conversation.

Instead of the verbal response I'm sure he was looking for, I merely arched an eyebrow and looked up at the "Welcome Transfers" banner at the front of the room and then back at him.

"Right," he quickly tried to recover, "of course. What I meant to ask was where you're from."

"Connecticut," I answered. Another curt reply. I wondered how many it would take before he finally walked away.

"Really?" He looked surprised. "Me too. What part?"

"New Canaan."

"No way. I grew up less than an hour away in Wallingford." He seemed excited to be standing on common ground.

"Small world." I smiled and looked away, scanning the room to find the group of girls still watching my every move. Even some of the guys started looking our way. Faculty included. Clearly, the guy really was a big deal.

I turned back to peer up at him through my long lashes. He had the kind of smile you see in toothpaste commercials. He wore a snug grey Boston College t-shirt, and as my eyes slid down his body it was obvious he spent a lot of time outside. The tanned skin over toned muscles made it clear that time was physical.

"Jock?" I guessed aloud.

He chuckled lowly. "I guess you could say that. I play football." The conversation continued, albeit one-sided with him talking about sports and me staring vacantly at absolutely nothing. I hated sports, and I didn't even try to pay attention.

Abruptly, he cut off his rambling. "I'm so sorry," he said apologetically, tilting his head to the side and grinning like a little boy,

"I'm just excited for the season to start. I swear I'm not just a good throwing arm."

"Prove it, Ryan-no-last-name," I sat back in the chair and crossed my arms and legs simultaneously, a smirk playing on my lips.

He seemed startled at my boldness. I was a bit surprised myself. I usually got dates by acting like all the other flighty girls. Batting my eyelashes. Flipping my hair. Playing stupid. Not this time. This time I was doing it my way.

"Herrington. And how about tonight?" he asked eagerly. I glanced again at the sign hanging at the front of the room.

"Right," he pinched the bridge of his nose and shook his head. "I meant Friday night."

"Perfect."

* * *

Our first date was like a scene from a romantic movie. Recycled material, but rehearsed and played well. He brought flowers and smiled sheepishly as he opened the passenger door of his black BMW for me. Impeccable manners, if a little on the traditional side. The restaurant he took me to was in a small brick building on a street that looked more like a well-lit alley. It was dimly lit—the soft, warm light that makes people look almost angelic. Again, impeccable taste, if a little clichéd.

We talked about everything. Growing up in Connecticut, the move to Boston College, and what seemed like every detail about his friends and family. His eyes lit up when he talked about his nine year-old brother, Max. I wouldn't have been surprised to hear that he volunteered at nursing homes in his spare time.

He wanted to know about me too, of course. I told him about my parents, the perks of being an only child, and how I'd spent the previous year traveling and taking college courses online, and finding myself. The conversation flowed freely and the awkward silence was non-existent. At least he wasn't just a pretty face.

After dinner we took a short walk through the North End before he drove me back to the safe, off-campus apartment my parents were happy to pay for. He walked me up to my door and I fished my keys from the bottom of my purse. Before I could slide the key into the lock, Ryan moved his hand to tuck a strand of my long blonde hair behind my ear.

"It was in your eyes," he explained with a small, impish grin when I looked up at him.

"Convenient," I returned his smile while calling him out. "But did you really need an excuse to touch me? Or do I need to tell you that I had a nice time while nervously biting my bottom lip?" I pulled the corner of my bottom lip into my mouth, mimicking what I'd just described. Once again my audacious nature seemingly left him a little off-balance.

His kiss was gentle; a whisper on my lips. I wanted a scream. And I wasn't the type of girl who believed in asking. When I wanted something, I took it.

I opened the door, shoved him inside, and kicked it closed. His blue eyes blazed with excitement as I pushed him hard up against the wall, pressing my body into his. Fisting my hands into his hair, I taught him how to kiss me. Deep and hard with the promise of so much more.

He tried to steer me further inside the apartment but I resisted, keeping him against the wall.

"Not as far for you to walk when we're finished," I panted, busy unfastening the button on his pants after making quick work of his belt.

"So you're just gonna toss me out after?" He sucked in a breath as I leaned in to run my lips across his neck. "No spooning?"

"No spoons," I breathed into his ear while running my fingernails lightly down his chest. "You want knives."

*　*　*

Ryan and I were inseparable. That is, with the exception of the time I spent reading boring finance texts off the required summer reading list and the time he spent doing football things. Being with him was unlike anything I had ever experienced. Despite the fact we were rarely seen together—I refused to attend anything sports related—somehow everyone knew we were together. Suddenly I was the sparkly, pink boa instead of the stealthy camouflage. While I enjoyed all the attention at first, living under a microscope got claustrophobic.

Not that it was difficult to convince him to stay in more. Until classes started. Between conflicting school schedules and football, we started seeing less and less of each other. Something had to give. I knew that people were like bones. Sometimes they needed to be re-broken in order to heal properly. So that's exactly what I did.

The backhanded compliment was the first weapon in my arsenal. If he brought me flowers they were nice, but not my favorites. If he made dinner the pasta was delicious, but maybe less salt next time. If we were having sex, I wanted it harder and faster. Everything was almost, but not quite.

Drill sergeants train soldiers by tearing them down and then rebuilding them. My method was similar. Well, the tearing down part anyway. But once you added in my second weapon—isolation—the results were nothing sort of miraculous.

That meant that friends had to go. His, of course. Friends were emotional crutches for broken people. I had acquaintances. What surprised me was how easy it was to separate him from other people. Bail on plans a few times and the calls and texts just stop coming. But it wasn't enough.

Soon I had him skipping classes and blowing off practice for the sake of our relationship. By the time Thanksgiving break came, he was failing three of his five classes and had been benched more games than he played. He brushed it off by saying that he had plenty of time to catch up and that I was worth it.

It was the week before winter break when I knew my work was done. Well, almost. I stared at him from across the beige Formica tabletop in the cafeteria. At first glance, he appeared unchanged. Beneath the surface, however, he couldn't have been more different. No longer the robust athlete he had been just a few months before, his smiles came slower and his eyes had lost their shine. He was hollow.

I had unraveled him one thread at a time—preparing him to knit himself back together—stronger, unencumbered by emotion. Only a single strand remained to hold him together. Me. And my scissors were ready.

"Ryan, we need to talk," I said slowly, watching his reaction closely.

"Sure," he said, taking my hand in his. "What's on your mind?" He was trying to play it cool but it was impossible to miss the shadow of fear that darkened his expression.

Pulling my hand away from his, I interlaced my fingers together and placed my hands in my lap. A visual show of separation was clearly necessary.

"This isn't working anymore, Ryan," I told him matter-of-factly. "You've changed." And he had. He was so close to reaching his potential now.

Tears began to pool in his eyes, and he was visibly shaking. "Look, Winter, I know I've been stuck in a rut lately, but we can get through this. Please. I love you." He looked at me with the saddest eyes I had ever seen. If that was the face of love, it was pathetic.

"You don't even love yourself, Ryan," I explained. "There is no way you can possibly love anyone else. Pulling my black leather bag over my shoulder, I got up from the bench to leave.

"Please Winter," he begged like a child, though there seemed to be little life left in the plea, "don't do this. I can change. I can be who I was before."

But I knew he couldn't. The light had gone out of his eyes.

I exhaled contentedly and turned to walk away. "No, Ryan, you can't."

That was the last time I spoke to him. He called, texted, and even stood outside my apartment for hours, but I ignored each attempt at contact. Before leaving for Connecticut for vacation, I kept tabs on his progress by eavesdropping on the gossip. I overheard a number of hushed conversations and whispered accusations around campus. Talks of how I'd publicly eviscerated him. Rumors that he got kicked off the team. It was all going exactly as expected. I drove home for break Friday after my last class, quite pleased with how everything had worked out.

There is only so much pain a person can take before feeling is no longer a suitable option. That wouldn't be an issue much longer.

* * *

The Boston College Eagles lost one of the biggest games of the season Saturday night without their star quarterback, and they found Ryan Herrington dead the next morning. He had hung himself. No pills or ill-place slits to the wrist. Not a cry for help. While not the progress I'd been hoping for at least it was decisive. There were rumors of a suicide note, but I was sure his parents had kept it under wraps. What I wouldn't have given to read it.

Even without the written condemnation, the haters came with pitchforks and torches. It started with whispers in the halls, but quickly escalated to libelous bricks being thrown through my apartment windows in the middle of the night.

At the urging of the police, the dean called and informed my parents of the situation. They were in Boston with a moving crew a few hours later. During the drive back home to New Canaan I decided I could either call this one a failure or accept that some people knew they were too broken to be saved. I chose the latter.

The Other Half
The prospect of living back in Connecticut with my parents was grim. Trying to cage a bird that's only just realized she can fly. Fortunately, another opportunity was quick to present itself. My uncle was an administrator at a university in Texas, and while the south wasn't my first choice, it wasn't living with my parents, either. A few strings were pulled, but within a few days, I was settling in to my aunt and uncle's guesthouse on their ranch in College Station preparing to start my first day of classes at Texas A&M.

I had lived in New England my entire life, and to say that moving down south was an adjustment was an understatement. Although my childhood had been one long exercise in fitting in, I had no intention of donning a mask of false southern charm. Texas was going to have to acclimate to Winter.

* * *

My mother had called it a fresh start. My father said it was a fantastic opportunity. My aunt and uncle insisted it was a clean slate. I didn't care about any of that. To me, it was new hunting ground, and I was looking for easy prey.

I found it the first week of school in a most unusual place. My aunt and uncle dragged me to a tailgating party before a basketball game one night after class. I had never seen so many people gathered in one place; I swore every car in the state of Texas had to be parked in those lots. There was also no shortage of school spirit. A blur of maroon and white t-shirts and hoodies as far as my eyes could see. I suspected my cardigan and pearls were a bit out of place and I smiled at the thought.

Quickly abandoning my relatives and their boring middle-aged friends sitting around a fold-up picnic table, I set off to explore my new world. It wasn't long before I came across what had to be the largest, most obnoxious truck in the entire lot. It was fire-engine red with orange and yellow flames painted across the sides and monster tires lifted at least four feet off the ground. It was an open invitation to ridicule.

"Clearly overcompensating," I mocked aloud to myself as I walked by.

"What was that?" A raspy southern twang shot back.

I turned to see a guy in faded jeans and black cowboy boots stepping out of crowd gathered near the back of the truck. His shaggy brown hair hung in his eyes and his tight, white t-shirt had seen better days.

"I said," speaking slowly and enunciating my words to ensure he understood, "that the owner of this truck must be overcompensating for something."

"Is that right?" he drawled with a crooked smile. "It just so happens this truck is mine. And if you wanna come on over here I can show you I ain't makin' up for nothin'." The wicked grin spread across his entire face.

"I'll pass," I replied coolly. *Too easy.*

"I thought this country boy might be too much for a city girl like you." He smirked, clearly trying his best at reverse psychology.

I laughed low and dark as I walked right up to him. We were standing so close I could smell the alcohol on his breath and feel the heat radiating from his body. Sizing him up, I saw right through the layers of bravado and badassery all the way to his insecure, bleeding heart. He was clearly emotionally stunted and probably went home with a different girl every night. I decided to take the chance. Call me an optimist, but the guy was already half-empty.

"What's your name, country boy?"

"Walker," he replied, his eyes raking down my body as if he were the predator. "Walker Dixon."

"Winter Blake," I offered, amused by how simple he would be.

The size of a man's ego is directly proportional to the ease with which you can crush it. When a man is humble, it's harder to break him down. Humility had obviously never been a virtue for Walker Dixon. He was everything that Ryan Herrington had not been. Essentially, an arrogant asshole. Thus, the appeal. Say what you will, but I felt that I deserved a bit of a break after Boston, and apparently, fate agreed.

After exchanging numbers at the tailgating party it took him two days to text me. It took me three to respond. I knew that everything with that one would be a power struggle. He was used to being the alpha male. That was about to change. The only way to fix him was to dominate him.

* * *

Walker Dixon didn't date. Or so he said. I told him to pick me up at seven. He showed up at five after and honked three times before finally walking up to the door. There were no flowers or chivalrous gestures. He was definitely the fuck 'em and forget 'em type.

That fact became even more obvious when we pulled up to a run-down diner on the outskirts of town. The place had fluorescent lighting and the menu was printed on an ordinary piece of paper and housed in a dirty plastic sheet protector. He looked shocked when I ordered the chicken fried steak instead of the salad I was sure he assumed the city girl would get. And I ate every single bite.

After the waitress dropped off the check a roguish grin spread across his face.

"Ever dine and ditch?" he asked in a hushed tone, looking around like a petty criminal.

"No," I said, not impressed with the childish game.

"Well, you're going to tonight." He leaned in conspiratorially. "Unless, of course, you want to pay for dinner."

"I'd rather not," I replied nonchalantly, recognizing this for the test it was. I wondered how many girls he'd suckered into buying him dinner; too scared to leave without paying.

A moment later he was out of his seat and heading toward the restroom.

"Where are you going?" I called out loud enough to blow his cover. He hurried back over to me with a face that screamed *what the hell are you doing?*

He bent low and whispered close to my ear, "I'm going to climb out the bathroom window. You wait a few seconds then follow me."

"In this skirt?" I smirked and arched an eyebrow at him. "You'll take the fun out of it that way. C'mon." I grabbed his arm with one hand and the check with the other.

"Excuse me," I snagged the attention of the woman making coffee behind the counter.

"Yeah," she turned to face us.

"Thank you for dinner," I said as I ripped the bill in half and tossed it onto the floor. I waited for her to say something and when she just stood there stunned, I turned on my heel and walked right out the front door, still dragging Walker behind me.

"Oh my...did you see her face?" His eyes were wild and his southern accent thick as we sped out of the parking lot. "That was amazing. I've done that a million times, but I've never gotten to see their reaction before. What do you want to do now? Rob a bank?"

"That's a little too Bonnie and Clyde for me." I shrugged. "How about a movie?"

"Finally!" He shouted like he'd won the lottery. "Something predictable."

"We'll see." I gave him a mischievous smile full of promise.

* * *

He paid for the movie, but I chose it. It was either a romantic comedy or horror, and I picked horror. Even if I wasn't planning to watch, I'd choose fear over love any day.

There were only a handful of people in the theater, and we sat alone in the back row. As soon as the lights went down I leaned in close and made my intentions known by taking his hand and bringing it to my thigh, brushing it slowly upward.

Not for the first time tonight he looked at me with a bemused expression. Not the brightest, that one. Recognition finally dawned in his eyes and a sly grin took over his face. He immediately took his hand from my leg and began undoing the button on his jeans.

"Easy, now, country boy," I said as though I was talking to an animal, sliding close enough to feel the heat radiating off his body.

"You won't be gettin' off easy." His voice was low and husky as he took my hand and placed it on the bulge in his pants.

"Give and take," I whispered in his ear, and then grabbed his fingers and slipped them under the hem of my skirt. I arched my back

13

in response to his touch as he quickly slid the lacy barrier out of his way. Moaning softly, I smiled to myself. He was clearly oblivious to the fact that he was going to give, and I was going to take.

* * *

We spent a lot of time together over the next few weeks, but I was beginning to get bored. He had been even less of a challenge than I had imagined, and it was time for me to move on. I knew he was ready when he began texting me randomly throughout the day. Every day. The guy who didn't date—treating me like his girlfriend. I did the most logical thing, of course; I stopped responding. The last thing I needed was for him to become so dependent on me he was incapable of functioning on his own. Been there, done that.

Things came to a head one night in a local bar. A supernaturally boring two-hour lecture in Business Ethics had left me wiped out, and I stopped at the place, known for their lax ID policy, to have a drink. It was also Walker Dixon's favorite spot.

I was perched at the end of the bar drinking a Vodka Cran and chatting with the guy next to me when I heard my name from across the semi-crowded room. I swiveled the stool around to find Walker striding toward me, his expression unreadable.

"So is this how you've been spending your nights, lately?" He gestured toward the man seated beside me.

"It's really not any of your business how I spend my nights," I replied matter-of-factly. "We had some fun, but I'm over it. You should be, too."

"Are you fucking kidding me, Winter?" he shouted. I stared icily at him for a few moments, watching the boyish mischief bleed from his eyes before finally turning my seat back around to face the bar. The sound of his boots was heavy on the wood floor as he stormed off a few seconds later.

I watched him from the corner of my eye the rest of the night. I'm sure he stayed just to prove to me I hadn't gotten the better of him. He slammed drink after drink and hit on girl after girl, making out with several over the course of the evening. He even managed to get into a fight with one of the girls' boyfriends. Fucking and fighting. He was perfect. I smiled to myself when he was practically carried out by one of the stupid twits, content that he was now completely heartless as I was.

⌒ ⁓⊱╬⊰⁓ ⌒

The Contender

If I believed in the Devil I would swear fundraising parties were his idea. Rich people paying a fortune to get dressed up in designer clothes and eat gourmet food all in the name of those less fortunate. Talk about irony. If I believed in God I can't imagine he would be pleased with that particular form of charity. Not that I believed in real charity anyway. Experience had taught me that people do what is good for them. And that's exactly what I intended to do. Forced to attend the gala by my aunt and uncle, I decided I could either sulk around the entire night, or I could make the most of the evening.

The event raised over a million dollars for some mentoring program sponsored by the university but was a monumental waste of my time. I had been wandering the grand room aimlessly listening to catty gossip about Botox and liposuction when I noticed a guy talking with my aunt and uncle a few feet away. He was turned to the side so I only saw his profile, but he was clearly closer to my age than theirs. Suddenly the night didn't seem so dull.

My tail twitching, I made a beeline straight for the trio.

"Winter." My uncle placed his arm lightly around my shoulder. "There's someone I'd like for you to meet. This is Emmett Parish. Emmett, this is our niece, Winter."

The Emmett Parish. I had heard his name on campus in various circles. An athlete. A scholar. A do-gooder. All excellent qualities for my particular purposes. What all the chatter had failed to mention was that he was also drop-dead gorgeous.

His face was like a sculpture, chiseled and angular. The contrast of his almost-black hair and sky blue eyes, striking. I found myself staring at him when a short girl with plain features and dishwater hair walked up and looped her arm around his as if claiming ownership.

"It's nice to meet you, Winter," his eyes sparkled beneath a heavy fringe of dark lashes. He smiled in lieu of a handshake, seeming to realize his arm was entangled with his date's. "This is Callie."

Callie nodded at me with a syrupy smile and seemed to tighten her hold on Emmett's arm. *He is mine* was rolling off of her in Tsunami-sized waves. Part of me was tempted to flirt with him in front of her just to see how she would react. Instead, my uncle asked some sports related question, and I took that as my cue to politely excuse myself.

I desperately wanted to leave, but I thought there was a chance I might actually get to speak to Emmett. A little while later, he approached me at the drink table.

"Where's your girlfriend?" I asked without hesitation.

"Callie's not my girlfriend," he corrected, his southern drawl low and deep. "We've only gone out a couple times. And she's still talking with your aunt. I think they're exchanging recipes."

"Sounds riveting," I said sarcastically, swirling the ice around my glass of sweet tea hoping to dilute it. "Southern women and their hospitality."

"Not your thing, huh?" he probed. "Your uncle said you were a city girl."

I smirked at him as though he should have been able to tell by looking at me and wondered what else my uncle had told him.

"What about basketball?" he asked with a crooked smile. "You could always come to a game?"

"Not likely." I turned my nose up at the idea.

"Not a sports fan?" he asked with genuine surprise.

"Understatement."

"What are you a fan of? The inquiry hung in the air in a moment, pausing our rapid-fire conversation. Good question.

"Control," I answered honestly.

His eyes widened in surprise and his mouth slowly turned up at the corners. "Well, that was honest," he admitted with only the hint of a southern accent that could melt butter. "I think I'd like to hear more."

Before I had a chance to respond, Callie strode up to us and took her place back at Emmett's side, the jealousy evident on her face. Not that I cared. But, I could swear I saw a twinge of disappointment flicker in his eyes before Callie dragged him off to dance.

I smiled as he walked away, thinking that he could be quite a challenge. I wondered if he was worth the effort.

* * *

It was a cold February day in the campus parking lot when fate made the decision for me. After a horrific morning of listening to my English professor wax poetic about love during a lecture on Shakespeare's sonnets, I finally got out to my car only to discover a flat tire. When it rains…

I was fishing my phone from my purse to call my insurance company when a nearby voice caught my attention.

"Winter, right?" I instantly recognized the deep drawl.

I looked up to find Emmett Parish walking toward me.

"Good memory." I smirked.

"Flat tire?" he asked, peering around me to look at my car.

"Observant," I mocked a little. "Not just another pretty face?"

"Emmett," he offered as though I could forget. "We met at the fundraiser the other night."

"I remember," I replied. This seemed to please him, as a roguish grin spread across his face.

Despite my protests that I was perfectly capable of handling the situation, Emmett made quick work of changing my tire. He didn't even break a sweat. Then again it was cold outside. He smiled and chatted the whole time he worked, seeming all too happy he'd stumbled upon me in need of assistance. Something told me he enjoyed playing the white knight, and I'd temporarily been cast as a bit of a damsel in distress. Eager to abandon that role, I thanked him and prepared to get into my car.

It took him a few seconds to respond. "You're welcome. Actually can I buy you a cup of coffee?"

"You're the one who fixed my car." I smiled up at him. "Shouldn't I be buying you coffee."

He inclined his head with a bashful expression, and we headed for the campus Starbucks, which was quite a ways away. The conversation flowed and, except for the moments spent ordering, we talked the entire time. I learned that he was a point guard and captain of the basketball team, though I had no idea what either of those things entailed, and he was kind enough to not bore me with the details. A psychology major with a minor in education, he was excited about getting his Master's degree and becoming a school counselor. He laughed with genuine amusement as he told me how everyone thought he was crazy for passing up a chance to play in the NBA to work with snot-nosed kids.

"I'm good at basketball, and it's opened a lot of doors, but working with kids is my passion," he said with sincerity. The guy really was a do-gooder.

"Everyone has a calling," was my only reply. He looked over at me for a moment then, his expression curious. He then wanted to know all about Winter. I gave him all the standard answers, but he was content with none of them. He wanted to know more. Not just the who, what, when, and where. He was trying to learn the why's and how's. His questions were probing and personal. He didn't just want to know my favorite color or food, but what I loved about my life and the things I would change. Definitely not your typical getting-to-know-you material.

If I'm being honest, some of his questions were not easily answered, despite my best efforts. But what did I expect from a psych major? By the time we finished our coffee, I could tell he was interested, and we had exchanged numbers under the guise of friendship.

But you know how I feel about friends.

* * *

We hung out several times before anything really happened between us. Studying. Coffee breaks. Long lunches between classes. Finally, he asked me out on an actual date. Apparently he was trying to be gentlemanly, allowing a suitable amount of time to pass between calling it quits with Callie and starting things up with me. I doubted I would ever understand dating rituals.

We ended up having a picnic dinner at a romantic spot on campus to watch the sunset. It was well played if you're into romance. I, however, enjoyed what we did in his Jeep afterward much more. He did, too.

It took all of five minutes for every student, and likely the faculty too, to know that I was dating Emmett Parish. He was a traditional guy and wanted to be exclusive.

I didn't really do labels, but if calling me his girlfriend would get me what I wanted, I would allow it.

* * *

Apparently the end of college basketball season is insanity. Literally. It's called March Madness. This limited my time with Emmett. I knew I would have to work fast if I didn't want to be stuck in another long-term fiasco. It was time to revisit my arsenal.

Backhanded compliments were like wine, and I poured generously. The problem was Emmett's eternal optimism. His confidence allowed him to focus on the positive part of my comments and seemingly ignore the rest. But I wasn't out. Not by a long shot. I don't care how secure he is, any man can be humbled in the bedroom. Or so I thought. I quickly learned it's hard to humble someone when you're busy screaming their name.

And I wasn't the only one undermining my efforts. If Emmett Parish was ship, I was an anchor, but all of Texas was his buoy.

Isolation would cure that. Except that the guy had no shortage of friends. Between basketball, classes, and living with his best friend, it was not easy to get him alone. And the harder I tried to isolate him, the harder he worked to include me in his various circles. None of my usual tactics were working. I was starting to think maybe he was trying to fix me as much as I was trying to fix him. If so, there was only one surefire way to break Emmett Parish.

* * *

I wouldn't normally resort to such a primitive method, as it was beneath me, but I had no choice. Emmett was the worst kind of broken. The kind that thought he was whole. It was going to take drastic measures to shatter that illusion. Luckily, drastic was my specialty.

Emmett was constantly busy. Basketball practice. Classes. Conference finals out of town. But with all of that, he still tried to carve out time for his girlfriend. Ever the sentimentalist. At his request, I started hanging out at his place at night while he studied. His roommate and best friend, Jared, didn't seem to mind in the least. Jared was the bookish sort, and it was pretty clear he might never have spoken to a girl if not for Emmett.

It was simple enough to make Jared like me. He wasn't blind, after all. And with Emmett's schedule so crazy, it made perfect sense for me to show up at their place now and then thinking he was home when he wasn't. It was too easy, really. You see, Emmett was Jared's only real friend—maybe his only real contact with the outside world. It was only natural that we should commiserate Emmett's absence together. With alcohol.

On a night when I was sure Emmett would be home late from practice, I showed up at their place nice and early. Plenty of time to let the vodka do all the work for me. We downed shot after shot. Well, he did. I stopped after two. After that it was an accidental touch, and then more on purpose until we were both naked and writhing on the couch. I had timed it perfectly.

Emmett walked in the front door that night and got the show of a lifetime. His girlfriend and his best friend going at it like animals. And no one but himself to blame.

I wasn't sure if he was more upset about Jared or me, and I didn't care. The look on his face when he saw the two of us together made it worth stooping to that level. He was a mixture of shock, disbelief, betrayal, anger, and self-loathing, and it was a priceless thing—to witness the moment the flood of emotion gave way to the safety of numbness.

Emmett left, and I couldn't get away from Jared fast enough. He wasn't much to begin with, and I thought there was a chance I had broken him, as well. Two for the price of one.

* * *

Watching the recap of the first round of the tournament should have been horrible, for a girl who despises sports. But it wasn't. You didn't need to know anything about the game to understand that not getting the ball into the basket was a bad thing. Even the newscasters held Emmett responsible for the loss.

The Aggies' season was over. And so was life, as Emmett Parish knew it. Feeling completely alienated by his team, he shut everyone out. Basketball may not have been his life, but his life was tethered to it all the same. When that fell apart, everything else collapsed around it. What was left was a man without the one thing that had threatened all my plans for him. Hope. But that was gone now. He was cured of the infestation of emotions that had held him down; made him weak. Eyes that had once burned with love, hate, desire, and contempt were now black and empty. My biggest accomplishment yet. I had stripped him down to the man he could become.

And he was glorious.

⁓ ⁓৪;৪⁓ ⁓

The Master

I finish my story, but continue staring out the window a moment before turning to face the woman behind the desk.

"So you see, Dr. Parks." I pin her with a satisfied smile. "You were wrong about me."

"Was I?" A small smirk plays on her lips. "How so?"

"You said I could only ever be a copy," I explain. "But I'm the original. They're the copies."

"Bravo, Winter." She finally nods at me, acknowledging my victory. More than that, she is celebrating it right along with me. "You have far exceeded all my expectations." A Cheshire cat grin spreads wide across her face, and I see something in her eyes I never noticed before.

My smile slowly fades, surprise taking over my expression.

All these years I assumed the vacant stare was a clinical detachment. A defense mechanism to ensure that she didn't get emotionally involved with her patients. I realize now I was wrong.

Her steel-grey eyes are shrewd and cold as always, and she laughs. A dark, hollow sound. "I'm surprised you're just figuring this out," she says, more relaxed than I have ever seen her. "We're normally quick to recognize our own."

I think back to the hours I spent in this place with her and suddenly, it all makes sense. Her dislike of labels. Her calculated responses. Even now I can see that she was imparting wisdom to me as I was so determined to leave her office that day. Simple reverse psychology.

"You never believed any of those things you said to me." It was a statement rather than a question.

"No," she shakes her head slightly.

"I suppose I should thank you," I say, still a bit in shock.

"That's not necessary, Winter," she replies coolly. "I'm pleased that you have become the woman I knew you could be." Detached, even now.

I haven't proved her wrong at all. In her eyes, I have simply lived up to my potential.

21

"Hour's up," she announces after glancing at her gold wristwatch. I grab my purse from the chair, but I can't steal my eyes away from this woman who helped make me the person I am today, and I stare at her a moment longer before preparing to step out of that office yet again. For the last time.

Finally convincing my brain it is time to go, I swing open the office door. As I do, I am startled to find three people just a few feet away. A man, a woman, and a young girl. A family. After a cursory scan of the mother and father my eyes come to rest on their daughter. Though her hair is dark and short and her skin a light shade of mocha, the black, cold emptiness I find in her eyes is like staring into a mirror. Not a copy, like the ones I've created. But an original.

Pulling my gaze away from the girl, I look back at Dr. Emilia Parks with a hint of admiration.

"You have your ways, and I have mine," she says with a hint of pride in voice, her expression unreadable.

I hold the door open for the young family and then close it behind me. I am leaving with the knowledge that she will continue to groom those of us fortunate enough to be born without the bondage enslaving the rest of you. As for me, an army of weak, broken boys lies ahead. I will make them soldiers; trained to break the emotional chains of those around them.

They say it's better to have loved and lost than to have never loved at all. They are wrong. But it will have to do.

The End

I'm a reader of fantasy turned writer who enjoys great characters and fascinating plot twists. I like bad boys, fast cars, and chicks who aren't afraid to talk back. When I'm not writing, I can be found teaching Pilates, being mommy to two fabulous kiddos, and just generally being a crazy sarcastic insomniac mess!! To learn more, visit: https://www.facebook.com/shannonmortonwrites

CAGED

A retelling of Rapunzel
by L.P. Dover

Once upon a time there was a girl who fell in love with a dream. She wanted to be a singer, to show the world what she could do. That person was me. I loved the way it felt to hear my screaming fans in the crowd as I walked across stage. I thought it would be enough. I had everything I ever wanted; at least that was what I kept telling myself. Instead of controlling my dreams, they controlled me. Or better yet, my agent did.

"What the hell is wrong with you? You didn't have that bad of a time at the party, did you?" Kye asked, his voice sounding frustrated.

"I'm just sick of going to these parties. They're your friends, not mine. Why can't I have a life of my own?"

"Really, Casey? You're going to argue about this again?"

Sighing, I dropped my purse on the couch and turned around. He shut the door and stared at me, crossing his arms over his chest. Kye Bender had been my agent for two years. During that time, my career had skyrocketed, but at what cost? He was thirty-three years old and determined to get what he wanted; he always got the job done. If he hadn't discovered me singing at a bar back home in North Carolina, I'd still be there serving drinks.

"I know I sound ungrateful, but I've given up everything. I miss being around my family and friends. I miss …"

He scoffed. "*Him,* right?"

My breath caught and I closed my eyes. I was glad he didn't say the name. It hurt too much to even think about the man I thought was my happily ever after.

Opening my eyes, I held back the tears. "I loved him, Kye. I thought he'd be able to handle all of this."

"Obviously, he couldn't or he'd still be here." He pulled me into his arms, and even though it felt good to be held, I couldn't find the comfort I needed. "You deserve someone who isn't threatened by your success. That cocksucker left you because he's a pussy." Huffing, I tried to jerk away, but he held me tight. "I'm sorry, I shouldn't have said that. I know it hurts you to talk about him. I just want you to

1

know I can be the man you need. It's no secret that I want you. I always have."

His grip loosened and I stepped back. He was a good looking man, always dressed to perfection with perfectly coifed light brown hair and gray eyes. There were always women trying to come on to him at the parties, but he never strayed from my side. Maybe it *was* time to move on, but why was it so hard to convince my heart?

"Don't you think it's a bad idea to mix business with pleasure? You're my agent, Kye."

His lips pulled back into a smile. "I don't see anything wrong with it." He snaked his arms around my waist, his body incredibly close to mine. Ever so slowly, he moved his lips closer, his gaze never wavering from mine. "Just think how powerful we could be together. Tell me you want this just as much as I do," he murmured.

"I don't know what I want," I replied, breaths coming out faster. His lips were about to touch mine and I didn't know if I should stop it from happening or give in. He didn't allow me much time before he closed the distance and I was sucked in. My body betrayed me and I opened myself up to him, returning the kiss.

Groaning, he pushed me toward the couch, his arousal pressing into my leg. "I've wanted this for so long," he growled low in his throat.

I broke away from his kiss, placing my hands on his chest. He stared down at me, his eyes heated and raw. "I don't think it's a good idea to jump right into the sex, especially since you're leaving in an hour to go to New York."

He huffed and then nodded. "You're right, it's not. But dammit to hell, I want to feel you wrapped around me."

Placing my hands on his chest, I gently pushed him back. "Just give me a little more time. When you get back next week we can talk about taking that next step. I don't want to move too fast."

"And we won't. We have plenty of time." Lifting my chin, he kissed me again. "Just know that once you agree to be mine, I'm not letting go. Are you prepared for that?"

Biting my lip, I smiled up at him. "I might be."

His eyes darkened. "So does that mean you'll be mine?"

My heart screamed at me to say no, but I wanted to feel loved again; I needed it. I had the love of my fans, but I wanted more. Kye was good to me and he was hot as hell, but he wasn't what I truly desired. The one man I wanted was someone who didn't want me.

"Yes," I breathed, wrapping my arms around his neck. "When you come back, I'll be all yours."

Scooping me in his arms, he held me tight. Hopefully I could learn to love him.

"Did you really agree to be his girlfriend?" Skyler asked, wide-eyed.

On the walk over to our favorite café, I told her everything that happened between me and Kye. We grabbed our coffees and sat down at one of the tables. She was my personal assistant but I considered her more of a best friend than anything. Her quirky style and friendly demeanor was what I fell in love with when I hired her. Not to mention she had about six different colors in her hair, which I always wanted to do to mine. However, being a country music star, I had to keep up appearances.

Skyler waved her hands in front of my face and almost knocked the hat off my head. I didn't realize I had zoned out. "Casey, you okay?"

Snapping back into reality, I nodded and fixed my hat. It was hard to avoid the press with Skyler around since everyone recognized her by her hair, but I tried my best. There was always someone around taking my picture. "Yeah, I'm fine. Sorry about that. What were you saying?"

She rolled her eyes. "I asked you if you really agreed to be Kye's girlfriend."

I shrugged. "He asked if I would be his and I said yes. I assume that's what it means."

She chuckled. "I'd say so. That man has been after you from the very beginning. Talk about sex on a stick if you ask me."

Nodding, I took a sip of my coffee. "That he is."

Narrowing her gaze, she tilted her head to the side. "Why do I not see you glowing? I've been dying to hook you up with someone and now you're taken. I thought you'd be happy."

"I am happy. It's all so new to me."

She studied me. "You're lying. I've been by your side every day for two years. What gives, Case?"

I finished my coffee and looked down at my phone. "Nothing, I promise. Now let's go shopping. I need a new outfit for Saturday's concert." Getting to my feet, I threw away my cup and waited on her to join me by the door.

Brows furrowed, she stopped in front of me. "Why are you acting weird? Is there something you're not telling me?"

Chuckling, I pushed her out the door. "I told you I'm fine. Now let's get out of here." We spent the rest of the day shopping and it was just what I needed to get my mind off of things. Kye texted me throughout the day which ended up helping me feel better. He was always there for me when I needed him.

"Do you want to go out to dinner?" Skyler asked.

We got in her car and I took off my hat. "Not tonight. I think I just want to get home and have a glass of wine. Raincheck?"

"Of course. I might do the same. What time do you have to be at the studio tomorrow?"

"Nine o'clock. You coming?" I asked.

She pulled to the front of my building and helped fetch my bags out of the trunk. "I'll be there, chickadee. Do you want me to bring you a blueberry bagel?"

My mouth watered just thinking about it. "That would be awesome. Thank you."

Biting her lip, she handed me my last bag. "Do you need help getting those into your apartment?"

I snorted and waved her off. "I got this, trust me. Go home and I'll see you tomorrow."

"Okay," she responded unsurely. I tried not to stumble going up the steps, and thankfully, I made it up without falling over my bags. I glanced back at her and she waved before getting in her car. Once she was out of sight, I pushed my way through the door and went straight to the elevator. Unfortunately, I didn't get very far before one of the bags broke, dropping everything to the floor.

"Fuck me," I hissed softly. Next time I knew not to be superwoman and let Sky help. The elevator door dinged and I heard footsteps approaching across the marble floor.

"Here, let me help you," a voice called out from behind.

Eyes wide, I froze and held my breath. Did I just imagine that voice or did I actually hear it? There was no way in hell I could ever forget that sound. When he dropped down beside me and I looked up at him, my whole world shattered. It was him ... Aiden, the guy who broke my heart.

For a split second, I was happy to see him, but then the past came back to haunt me. He looked the same as he did two years ago with his dark brown hair and crystal blue eyes. I used to think I could see his soul through his eyes. He was my first love and his betrayal went deep.

"What are you doing here?" I snapped.

Smile fading, he helped me with my bags and stood. "I thought I'd see you around town some time. I heard you were living here."

I grabbed my bags from him. "You didn't answer my question. What are you doing at my apartment?"

Blowing out a sigh, he put his hands in his jeans pocket. "You're not the only one who lives in these apartments, buttercup."

"Don't call me that." I started to stalk off and then stopped cold. When I turned around, he smiled. "You have got to be kidding me. You live here, too, don't you?"

He nodded. "I moved in last week. I've been traded to San Francisco."

Aiden Prince was one of the best football players when we were in high school and college. I knew he was playing for the Carolina Cougars, but I had no clue he'd been traded. I'd kept up with his accomplishments over the years, even though I wanted to kick myself in the ass for doing so.

Holding my head up, I stormed over to the elevator and pressed the button. "Good for you. I guess all your dreams finally came true."

The elevator door opened and I rushed in, only for him to join me. "Most of them, except one," he murmured. I didn't want to look at him because I knew I would break down. My heart still yearned for him and I hated myself for it. "What floor are you on?" he asked.

Closing my eyes, I took a deep breath. "Five."

He tried to take some of my bags, but I held firm and didn't budge. When the doors opened, he ushered me to walk out but I could feel him close behind. "You don't have to help me," I grumbled. "I can manage by myself."

"I know you can, Casey. All I want is to talk to you. You owe me that."

I glared at him over my shoulder. "I don't owe you shit."

"That's right, you don't. I deserve a whole hell of a lot more."

Not having a choice, I set a couple of my bags down so I could fetch my keys and open the door. Unfortunately, I didn't get to them fast enough. Grabbing my bags, Aiden dashed into my apartment.

"What the hell are you doing? I'm sure the NFL won't like it when I charge you for breaking and entering."

He set my bags down, returning my glare. "Honestly, I don't give a fuck at this moment." He stared me down and all I could do was stand there. There was so much I wanted to say, but couldn't. Huffing, he threw his hands in the air. "Why are you being this way? I didn't do a goddamned thing to you."

"What?" I gasped. "You can't be serious. You're the one who left me, remember?" Eyes wide, he froze, but then my phone rang; it was Kye. I rushed to the door and opened it wide. "I want you out, now."

He stood firm. "Not until we talk about what happened. I didn't leave you, Casey."

My eyes burned, the anger building in my chest. The last thing I needed was for him to rip my heart out again. He tried to reach for me, but I backed hard into the wall. "*Get out*," I yelled. My body shook and I couldn't hold the tears back. They poured down my cheeks and I gave in to the pain.

"Casey, please," he begged. My phone stopped ringing but then it started up again. Kye was persistent. Aiden sighed and started for the door. "All right, I'll give you your space, but this isn't the end." He stormed past me, disappearing down the hall. What the hell was I going to do?

Phone still ringing, I wiped away my tears, sucking the rest back. "Hey," I said, answering the phone.

"Hey, babe. You okay? You sound like you're getting sick."

I wished that was the problem. "I think it's just allergies," I lied.

"Spring time is the worst. Why didn't you pick up the phone?"

By the sound in his voice, it was as if he knew something was wrong. "I couldn't get to it in time. Skyler and I went shopping and I had my hands full. You caught me as I was trying to get in the door."

"Ah, I see. Are you ready to record tomorrow?"

Sighing, I sat down on the couch. "I think so. Hopefully these allergies won't be bothering me tomorrow."

"Take some meds and get some sleep. You should be fine. You need to get your rest before the concert this weekend."

"Will you be in town for it?"

"I don't know, but I'm hoping to be. If not, I'll see you Sunday."

I closed my eyes. "Sounds good. Right now I think I'm going to go to bed. I'll talk to you tomorrow."

We hung up and I shut my phone off. There was going to be no sleep for me.

Luckily, I sang better than I looked. My puffy eyes made it hard to see but at least I still had my voice. Everyone at the studio believed my story about being allergic to the dye in my new clothes. Maybe I should've pursued acting after high school. I did get the lead in two of my high school plays, one being *Juliet* and the other *Rapunzel.* Those were the good days.

"This album will be your best yet," my producer praised. His name was Marcus Cross, one of the best producers in all of California. He had bleached blond hair and golden tanned skin from being out in the sun surfing every day of his life. Smiling wide, he waved me out of the booth and I joined him and Skyler.

He patted me on the shoulder. "Go drink a glass of wine or twelve. You look like you need it."

"Gee, thanks," I grumbled.

He chuckled. "You're welcome. At least the rest of the week you can relax before the big concert."

Skyler handed me my bag and we started for the door. "True. I'll see you later, Marc."

When we got outside, I knew Skyler was going to say something. "Allergic to your new clothes? You expect me to believe that shit?" She followed me to my car and stood in my way before I could open my door.

Huffing, I stepped back. "No, because I know you're smarter than that."

"Then what is it?" she asked, crossing her arms over her chest. By the stubborn look in her eyes, I knew she wasn't going to back down.

I ran my hands through my hair. "Fine, I'll tell you. It'll save you from ragging my ass all afternoon." I took a deep breath and blew it out. "I ran into Aiden last night."

She gasped and froze with her mouth wide open. "Holy freaking shit balls. Are you serious?"

"Very serious, I'm afraid. It didn't go very well. I spent the entire night crying my eyes out. I didn't think he'd get to me like that."

She rolled her eyes. "How could he not? He's the love of your life, right?"

"Was," I stated.

"Either way, I know it couldn't have been easy. Weren't you two together all throughout high school?"

"And then some," I added. "In college, I always knew he'd make it to the NFL. It wouldn't have worked out anyway."

"Why not? What did he say?"

I shrugged. "I didn't give him much time to say anything. Everything happened so fast. I wasn't ready to talk to him."

Her voice softened. "Will you ever be?"

"I'm not sure. All I know is that he's living in my apartment building and there's no way I can avoid him forever. I just don't want him to know how bad he hurt me."

Sighing, she pulled me in for a hug. "Then don't. You're strong. I know you can handle this."

I squeezed her tight and let go. "I sure hope you're right. Trust me, my eyes can't handle anymore crying."

"Want to get a couple of drinks before you go home?" she asked, nudging me with her arm.

I wanted to, but I felt and looked like complete dog shit. "Not tonight, Sky. I really just want to curl up in bed and eat the hell out of some Ben & Jerry's."

Her eyes brightened. "I might just do the same." We walked over to our cars—which were beside each other—and she glanced over at me. "I'll call you tomorrow morning to make sure you're okay."

I smiled at her. "Sounds good. The only thing I have to do this week before the concert is appear at the morning show. Other than that, I'm going to take it easy."

"You need it, girl. Take a break."

She waved at me and got in her car. I didn't just need a break, I needed a long vacation. My heart pounded in my chest the whole way home. The last thing I wanted was for Aiden to see me looking the way I did. Luckily, when I pulled up to my building, I didn't see a car that resembled anything he would drive. He loved his trucks. I parked quickly and rushed inside, taking the stairs instead of the elevator. Once safe behind my closed door, I breathed a sigh of relief, only it didn't bring me comfort. My chest still ached.

Turning on the radio, I grabbed a pint of cookie dough ice cream out of the freezer and opened the door to my balcony. The night was windy and a tad chilly, but it was perfect. Back home in Charlotte, North Carolina, it would be humid and hot, even if it was late May. I didn't miss that at all, but I did miss my family.

My ice cream was almost halfway gone when a haunting sound caught my ears. It was one of the first songs I ever wrote. The only way I could get over Aiden was to sing my way through the pain and that was just what I did; the song was about him. Setting my ice cream down, I sang along with the song, reminiscing on the countless nights I stayed awake to write it. It was the first song of mine that earned a Country Music Award and a Grammy for Song of the Year. I never would've thought that a song clearly written out of heartache would be such a hit.

Closing my eyes, I sang the last few words of the song, my voice shaking. No matter how many times I sang it, I could never hide the pain.

"Every time I heard this song, it took all I had not to come out here and find you," a voice spoke out from behind.

Heart racing, I flew out of my seat, clutching my chest. "What the hell? How did you get in?"

Aiden stood there, leaning against the edge of the balcony. He glanced over the rail and then smiled at me. "I heard you singing so I climbed up. My apartment is the one below yours. I knew you wouldn't let me in if I came to your door."

"Are you insane?" I snapped. "What if you fell and got hurt? Your football career would be over in a heartbeat." I peered over the balcony and cringed. We weren't that high up, but falling three stories would definitely hurt.

"It would all be worth it to see you again."

I jerked my head in his direction. "Stop saying stuff like that."

He shrugged, his gaze solemn. "It's true. I've waited a long time to see you again. When I got the offer to trade to San Francisco I knew it was a sign. It gave me the chance to find you."

I crossed my arms over my chest. "Maybe you should've cared about that two years ago."

His smile faded. "I did. You were the one who gave up on us. I tried to make things work, but I wasn't good enough, was I?"

"Good enough? What the hell are you talking about? You're not making any sense."

9

He took a step forward, cornering me. "All I want is answers. You can call the cops and ban me just like you did before, but I have to know. What did I do wrong?"

The whole world felt like it was crashing in all around me. I was in a nightmare I couldn't get out of. I couldn't wrap my head around anything he was saying. He stared at me waiting for his answers, but I was lost.

I held up my hands, my body trembling. "Aiden, I have no clue what you're talking about. I never banned you from anywhere."

He scoffed. "I find that hard to believe considering you had me arrested. Luckily, my agent had my record wiped clean."

"When? How?"

Furrowing his brows, he studied me. I could feel the panic rising. "You really don't know, do you?"

I shook my head. "All I remember is the letter you sent me saying you didn't think we were going to work, that I would only drag you down. You said you had to concentrate on your career. It was the worst day of my life."

He stumbled back as if I'd punched him. "What the fuck? I never sent you a letter, Casey. I've always wanted to be with you."

I gazed up at him, my pulse racing. "So it wasn't true?"

Closing the distance, he took my face in his hands. "Hell no, none of it was true. I would never say anything like that. I wanted to marry you."

"That's what made it so hard," I cried. Holding me in his arms, I melted. "If you didn't write the letter, who did?"

He sighed. "Probably the same person who told me to stay away from you."

I jerked back. "Who?"

⁂

For two hours, Aiden and I held each other out on the balcony. I didn't want to let him go, even when I walked inside to fetch the letter he supposedly wrote to me. When he told me what happened to him, I couldn't believe it. "Why would my father do that?"

"I don't know. The day you left for California, I was all ready planning to come with you. I was going to surprise you, but before I could leave, your father showed up at my door. He said you needed space to be on your own, to build your career. And if I loved you I'd let you go. Basically, it was the same as this fucking letter," he growled, crinkling it in his firm grip. "After that, I came to California to find you. You never gave me the address to your other apartment and I knew your parents wouldn't tell me so I searched on my own. Your phone number didn't work when I tried to call."

"That's because I lost it in the move. Then after I got your letter, I broke down. When I got a new phone, I had the number changed. All I wanted was a fresh start."

He turned me to face him and my stomach fluttered like it always did when he'd look at me. I missed those feelings. His fingers brushed my cheek. "When I finally found out where you were, I was determined to see you. As soon as I showed up at your old apartment, I was apprehended by security. I was told I wasn't allowed in the building per your request. They had my name, description … everything."

Anger boiled in my veins. "And I had no clue. I can't believe my own family did this to me. They knew how much you meant to me."

"When's the last time you talked to your parents?" he asked, jaw tense.

"About a week ago, I think. So much has been going on I haven't kept track. They'll be hearing from me tomorrow though." If it wasn't past midnight back at home I'd call and wake them up.

He nodded. "What do you think they'll say?"

I shrugged. "I don't know. I just want them to understand how bad they hurt me. To go behind my back like that is unforgiveable. The past two years have been agony."

"No shit. Watching you on TV was the only way I could see you."

Cupping his cheek, I brushed my thumb across his stubble. "It was the only way I could see you, too. My God, I've missed you."

He moved closer, clasping a hand behind my neck. His breath was warm across my lips and I ached to feel them against mine. Biting his lip, he smiled, closing the distance. "Whatever happens, I'm not letting you go. We've wasted too much time."

Our lips connected and the spark I'd always felt between us fired through every fiber of my being. I opened myself up to him and let him claim me, relishing in the feel of his body against mine. We kissed for what only felt like minutes, but ended up being hours. "What happens now?" I asked, whispering the words.

The sun started to come up and he chuckled. "I'm going to go back downstairs and get some sleep. I have to be at practice in a couple of hours. When I get back, I want to continue what we started. We have a lot to make up for."

I kissed him again. "That we do. I'll see you soon. But this time, you're taking the door."

* * *

For the six hours I slept, it was the best rest I'd had in the past two years. I counted down the time until I'd see Aiden again. Unfortunately, I wasn't looking forward to calling my parents. Their betrayal hurt worse than anything. They were three hours behind since they were in North Carolina so I waited for them to get home. My heart thundered in my chest as I picked up my phone and dialed.

My mother picked up, her voice sounding excited when she answered, "Hey, honey."

"Hey," I replied, swallowing hard. It was so difficult to be angry when I could hear how much she loved me in her voice.

"Casey, are you okay? You don't sound right."

I sighed. "I have a lot on my mind. But there's something I want to talk to you and Dad about."

"What is it, sweetheart?"

My hands clenched around the phone. "Why did Dad tell Aiden to let me go?"

"Let you go? What are you talking about?"

I huffed. "Two years ago when I moved to California. Aiden was going to come with me, but instead, I got a letter with him dumping me. His story, however, is a little different. He says Dad told him to stay away from me. Care to tell me what's going on?"

"Oh, honey, there's no way your father could've said that to him. He loves Aiden just as much as I do."

"Aiden wouldn't lie to me, Momma," I snapped. Blowing out an angry breath, I closed my eyes and slowly opened them back up. "Where's Dad? I want to talk to him."

She sighed and I could hear the confusion in her voice. "He just pulled into the garage. I'll get him." I could hear my father come through the door and greet her, but then everything sounded muffled as my mom put her hand over the phone. She raised her voice, but I couldn't understand what she said. Then my father picked up the phone.

"I see you finally ran into Aiden. I knew he'd find you as soon as he moved there."

"And imagine my surprise when he told me the truth," I growled. Furious, I held the phone away from my ear and inhaled deeply.

He blew out a breath. "Casey, I know you're angry with me, but I need you to listen. I—"

"You're right, I am angry," I cut in. "Do you have any idea the pain you caused for both me *and* Aiden? How could you interfere like that? You knew we wanted to get married."

"I know," he murmured sadly. "But it was too soon for that. You needed time to grow, to become the star you are now. Everyone in the world knows you, Casey."

"That might be true, but I would've given it all up just to be happy. Aiden makes me happy, Dad. And I'm not going to let you or anyone else stand in our way. I would've been more successful with him by my side."

"We'll never know. But at least you have him now. I'm sorry I asked him to stay away. Kye pulled me aside and said it was the best thing to do."

"What?" I shrieked. "What does Kye have to do with this?" Surely I heard him wrong?

My father cleared his throat. "Kye was the one who thought I should talk to Aiden. He said he's had several clients fail in this business because they were being held back, mainly by their significant others. He didn't want to see that happen to you because he knew you had talent. Honestly, I didn't think it worked because he was adamant on finding you."

I scoffed. "And then he was apprehended by the police when he did. Was that your doing or Kye's?"

"Casey, I would never do that," he scolded. "I didn't realize it had gone that far."

Unable to believe what I'd heard, I sat down on the couch. Everything I'd known for the past two years was a lie. My father thought he was doing the right thing, but it was Kye who was really the deceiver. How could I have been so blind?

"So it was Kye," I stated.

"He was only looking out for you, sweetheart. The guy's done wonders for your career. Although, if he was responsible for getting Aiden arrested, I don't approve of that."

"You think?" I scoffed.

"What are you going to do?"

Closing my eyes, I leaned my head against the couch. "I don't know. It's gotten a little complicated."

"Why is that? You're not seeing him, are you?"

I groaned, regretting ever making that decision. All I had to do was wait a little bit longer. Then I wouldn't be in the mess I was in. "We kind of made it official before he left town," I replied.

"Oh hell, Casey. Does Aiden know?"

"No, but I'm going to tell him. There's no way in hell I can keep Kye as an agent now. Not after everything he did. When he comes back from New York, it's him I'm letting go."

"Are you sure that's wise? He works hard for you."

I couldn't argue with that, but I couldn't have him interfering with my life the way he did. "He does," I agreed, "but I can always get another agent. One that won't lie to me to get what they want."

"Good luck with that. He doesn't take me as the kind of man to back down."

He wasn't, but there was no way in hell I'd want him after what he did. It was over.

* * *

By the end of the afternoon, Kye had called me five times and each time I ignored him. I wasn't about to fire him through the phone. Given how angry I was that was just what I would've done if I'd heard his voice.

"Rapunzel, Rapunzel, let down your hair," a voice called out below.

Jumping to my feet, I leaned over the balcony and chuckled. Aiden smiled up at me, his hair still wet from football practice and dressed in a pair of black gym shorts and blue tank top.

"Ah, the memories," I laughed. "You did make a handsome prince, even if you did have to wear tights. How long did it take the football team to stop picking on you?"

He snorted. "Too fucking long. I wasn't about to let anyone other than me kiss you. A jab at my ego was a small price to pay."

I smiled at him. "So it was worth it?"

"You're damn right it was. So … what are you doing tonight? Want to grab dinner?"

My smile faded. "Why don't we cook something here? If we're seen in public, it'll attract too much attention."

"What's wrong with that?" he asked, narrowing his gaze.

The last thing I wanted was for Kye to see me and Aiden in the tabloids. "I'll explain everything, I promise. My place or yours?"

He pointed to his floor. "Mine. Go ahead and come down."

Pulse racing, I turned and started toward the door, nervous as hell. He deserved to learn the truth, but I didn't want to tell him about me and Kye. It wasn't like we'd really done anything, but the fact still remained … I almost slept with the enemy. When I got down to his floor, the door to his apartment was open. He held out a glass of wine.

"It's about time. I thought you got lost there for a moment." Taking the glass, I gulped it down and his eyes went wide. "Whoa, killer. Calm down. Rough day?"

"You could say that," I replied, setting the glass down.

He pulled me into his arms and kissed me. "Did that help?"

I giggled. "A little. Unfortunately, there's something I need to tell you."

His body tensed. "Go on."

Taking his hand, I guided him to the brown, leather couch and sat down. I felt at home in his apartment. It smelled just like him. Everything was the way I imagined it would be, all neutral yet masculine. "I talked to my dad today," I murmured.

His blue eyes softened. "How did that go? I know it couldn't have been easy."

"It wasn't, but he told me the truth. He admitted to confronting you about letting me go."

He blew out a sigh. "I half expected him to lie. I'm glad he was honest with you though."

I nodded. "He was, but that's not all. He admitted to doing that, but not about the police or the letter that was sent to me. He had no idea any of that happened."

"If he didn't do it, who did?" he asked, furrowing his brows. By the look in my eyes, I didn't have to say it. Jaw tensing, he turned and ran a hand roughly through his hair. "That worthless son of a bitch. It was Bender, wasn't it? I knew that fucker wanted to get in your pants. It all makes sense. He got me out of the way and worked his magic on you. Let me guess, he was the one who recommended you change your number?"

Sighing, I closed my eyes. It all made me sick to my stomach. "Yes."

"Goddammit," he shouted, jumping to his feet. "Where is he? That fucker's going to pay for this."

I gasped and held a hand over my chest. "He's in New York on business. He won't be back until the weekend."

"Please tell me you're going to find another agent. I won't be able to be with you without wanting to kill him. I don't want him breathing around you."

He was so enraged, his hands shook. Slowly, I wrapped my arms around his waist and laid my head down on his chest. His heart thundered in my ear. "You don't have to worry about that. As soon as he's back in town, I'm firing him. I didn't want to do it over the phone."

"Why not? You could be over and done with that bastard."

I blew out a sigh. "Not exactly."

Grabbing my arms, he pulled me away. "What are you not telling me?" I stared up at him, knowing the bomb was about to blow. "Spit it out, Casey."

"Fine, but just so you know it's not going to be as bad as it sounds."

His eyes went wide. "Please tell me you didn't fuck him," he spat.

"No," I shrieked. "I told you it's not that bad. Unfortunately, the day he left, I agreed to be exclusive. I didn't know you were going to pop back up into my life that same day."

Growling in disgust, he let me go and ran his hands through his hair. "What the hell, Casey?"

I grabbed his arm. "As much as it sucks, there's nothing we can do about it. We can't change what happened. I didn't want to move on but I felt like I had no choice. Kye will pay for what he did but I want to do it in person. He deserves to feel my wrath."

His body tensed. "And I want to be there when you do. I'm not leaving you alone with him."

Smiling, I took his hand and placed it on my cheek. "Always the protector. It's one of the things I loved about you."

"Loved? As in past tense?" he asked, running his other hand through my hair.

I leaned into his touch. "You know I still love you. I always have."

He moved closer, his lips almost touching mine. "Show me."

Heart racing out of control, I closed the distance and jumped in his arms. I didn't have to think twice. I wanted him, all of him. It'd been too long. Carrying me in his arms, he kissed me the entire way to his room.

"Are you sure this is what you want?" he murmured in my ear. The stubble on his chin made me shiver as he kissed his way down my neck.

"Yes," I breathed.

He lifted my shirt and dropped my shorts to the floor before undressing himself. His arousal pulsated in my hands when I massaged his thick length. Before I knew it, I was on the bed, his body covering mine. He kissed his way up my stomach to my breasts, suckling each one. My body shivered and I moaned as he pushed the tip of his cock into my opening.

"Please, Aiden. I can't wait any longer," I pleaded.

Chuckling darkly, he gently pushed the rest of the way in, keeping his raw gaze on mine the entire time. Our bodies moved together perfectly, his thrusts deep and hard. My breaths came out in rapid pants as my orgasm slowly started to build. Everything inside of me tightened and I moaned. I closed my eyes, but he growled low.

"Keep your eyes open, buttercup. I want you to look at me when you come."

Keeping my gaze on his, he drove me over the edge, my release making me scream in ecstasy. His grip tightened on my hips as he came inside of me, grunting with his final thrusts. Still connected, he pressed his forehead to mine and kissed me.

"I've missed you," he murmured.

My vision started to blur. "I've missed you, too. But I look forward to making up for lost time."

He moved his hips against mine. "That's what I plan to do now. I hope you got plenty of sleep last night. Because you sure as hell aren't getting any tonight."

Holding him tight, I squeezed my legs around his waist. "I'm good with that. Show me what you got."

"Gladly."

***

"Are you ready for your concert tomorrow?" Aiden asked.

Smiling, I took a sip of my wine and gazed up at the night sky. Three days had passed and the only time we'd been separated was when he had to go to practice. Other than that, I couldn't get enough of him.

"I'm always ready. You know singing has always been important to me."

His hand closed over mine, drawing my attention. "I know, buttercup. You've come so far. I just wish I could've been here to see you through it."

"Me too. But you're here now, that's all that matters." We finished our drinks, and then my stomach rumbled. "I do believe we need to get something to eat. What do you want?"

He pursed his lips. "We could always walk across the street to the café. I think it's time we stop hiding."

I looked down at my clothes and sighed. "All right, let's do it. However, I do need to change first. Let me run upstairs and I'll be right back." I didn't want to go out to eat in pajama bottoms and a tank top.

His gaze raked down my body. "You look great to me, but do what you want. I'll be here waiting for you." I kissed him quickly on the lips, and rushed out of his apartment and up the stairs to my floor. Everything was dark when I opened the door, and before I could turn on the lights, a set of arms grabbed me from behind.

I tried to scream, but a hand slammed over my mouth. "Ignoring my calls, Casey?"

Furious, I fought against his hold, and he let me go. I turned around and glared at him. "Maybe it's because I didn't want to talk to you. Now that you're here, I don't see the point in waiting any longer. You're fired."

He scoffed. "You can't fire me. You'd be nothing if it wasn't for me."

"You're wrong," I spat. "I'll be perfectly fine on my own."

"But you're not going to be on your own, are you? I know about loverboy downstairs. Did you tell him about us?"

"There is no us. My father told me what you did. It was you who tore me and Aiden apart. For that you can go fuck yourself." I stormed past him to the door, but he grabbed my arm, yanking me back toward him.

"You're mine, Casey." His grip was tight, his fingers digging into my arm.

"Let me go," I commanded. When he didn't, I tried to jerk away, but he pushed me to the floor. The breath whooshed out of my lungs, but as soon as I got in a good breath, I opened my mouth and screamed.

He slammed my head against the floor and everything grew fuzzy. It was like my muscles stopped working and all I could do was lay there. Aiden pounded on the door, yelling my name, but there was nothing I could do. No sound came out of my mouth. I thought he'd barrel through the door, but that didn't happen. Where did he go? I got my answer when I saw his arm hook over the railing of my balcony.

"No," I cried. Standing there waiting on him was Kye. Slowly, I got to my feet, but I was too late. Aiden glanced at me first, but then Kye came out of the corner and pushed him off the balcony, the sound of his body hitting the ground below making me scream.

Kye laughed and all I could see was red. "You son of a bitch," I shouted, racing toward him. I was no match for him. He grabbed me around the neck and hurled me across the room. Blood ran down my cheek from the gash on my head. I couldn't even feel the pain. All I wanted was to get to Aiden.

"You think you're so goddamn special," he hissed, grabbing something off the counter. I couldn't see what it was. His hands gripped my hair and he yanked, pulling my head back. His dark eyes stared back at me, the vein in his forehead bulging. "Let's see how you like this, you ungrateful cunt." My hair felt like it was being ripped out of my head, but it was Kye sawing it all off with the knife in his hands. Everything flashed before me and it didn't take long to figure out that he wasn't going to let me out alive. I didn't care what happened to me as long as Aiden was okay. "I did everything for you, but it was never good enough. At least now I know that no one else can have you."

As soon as he sawed the last of my hair off, I rolled across the floor out of his reach. Holding the knife in his hands, he didn't even look human anymore. He didn't look like the Kye I'd known for the past two years.

"What happened to you?" I cried.

He scoffed. "I'm sick of watching everyone get what they want. When I saw that you and that fuckhead were back together, I lost it. You're supposed to be mine."

I circled around the couch, the remnants of my long blonde hair on the floor. "How did you know?"

A devilish gleam sparkled in his eyes. "I have my ways. Why do you think I came back early? My contact was none too pleased to tell me you were fucking around behind my back."

"There is something seriously wrong with you."

The door was so close all I had to do was run to it and get out. However, the knife in Kye's hand had me terrified. It was a chance I had to take. Taking off toward the door, I grabbed the handle and opened it wide, screaming as loud as I could. Kye grabbed me around the waist and slammed the door. The knife skittered across the floor, but he had me bound underneath him. His hands wrapped around my neck, cutting off all breath. I tried to pry him loose, but he wouldn't budge.

We wrestled across the floor until everything started to turn black. The feel of cold steel against my fingers was my only salvation. My vision started to blur, but I gripped the knife and swung it down hard and fast, cringing when I felt it plunge into Kye's body. He roared and his weight lifted off my body, but it wasn't because of me. The floor thundered with footsteps and then I was hoisted into someone's arms. It wasn't Aiden. Kye fought with the police even though he had a knife stuck in the back of his shoulder. I breathed a sigh of relief when they handcuffed him and took him away.

"You're going to be okay, Miss Morgan. We'll get you taken care of," the cop murmured.

"Aiden," I whispered hoarsely. "Where is he?"

His face came into focus, but he wore a grim expression. "He's being loaded up in the ambulance now. I don't know the severity of his condition."

Tears streamed down my cheeks. "But he'll be all right, won't he?"

He sighed. "I don't know. I'm sure you'll know something soon. Right now we need to get *you* to the hospital."

He carried me down the stairs and as soon as we got outside, cameras flashed all around. *Please, God, let Aiden be okay.*

* * *

"I'm okay, I promise," I said to Dr. McCarthy who kept writing notes in my chart. He was a middle-aged man with salt and peppered hair and too many lines on his face from stress. They had me in a room, surrounded by nurses who checked my vitals every ten seconds. I grabbed one of them and she gasped; her name was Angel by the badge on her scrubs. "Angel, please. I need to know how Aiden Preston is doing. My blood pressure won't get any better until I know what the hell's going on."

She glanced at the doctor who lifted his gaze from my file. He walked over and nodded at her to step back. "I got this, Miss Richards. Thank you." The rest of the nurses walked out, leaving just me and him. From the look on his face, I could tell it would be bad.

"Just tell me, Doctor. I need to know how Aiden's doing. I haven't heard a goddamn thing."

"And I'm sorry about that, Miss Morgan. As a doctor, I'm concerned for your well-being as well. Mr. Preston sustained a head injury from the fall. Right now he's still unconscious. All we have to do is wait for him to wake up."

"How long does that take?" I asked.

He shrugged. "Sometimes it could be just a few hours or days. And in worse cases, it could be weeks or possibly never. Hopefully, it won't lead to that." I gasped and slapped a hand over my mouth. The thought of him never waking up terrified me. "I wish I could've given you better news," he replied sadly.

Before he could walk out the door, I called out, "When can I see him? I can't wait much longer."

He glanced back at me, his gaze sad. "I'll get one of the nurses to take you down."

By the time one of the nurses came to get me, my whole body was numb. I didn't know what to expect, but I had to prepare for the worst. As the door opened, I broke out in tears when I saw him lying there. His massive frame took up most of the bed, but his head was bandaged and he was bruised. The nurse wheeled me up to his side and quietly slipped out of the room. I held his hand and brought it to my cheek.

"Aiden, you have to wake up. I just got you back. You can't leave me like this," I pleaded. I waited for him to wake up, but he didn't. For hours, I sat with him and just talked, mainly about some of the stupid things we did in high school. We had so many memories together.

"Miss Morgan, you need to get your rest," one of the nurses murmured from behind.

I shook my head. "I can't leave him. Can I not just stay in here?"

She sidled up beside me and I looked up into her kind, hazel eyes. "You really love him, don't you?"

Sighing, I glanced back at his still form and nodded. "More than anything."

"Is he the one you sang about in "Lost Dreams"? He fits the description."

"Yes," I answered, whispering the words.

"I'm glad you two found each other again. That song always made my heart hurt. I could see the pain in your eyes every time you sang it."

"You've been to my concerts?" I asked.

I looked up at her smiling face and she nodded excitedly. "I've been to several. You're one of my favorite singers."

"Thank you. That means a lot."

"You're welcome. I tell you what though, if you give me free tickets to your next show, I'll let you stay in here as long as you want. I'll even bring a cot for you to sleep on."

I grabbed her hands. "I'll give you free tickets for a year. You have no idea how much this means to me."

She winked. "I got you covered. I'll be back in a few minutes." As soon as she left, I breathed a sigh of relief.

"I'm not leaving you for a second," I promised him. As carefully as I could, I climbed up beside him and laid my head on his shoulder. "I think I have a new song for us. With being in this situation, it sure can get your mind going. Do you want to hear what I have so far?"

I pretended he said yes and started singing. Every word that came from my mouth was from my heart. I sang and sang until I could barely speak. The ache in my chest made it hard to breathe. Burying my head in his shoulder, I held onto him and sobbed. He was my first love and I'd be damned if I was going to let anyone take him away from me.

"Shh, stop crying, buttercup," he murmured.

Gasping, I jerked my head up and stared at him. His blue eyes were open, but they were tired. "You're awake," I cried.

He tried to sit up and grunted in pain. When his gaze turned my way, his face darkened as he scanned my body. "What did that fucker do to you?" He lifted his hand to my hair that was now cut up to my chin, and then grazed them over my bruised neck.

"I'm okay. I paid him back with a knife to the shoulder and a lifetime in jail. It's over. I'm just glad you're alive."

"I couldn't leave you so soon. If I did, you wouldn't be able to dedicate that song to me. As soon as I heard it, I could feel myself coming back."

"Are you saying my song healed you?" I asked, chuckling lightly.

He nodded, his gaze serious. "I am. Without you, I was nothing. I don't want to be that way again."

Leaning over, I kissed him gently. "Neither do I. How about I make our next song with a happy ending? Does that sound good?"

His lips pulled back into a smile. "Perfect. That way I get the girl and live happily ever after."

"I think I can manage that."

The End

NEW YORK TIMES and USA Today Bestselling author, L.P. Dover, is a southern belle residing in North Carolina along with her husband and two beautiful girls. Before she even began her literary journey she worked in Periodontics enjoying the wonderment of dental surgeries.

Not only does she love to write, but she loves to play tennis, go on mountain hikes, white water rafting, and you can't forget the passion for singing. Her two number one fans expect a concert each and every night before bedtime and those songs usually consist of Christmas carols.

Aside from being a wife and mother, L.P. Dover has written over twenty novels including her Forever Fae series, the Second Chances series, the Gloves Off series, the Armed & Dangerous series, and her standalone novel, Love, Lies, and Deception. Her favorite genre to read is romantic suspense and she also loves writing it. However, if she had to choose a setting to live in it would have to be with her faeries in the Land of the Fae.

L.P. Dover is represented by Marisa Corvisiero of Corvisiero Literary Agency. To learn more, visit: http://www.lpdover.com

PUSS IN BOOTS
Retold
by Brynn Myers

Evin's heels clicked on the marble floor as she opened the glass door to Victor's office. She was annoyed by this midday distraction, but these types of interruptions were something she'd become accustomed to and unfortunately had to endure. It was her *job* after all. Evin was, for all intents and purposes, Victor's personal public relations specialist who was to be available at any hour of the day, according to his terms. It was just another thing she could add to her long list of grievances when it came to him.

As Evin passed Victor's secretary, she gave her a clipped wave before barging into his office. He'd been expecting her, so Evin could dispense with the formality of being cordial. Victor didn't even look up, in fact he seemed completely unaffected by her intrusion. As he sat behind his sleek modern desk, Evin couldn't help but think that for only being fifty-one, Victor looked aged well beyond his years. She was certain his ashen hair and sullen eyes were the byproduct of all his dirty dealings—cheating, lying, and scheming had to take its toll somehow. Evin smiled inwardly and thought, *Karma's a bitch.* "You summoned me?"

Victor sighed in exasperation. "Don't you think *summon* is a bit of a stretch, Evin? I simply asked you to come to my office to do a job. You still owe on your debt, do you not?"

"Thanks to you constantly changing the finish line, yes," Evin said as she sat in the chair across from Victor. "What's the job this time?"

Victor grinned. "Easy enough. I need you to transform a simple boy into a man of wealth and prestige."

"Oh, is that all?" Evin quipped.

"I owe a favor to an old friend, and this is *me* repaying my debt."

"This isn't *you* repaying anything. This is me doing all the heavy lifting and you taking all the credit for it," she spat as she slumped back into the chair.

"Same thing," he chided as he propped his feet onto the edge of the desk.

"And what do I get out of this?"

1

Victor narrowed his eyes at her, his intense stare speaking volumes as the two of them sat in silence. They remained in a visual stand off for several long moments before Victor finally relented. "Your debt will be cleared."

Evin gave him a smug look. "Really, or is this just another one of your tricks? Sounds too good to be true and you know what they say about deals like that."

"You'll do the job and stop complaining," Victor snapped. "Sometimes you are too much like your mother, Evin. It's your greatest and worst asset."

Evin glowered at Victor as he leaned forward and clicked a button on this phone. "Brooke, send in Marcus."

The door opened and in walked a tall guy with shaggy hair. Evin narrowed her eyes as she took in his appearance—t-shirt and jeans so wrinkled it looked as if he slept in them, and the Chuck Taylors he was wearing were ragged and splattered with paint. Evin didn't know what was worse, his disheveled look or the khaki canvas messenger bag he had slung over his chest.

"This is who I have to transform into a man of wealth and prestige? Impossible. No amount of money or Armani will change the fact that he looks like a stoner puppy who sits around playing video games all day." Evin seethed as she stood to leave. "No deal, Victor. I knew there was a trick in here somewhere."

"I'm sorry. Did I interrupt something?" the young man crooned behind her. "I can come back later."

Evin spun around and took him in again from head to toe. "Do you always dress like this?"

"Um. Yes. Mostly," Marcus said shyly as she paced in front of him.

Evin narrowed her eyes at him again. "Do you even like real girls or are you hard core into avatar chicks?"

Marcus pressed his lips together and furrowed his brows. "I like real women and don't have much use for computer generated females. I'm a software engineer who likes to build robots with my spare time," he said as he extended his hand, "Miss?"

Evin crossed her arms in front of her chest and glared at Marcus.

"Marcus, please excuse Evin. Sometimes she forgets her manners," Victor said as he stood and moved towards the two of them.

"Evin, this is Marcus Ames. Marcus—meet my daughter, Evin Keyes."

"Your daughter?" Marcus stumbled. "I see." He gave Evin a clipped nod. "It's nice to meet you."

"Marcus graduated summa cum laude from Columbia and has been highly sought after in the business world for his expertise in social robotics, Evin. He's more than just a boy, he's a man with a vision, and with your expertise in all things social and upcoming, he too can play among the corporate giants."

Evin shrugged. "Maybe, but the bigger question is who do you intend to pitch him to, Victor?"

Marcus stared at Victor and Evin, trying his level best to discern their awkward interaction. They may be father and daughter, but they seemed more like enemies than family.

"Donahue," Victor said simply.

Evin snapped her head towards her father. "You bastard."

"I'm sorry. Is this Donahue person bad?" Marcus asked sharply.

Evin huffed. "He's a real a real piece of work, but he'll give you all you need to be a major success. No wonder you're willing to clear my debt, Victor. The price for this job couldn't be any higher," Evin retorted as she continued to stew over her father's request.

"I think I've missed something," Marcus inquired.

"No, you've missed nothing," Evin spat. "I'll take the job but this is the last one, even if you change the terms." She waved her finger between herself and Victor. "We will be square, and we will be done. Understood?"

The edge of Victor's lips rose into a wry smile. "Understood."

"You better," Evin fumed before turning her attention to Marcus. "And you," she jerked her finger towards the door, "let's go."

Marcus looked at Victor, then at Evin who was walking out the double doors of the executive suite. "Um…o-okay," he said as he shuffled off after her.

"You'll be fine, Marcus. She'll do her job. All you'll need to do is listen to what she tells you and you'll be well on your way," Victor said as he watched Marcus try and keep up with Evin. "Good luck. You're gonna need it," he laughed under his breath.

"Where are we going?" Marcus asked.

"No talking. I'm thinking of all the places we have to hit today to get started with…well, *you.*"

Marcus scoffed but remained silent. When the elevator chimed, they made their way into the lobby. As they went through the glass revolving door and shot out onto the busy Manhattan Street, Marcus wondered why Evin was so hostile—not just to him but to her father and then towards whomever this Donahue person was.

* * *

It was lunchtime and the city was bustling with corporate types trying to grab a bite to eat and conduct business via their cells. Marcus found himself impressed by the speed to which Evin glided through the crowd in the heeled boots she was wearing. From his vantage point he couldn't help but take in how stunningly beautiful she was. She may have a wicked attitude, but her outward appearance was beyond appealing. Long blonde hair that fell in soft curls past her shoulders, an athletic physique that had his mind wondering what she looked like out of those tight black pants and loose fitting grey jacket. Yes, he was checking her out, taking in every detail of her appearance just as she did him. The only difference was—he did it with admiration instead of disdain. Had she really thought he wasn't into girls because of his outfit?

Evin took a sharp right turn into the Starbucks and nudged her way to the counter. When Marcus finally made his way next to her, she spoke for the first time since they'd left Victor's office.

"What do you want? This is gonna be a long day and you'll need to keep up."

"I don't drink coffee."

"What? Everyone drinks coffee."

"I don't," he said as he looked over at the barista waiting impatiently to take their order. "I'll have a tall hot chocolate, thank you."

Evin rolled her eyes. "Seriously?"

"Yes. I like them."

She ordered a vente latte and shook her head as she pulled cash out of the purse slung over her shoulder.

"You're getting a tattoo."

"No, I'm not."

"Yes. You are."

"But why?"

"Because women love a well-placed sexy tattoo. It'll get you laid every time," Evin said as she gave him a self-satisfied look before reaching for her latte.

4

"Okay," Marcus relented as he timidly looked at her, "but will it hurt?"

"Ugh! Not any more than I'm gonna hurt you if you don't shut up," Evin said as she shoved his tall hot chocolate at him. "And no more ordering these. Man up!"

Marcus' eyes widened as he reached for the cup, hoping to avoid the hot liquid as it shot out the small hole from the force with which Evin handed it to him.

"Hot chocolate," she muttered as she walked away. "Really?"

"Evin, wait."

"What?"

"I have no problem listening to you and doing what you say, but I need to understand something first." She put the cup to her lips and stared at him over the lid. "Why are you—or should I say why would you do this for me?"

Evin took a long slow sip before lowering the coffee from her lips. "Because I want to be free from Victor's demands and if you are my ticket, I'm gonna do my best work and make you the most desirable man in New York." She smirked. "And don't bother asking me anymore questions. My reasons are my own. I've told you more than you need to know as it is."

"I suppose I can live with that," Marcus said as he opened the door to let Evin walk through. As she stepped out into the crowd of people he mumbled under his breath. "For now, at least."

He wasn't sure why he wanted to know more about her, but he did. To him she was a puzzle. She was scattered with no clear pattern emerging as to whom or what she was, but he hoped once he got to know her he'd see the whole person. Would she be complete or lacking a missing piece? Only time would tell.

"You coming or are you planning on holding the door open for everyone?" Evin demanded.

Marcus gave Evin a slight grin and pushed his way past the influx of people piling into Starbucks and made his way over to her. "Where to first, my lady?"

Evin rolled her eyes. "Ugh. This is going to be harder than I thought," she said as she grabbed Marcus by the wrist and dragged him down Madison Avenue.

Evin and Marcus spent the next three hours shopping and revamping his look from geek-chic to GQ stud. If he was going to have any hope of snagging one of the New York elite bachelorettes and a coveted spot at Donahue Enterprises, he was going to need to look a lot less like Zachary Levi and way more like David Gandy—at least as far as Evin was concerned. Marcus, however, was fighting her tooth and nail on why he needed to change everything about himself in order to land an A-list job.

"You don't. You can stay this way and find yourself a nice girl, a simple job and a humble abode and live happily ever after, but that is not what you asked for, is it?" Evin remarked as she smoothed the back of the suit he was wearing.

Marcus turned towards her. "I didn't ask for anything, Evin. I simply handed Victor an envelope my father left me and he arranged the rest."

Evin scrunched her face in confusion. "I don't understand. Why would you just hand Victor a letter without knowing what was inside? Weren't you curious to know what it said?"

"My father recently died and in his will, he left my oldest brother the brokerage, my middle brother the real estate investments, and my portion of the inheritance was to be left in the hands of Victor Keyes. I was given specific instructions as to the time, date, and place I was to meet with your father—beyond that, I am clueless." Evin stared at Marcus quizzically. "About what my father intended for me to have, not a general cluelessness. Are you always so hostile or is it just towards me?" Marcus demanded.

"You misunderstand. This isn't about you. My frustration and anger is exclusively for Victor but in this instance, you are the byproduct of me having to deal with him."

"Well, I'm not your enemy, Evin, so I'd appreciate it if you stopped acting like I was."

She crossed her arms in front of her chest and watched as Marcus removed the jacket and headed back towards the dressing room. "Try on the jeans next and put on that black shirt with it too." Marcus turned to glare at her. "Please," Evin said blithely.

She watched him curiously as he walked away. It was the first time he'd shown any backbone. Maybe he was different than she'd first assumed—maybe she should give him a chance to prove he wasn't like every other male she knew.

For the rest of the shopping trip Evin toned down her venom towards Marcus and decided to learn all she could about his family and how he was connected to Victor. She wondered how his father had died and if he was a good man or as unscrupulous as her own. Marcus had talked about his brothers but Evin couldn't help but wonder where his mother was since he hadn't mentioned her. Evin had been away from her mother since she was a young girl and often thought what, if anything, would've been different in her life if she'd have been born to parents who were selfless instead of selfish.

Marcus walked out of the dressing room in the outfit she requested and her heart skipped a beat. The black button down shirt was tailored and fitted and unlike the jeans he was wearing this morning when she first met him, these fit him perfectly.

"Now see, *that* is the way jeans should fit, Marcus. Who knew you had such a great ass." Evin grinned as Marcus stared at her via the mirror. "This," she said as she smacked his ass, "this I can work with."

"How's everything going in here? Will you need any other sizes or do I need to arrange for alterations?" the tall redhead asked as she too stared at Marcus.

Evin smiled even wider. "See." She winked. "That's the reaction we're looking for, my friend." The sales girl blushed and Marcus stepped away from the mirror, embarrassed by the way the two women were gawking at him. "We'll take everything and he'll be back tomorrow to have the Dolce and Armani suits fitted. Let's say 2ish. Oh, and put it all on Victor Keyes account."

The sales girl nodded and moved towards the dressing room to gather the majority of the clothes before walking out and taking yet another look at Marcus. Evin had to admit, this part of the job was coming along nicely, but they'd only just begun his "transformation." He was still a major work in progress.

"Go get changed. We'll grab some food and then move onto the second half of our day." Marcus frowned and Evin reached up to ruffle his hair. "Part two."

"Oh joy," Marcus replied.

The two of them settled on stacked pastrami sandwiches at Carnegie Deli and it was nice. It was the first time they'd actually *talked* to one another. Evin had asked Marcus why he wanted to change and go corporate only to find out that he really didn't want to. With his father's sudden death, he felt like he owed it to him since he'd been such a letdown in comparison to his older brothers.

"What happened to your Dad?" Evin asked softly.

Marcus' eyes went to the table. "Heart attack. No warning, no chance to say goodbye—nothing. One day he was here and the next he was gone."

"I'm so sorry," she said as she touched his hand, but when Marcus looked at her curiously, she pulled back.

"So where's your mom?" Evin asked as she quickly took another bite trying to hide her concern.

"She passed away when I was a kid. It was just my dad and my brothers. Too much testosterone in the house with all the males jockeying for first position in Dad's eyes. He always said I was most like her—too soft hearted for Wall Street." Marcus paused, wanting to gauge Evin's next comment. When she remained silent, he continued. "No quip on me being a softie?"

Evin shook her head and gave him a sad smile. "Not everyone is meant to be cutthroat and cunning. Some are meant to try and change the world. There has to be a balance or we'd all cease to exist."

Marcus was stunned. Had Evin just let another bit of that granite guard down in a matter of moments? For fear of making her retreat, he chose his next words carefully. "I agree. That's why I focus on my work. I've been delving further into social robotics to find ways to make things easier for people. What about you? What is your ultimate dream?"

Evin shot Marcus a panicked look. *Oh crap*, he thought. *I've lost her again*. But instead, she bit her bottom lip. "No one has ever asked me what I wanted or dreamed of."

"Really?"

"I'm aloof, and most people think I'm a bitch."

Marcus coughed.

"It's all right." Evin grinned. "I have to be, in my line of work, or no one will take me seriously. I go from being the pretty blonde without a brain in her head, to the 'don't screw with me or I'll feed you your balls for lunch' blonde. The latter gets respect."

"So who are you really?" Marcus pushed.

"You know for a stoner puppy who sits around playing video games all day, you've got some stones." Evin smiled again. "Sorry about that comment by the way. I judged the book by its cover too quickly and I was wrong. You're all right, Marcus."

Marcus laughed. "Thank you, but you still haven't answered me."

Evin played with the french fries on her plate. "I'm just someone who wants to be free to live her life without expectations at every turn. I'd like a family, friends, and to be respected for who I am and not what I can do."

"Can I get you two anything else?" The waitress asked, breaking the moment between them.

Evin snapped back into her normal demeanor. "Nope. Just the check."

The waitress started to set the bill on the table but Marcus reached it first. "My treat, please."

"No," Evin argued.

"Yes and I want to ask for one other thing, Evin."

"You're pushing me, Marcus."

He laughed. "Can we start this day over—as friends?"

Evin sat back in her chair and crossed her arms over her chest. "Maybe." She grinned. "It would make you more bearable if we were."

Marcus laughed again. "Ditto."

Days turned into weeks as Evin and Marcus spent almost every day plotting and planning his grand entrance into the corporate/socialite world. Each event they attended was carefully orchestrated to get him in front of all the right people, which of course, only got him one step closer to Victor's goal of Marcus working at Donahue Enterprises. Evin was sure there was something in it for Victor or why else would he push Donahue, who dealt mostly in real estate investments, to hire a software engineer. There were plenty of other corporate heads that would kill to have someone like Marcus on their team.

The real issue, though, was that Evin wasn't completely convinced that Marcus was really set on following his father and brothers' footsteps of becoming a big wig among the business elite. He seemed content being the "MacGyver" of the robotic world. Some days he was ecstatic over the connections he made, while other times he seemed drained and uninterested. None of that really mattered, though, because all Evin had to do was get Marcus in front of Donahue so he could pitch his robotic concept and then she would finally be free of Victor.

"Hey, you home?" Marcus asked through the squawky intercom downstairs.

Evin didn't respond but rather just hit the buzzer to let him in. As he lumbered up the steps to the second floor, she unlocked the door and left it slightly ajar.

"I gave Bob a bagel on my way up and he said to say thanks for the coffee you brought down to him this morning," Marcus said as he stepped into her apartment.

Evin hit the button on the milk frothier. "Bob never lets anyone past the bottom step without the third degree. He must like you."

"Only you, Evin, would have a bum as a stoop bodyguard," Marcus teased.

"What can I say, I only work with the best," Evin grinned as she added the chocolate to the steamed milk and handed it to Marcus.

"Thanks," he nodded.

Evin had realized since their first encounter that Marcus' affinity for hot chocolate and being gentlemanly was just part of his charm. She'd also come to appreciate these traits as quirky rather than annoying. Evin had never met anyone like him and doubted she ever would again. So instead of trying to change him, she just let him be who he was. Evin knew all too well what it felt like to constantly be self-conscious about the things that made her unique.

"So what's on today's agenda?" Marcus asked.

Evin dropped a two inch binder on the table in front of him. "This." She flipped it open to the first page. "You need to familiarize yourself with all the people in here. We'll be seeing them several times this week and they are key to the final part of my plan."

Marcus snapped into business mode. "All right, who's most important?"

In the past weeks, Evin and Marcus found an easy give and take with one another. In the same way that she acknowledged his quirks, he too accepted her need to remain in control. She wasn't always all business, but at the moment she had to be.

"Her." Evin pointed. "This is Camille Perrault. She is the sister of Charles Donahue and like her scoundrel of a brother, she too is only out for one thing—whatever suits her fancy."

"She sounds lovely," Marcus teased.

"Oh, she is going to love you. You're fresh meat and with me by your side tonight, she'll want you even more, but Camille is not who I want you to get acquainted with."

"Who then?"

Evin flipped the page. "Her daughter. Christine Perrault, she's the polar opposite of her mother. Christine, unlike her family, believes in humanitarian causes and would be someone you'd like to connect with." Her last two words were said with a bit of a stammer.

"Are you trying to get rid of me, Evin?" Marcus grinned.

"Nah, but I knew you would eventually find someone who'd be something more than just your friend." She shrugged. "It was inevitable, right?"

Marcus' smile faded. "Yeah, I guess."

"Cheer up buttercup, I'll still be your buddy." Evin said with a half-hearted smile. "I just started liking you, besides, I have so much more to torture you about."

Marcus shook his head and laughed. "You can't get rid of me that easily. I'm like a bad penny; I'll just keep turning up."

Evin rolled her eyes. "Back to work. You have a lot of people to get to know before seven o'clock. Oh, and make sure you read up on the Desoto's, they too would be great contacts for you."

Truth be told, Evin had come to enjoy the time she and Marcus spent together, but their friendship hadn't been part of the plan—he'd just gotten to her, worn down her defenses, and now here they were—friends.

As Marcus started reading the dossiers for each of the people Evin planned on having him meet tonight, she finished making the final arrangements for the rest of the evening. She grabbed a few things out of the pantry and pulled two pots out of the cabinet. It was time to make the one thing she'd need to lure Donahue to her, not that she really needed anything. He had wanted her since he first laid eyes on her when she was sixteen and had made no secret of his desire to possess her one way or another. It sickened her that her father was willing to give him exactly what he wanted in exchange for Marcus' job placement, but then again, that was Victor. Evin had a plan of her own though, and if all went well, she'd give Donahue exactly what he wanted, or at least he'd think he accomplished his goal.

As Evin stirred the beeswax to melt it down, she watched Marcus as he flipped through the pages. Tonight was going to be an eye opener for him. Tonight, he'd meet all the people with the ability to make his dreams come true, but all Evin could think about was how lonely she'd be once he and Christine hit it off. She sighed and added the intoxicating scents into the perfume base.

"Wow, that smells great. What are you making?"

"Perfume. I don't really care for the store bought stuff. I prefer to make my own."

Marcus' brow quirked into an arch. "You never cease to amaze me, Evin."

She laughed. "It's just perfume, Marcus." Evin slid the pot off the flame and reached for the old pocket watch she used as a container. "Oh, a town car will pick you up at six then it'll head over here to pick me up. You good with that?"

"Yep. It'll be like a date," he replied without turning to look at her.

Evin almost spilled the wax mixture she was trying to pour. "No. Not like a date, like a business event."

"Yep, okay," Marcus said flatly as he looked at his phone. "Hey, I've got to run, but I'll see you at 6:15 for our *date*." He intentionally emphasized the last word as he kissed Evin on the cheek before heading for the door.

"Not a date." Evin called out the door of her apartment as Marcus took the steps two at a time. As she closed the door she said it again in her mind—*not a date, it's business.*

The door buzzed at six fifteen on the dot. Marcus always prided himself on being punctual and loved making sure Evin was well aware of his obsession with time. As usual she buzzed him in and waited until he knocked on her door. The only issue with tonight was that she wasn't completely ready. No shoes, back of dress unzipped, and she was struggling to put her earrings in as he opened the door.

Evin grimaced. "Sorry. Almost ready. I just need like five minutes."

Marcus just stood there in the doorway, never taking his eyes off of her as he closed the door behind him.

"What?" Evin replied nervously.

"You...you look beautiful," Marcus replied.

Evin smiled. "You're gonna have to work on your reaction to beauty, young man. Christine is a stunner." Evin reached for his chin. "So close this, wipe the drool, and help me finish zipping this," she said as she turned around.

Marcus stiffened at the site of the low-slung dress Evin was wearing. As he stared at the small of her back, his fingers fumbled for the zipper.

"Are you going to zip me up or what?"

"May I have option B? This dress is ah…"

Evin looked over her shoulder at Marcus whose eyes were fixated on her. "And just what does option B entail?"

Evin couldn't believe she just said that out loud but she did. It was an honest response to his question and with the way he was looking at her, combined with the way his hands were caressing her hips, she couldn't help herself. She wanted to know.

Marcus lifted his brows in surprise. He'd assumed she would've scolded him for even thinking such a thing, but the look in her eyes said something very different. Marcus reached for the strap on her dress but stopped for a moment, wanting to gauge Evin's reaction. When she put her hand on his and eased the dress down her arm just a bit, Marcus followed her lead, easing it down even further.

He couldn't believe this was happening. Evin was his ultimate fantasy. Him and every other man in New York that is. Every time they went out he had to fight the urge to pound the men gawking at her into the ground. She was alluring whether she was in her yoga pants or dressed to the nines. Marcus pulled her hair to the side and let his mouth explore as he kissed his way up her neck.

"Do you have any idea what you've done to me?" he said with a ragged breath.

Evin moaned as he nipped at her ear. "No, but I'm beginning to. Maybe you should continue so I can fully understand," she breathed as she leaned her head back to give him access to her lips.

Marcus didn't hesitate, his tongue slid between her parted lips as his hands roamed over her body. He wanted more; he wanted to strip her out of that dress and explore every inch of her. His body was burning with the need to mark her as his. Marcus pulled away but only long enough to slide the other strap off her other shoulder so the dress would fall to the floor. She was bare to him now, the only barrier between them were the black lace panties that hugged the curve of her ass as if they'd been custom made just for her.

Marcus wondered what had gotten into her and how this was even possible. Was this even really happening or had he simply imagined it once again?

Evin turned to face him and he pulled her close as the two of them devoured one another with their hands and lips. When Evin finally broke their kiss, they just stared at one another.

"I lost count of how many times I've wanted to do that," Marcus professed.

Evin chuckled. "Strip me out of a cocktail dress?"

"No." Marcus smiled.

"Then what?"

"Kiss you. Touch you. Hold you," he said as he held her.

"Well, I guess I have to confess that I've been wondering the same thing myself," she replied as she stared up at him.

Marcus kissed her again as he lifted her and set her on the edge of the counter. "I want you, Evin."

They were face to face now and there was no way either of them was going to get away without more explanation. The heat between them had been building for weeks, but now that they were here, neither knew exactly what to do.

Evin tried to break the tension as she ran her hands down the front of his shirt. "You know, for a nerd you certainly do take care of yourself. Who knew you had these abs?"

Marcus grinned. "I tried many times to get you to hug me close enough to feel them, but you always pulled away."

She looked into his eyes. "Because I was afraid if I got too close, I wouldn't be able to do my job and you aren't mine to have."

"And why not? Why can't I have you?"

"Because it's not part of the master plan. I'm just the person to get you to the finish line."

"Then I want to change the finish line."

"Marcus you can't. You're not the only one getting something out of this. I have to finish this job. I have to be free. Can you understand that?" Evin asked as she tried to squirm out of his embrace.

"I'll set you free."

She put her hands on his face and kissed him again. "You'll never know how much it means to me that you'd say that, but you're not the one who holds the key."

He buried his face in her neck, letting her scent consume him. He hated that she was right. At the moment he was just a software engineer with a middle grade job at some average company. How was he going to fix their situations without them following through with the plan?

"It's not going to always be like this, Evin."

"I say that to myself every day, Marcus, and yet every day I wake up and it is."

"So why let me get this far with you only to take it away?"

"Because I know that by tomorrow you'll be on to bigger and better things and I wanted to know, just once, what it felt like to be in your arms."

Marcus kissed her again. She gripped his hair and the two let themselves be consumed once more with the passion burning between them. The only difference now was that the truth of the situation could no longer be hidden—they both had a job to do.

Marcus helped Evin back into her dress but as he zipped it, he let his fingers linger another moment, unwilling to let her go. Marcus leaned down close to her ear. "Christine may be all you say, but I can promise you, no one will be more beautiful than you are tonight."

Evin shivered then turned to look at Marcus. Neither of them spoke. Instead they just let the seconds pass. Marcus pushed a piece of hair that had fallen behind her ear. "I know what the plan is, but for tonight, I'm grateful to have you on my arm."

"Thank you."

"You ready to go?" he whispered.

"Just need my shoes."

Evin looked at the clock and rushed to grab her shoes. "We're late, and I know how much you hate not being on time."

Marcus reached for her evening bag on the counter and held the door open. "I wouldn't trade a second of why we're running late. In fact, I'd just as soon stay here and finish what we started."

Evin sighed as she locked the door. "I'd love nothing more, but we have work to do. Get your game face on, and let's land you this job."

* * *

"Evin." Disdain dripped from the woman's voice. "Such a pleasure to see you."

"Always a pleasure to see you too, Camille."

"And who is this? Another one of your prey?"

"Oh," Evin droned, "hunting prey is for jaguars, not puma's."

Evin turned towards Marcus who tried to look unfazed but with his brows furrowed he wasn't really succeeding. "This is my friend, Marcus."

"Marcus, you may want to run far away from this one. She only leaves destruction in her wake. I'd hate for you to be another one of her casualties," Camille suggested.

Evin went to speak but Marcus reached for her hand. "I'm perfectly aware of who I am friends with, Ms. Perrault."

"Well, my, my, a man with backbone. Aren't you a breath of fresh air?"

"I didn't realize there was a shortage," Marcus retorted as he moved passed her with Evin at his side.

"By the way, how's your father, Evin?" Camille called out.

Evin stopped for a brief second but continued walking with Marcus towards the concierge. Tonight's gala event was going to be grand and the chances of running into Camille again once the event began was slim. She'd have too many other people she'd have to schmooze and annoy.

When they were out of earshot, Marcus leaned into Evin. "How does she know your father?"

"She was his whore...I mean lover," Evin corrected.

"Oh."

"I'll explain later. Right now, I'm going to need you to look alive," she said under her breath. "Tall man with the grey goatee, twelve o'clock. He's a great man with a head for business and a heart that wants to save the world."

Marcus glanced towards the fountain in the center of the grand foyer. "Ah yes, number two in the dossier. On it," he said as he adjusted his cuffs.

"Good evening, Mr. Desoto. How have you been?" Evin said, dismissing her and Marcus' previous conversation. "And where's your lovely wife tonight?"

"Oh, she's here somewhere, Evin. Probably writing another check to Christine if I had to guess," he laughed.

Evin laughed too. "Well, then I can only hope to be lucky enough to run into them both shortly." She turned towards Marcus and made the proper introductions.

"Marcus, Mr. Desoto owns one of the largest surgical robotic manufacturing companies here in the US."

"I know Evin is in the top of her field in public relations, so what is it that you do, Marcus?"

"Currently I'm a software engineer who dabbles in social robotics. I've made some real advances in the functionality of its everyday use, especially in relationship to its temperament and interaction with humans. I'm a great admirer of your work, Mr. Desoto. The things you've managed to do in the surgical field have been astounding."

"Marcus, would you care to join me at the bar," Mr. Desoto asked with a hearty grin, "There are a few people I'd like you to meet. I think they'll be very interested in the work you're doing.

"It would be my pleasure," Marcus replied before turning to Evin. "I'll be right back. Can I bring you back something to drink?"

Evin nodded. "Yes, thank you. I'd like a Boulevardier, please." Marcus scrunched his brows in confusion. She shook her head and smiled. "The bartender will know what it is."

As Marcus and Mr. Desoto walked away, Evin couldn't helped but feel relieved. The first connection has been made. Mr. Desoto was one of the most important businessmen Evin wanted Marcus to meet. He, along with his wife Margaret, were big contributors to any cause that helped people in need. In fact, this entire gala was centered on helping children's causes specifically; it was why she chose it over the others as Marcus' final introduction. Not only would tonight put Marcus in front of all the right people, but it was also the one event least likely to scar his soul—the truth was that the majority of people who attended these charity events, did it for the publicity instead of the actual cause.

Marcus was a kind soul with grand hopes and dreams for a better world. The least Evin could do was help him to fulfill those dreams, even if she had to be part of the majority who brought him here with the hope of bettering his social status. For her, it was okay that she was willing to sell her soul, but after all these weeks with Marcus, she didn't want any of her "truths" to infect him. Their kiss tonight was perfection, but like Camille said, she was destructive and whether she meant to or not, she'd hurt him in the end.

Just finish this job and move on. No attachments.

⁓ ⚬⁖⚬ ⁓

Evin and Marcus had a wonderful evening, meeting almost every person in the dossier except for two, Christine Perrault and Charles Donahue. Both, it seemed, had been tied up with benefactors rivaling for their time, but as they walked back towards their assigned table, Marcus ran smack dab into Christine by accident.

"Oh, excuse me. I wasn't paying any attention. I thought I saw an old friend and..." Marcus and Christine's eyes met.

"It was actually my fault. I dropped this and stupidly bent down to pick it up without realizing I was in the walkway," Christine replied. "Oh, hello, Evin. How are you?"

"Hi. I'm sorry about Marcus bumping into you," Evin said as Marcus bent to pick up the other papers Christine had dropped in their collision.

"Well, if I had to be clumsy and look foolish, I'm glad it was with you, Evin, and not one of the socialites. Can you imagine the gossip? I'd already be on YouTube," Christine joked.

They all laughed. "Marcus, this is my friend, Christine, head of one of New York's largest children's charities and the most eligible bachelorette this side of Fifth Avenue," Evin announced.

"Evin," Christine scolded. "Please. You know I hate all that."

"I know, but it was a 'proper' introduction, was it not?" Evin reached for Marcus' arm. "Christine this is my dear friend, Marcus Ames. Summa cum laude ..."

"Enough with the proper introductions, please just call me Marcus," he said as he extended his hand to Christine. "It's a pleasure to meet you."

As the three of them chatted about careers and the latest gossip, a man in a dark suit and a security ear piece walked up to them. "Miss Keyes, your presence is requested. Please come with me."

Marcus furrowed his brows at the large man's request.

"It's all right. I know what this is reference to. You and Christine go have a good time, I've got this."

Marcus still looked concerned but relented just a bit. "Are you going to be okay?" he asked as he leaned in to kiss Evin on the cheek.

"It's time for me to do my job and secure your final interview," she whispered. "Honest, I'll be okay. I'll find you tomorrow. Go enjoy the rest of your night."

He stepped back. Unwilling to agree, but the look in her eyes clarified she was back in work mode. "I'll call you in the morning then?"

She winked at him. "Don't do anything I wouldn't do."

Marcus shrugged. "Is that a short or long list?"

Christine tugged at his arm. "Hey, there is someone I'd like you to meet. He's an old friend from college who's starting a robotics company in Silicon Valley. I think he'd like to know someone with your talents, Marcus."

Evin winked. "Networking. It's the name of the game."

Evin rode the elevator in silence next to Charles Donahue's personal security guard. Evin may not have seen Donahue tonight at the gala, but it was now apparent that he'd seen her. She was being summoned. What was it with him and her father and their arrogance in demanding her presence? Evin pulled the pocket watch filled with her homemade perfume out of her bag and lightly dabbed it at her pulse points. The heat of her body would amplify the balm, thus intensifying its effects in a matter of moments. The man standing behind her shifted his stance and she grinned. It was working already. The perfume was merely to make her intended target more pliable to suggestion. Too bad it couldn't just do the job for her.

Evin put the watch away and adjusted her dress with a subtle shake. Another groan from him and the elevator door opened to the tower floor. She and the *muscle* walked down the corridor until they reached the Penthouse Suite. The guard knocked and locked his hands to wait.

"Come in," a deep voice sounded from the other side of the door.

As Evin walked into the room. She couldn't see Donahue but shivered inwardly at the feeling of his sordid energy.

"Take the rest of the night off, Jake, you and the rest of the crew. I won't be needing your services anymore tonight."

"Yes, sir. We'll return at 6 a.m. as usual. Have a good night," Jake responded as he nodded at Evin and turned to leave.

When the door clicked closed, Evin sighed. This was the part of the job she hated the most. As she walked around the corner, she saw Donahue sitting behind an ornate desk adjacent to the windows overlooking the city.

"Charles," Evin stated matter-of-factly.

"Have a seat, my dear."

"I'll stand."

"Oh, now that wasn't part of this deal. You want the boy to have a job high up in my company and in order for that to happen, you will need to become more flexible."

Evin scowled and moved to sit on the couch across from Donahue.

"You look stunning tonight, but I must say I am disappointed to not see in you in your usual attire."

"It was a black tie event, boots weren't exactly apropos."

"True, but I really do love to see you as you truly are."

"Which is?"

"My perfect little puss in boots," he said with a smug look on his face.

"You make me sick. You've been gawking at me since I was sixteen. All you are is a rich perv who uses people to get what he wants."

"And I do always get what I want, don't I?" Donahue laughed. "Which is why I'm going to need a few things from you before we can continue on with our *arrangement*."

"Aren't you taking enough?" she hissed.

"Enough would've been for me to have won you in the last high stakes poker match with Victor, but I was a little off my game that night," he said as he took the last sip of his cocktail.

"Excuse me?"

"Yes. It seems your mother and Victor have always been willing to barter when it comes to you."

"What the hell are you talking about?"

"You don't know?" Charles taunted. "Interesting."

Evin tried to keep her composure, but his words were threatening to be her undoing.

"Victor told me during one of his drunken escapades how your mother was so desperate to be free of him that she was willing to give you up in exchange for her freedom. You were just a young girl at the time and hadn't come into your own yet, but Victor agreed and took you away from your country life and brought you here to New York."

"You don't know..."

"Don't I though?" Donahue interrupted. "It wasn't too soon after that when you became his protégé and he became one of the wealthiest men in New York. Why is that, Evin, or should I ask, how is that? What makes you so special besides the obvious?"

Evin's mind reeled as she replayed the day she and Victor left her mother in their house in the Berkshires. She was crying and Victor was gloating, but when they drove away he'd told her this was only temporary, that as soon as she paid off her mother's debt, she was free to go back home. It was the reason she did the jobs, so she could save her mother.

"You're lying."

"Am I? He owned you for years, you were his most prized possession, but now for whatever reason, Victor has just *given* you to me. It's a mystery for sure but I never look a gift horse in the mouth."

"No one owns me," she snarled.

"You're even sexier when you're angry."

Evin flipped him off as she ripped her cell phone out of her purse. She swiped her code and pressed her thumb over her father's number. Loud noise played in the background as he yelled into the receiver. "What is it, Evin? I'm kind of in the middle of something."

"Look, you son of a bitch. I don't give a shit what you are doing right now. Tell me the fucking truth for once in your life."

Victor scoffed. "Ah, I guess my good buddy has shared a little too much information."

"So it's true then? You *bought* me from Mom as some payoff?"

"Gail was weak like that, and it's not as if I asked much of her either. Just a little insight into the future to secure a few business deals. I had assumed you were precognitive like her, but who knew you were so much more? If I'd had any idea, I would've taken you way before I did."

"I didn't think it was possible to hate you any more than I do."

"Finish the job, Evin, or your ego will be the least of your concerns. I've never seen you take this long to do a job. It's obvious that you've let your guard down with the kid, and I'd hate to have to tell Marcus who you *really* are." Victor paused. "Do we understand one another?"

She didn't respond. Instead she hung up the phone and glared at Donahue. It took a moment for Evin to focus her thoughts, but she'd managed to shift from being overwhelmed with pain and anguish at Victor's lies, to being determined and focused once again. She hated them both for this, but as of this moment, she wasn't doing this for them, she was doing it for Marcus. He didn't deserve to be screwed over. She may be poison, but he didn't need to know that truth.

Back to work, Evin. The sooner you got this over with, the sooner you can get away from everyone.

⁓ ❦ ⁓

Evin stood, kicked her heels off, and walked towards the desk Donahue was sitting behind. "So what is it you want so badly," Evin cooed as she sat on the edge.

Donahue loosened his tie and sat back in the chair. "I want you to fulfill my every fantasy. You have no idea the things I've imagined you doing."

Bingo

Evin smirked and while Donahue perceived her coyness as an agreement to his terms, she knew otherwise. She closed her eyes and let her mind take over. Evin was a telepath, her gift stemming from her mother's side of the family, and now she was going to use her 'talent' to trick this sick bastard into thinking he was having his way with her. When in actuality it would all be in his mind. Donahue would believe it to his core, that every fantasy he had ever had about her was coming true. Evin, however, wouldn't be anywhere near him. Instead, she'd be using his own thoughts to complete her task.

Moans and dirty talk filled the room as Evin's visions invaded Donahue's mind. She was disgusted hearing his voice and sickened by the images she was having to illuminate. Having had enough of his revolting images, Evin set the current vision on a loop and grabbed her shoes, slipped out of the door of the hotel room and leaned against the wall. She needed a break.

"So this is the way you secure jobs for people?"

"Marcus," Evin exclaimed. "How...how did you get in here?"

"I followed you because I was worried about you," he huffed. "Guess you were more than taken care of."

"But I..."

"Why, Evin?"

"It's not what you think. I swear."

"Yeah, I'm sure."

Loud moaning came from the other side of the door and Marcus scrunched his brows. "What's going on in there?"

"Like I said, it's not what you think. Please let me explain," Evin pleaded as she grabbed Marcus' wrist.

Marcus glared at her.

"It'll all make sense in a minute, but I need you to trust me and be quiet. Okay?"

He clenched his fists in hopes of trying to contain his anger.

"Please?"

"Well, this must be important if you're actually asking nicely." He pulled away from her. "I thought our kiss tonight meant something, Evin. I guess I was wrong."

Evin's eyes welled with tears. "It did, Marcus—it did."

All the emotion Evin had been trying to contain came bubbling to the surface with no filter to stop it. Marcus softened and pulled her into his arms. "I'm sorry, Evin. Please tell me what all this is. I'm listening."

"I'll explain everything to you, but in order for it to make sense you need to see this," she said as she opened the door.

As they walked into the main sitting room, Marcus' jaw dropped. There bent over the desk, humping it as if someone was beneath him, was Charles Donahue. His shirt was unbuttoned and pushed off his shoulders, while his pants were around his ankles with his ass bared to the world.

"Wha…" Marcus mouthed.

Evin put her finger to her lips and walked them back out into the hall. "He thinks he's having sex with me," she said as more tears streamed down her face.

"He thinks what? What the hell is going on, Evin?"

Evin bit her bottom lip, trying to steady herself. No one knew about her abilities other than Victor. It was what made her the perfect con artist. They perceived every single thing she implanted into their minds as truth. So no one ever suspected they were being had. Evin hated who she was, but it wasn't as if she had a choice. She *thought* she had been saving her mom, but now she knew, that too was a lie. Was anything in her life real?

Marcus turned to leave. "If you're going to stand there in silence I'm leaving. It's obvious you're trying to come up with the perfect lie to explain all this away, but I don't want to hear it. I thought you were different, Evin. I thought…" he stopped, "Forget it. It doesn't matter now."

"Wait. What I'm about to say isn't a lie, but I doubt you'll believe it anyway."

"Try me."

"I'm a telepath. I can make people see, think, and feel things based on what I project into their minds."

Marcus huffed. "Is that what you did to me tonight?"

"No!" Evin exclaimed. "That was real. That was me wanting you."

"Really?"

Another loud cry came out from the other side of the door. Donahue must've climaxed based on the expletives he was using with Evin's name intertwined amongst them.

Marcus slammed his fist into the door jam. "That sick bastard thinks he just fucked you in exchange for my job placement and YOU were the one to make him believe it! This is beyond fucked up, you know that right?"

"Yes," Evin whispered.

"I can't have you for real but he can have you in his mind?" Marcus raged.

"That's not true."

"Isn't it?"

Evin finished the final sequence of illusions by having Donahue fall asleep thinking he was completely sated. The last thing she needed was for him to walk out here and see her and Marcus arguing. When Donahue woke, she wouldn't be there, but then again why would she be, their agreement was complete. Evin wanted to focus on Marcus now and do everything she could to make him understand the real truth.

Marcus threw his hands in the air. "I can't deal with this. I don't even know where to start with trying to filter all this bullshit." He gripped his hair in frustration. "Has anything you told me been the truth or was it all just a continuous chain of lies?"

"Please, let me explain," she pleaded as she reached for him.

"No. I'm done. I wish I never brought that letter into your father's office, and I sure as hell wish I never met you." Marcus tugged away from her and stormed down the hallway to the elevator.

"I'm sorry, Marcus," Evin cried out. "I never meant to hurt you."

The elevator chimed and Marcus stepped in without responding. Evin slid down the wall and buried her head in her hands. As the tears streamed down her face, realization set in. She was truly alone. Everyone she had ever known had left her, used her, and dismissed her. Nothing could free her now.

It had been weeks since Evin had seen or heard from Marcus. She'd left him several voicemails and tried to stop by his apartment but had never been able to connect. She had, however, seen him and Christine in some pictures on Twitter. They were picking up where she left off. They were a couple now, it seemed. Evin should be happy, it was the job and she'd at least succeeded at one of the two tasks even if her heart was broken.

Victor called the day after her world shattered, only to tell her that Donahue altered the agreement, that one night wasn't enough and until he had Evin all to himself, he would not be hiring Marcus. Evin's response was swift—they both could fuck off. She was done.

Evin had also hired a private investigator to look into exactly what happened to her mom. It had been years since she'd heard from her. Victor would always tell her that she was in Monte Carlo or Fiji with a new boyfriend and was just busy, and while she was upset with her mother's indifference, Evin had foolishly believed his lies. The real truth, her mother committed suicide just after Evin's twenty-fifth birthday. Apparently, she was so wrought with guilt over the choices she'd made, she couldn't bear to live with herself. The investigator said she left a journal and that was how Evin finally came to know what really happened.

None of it mattered though. It changed nothing as far as Evin was concerned. Her mother gave her up, Victor used her, and her one chance at normal was now with someone else. It was time to move on. Evin had enough money saved in the bank to support her for years to come and with the sale of her apartment, she'd be able to buy a house near the beach somewhere. As long as it was far away from New York, she'd be good.

Evin poured a glass of wine and turned on some jazz. It had been a long day and she was looking forward to relaxing. She plopped on the sofa and flipped open *Travel & Leisure* magazine. "Maybe I need a vacation too," Evin grinned. "Hmm, I wonder what Seattle is like?"

A knock at the door startled her. No one could get into her building without being buzzed up. Evin looked through the peephole and sighed. She unlocked the door and stepped to the side as she opened it.

"Hi."

"Hi."

"Can I come in?" Marcus asked.

Evin waved her arm towards the kitchen.

"Thanks."

"So what brings you here, Marcus?" Evin asked as she set her glass of wine on the counter.

"What's with all the boxes? Are you moving or something?"

"I asked you first."

"I wanted to talk to you. And…" Marcus paused. "I wanted to apologize."

Evin's eyes went to his. "Not necessary. I totally understand."

"No, Evin. I don't think you do."

"Look, Marcus, I don't know what you are looking for me to say. I'm a horrible person, but at least I was able to do one thing right. I introduced you to Christine and that seems to be going well."

He snickered. "Yes, but it's not what you think."

"Look, a lot has happened since that night. I quit my 'job', she exaggerated with air quotes, and I'm packing because I'm leaving. I'm poison, and I know it, so I'm going to move to a place where no one knows who or what I am. Maybe then I can find some peace." Evin's voice stammered. "So whatever you have to say is irrelevant. I'll be out of New York soon enough and you can go on pretending you never knew me."

He stared at her. "I don't want to pretend I don't know you. I can't."

Now it was Evin who snickered. "And why is that?"

"Because you are the only woman I want to be with. You are the only woman who makes me feel, who makes me want to be something more than I am."

Evin's face paled.

"I'm serious. I should have never left you that night. I was an idiot. I was angry and I didn't handle things well," Marcus said as he moved towards her. "Is there a chance we could start again?"

"I don't know about that. I'm still all the things I was when you first met me, nothing has *really* changed."

"Hasn't it though?" He stepped closer. "You quit working for your father. That's not nothing. And these boxes…you're planning on moving to free yourself of any bad memories, but what if we were to make new ones—better ones?" Marcus pulled Evin to his chest. "I was a fool."

"I told you when we met I was a bitch but that it was just the façade and that's the truth. I have a heart and I can't bear for you to make me feel something more than I already do and then have you leave me again. I'm done with people leaving me."

"You've become a part of my soul, Evin." Marcus kissed her once, gently on the neck. "I have no intention of ever going anywhere again––at least not without you."

Their eyes met and words seemed irrelevant. Marcus kissed her slow and deep, savoring her sensual lips. The first time they'd kissed he was mad with a desire to have all of her but they had somewhere to be and too many obstacles before them. This time they had nowhere to go and nothing holding them back. This time he could take his time exploring every inch of her. When he was done, she would know exactly how he felt about her.

Evin pulled away from him. "But you're with Christine…we can't do this."

Marcus grinned. "Yes we can. I'm not with Christine, never was. She and I are just friends."

Evin furrowed her brows.

"Christine has a girlfriend for one, and two, she knew from the moment you walked away that night that my heart was with you."

"Wait, what? She has a girlfriend?"

"She does."

"I had no idea. Guess I'm off my game."

"She said she likes keeping her private life private, that her social life is about her work and not about who she is dating."

"So then what was with all the events and you two being seen together?"

"We're working on a project that will bring robotics into the children's hospitals. That *friend* she wanted me to meet offered me a job about fifteen minutes after he met me. Said I was perfect for the position and that he'd finally found the missing piece to his puzzle."

"Are you kidding me?"

"No. It was part of why I came looking for you that night. I wanted to tell you there was no need to go forward with locking in an interview with Donahue. I had just landed a six figure job without anything but my own skill set." Marcus grinned. "I've got a job, baby, a good one and you don't have work for anything again. I'm going to take care of us both."

"You can't," Evin interrupted.

He waggled his brows. "But I can."

She rolled her eyes at him. One minute a headstrong man going after what he wanted and the next his normal goofy self.

"I meant because of your father."

"Yeah, I now know the truth about that too. There was a second letter that came to my apartment about a week after I told the estate attorney about the job I landed. It explained everything."

"And?"

"My father was the reason Victor was able to be so successful in business. You of course played a part, but my father came first. Apparently, Victor was doing insider trading with Donahue and embezzling money from some very important people. They found out and in order to save his ass, he made a deal with my father—problems solved in exchange for a future favor. Victor agreed but secretly kept working on back door deals. I think that is where you came in. You, it seems, were his greatest secret."

"Yeah and the greatest lie."

"In my father's will, he told Victor to make me as successful as he was but with one exception, I was to be happy doing whatever I was doing and not bound to some convention of success. He wanted to make sure I had it all. A great job and a woman to fall in love with—have a family with. According to the note attached, my father made a promise to my mother on her deathbed to see me for who I was and not who he wanted me to be, that I was more like her and she wanted her legacy to continue on with me. He followed through with his promise because he loved her more than anything in this world."

"How did Victor react to you knowing the truth then?"

"He doesn't know I know about his connection to my father." Marcus grinned. "I lied. Told him exactly what he wanted to hear and he fell for it hook, line, and sinker."

Evin laughed. "Well played. So you have your job and your success, now what?"

"Now I bury your father with the truth, free the damsel in distress and live happily ever after."

Evin smacked his arm. "Be serious!"

"I am. Victor and Donahue will both pay for their crimes and I will be the one to make it happen. They will both be publically shamed and brought to their knees. In fact, it's already in motion—the beginning stages at least."

"And the damsel in distress?" Evin said sarcastically.

"You're in distress, right?"

Marcus didn't give her a chance to respond, instead he threw her over his shoulder and headed towards the bed.

"Put me down. You are being ridiculous."

"Nope. Can't until you tell me how you feel about me."

"Put me down and I'll tell you," she said as she smacked him on the butt. "Or better yet, I'll show you."

With that, he flipped her onto the bed and stared down at her. "God, you're beautiful."

Evin smiled as she sat up on her elbows. "Flattery will get you everywhere."

Marcus pulled his t-shirt over his head and climbed onto the bed, covering her body with his.

Evin was wearing a half top and her favorite yoga pants, the most comfortable thing she owned, but at this moment all she wanted was to feel Marcus' skin on hers. She didn't want there to be anything between them to block their connection. He must have read her thoughts because as his hands roamed over her body, Marcus stripped her out of both, leaving nothing but her matching lingerie set.

Marcus growled low. "I always wondered what you wore under that outfit."

"Did you now?"

"Oh yeah. School boy fantasy all the way, except now I'm a grown man with a way better imagination."

Evin laughed. "You're so crazy."

"Maybe, but I stand here before you with nothing but my truth. So what's yours, Evin?"

"Marcus, how can this work? We're so different from one another."

"Do you always have to over analyze a situation?" he teased. "Evin, I'm fairly certain I was willing to do anything for you the moment we met."

"What are you talking about? You fought me tooth and nail on everything and I was a total bitch to you."

"Yes, you were, but as that day went on I got to see the real you and that's when I knew you were more than who you pretended to be. That was the woman I wanted—that is who you really are," Marcus said as he hovered above her. "No excuses now. I'm not part of your job anymore, where does this leave us?"

Evin put her hands on his face and pulled him to her, kissing him gently. "It leaves us together, trying to figure things out one day at a time. I've missed you, and I can't imagine a future that doesn't include you in it."

Marcus grinned.

The End

Brynn Myers is an urban fantasy/paranormal romance author. After considering writing a hobby for years, she finally turned her passion and talent into a career. She came into the paranormal genre later than most but has always loved fairy-tales and all things magical. Using that love, she creates charmed worlds by writing stories involving passionate, strong willed characters with something to discover. Brynn lives with her family in the Brevard County, Florida area. To learn more, visit: http://www.BrynnMyers.com

RELL
A Modern Cinderella Story

by Amy Daws

⁘

**Dedicated to all the little girls out there
dreaming of their own happily ever after.
True love is wonderful.
But self-love is magical.**

⁘

Prologue

This was the fifth time I had seen the glowing woman in my dreams.

The first time she appeared, she handed me a huge mason jar of water with sunflower seeds floating in it. She chuckled when I pulled a face from the salty taste. Her eyes crinkled in a way that made you know she laughed a lot.

Another dream, we were flying. She carried me like a baby up to the top of the Rocky Mountains and laid me out in the sun. She nodded in a way that told me exactly what I was supposed to do.

This time, she simply stood beside me and handed me all of my sewing supplies. Every thread. Every needle. I couldn't see what I was sewing. The brights were too bright, the darks too dark. The contrast was so intense; I felt a twitching in my eyes. But it wasn't annoying. It was…enchanting.

The one image that was always clear was her familiar face, even though I didn't know who she was. Her cheeks were round and freckled with rosy circles. She had a tendency to constantly coif her short, bright white hair that had these perfectly sculpted curls like she'd just removed her curlers. Her lips were thin and angled downward, as if she was always trying to conceal a grin.

There was a warmth that emanated from her every cell. When I saw her in my dreams I felt immediately comforted. And happy. That was what she glowed with. Pure, unadulterated happiness all the way down to the dimple on her chin.

She looked at me like I was something special. To have someone look at me in anything other than disdain was a foreign concept for me.

1

Every time I awoke from a dream with her, I would be smiling. But as were most things in my life, happiness was temporary. Soon…the tide came in. And the crippling reality engulfed me again. Like a toddler crashing after a sugar high.

And the strangest thing of all…I missed her.

I missed the glowing woman…and we had never even met.

The real pain about the whole thing, the part that upset me the most, the part that made the hot tears come at night…was that I loved her. I didn't love anyone. Love wasn't an emotion that came in my sewing kit. Love just left you exposed to pain.

It was fragile.

Like glass.

<hr />

Blood dripped from my finger as I squeezed my throbbing digit between my thumb and middle finger. *Broke the skin.* I popped my index finger into my mouth and sucked the warm liquid. *Curses. Now I'll have to stop.*

I stood up from my sewing machine and walked over to the small rusty sink in my room. The pipes squealed in protest as I rinsed my hand beneath the cold water. My skin flamed red as blood seeped down the basin.

"I better get a bandage on this. MD will be none too happy if I get blood on her organza silk, Van Halen." MD was short for Mother Dearest: My lovely Stepmother. MD would stroke out if I got any blood on this fabric.

I grabbed a bandage out from the medicine cabinet and Van Halen watched my every move, slowly twitching his white nose curiously. A clear tell of judgment. That judgment was my only company most days so I wasn't complaining.

"It was a tricky stitch!" I argued, tossing the wrappers into the bin.

He licked himself and slid his paw down the white stripe of fur that streaked down the middle of his otherwise completely black face. He was clearly unimpressed by my excuse.

"You think I can do better?"

He cocked his head to one side, his eyes slanted further.

"You're right. You're always right. I can handle a blindhem stitch. I just need to get my game face on right meow!" I giggled and Van Halen starred at me, clearly missing my joke.

"Get it?" I paused. "Right meeooow?" I laughed again. Damn, I was funny. Or dehydrated. Probably both. But definitely funny. "Stop kitten around right meow, Van Halen! Cat is ridiculous!" I erupted into full on hysterics.

His nose twitched with boredom as he stood and stretched, dragging his claws across the scuffed wooden floor. He padded over to me, slid between my legs and flipped onto his back batting his paws up towards me. I bent over and picked him up with my non-bloody hand.

"If you need attention, you better go back downstairs. MD is probably jamming out to your namesake as we speak." I walked him over to the door and he mewed in protest. "Sorry, Van. I'm injured and on a huge deadline."

I opened my door and dropped him gently on the landing, relishing in the blast of A/C that snuck through the open door. My vision blurred suddenly, and I sucked in a big gulp of cool air. I was definitely overheated. Wiping the sweat from my brow, I shut the door and leaned back against it. It was nearly a hundred degrees in my small attic bedroom today.

The sun shone harshly through the open French doors that led out to a small, attached terrace. There was zero breeze coming in today. My bedroom was nothing but a glorified sweatshop in the summers. The rest of the four-story house was an arctic chamber of purified air conditioning. Air conditioning that I was not privy to. If I didn't love sewing so much, it would be utter hell up here every day.

I was currently working on an evening gown for MD. I made all of my stepmother's clothing, along with her two precious daughters, aka the Silicone Sisters.

In less than a minute, I peeled off my cotton dress and slipped on my favorite bikini. Even I had outdone myself with this little number. The bottoms were a diamond blue and revealed more of my butt cheek than was appropriate around small children. The top blended into a more royal blue and was a traditional triangle bikini fit with a fringe that hung down from the seams. Each tasseled strip of lyrca was embroidered with an intricate black stitching that took forever to apply. It was couture and it was one of a collection of swimwear that I had recently finished. MD hadn't gotten her grubby paws on any of these yet. If she had, they would be claimed for one of the Silicone Sisters faster than you could say *Hilary Duff*.

But it wasn't just the design that made this swimsuit a showstopper. It was the fit. Specifically, the special internal lining that I had created for the bust. About three years ago, I had this incredible foam material that form-fitted to you. The way I added it into my suit made you feel like you were wearing a perfect wonder bra that was customized just for you.

As a child, I was always making my own clothes. When I finally got the hang of sewing, I started designing swimwear—because swimming was one of my favorite hobbies. I made them all in the middle of the night to hide them from MD. Now I had twenty-four couture swim pieces hanging in my closet all with my unique interior mechanism.

Shaking off the nostalgia, I pulled out my topknot and checked myself in the mirror. My deep blue eyes popped against my long, straw-blonde hair and tan skin. Summers on our large country estate were bliss for sun-worshipers like me.

I stepped out onto the terrace and peered over the railing to make sure the coast was clear. When all was quiet, I threw my leg over and shimmied my nearly bare butt down the ivy-covered lattice. I dropped softly onto my bare feet, smiled, and then hauled tail around the house and into the open meadow towards the woods…

…where my sanctuary awaited.

Running barefoot was a skill I had mastered as a little girl. My father and I would go swimming in the spring fed falls nestled on our property. He always encouraged me to walk in the woods barefoot to toughen up my soles because the rocks in the water were extremely sharp.

"Not needing shoes means nothing can slow you down, Rell," he'd say.

He had an uncanny way of making grand statements about nothing. I never understood most of what he said. Now I would give anything to have that time with him again so I could ask those questions that still consumed me.

Time was a nasty thing. You never knew you needed more until it was too late. Now, the most profound memory I had of my father was his laugh. He would laugh so hard that he wouldn't make a sound. You couldn't even tell if he was smiling or laughing until that moment he would gasp for air. It was infectious. Whenever he laughed like that, my eyes would well with tears. It was an instinctual response to the sublime happiness that he radiated with that soundless laugh.

It was magical.

When he'd see my happy tears, he'd cup his large, calloused hands around my child-sized face and compose himself enough to rub the pads of his thumbs under my eyes.

"Rell, these tears are signs of your goodness seeping out to show the world," he'd whisper.

Again, a grand statement that I wished I would have asked more about. At fourteen when he died, I was just too immature to know how valuable those conversations would be to me as a twenty-year-old.

As I broke through the tree line and headed straight for the rocky cliff, I didn't slow down a single step. I knew these falls like the tips of my needle-pricked fingers. Without looking, I flung myself off the edge, screaming with ecstasy the entire thirty-foot precipice. With an expert dive, I plunged into the cool water. My achy limbs were instantly invigorated. I smiled beneath the surface, relishing in the sense of weightless freedom that water had always made me feel.

"That was some dive," a voice said as I emerged, gasping for air.

My bright smile instantly dropped. I screamed, swirling around to see who was there. Treading water only three feet from me, I locked wide eyes with a stranger who stared at me like he'd just seen a ghost.

"This is private property!" I cried, still attempting to catch my breath after my half-mile sprint.

I flicked my feet rapidly and swam towards the huge waterfall just ten feet away. Darting through the thundering stream, I pushed my hair back and looked over my shoulder to see if the handsome stranger was following me. His dark head was bobbing around, clearly uncertain what to do next.

"I'm aware," he shouted through the falls.

I reached the rocky plateau just as he broke through the heavy stream, wiping the water from his face. I heaved myself up out of the water and onto the jagged terrain.

"You're lucky you didn't dive ten feet to the left, you know. You could have killed yourself!"

I rolled my eyes and turned to face him as he treaded water. "Please. No one knows these falls better than I do." I paused as his eyes drifted slowly up my body. "Excuse you!" I cried, my jaw dropping at his nerve. For God's sake, he could at least attempt to show some common decency.

He chuckled shamelessly. "I'm sorry! Truly. That's just…quite the suit." He shook his head and in four powerful strokes, he gripped the ledge below me.

A surge of pride shot through me at his compliment of my design, but I knew that was seriously beside the point right now. "You really should get off of my…"

My words were lost to the falls as he pushed himself up out of the water and stood before me. My earlier indignation completely evaporated as I watched water drizzle down his rippled abs. His body was toned in a way that made you believe in magic. *Damn, do I believe in magic.* His biceps flexed as he raised his hands and combed through his jet-black hair that hung wet and wavy down his neck.

He had heartbreaker written all over him.

I closed my slack jaw and crossed my arms over my chest. "Who are you?" I asked finally, trying to ignore the way my body was reacting to this attractive stranger. *I'd never responded to anyone like this before.*

"My friends call me Prince," he replied with a lazy grin.

I laughed and glanced down, noticing how dangerously low his plaid board shorts hung. I connected eyes with him again and he squinted knowingly.

"Like the pop singer?" I asked with a smirk while noticing that his green eyes had a mesmerizing brownish hue around the pupil.

He arched one brow. "Like the last name."

I paused, racking my brain for why that name was so familiar. "So am I supposed to call you Prince? We're not exactly friends."

He smiled devilishly. "Give it a chance maybe." His eyes fluttered down to my chest again. I glanced down to try to see objectively what had grabbed his attention so much. My cleavage looked plump, just the way I designed it to, so I guess I couldn't blame the guy.

"You picked the wrong chick to flirt with. Princes don't do it for me I'm afraid."

I propped my hands on my hips trying to feign confidence when in reality, this guy was making me nervous as hell. But it was the good kind of nervous. The kind of nervous that made you feel alive. He laughed heartily, and I couldn't help but grin.

A bead of water dripped from his hairline all the way to his plump lips. His tongue slipped out, licking the moisture from his mouth and I swear I felt myself swoon. *Damn his charming boy-next-door qualities.*

"I'm very intrigued to hear what does do it for you," he said taking a step closer to me. He tilted his head down to catch my eyes that had drifted down to his abs again.

I swallowed slowly. "If you're talking romance…nothing. If you're talking something else." I stopped talking and bit my lip, delicately twisting my wet strands around my bandaged finger. If this guy was only after getting lucky, he would have better luck with the Silicone Sisters. But damn if I didn't fantasize of a situation just like this. *Maybe even dreamt it.*

He smiled and stepped toward me as I attempted to shake the déjàvu sensation fluttering inside my head. His eyes twinkled with mirth.

"Maybe we could start with your name," he inquired, his voice husky.

That playful smile of his was wreaking havoc on my insides. "You can call me Rell," I answered. A slice of pain pierced into my chest in that exact moment. My father was the only one that ever called me Rell. I have no clue why I just gave him that name. No one has called me that name since he died.

"Rell," Prince said, grabbing my hand. "What did you do to your finger here?" He stroked his fingers over mine, and a fission of electricity shot straight to my heart, erasing any flicker of sadness of familial memories.

"Tricky stitch," I said simply.

I glanced down at our entwined hands and a bright light glowed around them. I looked up at him curiously. He didn't appear to be noticing what I saw. But he did appear to be feeling something.

"Like sewing?" he asked, clearing his throat. "What do you make?"

"Everything." I pulled my hand from his and walked further into the cave beneath the falls. I needed a bit of space from this instant attraction between us or I would surely make a fool of myself.

My eyes squinted at the onslaught of moisture in the air over here. I loved this particular spot. It was the deepest part of the cave and dark, aside from the bouncing light that reflected from the shimmering water. The falling stream hit so hard here that a foggy mist filled the entire cavern.

My father used to take me here as a child and tell me to tell the mist my hopes and dreams.

"Your words will cling to the droplets of water floating in here, and swirl down into the stream to brew until the time has come."

"What time father?" I would ask.

"The time when magic becomes reality, Rell."

He was such a dreamer. I hadn't told these falls my hopes and dreams since he died. Now…I only came here to tell the mist my sorrows. Often times, I'd sit down here and not be able to tell where the mist started and the tears ended.

I closed my eyes and relished in the sensation of the water dampening my eyelids. I sensed Prince before I felt him. His shoulder brushed mine and despite myself, I peeped one eye open. He was standing next to me, eyes shut tight, allowing the falls to spray him just like I had. Damn he was handsome. His deep set eyes were dramatically lined with dark eyelashes. For a brief second I let myself dream about what it would be like to fall in love with someone like him. Then my heart heaved with angst at the sense of vulnerability that little fantasy shot through me. Like ripping stitches on an open wound: Extremely exposing and horribly painful.

Suddenly, one of his eyes peeked open, busting me staring at him. I awkwardly looked away and we both erupted into giggles. My earlier anxiety was quickly forgotten as I let the giggle turn into a full on belly laugh.

"You have a great laugh," he said, grinning ear to ear, his eyes twinkling. "You don't make a sound until you breathe. I've never heard anyone laugh like that."

He grinned at me in a dopey way that made it impossible to spoil the magical moment around us. The instant comfort I felt with Prince was odd. But I'd be lying if I didn't say that I appreciated the company of a friendly human as opposed to a judgy feline.

"So is that your thing then, Rell?" he asked, turning towards me and running his finger through the fringe on my suit. "Fashion?"

I swatted his hand away. "Excuse your hand, mister!" I exclaimed, grinning and sitting down to hang my legs into the clear bubbling water. He was quite bold, but it wasn't alarming.

"You were the one staring, Princess!" He chuckled good-naturedly while sliding down next to me.

I bit my lip to stop myself from encouraging this line of thought. I quite liked his nickname for me, but I seriously needed to cool off this chemistry. I hardly knew this guy!

"As a matter of fact, yes...fashion is my thing. This is my own design."

"Wow, you should be proud," he replied, nudging me.

A flitter of excitement shot through me both from his words and because our thighs touched. I couldn't help but marvel at how we'd just met, but touching him felt so incredibly *good*.

"Have you made any other suits?" he asked curiously.

I squinted and looked up into the falls like I was thinking, even though I knew every single swimsuit like it was a child I gave birth to. "Like...twenty-four."

"Holy cow! More than a hobby then! Do they all look like this one?" he asked, his eyebrows rose as his gaze dropped to my torso.

I bit my lip, suddenly shy. "Not just like this. But they are pretty cool. They are my babies." I shrugged my shoulders.

"Have you ever shown them?" he asked, lifting one leg out of the water so he could face me.

I mirrored his position. "What do you mean?" I asked.

"Like sold them in a store? Exhibited them in a fashion show?"

I laughed. "No...definitely not."

"Rell, if this one is any indication, you definitely should! You're obviously really talented." His eyes were wide and excited.

"What are you, some kind of fashion expert?"

"Hardly." He chuckled. "I'm pretty much married into the family business. Which is a lot less exciting. And a lot more frustrating."

"How so?"

He paused and contemplated silently for a moment. "I guess you could say my father expects me to be living what we're selling...and at only twenty-two years old, that's just...hard."

"I'm so not following," I replied, giggling at his serious expression.

He looked at me slyly out of the corner of his eye. "It's just my dad. He's lonely, I think, so he obsesses about me and my future."

A flicker of sadness cast over me as I wondered if MD has ever truly worried about me. "That doesn't sound too awful. What does your mother say?"

The sudden seriousness in his eyes made me nervous. "My mother is no longer with us. For many years now."

His expression was calm and collected. I could tell this was something he had lived with to be so composed about it. His eyes fell down to gaze at our hands nearly touching on the rock.

His voice was quiet. "So now my father has dedicated his life to helping me find my happiness."

"Why doesn't he just find love again for himself? That might take the spotlight off you," I offered helpfully.

He shifted on the ledge, kicking his feet back in the water. "He said that he had the great love of his life and you can never replace great love." Pursing his lips, he wiped the mist from his face, looking sadly up into the falls. "I have to agree with him there. My mother was pretty wonderful."

My heart lurched at the devotion behind his words. Beads of mist clung to his long lashes as orbs of reflected water danced on his face. He turned, smiling softly. Then, he reached up and stroked his thumb down my cheek. The tender caress was more than I'd felt from anyone in many years. My eyes shimmered with mist or tears...I couldn't tell.

He cleared his throat and let out a breath. "Have you been in love, Rell? A great love I mean?" His eyes were wide as he gauged my reaction.

I nervously looked away. I couldn't meet his gaze, but I could feel his eyes boring into me. The intensity behind his question was palpable. And the stinging in my eyes meant that I could no longer hide behind the mist.

"Can I be in love with my swimwear?" I smiled, and pulled my legs up to my chest.

"I think that's called passion." He eyed me sternly. "But seeing passion in someone is still pretty incredible."

His eyes were dancing on every tiny feature of my face, lingering on my lips. My breath hitched as his expression morphed. He looked at me like I was something special. Important even.

Leaning in I whispered, "But passion sure doesn't get you very far."

He scowled. "Passion is everything. Passion is what enables you to turn nothing into something. You just need the stepping point. You should go to that fashion party tomorrow night. Surely you've heard of it. Your designs would put the other designers to shame!"

I huffed out a self-deprecating laugh. "First of all, you've only seen one of my pieces! Second of all, you don't even know me. I'm a nobody from nowhere..."

"You're definitely not a nobody," he said seriously.

I rolled my eyes. "Not to mention, it's an invite only party, Prin—"

In that moment it all clicked. The déjàvu. The familiarity. The name, *Prince*. This was Bryson Prince. The son of Frederick Prince, the billionaire mogul and founder of princesbewed.com, a website dating platform! Their mansion was only ten miles north of our country home.

I stood quickly, backing away from him. You're...you're...Bryson Prince, aren't you?" I accused.

He shot to his feet, his body tense. "Yes. But Rell...I don't see why that—"

"You're a damn billionaire!" I interrupted. "What are you even doing here? Why would you need to trespass on someone's property?"

His face fell. "This is my family's property."

"No, it's not! This is my fath...I mean, my stepmother's property." Pain. Pain again. I hated that my father's things all belonged to MD.

"Wait, you're not Eva Taylor's daughter are you?"

"Stepdaughter! This property belongs to her. Us!"

He shook his head. "Not since last year."

I froze as his words settled over me. Surely my stepmother wouldn't have sold our land without telling me. Who was I kidding? That was completely something MD would do. I momentarily cursed my father for the umpteenth time for not having a will in place before he died six years ago. At such a young age I had no legal rights to any of his estate. Now, I still was nowhere near financially stable enough to purchase the property...let alone move out.

But it wasn't just the money that prevented me from leaving MD and her controlling ways behind. It was leaving what very little was left of my father's life. His legacy. His memories. Now I was losing the one place that was completely ours. These falls were special. I could feel myself beginning to implode.

"I have to go," I croaked and moved past Prince.

"Rell," he said, gently grabbing my wrist.

He stared at me with a look that could wreck me. *Pity.* Our bubble of attraction, connection, whatever it was had been good and popped now. I bit my lip to hold back the tears. The falls roared all around us, while the mist shimmered on his face.

"Please stop." I shook my head. "You've completely broken my heart…and we've only just met."

"How?" he cried, ducking his head to meet my downcast eyes.

"This land. These falls. They were all I had left of him. And now…" I pursed my lips to stop my chin from wobbling. "I've reached my quota on heartbreak, Prince. You have to let me go."

"I just found you!" He tipped my chin up so my blue eyes met his green. My gaze flashed between his worried eyes. They were begging me for something. Whatever it was, I didn't have it in me to give.

"Rell, please," he croaked. "I don't want you to run away from this."

What was he talking about? I was running away from nothing. Because nothing in this life was ever really mine. This entire situation just reinstated how very little I was worth.

"There is nothing to stay for," I muttered.

"Listen," he said urgently. "This land. These falls…they are open to you whenever you want. That is my promise to you."

I huffed and smiled sadly up at him. "Promises are as fragile as hearts. They're all bound to break. They may as well be made of glass."

***

That night, I threw myself into an extravagant swimsuit wrap that I had been working on for a while now. For me, swimwear was the one thing that still connected me to a time in my life when I was genuinely happy. Genuinely loved. The days I spent with my father at the falls were the happiest of my life. And the falls were the only place that my father ever told me anything about my mother.

"Only into the mist will we share these stories," he'd say.

My mother died when I was born, but the tales of their time together sounded magical. Recalling what Frederick Prince said about how you can never replace great love made me wonder how my father ever decided to remarry with Mother Dearest. It was my fourteenth birthday when MD and the Silicon Siblings moved in. My father died a week later.

After running from Prince at the falls, I didn't dare sleep a wink. My dreams were traitorous bastards when I was emotional. With my luck, Prince would show up in my dreams, or even worse…the glowing woman. I wasn't in the mood to be cheered up.

"Cinderella!" screeched one of the Silicone Sisters. I glanced to the video conferencing system by my door and Winter's round face filled the eight-inch screen. Her voice was hard to handle. She always sounded stuffed up due to a botched nose job she had when she was sixteen. "There's someone at the gate. Answer it!" she demanded. The screen went black.

"Well, Van Halen…because she asked so nicely." I stood up and Van Halen dropped to the floor with a growl.

I smoothed back my blonde hair and made my way down the three flights to the grand entrance. Our home wasn't a mansion like the Princes', but it was big enough to keep me busy as hell with MD's endless list of chores.

I buzzed in a teenage messenger through our security gate. I stepped outside as he approached holding an intricately carved wooden box. He handed it over and turned to leave without a word.

"Who's this from?" I called.

He shrugged and hopped back on his moped. On top of the box was a small square envelope with *Rell* inscribed on it.

"Cinderella!" Winter bellowed from inside. "Who is it?"

I quickly stashed the envelope in my shorts pocket and made my way to the sitting room. MD was standing next to a double wingback chair with a teacup pinched between her slender fingers. She was wearing a black and cream paisley dress that I had made just last week. Her presence alone made many flinch. She was extraordinarily tall and her face was long and angular. Her hair had started graying after my father's death and was always worn in a viciously tight bun at the nape of her neck.

Summer, my eldest stepsister, suddenly stepped in front of me in all her frizzy red-haired glory. "For pity's-sake, Cinderella! You sure are living up to your name right now! Look at your face!" she pealed in an annoyed tone.

I glanced at the mirror on the wall and noticed several smudges of soot on my cheeks. After I finished working on my wrap last night, I decided two in the morning was a great time to clean the five fireplaces in our house.

Rolling her eyes she snatched the box out of my hands. She scurried over to MD to inspect the contents. Summer was the spitting image of MD. Her long red hair was the only thing that really set them apart. Winter joined them to see what all the fuss was about. She was shorter and heavier with a short brown bob to match. Her face was mildly pretty, but the majority of it was medically purchased.

The three huddled around the box in a fury of excitement. As they cracked it open, several bubbles floated out of it.

"I knew it! I just knew them living so close would pay off eventually!" Winter squealed.

"Getting this invitation is our ticket in!" Summer mimicked Winter's excited tone. "Can you imagine? Landing Prince!"

"You will and you shall!" MD fawned. "Cinderella!" she barked as I attempted to sneak out. "How is the cream organza gown coming?"

"Very well, Stepmother," I replied. If this box was from Prince, I was dying to know what was inside my envelope.

"Good." MD set the box down and strolled toward me. "We have an event to attend tonight."

"What's the event?" I asked.

She held up her finger and waltzed over to the video screen beside me. "Down, Halen." She shooed him off the tall end table and pressed the video screen above it. Lupe, our chef and house manager's face illuminated the screen. "Lupe, we need hair and makeup for the girls this afternoon. I don't care if Eduardo is booked. Make. It. Happen." She turned back to me and arched a perfectly plucked brow. "We have the Princes' Fashion Mixer tonight."

"A mixer!" squealed Summer clapping her hands together and jumping up and down. Her tall, boney frame crashed into Winter and the two began shoving each other and shouting obscenities.

"Girls!" MD roared and they both stopped instantly. "Neither of you will get your chance with Bryson Prince if you show up fighting!"

"What do you mean?" I asked, clearly speaking out of turn as all three of them hit me with a murderous glare.

Winter came waddling towards me to join her mother. "Bryson Prince! The most eligible bachelor in Colorado. His father is throwing a mixer for him and to promote their new dating app that just launched. The party theme is high fashion! And best of all, we have a chance to date Bryson Prince!"

"But of course you wouldn't know who that is," Summer crooned, linking arms with her sister. "You'd have to be…someone."

Summer and Winter doubled over on top of each other in a fit of cackles. I rolled my eyes and then flinched as MD's eyes slanted at me.

"Enough girls!" she said, wrapping them in a stiff embrace. "Cinderella, you're going to need to alter the organza for Winter now. *My precious cobbler tart.*"

I pursed my lips as Winter giggled with pleasure at her mother's term of endearment. Winter was a good four sizes bigger than MD. This would not be easy.

"And I need a new original!" whined Summer. "This is a fashion party. I can't be in something old."

"I was getting to that *pudding blossom.*" MD smiled tightly and stroked her hand down Summer's red hair. "And of course, I'll need something new as well now that *Precious* is wearing my gown."

A sickness settled in the pit of my stomach. It was barely eight am and I already saw all three meals pulled from my belly. It would take a miracle to finish all of this in a week, let alone one day. I sighed heavily and turned to leave.

"Cinderella!" MD called out before I reached the steps. "You complete all of your tasks on time…and you may endeavor to attend. Your name was on the invitation, after all."

"But mother!" the Silicone Sisters cried in unison.

She arched a single brow at them. "She needs inspiration to work for, my dears." They instantly calmed and smiled meanly at me.

The elusive carrot.

He and I were good friends by now.

***

The prospect of attending a real live fashion show excited the hell out of me. This was what I did. This was my passion. To watch a show of this magnitude would be the experience of a lifetime! But the idea of seeing Prince again twisted my stomach into a thousand knots. A mixer? Was he really that focused on meeting someone?

I stepped into my room with Van Halen close on my heels. My hands shook as I ripped open the envelope. Inside was a micro SD card and a post-it note that said *PLAY ME*.

I popped it into the videoconference LCD screen and an image of Prince came up. I hesitantly clicked play.

"Hi, Rell. I know doing this on a video might seem strange, but I needed you to be able to see my face when I told this to you."

He paused and swallowed nervously. I couldn't help but smile at his obvious sense of discomfort. Damn, he was still hot. I had wondered if I imagined all of that yesterday. But here he was, wearing a fitted black t-shirt and his green eyes radiated straight into my heart.

"Look, I'm sorry about yesterday. You can't understand how much I wish I could go back and say things differently. I could care less about the land. So, I want to make it up to you. Tonight, there are three fashion shows scheduled to début their new lines at the party. You are the fourth."

"Now, Princess." He flashed a cocky smirk. *"Before you roll your eyes and shut this video down, please know that I had to pull about a million different strings to get this put together. It's already done so if you don't accept my offer, there will be twelve un-paid models and a fashion team furious with me for being booked for nothing."*

"All we need are twelve of your swimsuits. You said you had twenty-four…this shouldn't be an issue. You deserve a shot, Princess. No one even has to know they are yours if you don't want. All you have to do is get them here. Show up at 10:00, your models hit the runway at 11. Please.

"And Rell," he paused, looking down and knitting his eyebrows together. *"The only woman I will even care about seeing at that mixer tonight…is you."*

My heart thundered beneath my chest as the video went black. What did that last line mean? He had feelings for me? Impossible. We'd just met. Sure, there was some kind of…*something* between us. But it was nothing. It couldn't be.

And he didn't just want me to attend the party tonight! He wanted me to show my swimwear! Surely you can't just put on a fashion show without any prep work. It must have cost him a fortune to get this organized on such short notice.

I stood and walked over to my closet, pushing past the dresses to where I hung my swimwear.

A quiet voice in the back of my head said, *"Over half of them hadn't even been worn yet. They could form fit to the models perfectly. Tonight could be our chance!"* If MD and the Silicone Sisters were going to be there, then no one could know they were mine.

I sliced my hands through my hair as Van Halen snaked between my legs. "It'll take a miracle to get all my work done by tonight." I turned, eyeing the cream organza gown. "I guess if I'm going to go down, I'm going to go down swinging."

"Holy *Drew Barrymore*, I did it Van Halen!"

Van Halen mewed, his judgmental scowl perfectly in place. A satisfied smirk spread across my face as I appreciated my ensemble in the floor-length mirror. I was wearing a long, silver wrap dress. It was technically a swimwear design, but the off-the-shoulder straps had a formal feel about them. The bodice wrapped around my waist and clustered at my hip where a large, statement bow rested. There was a slit up to the top of my right thigh that gave the dress an elegant sex appeal that made it so much more than a cover-up.

My plan was to head to the party with MD and the Silicone Sisters, then rush back and grab my swimsuits when they were busy with the mixer. It was ten miles from our home, but I would hitchhike back if I had to. I hadn't been this keyed up for an evening in years.

I smoothed back my soft blonde curls and hurried down to find Summer and Winter primping in the foyer. Winter was in the cream organza gown that I had to let out. I ended up adding a sequenced tuxedo stripe down each side to make it big enough. It turned out pretty cool in the end. The alterations complimented her full figure perfectly. Summer was wearing an emerald satin gown, because I knew green looked great with red hair. Both of them looked hot, despite their scowling faces glaring up at me right now.

"What. Are. You. Wearing?" Summer growled through clenched teeth as I descended the final step. Her red hair was pulled back in a severe French twist that displayed the angry veins bulging on her neck.

"A dress. A cover-up sort of. But I think it works," I replied smoothing it down.

She marched toward me with Winter hot on her heels. Winter's brown ringlets bounced with each step. The two circled around me snatching the skirt into their hands and dropping it aggressively.

"This dress is awful," Winter sneered. Her face was screwed up in repulsion. "This is by far one of the worst things I have ever seen you design. Thank God you didn't try to give this to me."

Summer nodded adamantly and gestured to her own gown. "Although my gown tonight is a close second. It is so unoriginal, Cinderella. And for a fashion party? For pity sake, I'm embarrassed." She accentuated every syllable of the word through her pinched scowl.

"I've told mother that this is the very last time I wear anything of yours. It's all utter crap!"

My jaw dropped with shock. The Silicone Sisters had never been overly complimentary of my designs, but they had never given me feedback like this. "If you hate my work so much, why do you have me make all of your clothes?" I asked feeling like I had just entered the *Twilight Zone*.

"A favor to mother, of course!" Summer laughed meanly. "Are you stupid? Did you really think you actually had a talent for fashion design?" She burst into a hearty laugh, clutching her narrow waist in her boney arms.

"You've never even gone to college, Cinderella!" Winter seethed an inch from my ear.

"You can really be a fool," Summer said snidely into my other.

My neck snapped back and forth as they both circled me again. Their hands flailed wildly as they continued to pick apart every aspect of my dress.

Winter suddenly stopped inches from my face. "You have zero talent, Cinderella. Somebody needs to tell you." A cold detached look filled her features. "But Mother says since both of your parents are dead, we have to show you *pity*."

The mention of my parents felt like icy cold hands gripping and squeezing my heart until tears formed in my eyes. "Don't speak of them." My voice wavered. I bit my lip and unsuccessfully blinked back the tears that were slipping down my cheeks.

Summer's face joined Winter's. "Fortunately, there's really not much to speak of! Your daddy—" Summer stopped midsentence, chortling. "He acted like you were some prize. But—," she was laughing harder now. "It was all an act, Cinderella. Surely you've figured that out by now. He never thought you would amount to anything and he felt sorry for you."

"Why do you think he found our mother?" Winter added. "He needed someone to care about." She glared up at me from her squatty stature. "That's why Mother owns this home. And you don't. Not because there was no living will. The truth is, we were more important to your father than you *and* your mother combined."

I squeezed my eyes shut, willing away the flash images of my father kissing my head every night before bed. He'd give me two kisses. One from him and one from her. *My mother.* I never even knew her, but she was special to me. That memory had escaped me until this very moment.

My eyes stung with an onslaught of more tears, so I opened them. They trailed down my face, fast and furious. Just then, a foggy glow formed around Summer and Winter's faces. My balance began to waver. This wasn't a dream. This was my own living nightmare.

"No one loves you and you have no talent," Summer added and the two erupted into witchy cackles.

"Girls." MD's voice cut through my haze. My head snapped to find her leaning against the doorway. Her stance indicated that she had watched the entire scene. A quiet giggle escaped her breath when she tried to speak. "I told you to never tell Cinderella these things."

"It's been six years mother," Summer whined. "How long are you going to make us put up with her?"

"Enough." She strolled toward me in her scarlet-red chiffon dress. "As I said earlier, you are still very welcome to come tonight, Cinderella. That is…if you won't be too embarrassed by—" Her eyes dropped down to my dress without finishing her sentence.

My chin trembled. All three watched me with complete disdain. I stared back in wonder. Surely a flicker of empathy or feeling would show itself. Something. Anything! If either of them would have looked upon me with even the slightest look of compassion, I could have been saved.

Their faces only glittered with malice.

How had I lived with such hate for six whole years? Even if I had had the strength to stand up to them, I couldn't. They had armed their words as weapons and gave voice to that shred of self-doubt that I had screaming in my head every single day.

I wasn't talented.

I wasn't loved.

I wasn't anything.

I was a twenty-year-old charity case who still lived at home with her non-family because she had no one else in the world that gave two shits about her. How did I let Prince give me hope like he did?

Winter and Summer continued to giggle as tears rained down my cheeks. I swallowed around the painful knot in my throat. The damage was done. This was how pathetic I really was.

"I won't be coming," I uttered and walked shakily toward the front door past MD. "Thank you anyway."

As soon as the night air hit my face, I kicked off my wedges and balled my large skirt up in my hands.

Then…I ran. I ran to the one place that wasn't even mine to run to anymore. But I had no choice. I was being pushed.

⁓⁓⁖⁗⁖⁓⁓

Love was impossible. It was sick and twisted and wrong. Loving people. Loving what you do. Having passion. Anything you ever developed a true attachment to could only wreck you when it finally got around to striking you in the face.

Because everything always did.

I stopped at the top of the cliff, peering down into the falls with pure, undiluted pain. My dress whipped around me in the wind. It was torn and filthy from my sprint through the woods, but I didn't care. None of it mattered anymore. My designs. My dreams. My hopes. What a joke! I was nothing more than a seamstress. The dream of becoming a legitimate designer was all derived from lies. *From pity.*

Did anybody ever love me?

"Whyyyy?" I cried out, launching all the anger, resentment, disgust, and evil that was thrown at me tonight out into the rocky abyss. My lungs ached with my guttural scream as my voice echoed in the distance. "Why would you give me these hopes and dreams with no intention of ever helping me fulfill them? Why would you let me feel so alive for nothing? Nothing!" I cried out again and dropped to my hands and knees, dragging air into my lungs.

My vision blurred as my body was seized with sobs. I dropped to my elbows and cried into my arms like I'd never cried before. Not even when my father died. The loss of my father was a pure and innocent grief. This was a pain I didn't understand. The difference between mourning loss…and mourning hatred.

I wasn't sure how much time had passed before I suddenly felt my back and shoulders turn damp and cold. I looked up to see a huge cloud of mist surrounding me. My tears stalled instantly as I rose to my knees and analyzed the glittering droplets all around me.

The foggy mist swirled, increasing in speed with each lap. The vision before me was other-worldly. Then, the bubbles clustered and shifted into a familiar silhouette. With a huge burst of white light, I closed my eyes at the onslaught of water spraying my face. When I opened them and looked up, you could have knocked me over with a feather.

"Am I dreaming?" I whispered.

She shook her head.

"Am I dying?"

She shook her head again.

"Am I losing my mind?"

"A state-of-mind is fluid, like water, so that question is a bit harder to answer." Her voice sang with a pitch that warmed my heart. It was an older woman's voice with a weak tremble to it.

"Are you real?" I asked, tears forming in my eyes.

"I'm as real as your face is wet." She tilted her head and rubbed the back of her hand across my damp cheek.

It was the glowing woman from my dreams. I could see more than just her face now. She was short and round in a cozy grandmotherly way. Her cheeks were rosy and her mouth turned down in that obscenely happy way it always did. She was dressed in a long, pale blue cloak with a hood that framed her round face and white curly hair.

"What does this mean?" I asked feeling an overwhelming urge to run into her arms and cry.

"It means it's time, Rell," she whispered.

"Time for what?"

She placed her cool hands on both my cheeks. "Time for the dreams to stop and reality to begin."

I cried at her loving touch and she hugged my face into her waist. It was soft and supple, warm and inviting. It felt like a hold that a mother would give a child.

"Who are you?" I cried between sniffles.

"I am your Fairy Godmother, Rell. I have been with you for many years, and I am here because it is time." She giggled dreamily. "I've been listening to your hopes and dreams for many years. And for dreams to float, reality must sink."

My breath escaped me as she reached her hand out to mine and lifted me to my feet. She was a good twelve inches shorter than me.

"Have we met before?" I asked, curious about all of her appearances in my dreams and the feelings of déjàvu I had felt since losing my father.

She chuckled. "Well, it certainly wasn't a glitch in the *Matrix*!" She moved me to the edge of the cliff. "Come now, we don't have much time."

"What are we doing?" I asked nervously as we held hands on the rocky edge.

"We're grabbing your dreams."

Before I could ask another question, she jumped and pulled me down the bluff and into the dark waters. As soon as we were submerged, I felt different. I wasn't worried about time or holding my breath like I normally would have been. Time seemed to stand still. She crooked her finger and motioned for me to follow her. We swam deeper into the water, where the falls crashed to the water's floor. A flurry of bubbles pushed me through to the other side, near the cave.

There, we came upon a glowing light. The closer we swam to it, the brighter it got. Fairy Godmother stopped and urged me forward toward the light. All of a sudden, everything was bright white around me, like I was floating inside a cloud.

The water swirled and I noticed the fabric on my dress glittering at the hem. Pops of color shot off all around me. The colorful vortex spun up and up until I broke through the water's surface with a mighty explosion.

I landed straight onto my bare feet in front of our home. I looked around dazed and confused as to how I got here. But what was even more stunning was my appearance. And how dry I was.

"Remind you of anything?" Fairy Godmother asked, appearing from thin air beside me.

"I've made this dress." I touched my skirt delicately. I was wearing a diamond blue ball gown. The bodice was a strapless, sweetheart corset with navy blue rosettes layered over top of each other. The skirt was a shimmery light-blue organza with a navy overlay. I glanced at my reflection in the house window. The dress was large and simply dreamlike.

"But I only made this dress in my dreams," I said disbelievingly.

Fairy Godmother giggled while coifing her short, white curls.

"How…why?" I asked, touching my own hair as well. My blonde locks were curled and flowing down one side with blue ribbon laced into an intricate braid along my hairline. I'd never worn much makeup before. But in my faint reflection, I could tell it was dramatic and gorgeous. I barely recognized the girl staring back at me.

"Magic becoming reality my dear. I helped you make this gown in your dream." She smiled proudly. "And now your talent transcends the dream realm."

The word talent made my heart sink as my consciousness was flooded with earlier memories. That painful knot in my throat returned.

"Why the sad face, my darling?" She glided up to me as if she didn't walk on feet but on air.

"I don't have talent, Fairy Godmother. I so appreciate this but it's not...it's not any good." I was trying desperately to squelch the heartache of seeing my creation come to fruition. None of it mattered.

"Hush right now." For the first time since seeing her in my dreams, Fairy Godmother wasn't smiling. "Tonight, my dear. Tonight, you will see. You will see what evilness has been trying to hide from you. You go to that party. You show your work. And you will see." She chortled with excitement as a sleek stretch Mercedes pulled up to the house.

"But my—" I started as she shooed me into the backseat.

"Your designs are already there. Everything has been handled. Let your Fairy Godmother get her *fairy* on would you?" She tittered and tucked my dress inside the car door. "One more thing. I know you prefer barefoot...but—"

She circled her hands in front of her and a clear bubble formed. With a small burst of mist, two clear glass slippers appeared in her hands.

"This dress demands heels my dear. Hopefully this is a compromise." She winked dreamily and slipped the smooth glass onto my feet. "Go. Enjoy. Smile. Laugh. Live. Just...reach for that happily ever after. Because you...are *special* my child." A maniacal chuckle bubbled up out of her and her cheeks flashed rosier than usual.

I grinned incredulously. "Thank you, Fairy Godmother." I leaned out of the car and captured her around the waist in a tight hug.

She appeared to be taken off guard, and then relaxed. "It is my distinct pleasure." She stroked her hands down my hair and hummed with appreciation. "Oh! I almost forgot! You must be back by midnight. No exceptions." She pulled me back to lay her serious blue eyes on me. "This magic is a gift, not a guarantee. All you see before you will be as it was when the clock strikes twelve."

This was already more than I'd ever dreamed.

In a flurry of lights, champagne, people, and ball gowns, I found myself at a prime front row seat at the end of a runway. It was five minutes to eleven and when I gave my name at the gate, I was ushered quickly to my seat and told that everything was taken care of. My swimwear line would be waltzing down the runway any minute now and I was vibrating with anticipation.

"You came," a voice whispered into my ear from behind. I attempted to turn.

"No. Please," Prince said, placing his hands on my shoulders. "Don't turnaround. I've been staring at you from across the room for the last ten minutes and I'm afraid that if you actually look me in the eyes, I'll totally lose my nerve."

My eyebrows rose as a million butterflies took flight in my belly. "Your nerve should be well in tact considering all these women are here for you tonight."

He scoffed. "All they saw tonight was my head snapping in every direction looking for you. Kept me waiting long enough, Princess," he added with a playful growl.

I pinched back a smile. "I'm not really here for the mixer, Prince." I felt guilty at that admission, but it was true. Mostly.

He sighed heavily. "I know, Rell." His lips tickled my ear as he leaned in and whispered, "And while I'm incredibly happy for you and what we're about to see, I want to make it clear that I have ulterior motives."

I could feel his eyes on me now but I couldn't bring myself to look at him. My chest rose and fell with deep breaths as my mind dreamed of all the possibilities behind that statement. But too many people's words had power over me tonight. Tonight wasn't about their words.

Tonight was about my own voice.

"Well, suck it up." I grinned. "Tonight isn't about you."

A puff of cool air hit my neck as he let out a pleasant chuckle. He slid into the reserved seat beside me. "You look…beautiful."

I finally looked at his face and his eyes were bright and charming as ever. He was dressed in a fitted, warm-charcoal tuxedo with a black vest and bow tie that matched his dark wavy hair. He was looking every bit the Prince Charming tonight.

His expression morphed from amused to smoldering the longer we gazed at each other. I swallowed. Hard. I couldn't tell what was causing the most ruckus with my nerves: the fashion show that was about to start, or the way Prince looked at me, like if he didn't kiss me he might spontaneously combust.

Turning my gaze back to the runway I exhaled heavily to get a grip on these insanely overwhelming feelings. "I think I might be sick," I croaked.

"Don't. I was just back stage and...Rell." I turned back as his voice shifted. "I had a feeling you were talented but nothing could have prepared me for what I saw."

"Really?" I gasped in shock.

He shook his head in disbelief. "Do you really have no idea how amazing you are?" Our eyes locked again in a heated exchange as his words penetrated through all my fears and anxieties.

Clearing his throat, he added matter-of-factly, "I mean, the models didn't look half as good as you." I rolled my eyes. "Rell—" he started.

Just then the lights dimmed and three spots swerved to the stage.

"And now ladies and gentleman," the MC's voice announced through the sound system. "The surprise final show tonight. Introducing... Princess Pride Swimwear."

My head snapped to Prince and he shrugged his shoulders and grinned salaciously. I turned back to the stage, beaming with pride. This was really happening! A glowing rim of blue lights flashed around the perimeter of the floor-level runway.

"How much are you freaking out right now?" Prince asked, leaning into me as my eyes took in the huge crowd.

There had to be more than a thousand people here tonight. I nervously chewed on my glossy lip and Prince reached over and gripped my tightly fisted hands that were resting on my lap. I relaxed as he laced his fingers through mine. It had a comforting effect that I needed more than anything in this moment.

Suddenly, the music swelled and all eyes were on the draped curtain. The minute the first model stepped out onto the runway and the audience collectively gasped, I had my first out of body experience. I floated above and watched from afar as cameras flashed wildly. The audience was enraptured over each and every model pounding down the runway. The swimsuits fit perfectly, despite varying in shapes and sizes. This was exactly what my interiors were meant for. Whoever styled the models seemed to know my line, inside and out. It was exactly what I would have chosen myself. Large, soft beach curls and barely there makeup with a nude, glossy lip. Each girl commanded the runway with a fierceness that felt as though they were inspired themselves. It was incredible.

All too soon, the show was ending. As the models took their grand finale lap, the audience stood and cheered. *They were standing for my designs!* I stood with them and found myself crying uncontrollably. My shoulders shook as I watched all my pieces captivate an entire mass of people. I turned to Prince and giggled maniacally through my tears, baffled by what just happened. He turned to direct his applause to me, grinning from ear to ear.

The lights dimmed and I covered my cheeks in sheer exhilaration. Prince grabbed my wrists and pulled my hands down, turning me to face him. The blue stage lighting cast a stream of light over his face. I was stunned to see his eyes watery and red around the edges. Happiness, exaltation, empathy, and even honor were showcased all in one meaningful look.

Cupping my cheeks, my breath caught at the look of undiluted pride in his face. He slid his two thumbs softly beneath my eyes and gazed at me the way a man would gaze at the woman he's meant to spend the rest of his life with.

"Rell," he uttered. "I'm terrified that if I can't make you mine, it is *my* heart that will break."

Without a second thought, I cupped his cheeks and pulled his lips down to mine. I slammed my eyes shut tight and willed my body to live in this very moment. Fully and completely. My heart was leading my head and I didn't care how fragile any of it was anymore.

Our lips slid smoothly against each other's, tongues dancing a smooth waltz. He stroked my face reverently, as if he had hold of the most precious gift known to man. The fulfillment I was experiencing with this kiss was more than I had ever felt in my entire life. Simply put, *I felt cherished.*

It wasn't the moment of seeing my designs on stage fueling this passion. It was looking into Prince's eyes and seeing myself clearly for the very first time. Never had I felt such a sense of pride and possibility. Most of all, I felt like the risk of having my heart broken by whatever *this* could be between us was worth it all for *this* moment right here.

"Prince," I said, breaking contact. He pulled away for a second, appeared tormented and then crashed his lips on mine again. "Prince," I said again, giggling.

He pulled back and propped his forehead on mine. Breathing heavily, he said, "Rell, I need you to know—"

"I need to say something first," I interrupted.

His serious expression morphed into a wolfish grin. "By all means, Princess."

I smiled and pulled back so I could look into his eyes. "Thank you." I rubbed my thumbs along his jawline. "Thank you…for believing in me and giving me this gift. Thank you for honoring me this way."

"It's I who should be saying thank you. I've been resisting so many things in my life. But you're the first thing that I don't want to resist, Rell. I was convinced it wasn't the right time for me, no matter what my father wanted. But I was wrong. I just hadn't met you!"

"What are you rambling on about?" I smirked.

His eyes glittered with feeling. "Rell, I—"

The master of ceremonies cut into our conversation. "All right fashion fiends. Midnight is only moments away. Make your way to the north side of the estate for the fireworks display!"

My eyes shot wide. "I have to go!"

"Rell, you can't."

"I have to! I have no choice," I cried and balled up the hem of my dress. I'd have to run. Midnight was here and I wouldn't take advantage of this gift Fairy Godmother gave me.

"Rell, I need to tell you something," Prince said, gripping my waist.

"There's no time!" I yelled and dashed clumsily down the abandoned runway toward the backstage area where I knew the Mercedes awaited. Damn glass slippers! I paused to slip them off mid sprint and lost one behind me in the process. I saw Prince stuck behind a mob of people. He was yelling something at me but I couldn't wait. I would not break a promise to the one woman in my life that had ever cared for me.

Fireworks erupted into the skies as I struggled to catch my breath inside the Mercedes. At the same time, water began dripping from the ceiling of the car. The drip turned into a waterfall and before I knew it, I was floating down the falls in my original torn, grey dress. I hit the water with a mighty splash and gasped for air as I breached the surface.

I guess Fairy Godmother wasn't messing around.

As I made my way downstairs the next morning, I overheard the television blaring from the sitting room. I paused, tucking myself beside the doorway so I could catch a glimpse. Video coverage of the models in my swimwear last night was situated over the shoulder of a male newscaster as he spoke.

"Major national retailers are pressing the Prince Estate to reveal the name of the secret designer behind the swimwear line charmingly dubbed 'Princess Pride Swimwear.' The collection was a surprise addition to last night's show that has everyone reeling. The Prince Family has yet to release a statement. It leads the greater Denver area to wonder…who is this mysterious Princess?"

The video switched to a full screen shot of Prince and I kissing at the show. It was a faraway shot and my face was in the shadows, but there was no doubt of the passionate exchange between the two of us.

"Who is that whore?" Winter screeched.

"Mother!" Summer whined. "I did everything right. I giggled, I touched him. I told him all about every single one of my hobbies. I even told him about my pet toad that died when I was twelve!" She flopped down onto the white sectional sofa and crossed her arms moodily.

"I told you. It doesn't matter," MD crooned, "Cinderella!"

I jumped as she caught me loitering in the doorway. "Yes M…Stepmother?" I replied, walking in to greet her.

She strolled toward me with that intimidating swagger she had. "We'll need styling today. High-end casual. We have a special guest coming over this evening."

"Who would that be?"

"Bryson Prince of course! He was quite taken by our Summer last night. I've invited him over for dinner," she replied.

"Bryson Prince is coming to see Summer? But…that girl in the news," I said, feeling a stab of possessiveness.

"Paalease! Did you see her? She was trash," Winter snorted, flicking through the TV channels while chomping on a huge licorice rope.

"Girls, go get ready!" MD ordered. They both shuffled past me, shooting nasty glares the entire way out.

MD stepped even closer to me now, her face taught. "That girl was nothing. Bryson was just a boy trying to sow a wild oat before he commits to someone proper. Do you honestly think Frederick Prince would let his son date a nobody like her?"

"You didn't even know her," I argued defensively.

"If she was somebody of importance, we would know. Use your head, Cinderella! That mixer last night was for Frederick Prince to put the right girls in his son's path. They won't stand for a no-name floozy on his arm in society, holding him back. Summer is much better suited for him. Even his father agrees."

"His father?" I whispered. If Frederick Prince wanted someone like Summer for his son, that certainly wasn't me.

MD's eyes squeezed into slits at my emotional reaction to this information. "People must know their place, Cinderella. They must know reality. Hopes and dreams only ever end in heartache."

Her words were the nail in my coffin.

As I closed the door to my attic, a sense of melancholy fell over me. I was right back where I started: Contained to an attic in the shadows making clothing for others.

Did Prince really ever think I could be a substitute for Summer? Or was MD right? Maybe I really was just a distraction for Prince? Did I seriously get played?

A few hours later, I'd styled the Silicone Sisters and was finishing a scarf at MD's urgent request. Van Halen was blasting in my ear buds and with every stitch I dropped, my pity party quickly turned into a rage-fest.

I glared moodily at my glass slipper. The one reminder of what a sham last night really was. I had to start putting my foot down. I had to get out from under MD's thumb. I was done allowing people to put me in my place. They were all going to hear my voice, once and for all.

From my lap, Van Halen suddenly grew tense, his black hair standing up on his back. I turned to see what caught his attention and found MD rifling through my closet.

"Thief!" she bellowed. A silver pair of scissors caught the light just as they slide through a black one-piece swimsuit.

I ripped my ear buds out and jumped to my feet. "No!" I bent over and picked the pile of shredded pieces up off the floor. They were all the suits from last night. I didn't even know they all had made it back into my closet. Fairy Godmother maybe?

"You stole these from the show last night!" MD towered over top of me, her crooked finger stabbed hard into my chest.

I clutched my designs protectively. "I didn't steal them! I created them!"

"You honestly expect me to believe that, Cinderella?" She grabbed a wayward bikini top from the floor and with a mighty yank, ripped it into two. "You're lucky I'm not turning you in. You can't expect me to believe you have this kind of talent!"

"I don't expect anything from you!" I screamed, breathing heavily. My eyes scanned the scraps of my life's work splayed all around me. "You made it clear as glass last night how very little you believed in me."

"You sound just like your father." MD's chin dropped.

My jaw clenched with barely contained fury. "You knew nothing of my father."

"I knew plenty of him. He was a damn dreamer! And all that got him was six feet under. And if I need a reminder of him, all I have to do is look at your face." She may as well have spit at me. The poignant pain behind her cloudy grey gaze was palpable.

She cracked her neck and continued. "Can you *fathom* what it's like living with a constant reminder of all you've lost?" She harrumphed. "Idolize him all you want, Cinderella. But he's gone and I'm all you've got. And if you think that Bryson Prince is interested in you, you're more pathetic than I thought."

I looked at her in horror as realization dawned on me. She knew it was me all along last night. Pushing past me, she slammed the French doors shut that led to the terrace. She then pulled out an old skeleton key from her pocket and turned it in the lock.

"What are you doing?" I asked as she moved toward the stairs next. Already I could feel the heat in the room increasing.

"You think you're good enough for a Prince?" She guffawed. "You're dreaming."

Sensing danger, Van Halen suddenly scurried past me and out the door. Before I could realize what was happening, MD slammed the door and locked it, trapping me into my own personal sweatshop.

"No," I whispered. "No!" I screamed. "You can't be serious!"

I ran to both doors, shaking the knobs. Panic consumed me as beads of sweat drizzled slowly down my temples. This couldn't be happening. This couldn't be real. I buckled over, dropping to the floor.

"Fairy Godmother," I blinked back tears. "It's time for magic to be a reality again...or however you said that before." I looked all around the room for any sign of bubbles, water, mist, brightness, anything.

I grabbed the glass slipper off my sewing desk and squeezed it to my chest. "Please. Please. Please!" I screamed the last one and felt the slipper crack in my grip along with all remaining hope in my heart.

Loud voices filled the room, waking me from a fitful sleep. When my eyes opened, I found myself on the floor and the light in the room was golden. How long had I been out? I sat up, drenched in sweat.

I glanced over to the noise coming from the videoconference screen and Van Halen's white striped face filled the frame. He was licking the LCD screen in the sitting room downstairs and had activated the touch screen. I squinted at the action taking place behind him, certain I was hallucinating.

"As I said, Bryson," MD continued, "Cinderella left for fashion school overseas this morning. It was an incredible last minute opportunity."

"She really just left?" He sounded bereft.

"That girl is as selfish as the sun is warm." She chuckled. "You're better off without her and you know it, my dear. She is inconsequential."

Her words cut me. Just then Summer and Winter sashayed into the room.

"Bryson, so nice of you to come see me again!" Summer said, snaking her arm around his.

"Summer?" he asked, sounding confused. "You're the one I called security on last night." He pulled away from her nervously.

"What?" Winter screeched, obviously excited by the prospect of her sister being less than perfect.

"You had pictures of a dead toad with you," Prince exclaimed. "It was...alarming."

Summer's face turned fiery red and Winter erupted into belly-shaking cackles. "He was an important part of my life!" Summer roared which only caused Winter to laugh harder.

"Bryson, never mind any of that. You two are really very compatible—"

"Enough!" Prince shouted. "Someone had better tell me where Rell is right this second!"

"Rell? Is that what you call her?" Winter bellowed, falling over and laughing uncontrollably. "What a stupid name. She's locked in the attic where she belongs."

"Winter!" MD and Summer both shouted in unison. Winter's face dropped as she realized what she just let slip.

Prince's face turned horrified as he pushed past MD and ran out of the room. MD and Summer chased after him and before I knew it, I heard steps thundering toward me.

"Rell!" Prince shouted, banging on the door.

Before I could muster the energy to stand, a loud cracking sound echoed in the small room. The hinges splintered and the door flew open, revealing an out of breath Prince.

"My God, Rell," he said, dropping onto his knees beside me. "It has to be a hundred degrees in here!"

The blast of cool air that accompanied him was life changing. He helped me stand and the look on his face was enough to make me sick if I wasn't already. MD and the Silicone Sisters scampered in.

"Cinderella," MD cajoled. "I'm surprised—"

I held my hands up to stop them in their tracks. "Save it, Mother Dearest. I'm done with the wire hangers." She looked completely clueless by my movie reference but I couldn't care less.

"I'm getting you out of here, Rell," Prince placed his hand on the small of my back.

"No!" I flinched away from him, renewed energy overcome me. "I don't need your sympathy, Prince. I'm not a charity case."

He looked at me like I'd shot him. "Rell, I have no idea—"

"I know everything, Prince," I groaned. A flicker of sadness cast over me as I took in his confused face, but I had to stay strong. "I know your father has expectations for you. And those don't include me."

"What on earth?" he cried, raking his hands through his hair in frustration.

It killed me to say it, but I had to do this. None of this was real. It was all a dream that I allowed myself to get caught up in.

"I don't know if you were just passing time with me or if I was just a mistake. I don't even care. Just do what you have to do. Have Summer. Have Winter and Spring too! Because the only thing I care about right now—the *only* thing I won't let any of you mess with anymore…is my heart."

I bent over and picked up the cracked glass slipper on the floor. "I told you hearts were fragile, Prince. That's why I am going to start protecting mine right now."

"Rell, my father just wants me to find great love like he did!"

"Don't speak of love!" My voice cracked with heartache. I threw the slipper to the ground, feeling empowered by the shattered glass all around me. "I knew love, Prince. I heard it in my father's voice when he talked about my mother. I saw it in his eyes when he kissed me goodnight."

I turned back to MD. "I don't know how you lost sight of that." MD's nostrils flared as I stepped closer to her, staring her down. "But I forgive you. Your heart broke when he died, and I think you lost yourself. I hope someday you can learn how to love again and teach your daughters."

Summer scoffed. I looked to her. "Your day will come, Summer. The day when you realize how very sad your life is with all this hate in it."

My eyes stung with the approach of tears. I turned back to Prince and was blown away by the desolate look in his eyes.

"Don't feel sorry for me, Prince." I clenched my hands to my chest as two tears escaped and slid down my cheeks. "I'm lucky. My dad was a great teacher so I know how to love!

"I thought I saw love with you, but it's okay." I smiled sadly and stretched my arms out wide, backing toward the door. "I've got this now. I love me! And I haven't been able to say that for a long time."

Prince's expression morphed into panic as I turned to leave. "Rell—" he cried, but I cut him off again.

"I will just have to be enough."

In only my white underwear and bra, I found myself standing inside the cave beneath the thundering falls. *My special spot.* I pushed the cool mist up my face and down my soaked hair, relishing in every droplet.

"Well," I said out loud. The mist clung to my lips and eyelashes. "It's time! I'm ready for my dreams to become my reality."

I waited expectantly for the magic I saw with Fairy Godmother to begin. Nothing happened.

"I'm done doubting myself. I know I'm talented. I know I can create. I love myself. I'm ready! I'm ready for my dreams to float!" Still, nothing happened.

I looked down at my feet, feeling a new depth of sadness at how utterly alone I was. "I thought that my dreams would be more than fashion. More than design. I thought I could find the love that my father told me of right here." I pointed down to the rock. "But it's fine. My true love can come from my own two hands." I looked meaningfully at my fists. "I can be happy with just this."

"What if you can't?" A voice called through the falls.

I saw Prince's silhouette bobbing on the other side as he prepared to push himself through the stream. Black strands of hair clung to his face as he laid those gorgeous green eyes on me once again.

"Prince—"

"It's my turn now," he snapped, swimming straight towards me.

He carefully hauled himself out of the water and stormed up to me in a blaze of fury. Anger and passion radiated off his chiseled abs as he stood before me in a pair of soaked cargo shorts.

"You *seriously* think I want Summer?"

I tried to respond but he cut me off, stepping so close to me I had to tip my head back to look at him. "If you think I want any of this life without you, you're dead wrong," he cried, thrusting his hand through his hair.

"Prince, you don't need to do this." I looked down, clutching my arms across my belly to gain control of my emotions.

"Rell, I am in *love* with you!" he roared, his voice echoing off the cave walls. His breath heaved with his declaration. "That is the only thing I *need* to do. Don't let whatever manipulated crap that wicked stepmother of yours said taint that!"

My mind wanted to run for protection, but my heart soared at the hope behind his words. I opened my mouth to speak, but no words came.

He reached out and gripped my wrists, touching his forehead to mine. "I fell in love with you the instant your head came up for air in the water that day." Staring down at our hands, he continued. "I breathed with you in that moment and I finally knew what my father meant by a great irreplaceable love. That is all he's ever wanted for me. And I've found that. *With you.*"

He sighed heavily and peered up through his thick, dark lashes. "Rell, this is the kind of fairy tale love that you feel in your gut and ache for until you can make it come true."

I tilted my head back and looked closely into his eyes. My heart skipped a beat at the clear devotion I saw there.

"Are you a dream?" I asked on a whisper.

"A dream would pale in comparison to this incredible reality. I know we hardly know each other, Rell. But if you would open your heart to me, I could show you." He laced his fingers with mine and pressed them against his chest. "I believe in love at first sight. But only with you. Tell me I'm not alone."

As I squeezed his hands back, a cloud of mist swirled around us. Refusing to break eye contact, we both studied each other as a fantastical magic surrounded us, playing tribute to our heartfelt exchange.

"You're not alone, Prince," I finally replied. "I am in love with you too."

It was all I could say. It was all I felt. In that moment with him, hopes, dreams and love commanded me.

"I was hoping you'd say that, Princess." His mouth split into a broad grin as he reached into the cargo short's pocket and pulled out my other glass slipper. The one I left behind last night.

I smiled and reached out to touch the smooth glass in his hand. The meaning behind this small gesture made my heart sore.

Gazing seriously into my eyes, he said, "I'm never going to let this one break, Rell."

He dipped his head and captured my lips in a swirling, all-consuming kiss. With the slipper nestled safely between us, I tipped my head back and gave him all of me to protect and cherish.

"I think I want to marry you," he murmured against my lips.

I smiled. "Let's try a date first, Prince Charming."

And so we stood there, kissing in the mist...because it was time. Finally our very own hopes and dreams had become a reality.

And the best part was: Our happily ever after had only just begun.

~~The End~~
The Beginning

Amy Daws is a contemporary romance author who loved dipping her toe into the world of fantasy for this modern day Cinderella story. If you loved her contemporary style, check out her award-nominated adult romantic comedy series, The London Lovers Series. It's emotional, and self-deprecating, with lots of humor sprinkled in. To learn more, visit: http://www.amydawsauthor.com

CASTING CROWNS AND OTHER CURIOUS THINGS
A retelling of Alice in Wonderland
By Elizabeth Montgomery

She said I'd never hold the crown.
    She said I was a stupid girl.
    A stupid girl that would lose her head.

    I swear, the Red Queen will regret her outlandish words the day I hold her bloody head in my hand... crown and all.

* * *

Most Wonderlandians try to escape this horrid place the Red Queen called home. Not me. The people of this land acted as if they worshiped her, but it was just that: an act. They were terrified of her and her bloody reign. They'd bring her flowers, potions, teas and crumpets in hopes of surviving one more day in this tragic wasteland. It wasn't always this way, though. Once, Wonderland was a place where your best dreams came to life, the flowers were your friends and the dragonflies didn't try to kill your family. Those days were long forgotten under the reign of the Red Queen. Now the streets were filled with blood, savage beasts, and darkness. This land was no longer a place for happily ever afters. It was a place of nightmares and death.

    Not only did I find my way inside, but down into the secret tunnels. They led into a dark and dusty castle cellar. I explored cobwebbed tunnels and dead ends, until I finally found a small opening in a stone wall. A screeching voice reverberated above me. That voice could only belong to one person: The Red Queen.

    I was directly under throne room.

    The opening was no bigger than a rabbit hole. But I was determined that the Red Queen would eat her words. Arms first, I squeezed through the opening. Once out of the tunnel, I climbed atop a few scattered stone blocks. On my tiptoes I peered through a small fissure in the mortar between the ceiling and the back wall.

1

The Red Queen
Blood spilling savage
Ruler of Wonderland
Loves hearts and all things red,
especially when the red things spill from the bodies of her enemies.

"Fetch me my tea, Richards," the Red Queen's voice squawked like an angry crow.

"Yes, your majesty. Is there anything else I can get for you?" Richards's tight voice echoed through the grand room.

"If I wanted anything else I would've ask for it, you idiot," she spat condescendingly.

Richards cowered. He quickly recovered and hurried past the Red Queen and escaped through an old wooden door. The door groaned as he pulled it open and bustled behind it, disappearing from sight.

Richards
The Red Queens man servant,
in more ways than
he wishes to be.

Richards couldn't have been much older than me, but the few years he'd spent with the Red Queen had done a number on his looks. A deep, twisted purple scar trekked across his eye and down the length of his face. A reminder of the Red Queen's temper. Rumor in the woodlands was that Richards's face fell victim to her majesty's razor sharp nails after he spilled a tray of brudleberry crumpets into her lap; it was said his cries for mercy could be heard from outside the castle gates and into the village. She broke his spirits. Literally. No longer a confident young man, he hunched over. Dressed in a tattered button-down he carelessly tucked them into his potato sack pants.

Before the Red Queen claimed him as hers, Richards was well known amongst the ladies of this land. Swoons filled the street as he walked past, along with estrogen—it was quite the scene when Richards left his small crooked purple house. Needless to say, the Red Queen didn't take kindly to someone attaining more attention than her, so she had her cardsmen grab him one night as he walked through the village after a midnight rendezvous with one of the Spratly sisters. Once in the Red Queen's clutches, she threatened to behead everyone he ever loved if he didn't stay with her as her servant. Obviously he took the deal.

Adjusting my footing, I stared through the crack in the wall. The Red Queen was perched upon her golden throne. Her legs rested carelessly upon the arm as her long, black ball gown, plentifully adorned with brilliant heart-shaped rubies, dangled to the floor. The stones pulled in small bits of light that crept through the large stained glass windows that bordered the ceiling, making the space around her shimmer. The sparkle almost made it look like a happy place to be. I knew better.

As the Red Queen sat there picking at her pointed fingernails, she chatted up one of her cardsmen about the fate of a prisoner. It was like she was discussing which jelly she'd prefer on her toast as she debated what his head would look like as it rolled from his shoulders. She was a sadistic bitch.

Cardsmen
Ruthless, spear carrying, blood thirsty
mercenaries belonging to the Red Queen.
Their paper bodies cannot be torn,
But they can be set ablaze.

The prisoner the Red Queen was speaking of was one that I was going to set free— Tyden would never meet the Red Queen's fate. He was my reason for treason. His crime? Loving the Red Queen's sworn enemy: Me.

Alice (Me)
An ordinary girl with an extraordinary mind.
Hated by the Red Queen.
Prophesized to rule Wonderland by the seer.
Always dressed in blue,
it's the color of all things wonderful.

I closed my eyes and thought back to the moment the Red Queen took him from me. Unbeknownst to Tyden and myself, the Red Queen had sent her army of cardsmen to retrieve him on the night we were to seal our love in the most intimate way. Two bodies becoming one. The air was thick with lust, swirling around us as his jet black hair fell across his left eye and swooped down to the corner of his devilish smile. The moonlight from the window cast dancing shadows across his bare body, calling attention to each flawless muscle as he sauntered toward the bed and knelt down over me. The weight of his body on top of mine felt magical, his hands gently wrapped around my middle sending a wave of electricity through to my spine. There was nothing more than a breath between us when a thunderous roar rang through the forest, shaking the walls of his home. As if we were of one mind, Tyden and myself leaped to our feet and raced to the small window across the room. It was a mob of cardsmen that followed behind the two headed black beasts, their hooves pounded the earth as they pulled behind them the notorious black carriage. They were taking aim directly at Tyden's home.

Tyden
Son of the Mad Hatter
Lives outside of the main village
Secretly makes potions and
sells them to the Wonderlandians
And last, but not least, the love of my life.

The front door burst open. Splinters of wood shot from the door frame, impaling anything in their path. The cardsmen had arrived. Vials of smoke were slammed to the ground, making it impossible to see. Their boots slammed the floor with every step as they piled into the small house. Tyden was no longer beside me, nor did I know where he went. I could only imagine he had gone to fight the intruders. Sliding down to the floor, I felt my way to the back of the room and hid behind a large leather-strapped trunk. I wanted to throw my hands over my ears at the sound of flesh being pummeled. It made me want to throw up, but then a pleasant sound came and made me feel a bit better; the sound of crumpling paper. After a few moments, the smoke dissipated and I seized the opportunity to glance around the base of the trunk; I almost wish I hadn't. Tyden put up a fight, grabbing the paper soldiers one by one, making contact with every swing of his fist. He ducked and dodged the cardsmen's attempts to grab him. His upturned lips taunted the paper bodied soldiers.

A boisterous voice belonging to one of the cardsmen echoed through the room, "Where's the girl?"

My hand came to rest over my mouth as I saw Tyden's face turn grim.

They were here for *me*. Not him.

I quickly tucked myself back behind the trunk. My breaths turned shallow as my heart pounded in my bare chest.

Tyden was stronger than any man I had ever known, but it wasn't enough to overcome the legion of cardsmen that flooded through the gaping void where a door once stood. After his hands and feet were bound by the vines they used as rope, he was pulled outside and shoved into the black carriage driven by the two-headed beasts. He was sure to be chained and thrown into the bowels of the castle; to be brought before the Red Queen by the next afternoon. All the other unfortunate Wonderlandians who had the displeasure of riding in that coach had met a similar fate

My chest heaved as I held back the sobs that so desperately wanted to escape. My face drenched from the uncontrolled tears that poured down my face as I watched the love of my life taken from away. I wanted to scream. I wanted to kill them all. Most of all I wanted him back and that was exactly what I planned to do.

When the pounding of the hooves were far enough out of earshot, I climbed out from behind the chest. I threw on my clothes and bolted out of the hollow entry. I pushed myself to run faster, harder, to hold back the tears that threatened to spill over. As I got closer to the main village, I could hear the people and creatures cheer as the black coach carrying Tyden rode through town. It was the law to cheer when a black coach passed by, even if it contained someone you held dear to your heart. Any Wonderlandian who broke the law would meet the same fate as the unfortunate soul occupying the carriage. Death.

* * *

As I shook the thought of that tragic night, I focused my thoughts back to the tunnels of the castle I was standing in. A shift in movement behind me caught my eye. I crouched down low and swiftly ducked into a darkened corner. One of the Red Queen's cardsmen passed by the small rabbit hole I had wriggled through.

"Are you sure you saw someone come down here?" the cardsmen asked, his voice gruff and hurried.

"I-I thought I saw a girl," a small voice said. Just then, a girl no bigger than a wonderweed walked past the opening and stopped. "You know, *the* girl? She was wearing the blue dress that the Red Queen told us all to look for. I know I saw her, I really did," her voice faded with every other word, as if she was turning her head back and forth, looking for me.

"I don't see anyone. You're wasting my time, you ridiculous girl!" he boomed.

I jumped. A few pebbles rolled to the ground.

"Wait, what was that? Did you hear that?" the girl asked.

The paper-bodied cardsman held his lantern close to the hole, the light illuminated the red hearts that decorated his flat, cream colored torso.

"THE GIRL! I found her!" he shouted before he blew his whistle over and over, alerting the other cardsmen.

It was fight or flight; I didn't have wings so that only left one option.

Without a second thought, I pushed off the wall with all my strength and barreled toward him. I snatched the lantern from his gloved hand while he was distracted with his obnoxious whistle blowing. I smashed the top of the globe. Oil spilled onto the cardsman that had managed to shimmy himself halfway through the small hole, leaving him in a bad position: stuck.

"What are you doing? Stop it!" he screeched as he tried to get away before the flames lit him up. All it took was the corner of his paper body to catch fire and within seconds he was engulfed in flames. Embers flew around the room and when they settled he was nothing more than a pile of ash, scattered on the stone. I stood there for a moment with a small sense of satisfaction as I stepped through the ashes.

I crawled out into the main hall, my skin and dress now covered with streaks of dark grey soot. I looked down both ends of the tunnel, waiting for the other cardsmen to come and finish the job this one had failed. None came.

The brown haired girl that had brought the cardsman down sat against the wall across from where I stood, her body trembling, as she held her head against her knees. Her back heaved. The heavy sobs caused the hem of her bright pink dress to shiver.

"What's wrong, child?" I asked.

She pulled her head up. I offered my hand to her, but she recoiled.

"Are you going to kill me now?" she asked, her bright green eyes completely waterlogged.

"Oh my, no! I'm not going to kill you." Jarred by her words, I stooped down so we were eye level. "I think you can help me, sweet girl."

"I can?" she asked as she wiped the tears from her swollen eyes.

"I hope so." I smiled at her, pushing a loose strand of hair behind her ear. "Are you ready to do some good deeds?" I asked as I dusted off some the cardsman's ashes from the front of my dress. It was slightly morbid to have the by-product of murder strewn about your person.

"I would like that very much," the girl said as she pushed herself up to her feet. "I am truly sorry by the way, I just wanted her to like me, you know. I thought if she liked me she wouldn't find a reason to separate my head from my neck."

This girl was a prime example of why Wonderland needed to change. She was too young to know how remarkable and magnificent Wonderland could be, all she had ever know was this evil.

"What's your name?" I asked, not wanting to entertain her morbid thoughts.

"Celia." Her sparkling green eyes held a hint of sadness.

"I'm Alice. Nice to meet you, Celia." I took her hand in mine. "I think we should go this way. We have to be quiet though, can you do that?"

She nodded in response, already honoring the silent pact. A few minutes into our walk, I realized I had no idea where I was. I needed to get my bearings; I needed to find a door that would lead us out of the bowels of this castle.

As if the gods were smiling down, a big wooden door came into view around the next corner. We stood and stared at it as if we were waiting for it to magically open.

"Are you going to open it or should we just stand here and admire what it could have been?" Celia whispered.

"Cheeky." I smirked.

She giggled but stifled the laugh with cupped hands. I bumped her with my hip, sending her petite body gently colliding against the wall beside us. We both gasped when we heard a loud crack. There was no way she hit hard enough to break the wall. A scraping sound filled the air, like two stones being dragged across one another. All laughter ceased. I grabbed the girl and fled to the shadows on the other side of hall; in Wonderland the shadows were your only protection. We sat there, watching the wall she had bumped into recede into the floor, leaving behind a cloud of dust.

"Do you think it's a trap?" she asked as her body began to quiver.

"I'm not sure," I replied as I bit the corner of my lip. This was another one of those doomed if you do, doomed if you don't situations. "You stay here, I'm going to, umm, well, I'm going to go see what's in there." I sat her down in the safety of the shadows and walked to the entryway. I strained to get merely a glimpse into the darkness.

In the distance was a glowing blue rondure. It was small, but bright. Yet, it illuminated the back wall, revealing shelves that held assorted boxes. The path in front of me, though, was still shrouded in darkness. I had to use my hands to navigate across the room. Suddenly, a sharp pain sliced through my thigh. Sucking in a deep breath, I released it as I bent down and ran my hands over what felt like spikes and blades. Even though I couldn't see what had jabbed my thigh, I knew I had to be more mindful of my steps in this room.

The source of the blue light revealed itself in the form of a small potion bottle. Corked at the top, its bulbous bottom was full of the brilliant liquid. Reaching out for it I noticed a small ribbon tied around its neck with a sizable label attached. The words 'DRINK ME' were penned on the label in thick black ink, bleeding slightly at the base of each letter.

I learned my lesson the hard way on drinking out of vials that instructed me to do so, last time I did this I was the size of a sheetle beetle for a week. Instead of complying with the label's demand, I used the light from the bottle to guide my way back through the room, which I could now see was the Red Queen's arsenal. Weapons covered the room from wall to wall. A gasp came from the doorway as I saw Celia, wide-eyed, standing there, mouth agape.

"What *is* this place?" Her words were softly drawn out in adoration as she crossed the threshold, her bright eyes wide as she took in her dimly lit surroundings. She ran a single finger across the blade of an axe that had been discarded carelessly onto a table by the front of the room.

"I'd say this is our saving grace, Celia." These weapons could be what keep us alive. "Grab what you can carry."

I picked up a few daggers and slid them into the ribbon that was tied around my waist, leaving them secure while easily accessible. I looked over to Celia, who was dragging a mace bigger than her head.

"When I said grab something you can carry, I meant *discreetly* carry." I pointed down to the weapon behind her.

"Oh, I suppose that would make more sense." Her voice came out as a whisper as she dropped the handle, reached across the table next to her, and grabbed a small green pouch. "This should do then."

"What is that?" My brow was tight with curiosity.

"Well, I've seen the Red Queen's sidekick kill people with it, so it must be something good. He always pulls the green pouch out of his pocket right before someone dies." She examined the pouch, turning it from side to side.

I walked over to her and popped the button that held it closed. I nearly choked on my own breath when I saw the corner of the contents sticking out. A vial no bigger than my thumb filled with a black, smoky liquid that swirled inside the walls of the glass.

"That...don't...Celia, close that now," I said as I regained my composure. "Do you know what that is?" I picked up the green pouch between two fingers, mindful of its power.

"No, I just know that it's bad, which in our case is good right?" she asked proudly.

"Well, yes and no," I said, leaning up against a stone pillar. "It is good that we have it and not the cardsmen. This vial changes the person that's in possession of it. It *can* be used for the power of good if the right person gets a hold of it, but if not it can turn the purest heart black as night."

"Is that what happened to the Red Queen?" Celia asked as she continued to stare at the pouch.

"I think the Red Queen was born with a black heart," I winked and shoved off the pillar. "Okay, let's go get Tyden from the stocks."

"Is Tyden your friend?" Celia asked as she grabbed a stray knife hanging on the wall by the door, slipping it into the same place on her dress that I had mine.

"Tyden, well, he is my happiness. He is the smile on my face each morning. The reason I know what it feels like to be alive." I felt a lump climbing my throat. As I stepped back into the tunnels, I shook the thoughts of him and focused on my mission. Looking toward each end, I stood and pondered which way to go. Everything outside the castle had signs pointing this way and that. Those sure would've been helpful down here in the musty bowels of the castle. I counted to three then chose left.

"I know how to get to the stocks," Celia chirped, "But you will have to go through the throne room to get there." The small girl was on my heels, her little brown shoes clicking with every step.

"Well, I've wanted to meet that bitch face to face for a long while, Celia." I didn't want to face the Red Queen without Tyden by my side, but if I didn't he may die and a life without him really wasn't a life at all. He was worth the fight. He was worth dying for.

After a few twists, turns, and round-a-bouts, we made it to the service doors that Celia said would lead straight up to the throne room. I took a few deep breaths; knowing that your death potentially sat on the other side of any door was a somber thought. But knowing that the man you love could possibly wrap his arms around you again helped to ease the sick feeling currently churning in my gut.

I remembered the blue bottle I had slipped in the pocket of my dress, contemplating for a bit whether to take a sip.

"Celia, you are to stay down here no matter what. No matter how awful it gets up there, you do not come up. Do you understand?" I ran my fingers through her thick brown locks and down her plump, rosy cheek, leaving my hand to rest at her jaw line. Celia was such a beautiful child, something about her felt like home. A safe place.

"I'm not as useless as you think, Alice." She giggled and ducked under my hand as she swooped past me and up the stairs, rounding the corner at the top.

"Celia stop!" My words slid across my teeth in a loud whisper as I slipped the bottle back into my pocket and took off after her up the stairs.

"What is this?" My body froze at the sound of the Red Queen's icy voice, "Where did you come from child?"

Dammit.

I had no plan.

Nothing.

"I fell into a wall down in the tunnels and found this." Celia's small voice echoed in the grand room. The only thing that she had was the knife she plucked from the wall on her way out of the weapons room.

I was at the top of the stairs, no more than a stone's throw from the Red Queen herself. All it would take was a few steps for me to be in her sights, the battle to begin, and someone's head to roll.

"Why were you in the tunnels? Have you not been educated on the *rules* I have for children in *my* home?" Her drawn out words escalated in pitch, followed by the sickening sound of smacked flesh and a scream that came from Celia. My feet started moving before my thoughts could catch up.

When I came around the corner, Celia was motionless was on the floor, her hair splayed across her face.

"What did you do?" I screamed at the Red Queen as I fell to my knees beside the small girl, brushing her hair away from her face.

"Alice? How kind of you to join us." The Red Queen's words dripped with mockery. She stood at the forefront of her oversized throne, glaring down at us in disgust. It was as if we had defecated in her breakfast oats. "Guards!" she shrieked. Her eyes turned to slits as she called for her cardsmen.

The floor trembled as the paper army converged on the room. Panic rose in my chest… until I remembered the green pouch and the blue vial in my pocket. Reaching into the front of my dress, I flicked the small flap open with my thumb and pulled out the vial filled with the black smoky liquid.

"Call off your guards now, Queen." I held up the vial and rose to my feet. An overwhelming sense of valor came over me. I stepped toward the Red Queen, stopping only a few feet back from her faltering arrogant stature.

"Wha–where–how…" the Red Queen stuttered and stumbled backward, her face twisted as she tripped into her throne, catching herself on the arm before her ass landed flat on the floor.

"Call. Them. Off." I spoke through gritted teeth as I held the bottle up.

"Richards," she called out over her shoulder, her eyes never losing sight of me. "Bar the door."

Richards shuffled in from a tall wooden door behind the throne. "Yes, your majesty." He walked to the large double doors adjacent from the throne, pulling down the thick wood plank that secured the doors shut.

"Now, can we have a chat, my dear Alice?" Her voice was laced with poisoned sweetness.

"You want to have a *chat*?" My head fell back with laughter. "About what, *my Queen*? About how you have vowed to kill me? About how you have Tyden in the bowels of this hell hole you call home?" I threw my hands up, gesturing around us. "Or perhaps you'd like to chat about the horrible place you have turned Wonderland into. Please, enlighten me on what *you* would like to chat about, your majesty." My last words came out in a hiss, mocking her royal highness.

The Red Queens lips pursed as her face grew tight. I questioned myself on the amount of courage I had gained until I felt a damp spot on the side of my dress. I wanted to look down, but didn't dare break eye contact with the Red Queen. I'd likely lose my head that way. I must've broke the seal on the blue vial when I grabbed the green pouch. That's when it hit me.

Courage.

That's what the blue potion was!

I pulled it from my pocket and dropped the black vial back into its home, popped the broken cork the rest of the way out and dumped it down my throat.

"NO!" The Red Queen screamed and lunged toward me, throwing both of us to the polished stone floor. The impact sent a streak of pain through my chest. She held her torso up slightly off the ground with one hand, swinging her other open palm towards me. My head whipped to the side avoiding the strike. A near miss, but a miss for her majesty nonetheless. The Red Queen reared her hand back again, this time balled into a white-knuckled fist. Without thinking I reached up and caught her next blow in the palm of my hand, clenching her balled fist in my grip. The Red Queen's face twisted in confusion as she struggled to get free.

My body buzzed to life. A wicked smile spread across my face. I laughed sadistically. "You think you can kill me, you wretched old hag? You are nothing more than a washed up has-been, a fool in a court of jesters. Now get up." I grabbed a handful of her bright red ringlets, ripping her off of me and rising to my feet.

The Red Queen followed suit, standing before me, her fists clenched at her sides. "You have made an enormous mistake, my dear stupid girl." Her face was inches from mine, eyes filled with fiery hatred as she reared back and raked her razor sharp nails across my face.

I jumped back with a hiss, holding my hand to my cheek. The crimson liquid staining my palm was the last straw. "You shouldn't have done that." I lunged toward her. My fist collided with her jaw.

She spun around, kicking me in the stomach before I could move. I sucked in a deep breath. Pain radiated through my body.

"Should I call the guards back?" Richards's small voice asked from behind us.

"Oh no, Richards. This one is mine." Her face twisted up into a menacing grin. Faster than I could react, her hand snaked out and wrapped around my throat. "I'm getting bored with this blow for blow charade you have going on, dear Alice. Let's get this over with once and for all."

My feet dangled off the ground, the world around me spun and began to fade into a blur. This couldn't be how it ended; it couldn't be this easy for her to win.

The black vial.

With everything I had left, I sunk my hand into my pocket and pulled it out, flipping the top open. I splashed it in the Red Queen's face. Her hand quickly unwrapped itself from my neck. A thick black cloud, very much like the one I saw in Tyden's house, erupted and encased the Red Queen. Her screams were muffled by the dense smoke that churned around her body.

I gasped for air, palming my throat as I staggered over to where Celia had been lying. She was gone. I scanned the room. Wringing his white knuckled hands, Richards paced behind the throne. He glanced at his master every few seconds. He looked lost, waiting for her to give him orders.

A familiar quake shook the ground. The tall wooden door began to rattle from the incessant vibrations.

"It's going to be okay, Alice," a small voice said behind me.

I turned but saw no one. The Red Queen struggled to get free from the black cloud she was still contained in, smoky tendrils reaching out as if they were looking for something to grab on to. Sparks flew out of their vapored ends the closer she got to where I stood. Black streaks had taken up residence in the form of spider-webbed veins from her face to her fingertips. The Red Queen seemed to no longer walk, but float across the pale stone floor.

"My dear Alice, thank you for your astonishing gift." Her penetrating voice echoed louder than before. "While it was a painful transition, I'd say this was the best present I have ever received."

As she twirled around, rings of smoke twirled with her, creating a tornadic effect. This wasn't supposed to happen! The black vial was supposed to kill her, not empower her further! My thoughts raced to come up with a plan--a plan that would keep my head attached to my body.

I had basically given all of Wonderland a death sentence by creating a ruler so wicked her veins were filled with evil. There had to be another way!

"There is another way," the same small voice said behind me.

"Where are you, Celia? I know it's you." My voice shook as I dodged one of the tendrils shooting out from the Red Queen's smoke. The black cloud was yet another prisoner of the Red Queen, bowing to her commands.

I am you. I was the courage you needed to find, but already possessed, the voice was inside my head now, *Do not overthink it Alice or your brain could get scrambled, leaving me in quite the predicament.*

Scrambled. Celia. Alice. The letters scrambled. A wave of solace washed over me as I dodged another one of the smoky outstretched curls.

"You *are* me, which means I'm you. We're one," I stared at the ground as my words fell out in a whisper. It was then I realized how to defeat the Red Queen.

My head flung up, meeting the Red Queen's gaze, "Richards isn't real, is he *Charrdis*. That was your name before you were crowned, right?" I asked the Red Queen. "I remember it because of how silly it sounded to me when I was a girl. Charrdis," I taunted. "What kind of name is that anyway?"

The Red Queen tried to cover her horrified expression with a tight lined smile. "What did you just say?" Her strangled words came out one at a time. "You're nothing more than a peasant. You do not have the privilege to call me by my former name, stupid girl."

I kept my distance from her, slowly circling backwards as she hovered in the black misty cloud.

"He's *nothing more* than a projection of you, the smallest part of you that remained good through all the darkness, the sliver of light in your tainted miserable excuse for a heart. You couldn't stand for it to be a part of you so you cast out that part of your soul and sent it to mingle with the commoners. You couldn't stand it when he was accepted and wanted by the very people who loathe your very existence so you had him seized and made him your slave. Ironic, really—you are your own slave." I grinned as she hovered, her cheeks turning a fierce shade of red between the dark veins that branded her face. "The potion that was in that bottle made the outside match your inside, didn't it?" I asked as panic continued to race across the Red Queen's face. "Your beauty has faded, and your soul is exposed. You're pure evil now, and that alone is a life sentence even *I* wouldn't wish upon you." I rambled on in an attempt to keep her distracted long enough to move next to her oversized throne where I spotted a set of skeleton keys. If I could get to them I could take off and find Tyden.

A loud noise came from the other side of the room. The Red Queen whipped around. "Richards!" she shouted. "Is that you making that awful racket? I'm trying to kill the girl, so if you wouldn't mind keeping it down back there, I'm sure that the rabbit can wait." Her words turned to nonsense as she chuckled. She whipped back around, the cloud swirling in sync with her movements.

I dove for the keys that hung on the back of the throne, landing on my side, keys in hand. "Put those down!" The Red Queen's voice was now frantic.

She thrusted her body forward. Her head snapped back while she remained cemented in place as if the black swirling tendrils had locked her into her own prison. Her torso whipping side to side as her black veined face flung around erratically. "What's going on? What did you do to me?" She continued to wriggle and strain against the power of the cloud that held her, suspended in its swirling vortex.

"Ahh, the hexan cloud. That won't be easy to get out of, your majesty," a deep voice came from the other side of the throne. I glanced in the direction of the familiar voice and saw Richards casually walking across the room as if he was taking a Sunday stroll through the Dragleberry fields.

"Richards? But how can you still be here? The cloud should have taken you away, unless…unless you *are* real," I said, slightly taken aback at the sight of Richards's actual height and dapper looks. He was no longer hunched over wearing rags; he was dressed in a royal blue suit and his dark brown hair was swept to one side of his face.

"You see," his voice was low, albeit powerful as he made his way to the Red Queen and slowly circled her like a beast stalking its prey, "when you threw the hexan potion onto Queeny here." He flicked his wrist towards the Red Queen. "It unlocked my bond to her, severing ties with the small bit of good she had inside of her: Me. Since I was a part of her that she had manifested before the spell took over, I was able to remain tethered to Wonderland, opposed to being condemned to her darkness."

The Red Queen struggled to break free of the hexan cloud, screaming and demanding for her cardsmen to come and save her. But as they came in the throne room, one by one, they stood at attention, but faced Richards instead.

"You said it won't be easy for her to get out, which means there *is* a way." I fidgeted with the skeleton keys .

"Yes, and while it is unlikely that it will happen, to break the curse she will have to convince her own heart to love something other than herself," he said matter-of-factly as he walked toward the line of cardsmen. "Attention, guards," he calmly said; the floor vibrated when the paper army stomped one foot in unison. "You will escort this young lady down to the stocks and free the man that is being held prisoner. If any harm comes to either of them I will set you all ablaze. Understood?"

A unified "Yes, Sir Richards" was spoken by the cardsmen. They fell in line behind one another, stopping just short of where I stood.

"Are you ready, dear Alice?" the leader of the line spoke.

"Well, yes," I said, slightly confused and a bit wary of the cardsmen, whose only goal not long ago was to kill me.

I glanced over at the Red Queen. She continued to struggle against the black cloud that had entangled her.

"The first five will escort you down. It will take the rest of the army to accompany the Queen," Richards said over his shoulder as he gave the five chosen cardsmen a once over.

"Accompany me where?" The Red Queen's frantic words were followed by a crazed smile. "Richards, what about all the good times we had? Does that mean nothing to you? I didn't treat you poorly. We were a team, we *are* a team."

Her poor attempt at kindness resulted in an uproar of laughter from Richards.

"Good times?" He stormed toward the Red Queen with long strides, his arm raised in the air and finger pointed. He shoved his finger into her face. The black tendrils shooting sparks all around him but never touched him, "You mean when you forced yourself upon me? Or when you scarred my face because I spilled your crumpets? Or let's see, when you used me as a footstool for five hours because your feet were tired from walking to the other end of the fucking throne room?" Spit flew from his lips as the words fled through his teeth. Veins in his neck bulged out with every word.

"I–I didn't know you felt this way, my love." Richards reared back and smacked the Red Queen across the face so hard the sound reverberated off the walls. Her mouth opened, but no sound came out, only a deep inward gasp. No screams, no words, just hot, stale air. Richards ran his hands down his face and cocked his head to the side; he stared at the Red Queen as a single tear ran down her porcelain white cheek. "I just didn't know, Richards…"

Her words were cut off by his hand cupped across her mouth, "Shhhh…hush now, Charrdis. It's your turn to listen," Richards leaned in and blew into the black smoke, sending a ribbon over her lips and sealing her mouth shut. He clasped his hand around her jaw, pinch the black veined skin between his fingers and pulled her face closer to his, "The only way to undo this is to find love in your heart—love for someone other than *yourself*. And that, my dear Charrdis, is going to be a bit difficult down in the stocks with only me to keep you company. A little known fact," he paused and let go of her face as he dropped his hands, clasping them at the wrists, "I hate everything you have done to me, but," He looked up at her with a raised brow and a crooked smile while he lazily shook a finger toward her, "I don't hate *you*. I know there is hope for you—albeit small, it is there." As Richards continued to speak, the Red Queen's eyes filled with the same black lines that had encroached upon her face. "If I was manifested from you, there is proof that you were once good, even if just a whisper of good remains, you need to find it, you need to *feel* it. I remember when you—we—were younger and you would frolic through the bumbleberry fields, not a care in the world. You would save the beetles that got their wings caught in the sticky vines and set them free. You cared. I remember the conversations we had with the daisies and the daffodils, do you remember any of this? Or has your heart become so blackened that all your memories have gone dark?"

The Red Queen cast her eyes to the floor. A droplet of salty regret fell from the corner of one eye to the end of her nose before it dropped into the black misty ribbon below.

"All right then," Richards clasped his outstretched hands in front of him, "Without further ado, let's free the prisoner. You five take Alice down and release Tyden," he said to the five cardsmen standing by me as if we were about to attend a grand celebration. "And the rest of you form a circle around the *former* Queen and bring her down, but be mindful of the sparks; your paper bodies will go up in a flash if you move too quickly."

The Red Queens head shot up, eyes wide at his last words, her head shaking from side to side as if she wanted to say something, but the hexan cloud muted her.

The cardsmen led me to the door that was just behind the throne and to a set of spiral stairs. As I rounded the corner at the bottom, I froze. I hadn't expected the stocks to look like this. It was a long, dimly lit hallway lined with wide doors on each side. A small window had been carved out at the top, eye level to the cardsmen that stood beside each one of them.

"Which one is he in?" I asked as I stood on my tip toes peering in every door as we passed.

"This way," the lead cardsman said as he hastily brushed past me.

"You may need these." I held up the keys as the cardsman stood in front of a pale yellow door with chipped paint.

The sound of the lock clicking in to place as he turned the key had my heart pumping loudly; it felt like every second was an hour. Finally, the creaking of the door echoed down the seemingly endless hall as I pushed past the cardsman and into the room where Tyden lay on the floor, petrified.

"Tyden!" I cried as I fell to my knees beside him. He lay there curled into himself, his clothes covered in dirt and blood, his eyes swollen and bruised.

I pushed a few strands of hair out of his face, he hastily jerked away from me as he bellowed, "No! Get away from me!"

"It's me, Tyden. It's Alice, you're safe, I'm here." I softly spoke, but kept my distance.

"Is it really you?" His raspy voice was almost unrecognizable.

"Get him some water. Please!" I asked the cardsman that stood at the door.

Within seconds, a pitcher of water was brought into the room. Tyden pushed himself up with a wince, took the whole pitcher and guzzled it down. He wiped his mouth with the back of his shirt sleeve as he heaved a breath inward and struggled to stand.

"Let's get out of here," I said to him as he steadied himself on his feet. "But first, there is something I have to do before we leave."

"Shouldn't this be the other way around?" he jested through a pained chuckle.

"What's that? The whole me saving your ass thing? Yeah, I'm sure there will come a time when you can repay the favor." I winked and wrapped my arm around his waist as he rested his head against mine, placing a gentle kiss at the top of my brow.

The cardsmen that were in charge of bringing down the Red Queen shuffled through the narrowed corridor as we stood idly by, moving from the doorway to give them access. She didn't put up much of a fight. The hexan cloud had removed itself from her mouth and feet, allowing her to walk on her own accord. Her face was riddled with defeat. The black lines still prevalent in her downcast eyes and continued the length of her visible body. The cardsmen shuffled out of the room they had ushered her into and shut the door. I walked over and looked into the small window to see the dissipating smoke. The hexan cloud had freed her, but didn't leave; it hovered over her, ready to pounce back on her at any minute.

"Is this the end?" the Red Queen asked. She never looked at me, but she knew I was there.

"No," I replied flatly. "This is the beginning of a new day, a day that will bring the wonder back to Wonderland. For this reason alone, your head will remain attached to your neck. I want you to see what I do." I smiled at her as she sat in the same place Tyden had been not too long ago. "Looks as though the seers were right after all, I will fix what you broke. The land. The spirits. I will make it right again. For what it's worth, I do hope you find peace within yourself."

Her head hung low. Her once brilliant ball gown was now dull and tired, tattered and torn.

"Someone will be here to tend to you," I said as I had begun to walk away, but then stopped. I needed to hear one last thing from the woman who was to reside in the bowels of her own prison.

"Hey," I looked back through the opening in the door.

"What is it, stupid girl?" Her voice was broken.

"How does it feel?" I asked.

"How does *what* feel?" she snapped, her head swinging around as she glared up at me.

"Losing," I whispered and shut the door to the small opening, locking it in place and giving the key to the one person that would be responsible for keeping her alive: Richards.

"You know, Richards, if she dies you're free, but you won't be able to see her face when she realizes she is no longer in control. It may take a few days, maybe even a week or two, but it will happen and I hope you get to be the one who witnesses it." I dropped the key in his hand. "Just don't go mad. It's how people lose their heads, I hear."

Richards chuckled as he palmed the set of keys, "I do like the way my head sits atop my shoulders. I will do my best not to let it fall off, my Queen," he said as he bowed in front of me, holding out the royal crown. "It has always been yours, dear Alice. You were meant to be the

Queen since the day you were born; it's in the prophecy that the seers scrolled."

"So I've heard." I attempt to collect my thoughts. "Richards, I don't know the first thing about ruling a pack of rabid field, what am I to do with an entire kingdom?"

Richards came near and placed his hand upon my chest. "With this," he said with a smile. "You, my Queen, have a heart big enough to put the Wonder back in Wonderland, and I will be here to help you every step of the way."

Tyden took the crown in a shaky hand and placed it atop my head. "Wow." His words a mere whisper.

"What? I look ridiculous right?" I wasn't sure what to say. I had just been given a kingdom that was in pretty bad shape. I had no idea how I was going to fix it, but what I looked like in the royal headdress was what fell out of my mouth. I chuckled to myself; this will be interesting for sure.

"You look beautiful," Tyden said, his voice still weak, but his eyes had life in them again.

"Why don't you go see your new room, your majesty? I will have the bell maids change out the bedding and make you curtains to your liking." Richards was definitely going to come in handy if I was going to accept the royal title.

Tyden's hand slipped down from the small of my back and fell to rest at my rear. "Where did you say that room was again, Richards?" I asked as Tyden's head fell back with laughter.

"The cardsmen will give you the grand tour. I'm assuming you know your way around the tunnels, so just the upper levels should do," Richards replied. "Oh, Tyden, here is something to help with the weakness." Richards handed him a small bottle of sparkling purple liquid. "Don't drink it all at once or you will tear the castle down just by walking."

Richards sat outside of the Red Queen's cell; perhaps he hoped things would turn out differently for them, that maybe she would find it in her to change, maybe he would convince her that she wasn't all bad. I didn't have as high expectations, but with her detained, I had the opportunity to make a difference in this land, to make it beautiful again. It would take a lot of work, but it would get done.

Right after we found that damn bedroom.

The End

Author Elizabeth Montgomery was born in Williamsburg, Virginia and raised a hop, skip, and a jump away in Yorktown, Virginia. Paranormal inspiration was easily obtained during her childhood in these colorful towns. This helped to spur her love of Paranormal romance stories, but she also enjoys reading YA and NA. To learn more, visit: http://www.ElizabethMontgomery.com

HANSEL & GRETEL
A twisted retelling
by Cameo Renae

What a bitch!

Stepmother? I spat at the word.

She didn't warrant or earn the title. The entire thirteen years my brother, Hans, and I were forced to suffer with the beast, she'd never shown a bit of motherly love toward us. Every single day we questioned if she was the primordial *spawn of Satan*. And without fail, at the end of every day, the answer was a resounding *yes*.

What our dad saw in her…we had no idea. He was her complete opposite. Kind. Generous. A decent human being. But he was also soft and naturally destitute of vision. For God sake, the woman was manlier than he was. The thought of her sent a shiver up my spine.

After our *real* mom had died, things went downhill quickly.

And then…the apocalypse happened.

A massive solar storm erupted and entered the earth's atmosphere, completely collapsing the national power grid, shutting down all navigational and communication systems across the globe. Millions were thrust into darkness.

But that wasn't the worst of it.

Over four hundred nuclear power plants were operating across thirty countries. Very few had backup generator pumps which relied on large tanks of water for cooling the containment shells. Within a span of about ten days, nuclear fuel melted through containment rods, spewing massive doses of radiation into the atmosphere.

To help keep global panic to a minimum, the governments offered people hope in the form of a vaccine. An anti-radiation vaccine. Despite the lack of testing or results, it was approved, mass produced, and distributed to shelters across the globe.

But we didn't have to worry about any of that. Before the terror was widespread, our father, an electrical engineer, took us to an underground bunker he'd secretly built and stocked. The shelter was small, and after thirteen years of surviving, it had become much smaller. We were now to the point our food supplies were dangerously low.

Through Morse code, our father learned the topside was safe to return to, but we were screwed. My dad built our survival bunker in the middle of the Alaskan boonies, at least twenty miles in any direction from civilization.

In recent months, my brother Hans and I kept our eating to a bare minimum. Because of it, we were slowly becoming emaciated. We'd gone to the topside several times to look for food, but there was nothing but dry, barren land as far as the eye could see.

⁓ ⊹⊹ ⁓

My name is Greta. I'm seventeen and was raised by my brother, Hans, who is nineteen. We don't look too much alike, aside from the same dark brown hair and brown eyes, and he's about a foot taller than me.

Our stepmother hated us. From the time we arrived in the bunker, she made sure our father kept busy with her matters. Every time he showed a bit of attention toward us, she became infuriated and we would get punished. We never forced either of their love or affection. Hans and I had each other, and that was enough. I was thankful for my brother.

We overheard her whole conversation with our father while lying on our old, worn cots in the adjacent room. She wanted him to take us to the topside to search for food, and not return until we had. In other words, she wanted us gone and dead.

The burly wench!

It took everything inside of me to bite my tongue and not scream curse words. She had it coming. After thirteen years of putting up with her crap, I was at my limit. The only reason why we kept quiet was because of our dad.

My pulse thrummed so loud I could hear it in my ears; my face burned with fury, and my hands balled into fists so tight my nails dug into the skin.

"Relax, Greta," Hans said quietly, knowing me too well. "Don't let it get to you."

"How can I not?" I huffed. "Why doesn't Dad ever stand up to her?"

"He's tried, and you know how that ended," he sighed. "It's time we left anyway. We've survived hell for all these years, topside shouldn't be much worse."

I rolled over, boiling with rage. "We'll die up there."

"If you think that way now, you're already dead." His brow raised and his head tilted to the side.

"Whatever," I complained, knowing he was right.

"I have something that'll help us, at least for a little while."

My head whipped over to him, and I mouthed, "What?"

He grinned placing his finger to his lips, then carefully lifted his pillow. Under it were six MRE's. The beast said we were out of MRE's months ago, so we'd been living off of miniscule portions of rice and beans.

"How the heck did you get those?" I whispered.

He grinned and shrugged. He wasn't going to tell me, and I didn't care. I was just glad we weren't going up without food.

I quickly calculated our survival rate. If rationed wisely, we could live off of those six MRE's for almost two weeks. Our dad told us there was a small town about twenty miles north. If we walked at least five miles per day, we would be there in at least five days. Hopefully less.

"Try and get some sleep," Hans said closing his eyes.

"You too," I exhaled, staring at the same gloomy, colorless wall I had for over thirteen years.

The next morning after packing water and survival necessities into our packs, our distraught father led us to the topside and told us what we already knew. We didn't give him any trouble, knowing he had to deal with the beast.

He gave us each another flask of water, and tucked under his shirt he pulled a few dehydrated fruit packets. Then, he handed Hans a machete, and me a dull ax.

"What am I supposed to do with this?" My face twisted as I held it up.

"It will help you chop wood and tinder for a fire," he replied.

"Fine," I sighed, knowing it would take a considerable amount of effort to cut anything with the blunt blade.

Hans giggled so I walked away.

"Greta." My dad's hand grabbed my shoulder, stopping me, so I spun to face him. "I'm so sorry." His eyes watered, which made my hardened heart soften just a bit. I blamed him for all the years he didn't stand up to the beast.

"I pity you, Dad. You don't deserve this life and the way she treats you, and she doesn't deserve you. One of these days you're going to have to stick up for yourself." Not wanting him to see the tears welling in my eyes, I walked away.

"Don't worry about us," Hans said.

"Be safe son, and please take care of your sister. I pray you find food. Just keep north and if you stay straight, it should lead you to the town."

"All right," Hans said, hugging him.

As we walked away, he called after us. "I love you both. I always have."

"We know," Hans answered.

"We love you too," I added.

A smile rose on his face, right before the beast's voice blared from the bunker, calling his name, and instantly severing the moment. The sound of her shrill voice pierced my ears, making them ache. And just like that, our dad disappeared into misery.

<hr />

By midday, we'd walked a few miles, but our frail skin wasn't used to the sweltering sun. The exposed areas of our bodies had become bright red and blistered. Our throats were as dry as dust, and our lips were cracked and bleeding.

I was teetering. My tongue was swollen, my eyes were burning, my head throbbing, and the few sips of water I did take made me nauseous.

We'd left one hell and entered another. The land around us was barren and bereft of life. It was eerily silent and completely motionless. Every step felt weighted, and every breath was agonizing. The heat from the ground scorched our tired, blistered feet.

Hans didn't complain, but I knew he was also suffering the effects of the sun. I could see it in the way his steps slowed, and how he was hunched over. We were both dehydrated, fighting our own demons, and there was no shade to rest under.

The wilderness was gone, and all that remained were snags; corpse remains of scorched and petrified trees, twisting in agony as death swept over them. Walking amongst them was haunting.

I stopped briefly for water, sitting on the scalding ground, resting my aching back onto a dead stump.

"We shouldn't stop," Hans urged. "We need to keep moving."

"I can't. If I walk any further, without resting first, I'll pass out."

Hans gave in and plopped down next to me. Then he opened his pack and took out one MRE. "Beef ravioli, or beef ravioli?" he asked, holding it up.

Figured. It was the beasts least favorite.

"Beef ravioli sounds like heaven."

Hans gathered a few dried branches and made a small fire using a flint stone he'd packed. He took out a metal cup and boiled a little water, then poured it into the pouch.

"Eat up. It's all yours," he said handing me the bag and a plastic spoon.

I ate half and gave him the rest, knowing he was just as starved as I was.

After he finished, Hans stood, and his eyes narrowed toward the north.

"What is it?" I asked.

"It looks like smoke." His voice carried a glint of excitement. "Someone's made a fire."

In the distance, wispy plumes of white billowed into the bright sky, and the more I focused, I could tell it was only about a mile away.

"Maybe they have a place to rest and some food," I said, a little delirious.

"Maybe they do." Hans was an optimist and always managed to keep our spirits high, even during our lowest lows. "Let's go find out."

With food and water in our bellies and a renewed hope, we set off.

As we came closer, Hans insisted we be discreet. The topside had changed, and we hadn't had interaction with other humans in years. Thirteen years of survival can do strange things to people, and he wanted to make sure we were safe. I didn't argue.

We soon spotted a small cabin resting quietly in the middle of nowhere. It was quaint and appeared well kept.

Quietly and carefully, we snuck closer until we could see it clearly. In front of the cabin was a large sign stuck in the ground with words painted in bright red:

FOOD AND SHELTER HERE!
ALL SURVIVORS WELCOME!

Behind the sign, set against the house, was a long table with dozens of canned goods neatly stacked in rows on top of each other. Next to the cans were dozens of filled water bottles.

The front door squeaked open and a girl came walking out wearing a yellow dress. She had a pretty face and seemed around our age. Silky brown hair fell down her back, shimmering in the sun.

She added a few more cans to the table, then grabbed a bottle of water, twisted the cap off, and took a sip. She then closed her eyes and leaned her head back, letting the sun touch her golden skin. After a minute, she walked back into the cabin and closed the door.

"Do you think it's safe?" I asked.

Hans had an odd look on his face. "It looks fine from here."

I glared at him. "Are you looking at the situation or the girl?"

He shrugged. "Both."

"Yeah, that's what I thought," I snickered. "Don't let your heart loose on the first eligible girl. Look what happened to Dad."

"Grab your stuff and let's go," he exasperated.

I stood, throwing my pack over my back. "I'm just saying."

"Well, as your older brother who raised you, I'm asking you to trust my judgment."

"Fine."

As we neared the cabin, we caught an aromatic scent we'd become unfamiliar with; the smell of *real*, home-cooked food. It wafted in the breeze making our mouths water.

We walked up to the table and stood there, gawking at all the cans of unopened food.

Hans was about to knock on the door when it opened and the girl in the yellow dress stood in the doorway, frozen in her tracks. Her eyes were filled with panic and fear, and then all of a sudden, the cans wrapped in her arms dropped to the ground. She stumbled backward and fell on her bottom.

Hans held his hands up in the air and slowly stepped toward her. She cowered away from him, making him stop.

"Hans, you're scaring her," I piped.

"We're not going to hurt you," he said kindly. "We saw your sign and came for food."

She didn't say a word, but her body was trembling. She jumped up, ran back inside, and slammed the door shut.

"Way to make a first impression." I teased.

"I didn't know she was gonna walk out the door," he puffed. "She looked terrified of us. I guess she wasn't expecting to see any survivors."

"We're probably the first she's ever seen."

We stood still and waited a good five minutes. When she didn't return, I finally motioned for him to knock. Hans shook his head, but reluctantly went and knocked on the door anyway.

I stood next to him as the door creaked open.

This time, an older woman, possibly in her mid-fifties, came to the door. She greeted us with a broad smile. Her face was weathered and worn, and she had salt-and-pepper hair which was pulled up into a messy bun. Her eyes were a dark blue but a little smoky.

"Hi ma'am," Hans greeted her, extending his hand. "My name is Hans and this is my sister Greta."

"Survivors!" she exclaimed, thrilled to see us. "I didn't think there'd be many survivors around these parts. My name is Peg. It's nice to meet you."

"Nice to meet you too," Hans replied. "My sister and I left our bunker, a few miles south. We're heading to a town about fifteen miles north to look for food for our family. On our way, we spotted the smoke from your chimney and followed it here. We saw your sign, so we thought we'd come and rest for a while if that's all right with you."

"Well, we're more than glad to have you," she chimed. "How many are in your family?"

"Just our father and…" Hans paused and gave me a knowing glance. "…his wife."

"Ahhh. I see." She sighed and shook her head. "The evil stepmother?"

I rolled my eyes. "Evil is an understatement."

The old woman laughed.

"Your house smells wonderful," Hans said.

"Yes. Yes, it does," she replied. "We were lucky. We set a trap the other day and actually caught something. My husband and son were avid hunters and trappers. We didn't think we would find anything out there, but I guess we were wrong."

"What'd you catch?" Hans asked.

"Something we can eat," the woman chuckled. "I was excited to bring it home and cook it. And let me tell you, it tastes even better than it smells." Her face lit up. "And wait until you see my garden. Everything in the stew is freshly grown. I planted them with seeds I'd kept from before the apocalypse. It took us a while to dig past the poisoned earth, but we eventually hit rich, fertile soil. We've got quite a crop out back if you'd like to go see," she said.

"We'd love to," I replied. "I'd like to have a garden one day."

"Well, it's possible, and I have proof."

The girl in the yellow dress slowly stepped into our view. She stayed deep in the background of the cabin, her wide auburn eyes swirled with a mixture of fear and sadness. Then, she did something completely unexpected. Her eyes froze on mine, and she shook her head slightly.

Was she telling me no? What would she be telling me no to?

The old woman caught me glancing over her shoulder and craned her neck back. The girl immediately put her head down.

"Have you two met my daughter, Mary?" she asked.

"Not formally," Hans answered. "I think I scared her."

"She obviously hasn't been around many people, so seeing you made her jittery. And, she's very timid. Aren't you, Mary?"

Mary nodded. Her eyes still glued to the floor.

What the hell was going on?

"We understand not being around people. You're the first we've seen in thirteen years," I said.

"Well, why don't you both come in for a hot meal? The stew is almost done and you both look famished. Then I'll take you on a short tour of my garden out back."

"Thank you," Hans said. "That's very generous of you."

"It's our pleasure to have such lovely company. I'm sure my husband and son will be thrilled to meet you," she added. "Come, sit down and make yourselves at home. Mary, why don't you go outside and bring in a few bottles of water?"

Mary moved quickly toward the door. Then I noticed she had a long chain clasped around her ankle which was attached to a pipe on the wall.

I nudged Hans, trying to point it out, but the old woman came and set two steaming bowls of stew in front of us. The smell of meat, vegetables, and spices simmered in sauce instantly deadened my thoughts.

The woman stood in front of us, slapping both hands flat on the table. "Well, dig in," she said with a toothy smile. "Let me know how it tastes."

I took a scoop, and as I lifted the spoon, I saw a piece of carrot, a pea, and a piece of meat. As I raised it to my lips, Mary came sprinting from the door and slapped the spoon from my mouth.

Shocked, I sat there frozen, gaping at her.

"Why did you do that?" Peg barked. She smacked Mary in the face, and she fell into a heap on the floor. "I don't know what's wrong with that girl. She's never acted inappropriately before."

"Why is her ankle bound?" I asked, drawing Hans's attention to it.

"It's for her protection. She wanders in her sleep. A few weeks ago I had to go searching, and found her almost dead, lying on the dirt a mile away."

Then why is she bound when she was awake?

Peg bent over and un-cuffed Mary's leg, tossing the chain to the side.

"Why doesn't she talk?" I asked.

"She's mute," Peg answered.

Hans stood from the table. "I think we should leave. We still have a ways to go before we reach the town." The deep lines in his brow and the twisting of his hands showed me he was just as uneasy as I was.

"I came from the town a few months ago," Peg replied. "There isn't much left. I was one of the survivors from a family members bunker right on the outskirts. My husband and son refused to go underground and took the government vaccinations instead. A few months ago I made my way back and found them here. They were barely alive; their bodies were so weak they could hardly move. It took a lot of hard work to get them healthy again. Even now, they're still on the mend."

"They survived on the topside all those years?" Hans gasped.

"Yes," she said sadly. "But it did a lot of damage to them."

"Where are they now?" I asked.

"They're out back," she said. "You wanna meet them?"

"We don't want to bother," Hans replied. "We should be going before the sun goes down."

"Nonsense. They'll be thrilled to know there are survivors around here." When Hans didn't answer, she added, "Well, at least come see my garden before you leave. I'll give you a few fresh vegetables to take to your family. And I could use your help carrying a few buckets out back since Mary isn't much of a help."

Hans glanced at me.

"Pretty please," Peg begged sweetly.

"All right," Hans responded.

"Thank you," she bubbled.

As we followed her out back with the buckets, Hans and I made eye contact. I threw my pack over my left shoulder and readied the ax, just in case. Rounding the corner we witnessed her garden, and it was just as amazing as she said it was. Rows and rows of carrots, cabbage, green beans, potatoes, and herbs. It was the most amazing thing to witness; an oasis in the middle of the desert. Life amidst death.

"Wow. This looks like it took some time and a lot of hard work," I said.

Her eyes softened as she looked at her masterpiece. "Yes. A lot of blood, sweat, and tears. But the bounty has made it worthwhile."

Hans looked around. "Where is your family?"

"Probably down in the cellar, resting from the heat." She smiled. "We've got bottles of wine and pop down there. I'll give you a few bottles to take back. I'm sure your dad would appreciate it."

"That would be nice," Hans replied, not wanting to offend her.

"Could you please help me pull the hatch open?" she asked. "It's much too heavy for an old woman like me."

Hans handed me his pack, and I held it to my chest with the handle of the machete in my grasp. Then he walked up to a large cellar door in the ground and yanked it open. Once free, the old woman pulled a gun from her back and aimed it at him.

I withdrew the machete from the pack and stepped toward her.

"Stop," she hollered, pointing the gun at Hans. "Come any closer and I'll blow his head off."

"What are you doing?" I cried, backing up.

"Surviving," she answered. "Now drop the damn blade."

I released my fingers from the handle of the machete and watched it fall to the earth, along with any chance of freeing ourselves. She took our packs and forced us down into the cellar, keeping the gun pointed at us as we descended into the darkness.

I gagged as a rotting stench burned my nose.

Once we were all down, she pointed to a corner of the room. "Move," she snapped.

When we didn't listen, she fired a warning shot at the ground in front of us. Hans and I immediately backed up. As soon as our backs touched the wall she hit a lever, dropping large metal bars around us.

Hans threw himself at the bars, but they were too strong. We were caged, like animals.

Screams and growls erupted from something on the other side of the bars.

"What the hell is that?" I backed away from the noise.

The old woman clicked on a flashlight and lifted it, illuminating the area to the side of us.

I screamed, falling backward as I stared at two monsters. They were horribly pale, and their bodies severely atrophied. Milky white eyes sunk deep into their sockets. Their skin was coarse and scabby. Growls and screams raged from rotted mouths.

"I'd like you to meet my husband and son," the old woman said with a broad smile. She slowly stepped forward, stopping only a few feet from the cage.

A decrepit limb shot out at her face. Its bony fingers rabidly clawed at her.

The old woman took hold of the hand and kissed it.

This bitch was crazy.

"Are you hungry, dear?" she asked the creature.

It answered with horrifying screams, still trying to rip into her.

The second creature, which appeared to be the younger, was just as eager. He thrust his gaunt arms and sharp, filthy nails at her.

"Yes. Yes, I know you're hungry," she cooed sweetly.

She backed up and pivoted, shining the light on a piece of meat hanging from a rope.

"Oh my God," Hans exhaled, his voice shaking. "That's a body."

"What?" I gasped.

Terror ripped through me as her light shined on a human corpse strung upside down. Its head was severed, as well as its right leg and arm.

Bile immediately rose in my throat, and I dry heaved.

"You're a smart, young man." The woman laughed wickedly, pointing the flashlight at us. "By luck, this man came knocking on our door a few days ago and just in time too. My boys were starving and won't eat the delicious vegetables from my garden. It seems they've only got a taste for raw meat these days."

"They aren't human," I screamed at the top of my lungs. "They're monsters!"

Her face contorted into something horrifying. Something evil.

"They're my family!" she bellowed back, spittle flying from her mouth. Then her finger pointed at us. "*You* are here to keep them alive.

But first, I'll have to fatten you up. You're both much too skinny and wouldn't last more than a few weeks."

"You can't do this," Hans yelled. "We're survivors, just like you are. *Our* family is depending on *us* to bring back food."

"Well, hopefully, they'll come this way. That'll be even more fresh meat for my boys."

She grabbed a wide, serrated knife off the wall, and carved huge chunks of flesh from the corpse's side. As she tossed the meat into the monsters cage, they went wild like ravage beasts, clawing at each other for the pieces.

I looked away, pulling my shirt above my nose. It was a poor attempt to keep from vomiting. This place was worse than a nightmare. The air was thick and rancid. The ground was covered with straw and stunk like mold.

Hans came and sat next to me. "We'll find a way out of this," he said, but his words were shaky and uncertain.

I shook my head, unable to speak. Tears filled my eyes for the first time in years. I couldn't remember the last time I'd cried, but seeing the dead body, and being caged with monsters and a crazed woman, drove me to the edge of my emotions.

We were going to die next, and there was nothing we could do. We were helpless.

"Eat up boys," the woman cheered, before sawing off the other arm and tossing it into the cage. I covered my ears as the mutants tore into the flesh; the sounds they made while feeding were savage.

They were vicious. They were monsters. And this was hell.

The woman came and dangled pieces of bloody flesh in front of us.

"Want some?" she teased. "You said it smelled wonderful in the stew, and I know you would have loved it if Mary hadn't rudely hit it away from you."

"You're sick," Hans spat. "We'll never eat another human."

"Oh, I wouldn't be too sure of that. In a few days, you'll be starving and begging for it. And once you taste it for the first time, you'll crave it." She laughed loudly and flung the last piece of meat into the monsters cage. "I'll have Mary bring you some food."

"We don't want your damn food," I cursed.

"We'll see." She snickered, climbing up the ladder. "We'll see."

As soon as the cellar door shut, we were back in complete darkness.

"What have we done?" I sobbed. "She's a murderer, and they're all cannibals."

"I'm sorry, Greta. It's my fault," Hans said, placing his hand around my shoulder. "I should have used better judgment."

"It's not your fault," I said. "We both let our guards down."

"There has to be a way for us to get out of here."

"Wait," I sniffled. "She said she was going to send Mary down with food. You need to try and seduce her. Get her to like you, and then maybe she'll help us."

"How would I seduce her? Does she read lips?"

I gawked at him, baffled at his response. "Hans, she's mute. She can hear you perfectly fine, she just can't answer you."

He paused and then shrugged. "I knew that."

"Yeah, sure. But it seemed like she wanted to help us. Why would she shake her head at me, or keep me from eating the stew?"

Hans nudged me. "Maybe *you* should talk to her. She seems to like you better."

"No," I rebutted. "I saw a look in her eyes when she first saw you. Something beyond the horrified expression. Something only another girl would understand."

"You did?" His face scrunched.

"Yep. And I think with a little work, she'll fall for you."

"I'll give it a shot, but you do realize I haven't been around *any* girls, aside from you and the beast."

"Just smile. She'll dig your big, goofy smile."

"My smile's not goofy."

"Oh, it's downright goofy," I teased.

Hans wasn't ugly and had a very charming, witty personality. I was banking on that fact, so he'd be able to use it to his advantage and get Mary to free us. If anyone could do it, he could.

My head was about to explode from the constant bursts of rage from the monsters. Their high-pitched screams pierced my eardrums. Every few minutes they would fling themselves against the cage, stretching their limbs, attempting to reach us.

After countless hours, they should have figured out they couldn't get to us. But no. These monsters were obviously brainless, and their incessant explosions kept us up all night. If I had anything other than straw around me, I would have hurled it at them.

The next morning we heard the hatch open. Sunlight flooded the cellar making our eyes ache. The monsters went wild again while Hans and I stood, watching Mary climb down the ladder.

"I'll give you five minutes," the old woman shouted from above. "Do what I tell you or I'll lock you up and you'll get no food today."

God, she sounded like the beast.

Mary was wearing a blue dress with a large, brown sack thrown over her shoulder. Her hair was tied back, and simple white slip-on shoes were on her feet. Once she reached the bottom, she quickly set the bag down to empty it.

"Don't forget to feed your dad and brother!" Peg hollered down.

The monsters were going crazy, bashing against the cage, growling, and screaming. I could barely think and felt like my head was going to explode. Those freaking damn mutants were getting on my last nerve. My fear was quickly transforming into rage. If I had a gun, I'd blast a hole in each of their heads just to shut them up and put them out of their misery.

Mary knelt and unfolded a napkin. Inside were baked morsels which looked like cookies. The sweet aroma drifting from them was mouthwatering.

I nudged Hans and he walked toward the bars to meet her.

When she handed him the cookies, he carefully took them from her; his fingers lingering on hers.

"Thank you," he whispered.

She glanced up and caught his stare; her face flushed pink. She awkwardly looked away before pulling two Tupperware containers from her sack and placed them on the ground next to the cage. I almost threw up in my mouth as I realized what they were. There was no freaking way I was eating cannibal stew.

"Hurry up!" Peg hollered from outside the cellar.

She was also getting on my last nerve.

Hans wasn't making any progress with Mary, so I stood at the bars and whispered, "Mary, you have to help us. Please."

Her eyes widened with trepidation. She shook her head.

"If you don't help us, we're going to die and end up like that," I urged, pointing to the corpse hanging behind her.

"Sorry," she mouthed. She then opened her mouth widely.

"What the...?" Hans went pale.

I gasped and threw my hands over my mouth.

Mary's tongue was gone. Like gone, gone. Like it was cut off, gone. Now we knew the real reason why she was mute. It was because she didn't have a damn tongue.

"Mary, you have to help us get out of here," I begged. "We'll take you with us. We will take care of you and make sure she'll never hurt you again."

She wouldn't listen. She was too afraid, and it was written all over the furrowed lines in her brow.

"Mary!" the psycho screamed down.

Mary hurried toward the corpse, grabbed the knife off the wall and began sawing at it, severing flesh from bone. I could see the disgust in her eyes as she threw the raw meat into the cage. When she was done, she wiped her bloodied hands on her dress and wiped her teary, red eyes on her sleeve.

She didn't look at us again. Instead, she walked straight to her empty sack, picked it up, and quickly climbed back up the ladder.

When the hatch closed and we were back in darkness, I suddenly felt nauseous. The room was thick with an overwhelming hopelessness, suffocating me.

No one knew where we were, and the only one who cared, couldn't do a thing. Even if he did come, he'd probably never find us, or worse...end up another victim.

"We'll never get out of here," I said, swallowing my despair.

I walked back to the far corner of the cage and slumped down. There were tiny cracks in the cellar door which allowed a few rays of light to filter in. Once our eyes adjusted to it, we could see the room a bit better.

"You should try these cookies," Hans moaned, taking a bite. "They're amazing."

"Why? So she can fatten us up and feed on us longer? Screw that."

"What do you think happened to Mary's tongue?" he murmured before taking another bite.

"I don't know. Maybe she talked back? Maybe she voiced how wrong it was to *eat* another *human being*? I wouldn't doubt her mother dearest cut it off and fed it to her dad and bro over there. Who knows? They're all freaking weirdos if you ask me."

The monsters in the adjacent cage were going crazy again. They'd finished their meal and were still ravenous.

I grabbed a Tupperware, popped open the lid, and walked toward them, standing just from their grasp.

They were the most ghastly, horrid things I'd ever seen, with barely any resemblance of humanity left. Whatever happened to them on the topside severely mutated them into these hideous monsters. They were now the things nightmares were made of. They were unadulterated evil and wanted nothing more than to rip us to shreds and eat the flesh from our bones.

But while they were terrifying, they were also annoying as hell.

I flung the stew at the monsters and let them have at it, but it only quieted them for approximately six seconds.

"Greta, look." Hans pointed at something under the straw, about a yard from the edge of our cage. It appeared metallic.

"What is it? I asked.

"I don't know, but maybe we could use it to get out of here."

He stretched his arm against the bars, but it was just beyond his reach.

"Move, big brother," I said, tapping his shoulder.

"How are you going to get it? Your arm is way shorter than mine."

"Yes, but my leg is longer, and thanks to the beast, it should be thin enough to fit through the bars."

I slid as close as I could to the bars and sure enough, my leg slipped right through without a struggle. I pressed my heel on top of the metal object and dragged it back toward us.

Hans grabbed it and lifted it up.

"It's a hook," he said, observing it.

It was a large metal hook with a sharp point on one end.

"Do you think we can use it to catch the lever and get free?" I asked.

"I don't know. That would have to be a pretty accurate throw."

"It's not like we have anything else to do down here." I was willing to try, no matter how long it took.

"We'll need something to attach it to, so we can yank it back."

I glanced over to the monsters. "They're both wearing belts," I noted.

He looked at me with narrowed eyes. "And how the hell are we going to get the belts off of them?"

"Well, they'd obviously have to be dead," I scoffed. "And we finally have a weapon to kill them with."

"This?" he asked, holding the hook up like it was part of his limb.

16

"Yep." I nodded.

Hans held the hook out to me and raised his brow.

"What? You want me to do it?"

He shrugged, still holding it out. "It was your suggestion. Knock yourself out."

I sucked in a deep breath and thought about it for a minute. These monsters were the reason we were locked down here in the first place, and I wasn't going to sit here and willingly add myself to their menu. This was it. The psycho woman up top was already planning our executions.

It was either them or us.

I snapped myself into some kind of survival mode, then snatched the hook from his hand and headed toward the cage.

"Greta, what are you doing?" he piped.

"Taking out our enemy," I informed.

The larger of the two mutants charged toward me, thrashing against the bars, stretching its osseous, filthy fingers toward my face. It's rotted mouth snapped open and shut, wanting to sink its teeth into me.

Without hesitation, I raised the hook above me and slammed it down against its head. The sickly sound of bone splintering echoed as the hook penetrated through its brittle skull. I yanked the hook back and watched the point exit from the socket of its right eye. It's eyeball burst, liquid and jelly hung down the side of its face as it wailed.

Eye juice splattered on my arm, so I screamed in horror and released the hook. Realizing what I had done, I stumbled backward. The mutant's milky eye went wide as it dropped to its knees; its lifeless body fell against the bars.

"Oh my God. Oh my God. Oh my God," I babbled. "I just killed it." A shiver ran through my body as I wiped the dead mutant's fluid from my arm.

The smaller became even more aggressive, attempting to force its limbs through the bars to reach us.

"Hans, that one's yours." I pointed.

"You left the hook in the dead one's head. How the hell am I supposed to kill it?"

"Go pull it out," I said flatly.

"You shoved it in there. *You* go pull it out."

All the blood mixed with brain and eye goop flowing from its wounds was enough to make anyone want to leave it alone.

"I killed the thing. The least you can do is pull the hook out…*big brother*," I smirked.

He growled at me. "Then get the other one to move away."

I headed toward the second mutant and stood just beyond its grasp. As I led it away, its hatred for me was evident and seeped from its milky eyes.

I kept its attention on me while Hans quickly made his way over to the dead one. He moaned as he tried to dislodge the hook. I could hear the brain matter being pushed around, squishing. Then he gave a loud yell and yanked, finally setting the hook free.

"I got it," he said excitedly, holding the dripping, bloody hook.

"Great. Now hurry up and put this one out of its misery."

There was movement above us, and the cellar door creaked open. Light flooded in, and we squinted as Mary came down the ladder. The brown sack was back over her shoulder, and I assumed she was bringing us lunch.

When she reached the bottom, it only took her a moment to figure out one of the mutants was dead.

"We're sorry," I lied, trying to speak softly.

"Hurry up, you stupid girl," Peg bellowed down.

"God, she's a bitch," I exhaled. "I can't believe she's your mother."

Mary's eyes froze on mine. She shook her head again.

"No?" I asked. "She's not your mother?"

Her eyes watered as she continued to shake her head.

"Now it all makes sense," I breathed. "Help us, Mary. Please. We'll take you away from here."

Mary paused for a moment, and then ran to the ladder and started screaming and pointing at the cage.

"What the hell is it?" Peg called down, but Mary kept hollering. "If I come down there for nothing, you'll rot in your room."

Mary betrayed us. She wasn't going to help. She was too far gone.

The ladder creaked as Peg made her way down with a rifle strapped to her back. When she reached the bottom, Mary moaned loudly and pointed to the dead mutant.

Peg's face dropped as she ran to the cage.

"Baby?" she screamed, her face twisted in torment. Tears poured from her eyes and snot from her nose. "What happened to him? What have you done to him?"

She reached for her rifle and pointed it at me and then Hans.

Mary let out a howling cry and jumped toward Peg, knocking the gun from her grasp as they wrestled on the ground. Peg wrapped her hands around Mary's neck. Mary's eyes rolled back as Peg slowly squeezed the life out of her.

Hans reached out and grabbed the gun. "Let her go," he yelled.

Peg wouldn't answer, so Hans aimed the rifle and fired off a shot.

Peg's body stiffened, and then dropped to the side. Blood seeped from a wound in her back. Mary pushed her away and ran to the wall, then pulled the lever, setting us free.

Hans ejected the casing from the rifle and reloaded it, then pointed it to the smaller mutant.

"Wait!" I exclaimed.

"What?" Hans turned with a puzzled look on his face.

"I have a plan."

Before we left, we opened the mutant's cage. The creature didn't even realize it was free, so we quickly made our escape, leaving the vile underground room.

"We should burn the place," Hans remarked.

"We will, but first we need to go get dad and the beast."

Hans nodded with a grin.

We stocked up on a few things before we left, knowing the trek would only take a few hours.

———— ❦ ————

When we reached our old bunker, we introduced Mary to our dad and the beast. The beast glared at her, but our dad greeted her kindly. Then, we showed them a few of the canned goods, and water bottles as proof of supplies.

Then, I did something I probably shouldn't have. I offered the beast a small Tupperware of stew, which I knew she wouldn't share. She practically inhaled it and wanted more, and I told her there was a whole pot waiting for her.

We continued to tell them about the quaint little cabin, the garden, and a cellar filled with wine. We knew the beast loved wine.

In a matter of an hour, they were packed and ready to go.

The beast complained the whole way, barking out orders, and made us carry all of her things. When we finally reached the cabin, her first words were, "Where's the wine?"

"I'll show you," I said nicely.

Hans gave me a glance, and I gave him a head signal. Then he began to tell our dad about the hunting rifles in the cabin, and led him inside.

Mary stood and stared at me.

"Mary, you can go inside with them," I said.

She nodded, then slowly followed after Hans.

"Are you going to take me, or not?" The beast roared.

"Yes, right this way," I said leading her toward the back. When we reached the cellar door, I stopped. "There's a lot of wine down there to choose from, and I don't want to pick the wrong one."

"I hope you're not just lazy," she snarled. "Just get the damn door open, and I'll go down myself."

"All right," I said, smiling inside.

I yanked the door open and let it drop to the ground, then watched her climb down.

"What's that god awful smell?" she griped.

I kept quiet.

As soon as she reached the bottom there was a loud growl. The beast screamed and stumbled backward into the ladder. In a flash, the mutant was on her, overpowering her to the ground. Then, it sunk its teeth into her shoulder, ripping off a chunk of flesh.

The beast screamed as blood poured from her wound; her eyes desperate, looking to me for help.

For the split second I thought about helping her, Mary appeared at my side. She stood quiet, staring at me through her wide, auburn eyes, and slowly shook her head. Then, she bent down, lifted the cellar door, and slammed it shut.

When the screams died down, we torched the cellar, finally ridding ourselves of the beasts and monsters which haunted us all these years.

When Mary and I entered the cabin, Hans and my dad were sitting at the table.

"Where's your mom?" he asked.

"She's *not* our mom," I replied. "And something horrible happened to her. She fell down the ladder to the cellar and broke her neck. Then, a lantern tipped over and set the whole place on fire. We couldn't save her."

My dad's face twisted, and he stood from the table.

"It's too late dad. There's nothing we can do," I said.

Mary stood quietly beside me.

My dad's brow furrowed, his head bowed for a few silent moments, and then, to my surprise, he was fine.

That night, around the dinner table, Hans, Mary, my dad, and I sat. We talked and laughed about life and the future, without interruption. Well, all of us except Mary. She remained quiet, but the smile on her face spoke louder than a thousand words.

We were finally free.

At least for the time being.

And we were happy…in our quaint little cabin, with a garden out back, in the middle of nowhere.

The End

Voted 2013 Break Out Author by Young Adult & Teen Readers, and 2013 Book of the Year (Hidden Wings).

Cameo Renae was born in San Francisco, raised in Maui, Hawaii, and recently moved with her husband and children to Alaska.

She's a daydreamer and a caffeine and peppermint addict who loves to laugh, loves to read, and loves to escape reality. One of her greatest joys is creating fantasy worlds filled with adventure and romance and sharing it with others.

One day she hopes to find her own magic wardrobe and ride away on her magical unicorn. Until then...she'll keep writing! To learn more, visit: http://cameorenae.com

REAL BOY
A retelling of Pinocchio
by Kellie Sheridan

"Wait, what?" I pull my hand back, gawking at Paul.

His jaw remains tense, but his expression offers no hints. A few seconds ago he was holding my hand and gazing into my eyes. Everything was fine, good even. Now he's watching me like he thinks I might break. Or implode. He's frowning, pity shining in his eyes.

"Angie, you know how much I care about you. But these things can't always last forever. It's time we both move on."

He's really breaking up with me?

This doesn't seem possible. Doesn't seem real. Where the hell is this even coming from? Last month we were talking about the idea of moving in together. What changed?

"By moving on to new things, what you really mean is new people," I accuse.

He glances downward and then makes a point of looking anywhere but back at me. There *is* someone else. Paul shakes his head pathetically.

What did I do wrong? How did we get here?

"Don't lie to me. Not now. At the very least, you owe me the truth. How long has this been going on?" I know I should just shut up and let him fill in the rest. However, I'm being bombarded with waves of panic, shock, anger and humiliation all at once. I barely even feel connected to my body anymore, let alone my mouth.

"Nothing is going on. Nothing happened, we've just hung out a few times. But I know it's not fair to you to keep doing this. We're both better off if we simply cut the cord."

My hands clench into fists on the table, so I pull them down to my lap. I desperately want to play it cool, but I can't keep my voice steady. "Hung out a few times. When?" None of this should matter. I'm better off without the sordid details. But what I really want to ask is who it is he's been hanging out with. I'm not sure I'm ready to hear the answer to that.

"No one you know. Angie, I'm sorry, this just…"

1

Paul and I have always been the type of couple who at least checks in a few times a day. I always have some idea of where he is or what he's getting up to. At least, I thought I did. My brain spins through the last few weeks, looking for any sign of a crack in his story.

"Is it Kathy?" I ask without thinking, my mind frantically putting pieces together. All those late nights at the office with "the team." He swore he didn't see her like that. I've never even seen a picture of the woman, but she always seemed to come up in his work stories.

Paul's head slumps down in either shame or defeat, I can't tell.

I don't care.

It's not even nine by the time I get back home, thirty minutes after the movie I thought we were going to see is set to start. I can't help wondering if he's there for her.

I still haven't cried a single tear, but I know the floodgates will open.

I trusted him. Again and again, he lied to me. Maybe I should have asked more questions, but I didn't think I had to.

None of this feels real. I should be collapsed in a heap on the floor. Instead, all I want to do is make this better. Not for us, just for me. To do something to fix the hole in my soul that Paul scraped out.

It takes less than an hour to clean my tiny apartment, including the wine breaks, a treat I usually reserve for the end of every term. Another forty-five minutes (and two glasses) to reorganize my closet and drawers.

It's still not enough. Having a clean apartment won't fix that I won't have anyone to call tomorrow morning and say hello to. No one to meet up with after work to tell about my day. Work. Right. I call the antique shop I work at, leaving a message for the opening manager tomorrow to say I won't be in.

Then I dust all of my furniture. I'm not sure I've ever dusted anything before and still it only takes ten minutes.

I open a new bottle. This one is a gift from my aunt that had been hiding at the back of my closet, and finally settle in at my desk and open up my laptop. Maybe retail therapy is the way to go.

I'm looking at exotic teas when an advertisement in the sidebar catches my attention. A smiling woman, her hair perfectly curled and her teeth perfectly white, has her arms wrapped around the shoulders of an equally perfect man. Except, he's not a man at all. They're advertising one of the newer models of synthetic companions. Androids, technically, but all the big companies avoid calling them that. As if that can make us forget what they are.

Synths have been a big deal in Europe for a couple of years now, finally reaching prices that make it possible for people other than millionaires to have bots in their homes and offices. They estimate that by 2035 there will be an average of one in the majority of American homes and businesses. And yeah, that accounts for the base models that will be cleaning schools and homes, or picking up our trash, but there's no denying that they are changing everything.

Maybe having one could change everything for me.

I don't really even realized that I've typed a few phrases into my search engine and pulled up a whole page of images of the latest synths models. That, coupled with a few well-placed reviews, definitely has me considering all the possibilities.

There are already more synths manufacturers in the U.S. than I can count, with a variety of reviews and prices. The one thing that remains consistent is just how real every single unit looks. Maybe not completely human, but closer to real life than movies from the last fifty years or so would have had us guess.

I find one designed for home care and tutoring children, with eyes nearly the same color as Paul's.

I close my screen with a snap. While more wine is tempting, I'll settle for sleep. Everything will look better in the morning. Maybe Paul will have come to his senses and it will be like none of this ever happened. This will amount to nothing more than a temporary nightmare.

I wake up the next morning, and everything is absolutely not better. I'm finally feeling all the things I'd pushed away the night before.

Every cell in my body hurts. Every single particle that makes up my body is enraged. Things were so perfect only a week ago, and now this is my life? He never cared about me at all. He couldn't possibly love anyone but himself.

But time doesn't stop passing. I can't just sit here and do nothing for a minute longer. I won't let anything like this ever happen to me again. Ever.

Practically on auto-pilot, I pull my laptop over from my desk and into bed with me. It starts up right where I left off the night before. Synths.

And I know exactly what I want.

CPRJ Robotics advertises the perfect companions. Not only can you pick out the desired traits you want—without even thinking about it I select the "loyal to only one user option", and when Kathy Miller's smug face flashes before my eyes. I also select an inclination toward total honesty—but they offer a "Real Boy" upgrade, which promises to enhance the emotional connections of synths with their female users, mimicking an ideal real world relationship.

I know my friends would mock me relentlessly for this, even think it was a little creepy. But right now, I couldn't care less about what anyone else thinks. I need this.

My only real hesitation comes with the checkout cart. And the final price tag. Synths usually run at about $3000, already a ridiculously high price for most people, let alone someone like me who is surviving on scholarships and government aid while I finish my degree. But the add-ons I've included have nearly doubled the price. I have the money, thanks to student loans, but I am kind of counting on that money to pay my rent, keep me fed and provide for my education.

Fuck it.

Complete purchase.

I get a momentary thrill, knowing what I've done. But my heart quickly plummets back into my chest. The estimated time until delivery is six weeks. Pretty damn fast, all things considered. But still far too slow.

***

Six weeks fly by. The first two pass in a blur, the third is all about picking up the pieces while a dark cloud hovers over me. It isn't until the fourth week that I start to feel like myself again. At the beginning of week five, I meet my dream guy on an impossibly windy day.

"Excuse me." A deep male voice says from somewhere behind me. A moment later I feel a hand gently tap my elbow and turn to see who's speaking to me.

"I'm sorry?" I ask, feeling ridiculous as the wind whips my brown hair in a cloud around my face. I force a laugh as I pull it aside to gaze up at the guy holding my recently escaped hat. "Shit, thanks."

I take my red cap back from him and turn to continue my escape from the weather into Heather's, my favorite local caffeine stop, only to see that my hat's rescuer is headed the same way. I hold the door to the café open for him, not thinking much of the whole experience. That is, until he grabs the last free table.

He's cute. Brown hair, big brown eyes that are watching me as I survey my table options, and lightly tanned skin.

I mean, what could it hurt to ask if he wouldn't mind sharing his table. I haven't so much as looked at a man in over a month—during which time, Paul hasn't contacted me even once—and it's not like I'm proposing marriage, just a temporary solution to a lack of seating problem.

"Do you mind?" I ask, nodding my head toward the chair beside him. "No pressure. You've already saved me once today."

"No, please. Sit. I can't imagine you want to head back outside any time soon." He smiles up at me, leaving a small dimple in his left cheek.

"Thanks. I'm Angie," I say, extending my hand once I've put down my coffee and over-sized purse.

"Jack."

After two more weeks and five awesome dates, I've practically forgotten all about my disaster of a relationship with Paul. And the night it all ended. I've been tactfully avoiding my bank balance, picking up a few extra shifts where I can to put off the inevitable implosion of my finances that much longer.

But when I get back to my apartment after a tedious study session to find a six and a half foot tall shipping crate sitting in my living room, it all comes rushing back. A big, green CPRJ Robotics logo adorns the side of the box.

He's here.

I key my account pin number into the security panel on the side of the crate, and the box springs to life in front of me. Within seconds, the front panel has slid aside. A towering, muscled figure stood before me. I gasp and stumble backwards, but the male figure in front of me doesn't move. His eyes remain cold and lifeless. I take a shaky breath, remembering that he isn't active yet.

Holding my phone out to the instructions chip on the side of the box, I downloaded his manual. Only once I'd done a quick read-through of the first chapter did I allow myself to really look at what I'd been sent.

There he was, standing in front of me. In the flesh. More or less. Every facet of his form was perfect, from the curve of the muscles in his shoulders to the shape of his jaw. And even as he stood before me, eyes closed, still waiting to be activated, he managed to look more alive than I had ever imagined. For all intents and purposes, he was exactly what they had promised. He was real. And he would love only me.

Which is exactly what I had thought I'd always wanted. But instead of imagining how the celery-green eyes I'd ordered would look in real life, it's Jack's face that springs into my mind.

What was I thinking?

What would Jack think of me if he knew about this?

I wonder if he's going to be as lifelike as they say.

The last thought darts into my mind unbidden, my curiosity easily getting the better of me. I have the latest and greatest of modern technology sitting here in my living room.

Maybe I can re-purpose him. Make him less of a companion and more of an assistant. I could definitely use the help. Between work, classes, assignments and errands, I *certainly* could use the help.

It's not like I can return him. He was designed specifically for me. Maybe I can sell him second-hand, find someone to alter his personality profile or whatever. But I wouldn't be able to do even that much without knowing what it is I'm selling.

I can try him out for a few days. See what happens.

Mind made up, I puncture the plastic wrapping that protects my synth's skin from dust and peel it away, and leaving what appears to be a sleeping human man standing in front of me. He's fully charged and ready to go.

I press my hand into his chest, only his white cotton t-shirt remaining as a barrier between us. A gentle buzz tingles under my hand as the activation process starts. His chest inflates slightly and his eyes open. They're exactly the shade of green I'd imagined they would be.

"Hello." A deep voice resonates from his chest, and somehow I can feel warm breath on my cheek. I drop my hand and step away.

"Hello?" It's more of a question than I mean it to be. I should have done more research on how this was supposed to work, what I could expect.

Awkwardly, the synth in front of me steps from his packaging and into my living room, but it's only a matter of seconds before he goes from fumbling to confident, finding his balance.

"It's wonderful to meet you. Are you my prime user?"

"I guess so. My name is Angela, or Angie."

As soon as I say my name, the synth's expression shifts from one of pleased curiosity to unbridled enthusiasm. "Angie! I can't believe you're here. You're even more beautiful than I expected."

I glance down at my crumpled t-shirt and old jeans. "Thanks. It's nice to meet you too. What am I supposed to call you?"

"That's entirely your choice. You're welcome to name me, or I can pick a designation from a list of randomly generated male names."

"Could you give me some options?"

"Certainly." His—its, I don't know—head tilts slightly to the side. "Abbott, Mitali, Jason, Fathi, Cadmus…" The list continues endlessly, while all I can do is stare in shocked silence.

"Cruz, Liang, Tyler, Gage."

"Tyler works," I finally sputter. "No, how about Ty?"

"Ty it is."

Ty. I look at the robot and mentally place the name with his face. Only then does he start to seem a little more like a person and less like a creepy, walking computer. He's moving around, studying my apartment, though not touching anything. I have no idea where I stand on the debate of whether synths like Ty have feelings or true thoughts or anything else that isn't just a result of programming, or if all humans are is a result of biological programming.

I can't keep him, not for long. Still, he's already looking at me like I'm the best person he's ever met… which could easily be the case if he's never truly met other humans, and if there's even a chance that my unceremoniously selling him to recoup whatever cost I can will hurt him somehow, the least I can do is explain.

"I have to tell you something." Immediately, Ty stops what he's doing and looks at me, looking directly at me in a way that Paul never really did. "I've gotten myself a little stuck, and I'm not completely sure what I want to do, but you deserve to know what's going on."

"If there's anything I can do to help, I'm happy to do it."

"I'm not even sure how much to tell you or where to start."

"Why don't we sit down, and you can tell me whatever you think is important. Do you prefer tea or coffee? I can make you something."

"Tea," I reply without meaning to. I have tea maybe once every couple of months and live for coffee. But I still can't think of coffee without thinking about that day at Heather's, and I want to avoid mingling that memory with whatever is going on here tonight.

We talk for hours. The story about how I came to order him quickly spirals into the history of Paul. And then the history of me. And school. And work. Ty listens and even makes a few jokes. The first couple fall flat, but it doesn't take him long before he completely understands my sense of humor.

Not once do I mention Jack. He's not a factor in any of this.

In the end, I opt to give myself a few days to think on all of this. Even though I've had all this time I don't have the slightest idea what I'm supposed to do next. I mean, I know what the smartest option probably is, I just don't see how it could hurt to take more time to really explore the possibilities.

***

Jack's apartment always smells amazing. At least it has the two times that I've been over so far. He lives closer to the school than I do, even though he graduated from their culinary program two years ago, and I've yet to even consider passing up an invitation to let him cook me dinner.

"Come in, come in!" He places a hand gently on the small of my back, ushering me inside before taking my heavy, fall coat. "You like Italian, right?"

"Is there anyone who doesn't like Italian food?" I give him a look that quickly evolves into a full on grin. "Yes. I like Italian. Pizza to pasta to… other Italian food? I like it all."

"Ever had Prosciutto?"

"Well, I've never even heard of it, so probably not. But I trust you."

As soon as I say the T word, a knot works its way into my stomach. Trust. There's so much I know I should tell Jack tonight. Three hours ago as I was printing out my latest essay, I was convinced I'd be doing that tonight. Even though I know how he'll react. Even though I have no real obligation to tell him anything. I'm sure there's so much he hasn't told me yet, we've only known each other for a few weeks.

And still, I know I should at least mention that I have an adoring robot at home waiting to help me with absolutely anything I need. He loves me, at least as well as he possibly can. And I need to get rid of him. And it was a moment of weakness.

And I'm rambling inside my own head as Jack stares at me expectantly. *Did he ask me something?*

"Sorry, what was that?" I ask.

"Did you want anything to drink?"

Dinner was perfect, surprising no one. We end up perfectly, wonderfully full, curled up together in his bed watching sitcom reruns.

I should tell him.

Jack's hand is resting ever so softly on my thigh. I snuggle backwards, inching as close to him as I can be until my hips are tucked against his, and the top of my head rests under his chin, scratching gently against the day old stubble on his neck.

"I've been thinking," Jack whispers, right as my eyes have started to drift closed. At once, they pop open, the possibility of sleep already long gone. My body groaning in protest, I flip over to face him.

"What's up? Is everything okay?" An image of Paul sitting across from me at the restaurant, mouth in a firm, unforgiving grimace, flashes through my mind.

My panic must show on my face, and at once Jack squeezes my hand. "Everything is perfect. These past few weeks have been incredible. Don't you think so?"

In answer, I lean over and slowly press my lips to his, murmuring happily.

"I know it's cheesy and have no clue if people still do this. I was wondering if maybe you wanted to make this official. Be a real couple, whatever that means."

"Exclusive. Boyfriend and girlfriend. All of that?"

"Exactly." Jack's gaze locks onto mine, and I can easily read how nervous he is to ask this, though I can't imagine why he would be. I honestly wouldn't change a thing. He's chivalrous, smart, and easy to talk to, he feeds me and is willing to share his Netflix password. He also snores, leaves laundry all over the floor of his bedroom and is completely clueless about all things historical—what I'm majoring in—

and yet somehow he manages to make all of these things impossibly endearing.

"I'm in if you are." His face relaxes into a contented smile. Looks like that was the right answer. This time it's him that kisses me, leaving my entire body humming.

***

"Welcome home, Angela."

The voice greets me as soon as I close the door to my apartment for the first time in nearly a day—having gone straight from Jack's place to school this morning. A few seconds later, Ty strides in from the bedroom.

Every surface of my home is spotless, and there's not a single piece of laundry on the floor. My place hasn't been this clean since the night I placed the order for Ty.

I've been walking on clouds since last night, lost in a world of me and Jack. I'm too happy to even be worried about the hole I'm digging myself into it and the android at the center of my problems.

"Hey, Ty! How was your night?"

"Lonely without you. I didn't know that you wouldn't come home. So I watched the first season of *True Blood* while I was waiting, organized your bookcase by author, cleaned out the cache on your computer, and pulled some research for your upcoming paper on Roman laws at the beginning of the Common Era."

"Oooh, what did you think of *True Blood*?" I'd mentioned it to him a couple of nights prior when we were chatting about all of my favorites, from books to TV to movies, and he'd promised to watch it whenever he had some time to spare. Which happened pretty quickly, seeing as he's not doing much besides waiting around for me to come home all the time. Maybe I should apologize for not letting him know I wouldn't be home, but he doesn't seem too bothered by it, and his programming has to allow for unexpected changes in schedule.

"I can see why you like it so much. Maybe we can watch an episode together tonight?"

"Great idea. I'm going to shower first, but I'll meet you on the couch in a few."

Ty grins at me before turning to the kitchen, presumably to make popcorn. It's now part of our nightly ritual. These past two weeks with him have been nothing like what I expected. Ty is strange and undoubtedly something other than human, but right from that first night I knew that he cares about me. Honestly, I'd worried that it would have been a little creepier, but he's always kept a respectful distance.

Which doesn't change that I'm going to have to say goodbye sooner or later. The longer I wait, the less I'll make back, but I haven't been able to bring myself to pull the trigger yet.

One more week. One more week and I'll put up an ad. Maybe I'll even bring Jack into the loop on all of this. He's better with tech stuff than I am and might even know how to go about wiping Ty's personality.

The thought hits me like a punch in the guy. Ty has turned into an unlikely combination of best friend and personal assistant. He has been exactly what I needed him to be, even if I didn't know what it was I needed when I first placed the order. But I can't keep him. I'm not even sure I can admit that I ever had him. I know how this looks. I know what this is.

"All set?" Ty asks fifteen minutes later as I make my way back to the couch, now wrapped in a bath robe.

We easily settle into our usual spots on the couch with the popcorn bowl sitting between us. Ty lets himself slouch back into the cushions. Even though I know that he has no nerve endings or real feelings at all, I swear I can see his muscles relax as a sigh escapes his artificial lips.

Three episodes in and the popcorn is long gone. I've curled up on the couch, taking over two of the three cushions and leaving Ty squished into the opposite end of the sofa. As the credits scroll through, I shift over and let myself stretch out completely until my toes touch the opposite arm rest, leaving my feet on top of Ty's not quite natural feeling knees.

"Time for bed?" Ty asks. "You look tired."

"You know, some women might find that insulting. But I'm fine, it's just been a long week."

"Good to know. And you're sure everything is okay? School? Work? You've been home less than usual. Maybe there's something I can help with."

"I promise, I'm fine. Downright happy even. Things have been crazy, and a bit of a whirlwind, but really good. School's hectic but good. Jack is amazing. Work is fine. Zero complaints."

"Jack?" Ty tilts his head to the side, which always reads to me like it's a motion programmed from a confused puppy more than a real human man. But it's quickly becoming Ty's signature move, especially every time Jack is mentioned. Which has to have been at least half a dozen times by now. It's not like I've kept him a secret. For whatever reason, this is simply the one thing about my life that Ty can't seem to retain. Or refuses to retain, though I'm not sure if that's even possible.

"The guy I've been seeing. Cooks, exercises for fun like a weirdo, great hair. That one."

Ty nods but doesn't say anything, and for the first time an awkward silence starts to settle between the two of us, reminding me that nothing about our relationship is conventional. He's everything I needed him to be, but in exchange I'm supposed to be everything for him.

Maybe I've let this go too far.

"I'm glad you're happy," he finally responds. "That's all I want."

"Are you happy?" I ask, my own curiosity getting the better of me. Or maybe I just want him to let me off the hook for leaving him alone for days at a time, knowing he has nothing else to truly focus on. Nothing else he even wants to be focused on. "Can you feel happiness? Or anything like that. How does it all work?"

"Of course. I'm happy whenever you're here. I'm happy when I'm learning something new. I'm happy when I'm out exploring. And if I'm not happy, or I'm bored, or not needed, I can just rest until I am."

"Promise? You aren't secretly plotting the beginning of the robot revolution?"

"I would never lie to you." And I remember that he can't. Ty is what he is, and he was made to be honest.

"I should get some sleep." I start to pull my feet off the couch to sit up, but lightning-fast, Ty reaches out and gently grabs my foot.

"I learned a new technique today, hopefully it will help you relax. Then, while you're sleeping, I can proofread your next paper."

I tug my foot slightly, but his grip doesn't loosen. "I'm fine really. I need to get some sleep." Tiny hairs raise on the back of my neck despite this being a perfectly normal Tuesday night.

"Let me guess, not a no on the proofreading." Ty winks in a way that only the very charming and handsome can pull off. And seeing how he's essentially offering to do my homework for me, I can't help laughing, letting some of the tension I'm feeling slip away with my breath.

"Only if you really want to. There's always more *True Blood*."

"You forget, mere mortal. I can do both at once. Email me your paper, and I'll send it back when I'm done." Ty's instructions came with a personalized email that I can use to send files directly to Ty's system for him to process, learn, or whatever needs to be done.

"Well, thank you."

I slip into bed feeling more confused than ever. My thoughts are racing at a mile a minute, and it's only moments before I drift off that I even think to wonder what Ty meant when he said he was happy when he went out exploring.

⁂

The cork pops off the champaign, shooting off the balcony and down toward the parking lot of my building. Thankfully, we're only seven floors up so it's not about to hurt anyone. Not that I would have thought of that in time. This is our third bottle after all.

"To you!" Jack cries out, looping his arm around my waist as he pours more booze into my glass.

It's the end of the semester, and I've managed not to fail anything, lose my job or completely run out of money. I don't know how it happens, but the ends keep meeting. I have yet had to resort to ramen.

"To me!" I take a small sip, focusing more on enjoying the moment than getting any drunker. The last couple of months have been unexpected, but really kind of wonderful.

Of course, maybe things would be a little simpler if I didn't have a synth in sleep-mode tucked away in my closet. I've only been activating Ty about once a week, when I need the help, or start to feel guilty about keeping him here like this. I can't even tell if this is a good thing, a healthy thing, or if I'm being horribly cruel.

I've tried to sell him twice, but both time's I've backed out at the last second, hoping to recoup more of my money. No one seems willing to pay more than half of what I did. Or maybe I'm waiting for the *right* buyer.

"Hey, can I talk to you about something? I've been…"

"Oooh!" Jack interrupts me, completely severing my already stilted train of thought with his trademark enthusiasm. "Tomorrow I'll take you out to the aquarium. We can celebrate some more."

"That sounds perfect," I say with a giggle. I don't have any particularly strong feelings about fish, but Jack's excitement is contagious. Life is good.

It's not long before Jack and I are intertwined again, making our way for the bedroom. This time though, instead of pulling my shirt up over my head, he pulls me past my dresser, the closet and a small pile of laundry to bring me down to a sit on my bed.

I nuzzle his neck with my nose, still desperate to be close to him until he pulls away slightly, temporarily stopping my heart. "What's wrong?"

"Wrong?" Jack's dark eyebrows shoot up. "Nothing is wrong. It's hard to imagine anything being wrong. I'm completely in love with you."

This time, I'm sure my heart has stopped completely.

"I love you too," I whisper, once I remember to breathe.

I might just be the luckiest girl in the world.

* * *

I shuffle along through the crowd, my hand laced through that of my aquarium tour guide who is happily pointing out various fish whose names I'll never remember. This has been more fun than I thought it would be, even if I wish it was just me and Jack in this glass wonder.

"Nemo fish!" I point out a bright orange fish swimming by with his buddy. Jack offers me a dramatic eye roll. "Clown fish, even I know that one. But points for effort?"

"Always. What about Dory, what's she?"

"Ellen fish?"

"Close. Blue tang."

"I will not remember that at all," but I give Jack's hand a squeeze so he knows I'm not nearly as exasperated by all this as I'm trying to let on.

"There you are." A strong hand taps me on the shoulder. I drop Jack's hand to spin around and come face to face with Ty. Ty who is still supposed to be locked away in my closet, fast asleep.

14

"You know a synth? How did I not know this?" I turn back to see Jack's face lights up in an enormous grin. "This is so cool!"

"Yup, we go way back." I smile as naturally as I can, silently freaking out. How did Ty get here? Why would he even... my mind can't make sense of anything I'm seeing right now but two sets of eyes are watching me expectantly, both looking so genuinely happy to be here with me that it's almost unnerving.

"Ty, this is Jack." All at once, Ty's expression shifts from friendly to unreadable.

"Hello," Jack says with a smile.

"Your shirt doesn't suit your complexion."

One heartbeat. Two. No one says anything, so I have to. "Ty can be a little on the honest side. He doesn't mean anything by it."

"Okay."

More silence. I can't whisk Ty away from here without raising a lot of questions I'm not prepared to answer. I also can't keep standing here waiting to see who is going to make this situation worse first.

"Do you know anything about fish? Jack's a bit of an expert, for whatever reason."

Ty shrugs. Keeping his eyes locked on me, he is practically refusing to look at my date.

"Well, we've always got room for one more on the Jack Lyons Grand Aquatic Tour."

By the end of the tour, both Jack and Ty seem to have calmed down a bit—Ty from whatever it is that brought all of this on, and Jack from his inexplicable fish-fact high.

"Are you still coming back to my place?" Jack asks as we escape back out into the fresh air, with Ty a few paces behind us.

"Nah. I should get back. Stuff to do. People to see. All that." Robots to troubleshoot.

"All right, no problem. I'll see you on Friday night then," Jack says."

"Wouldn't miss it."

We both pause, and I inhale ready to say it first, but of course he makes it so I don't have to. "Love you!"

"Love you, too."

And once again, we're grinning like idiots. I wonder how long it will be before the novelty, or this fluttery feeling in my stomach wears off. I hope never. We kiss quickly as I'm hyper aware of our audience, one member in particular, but I miss Jack as soon as he's gone.

"Ready to go home?" Ty asks once our third party member has crossed the street to the monorail station.

"What are you doing here?" I hiss. "How did you even get here?"

"You needed me, so I found you."

"I needed you?"

"You're making a mistake."

"Wait what? I'm beyond confused. Why. Are. You. Here?"

"I came to get you, to bring you home. He's not good enough for you."

"Jack?"

"Of course."

"You don't know anything about him."

"I know you, Angie. I only want what's best for you."

"What's best for *you*, you mean. The more I see of him, the less I see of you."

"No. You're my main priority here. I wouldn't lie to you. Couldn't."

Maybe true, but he's also not supposed to be able to leave his charging station on his own either. I'm not sure what to think anymore.

Maybe this counts as enough of a glitch to justify a refund.

"We'll talk about this later. For now, I need to get home. I'm tired." I also don't want to be responsible for mildly crazy robot-boy out in public. So there's that.

I leave Ty watching *Sons of Anarchy* on the couch, claiming I need to go study in my room. Instead, I'm frantically researching synths going above and beyond their initial programming. Everything I'm reading swears up and down that stalking their users is way beyond the scope of the base model capabilities.

And yet. Here we are. Somehow he's become far more than he was meant to.

Clicking back through my emails, I eventually find my original order. Which is when everything finally makes sense. Even if my victory is slightly tainted by the bolded print informing me that refunds after thirty days are a no-go.

Ty isn't acting like a synth. He's acting like an honest to goodness, jealous boyfriend. A real boy. Albeit, not one I think I'd be able to deal with. Or want to deal with.

I need to uninstall whatever it is that's making him like this. Not for the first time do I wish I had someone a little more tech-savvy I could ask for help.

That's not an option, and I can't leave things like this any longer.

I click download on an auto-updater.

"Ty," I yell, not getting up from my seat, but changing what's open on my screen. "I'm heading to bed. If you're up for some recharge time, I've got an update I'm going to send you."

In less than a minute, he's standing in front of my desk. He's hovering in the same way he always does, but now it feels tainted. More controlling than concerned.

"Do you really think you love him?" Ty asks as he locks his feet into position on the charging station.

I blink twice. He'd been out of earshot when Jack and I had said our goodbyes earlier.

"How do you know about that?"

"You told him. Last night. That you love him too. I believe you're mistaken."

"I... don't know. Things like this are complicated."

Ty smiles. I quietly shudder. "I understand better than you think I would."

<hr />

My phone buzzes in class even though I could have sworn I have it on silent. A few people sitting around me in the lecture hall turn to look, so I make a point of ignoring it. Maybe everyone will think it was someone else.

And maybe I get away with it. Until it buzzes again. No one ever texts me at this time of day, so I can't help but check. What I read has me abandoning my laptop and books to sprint into the hall.

You tried to erase me.

There's no number or name attached to the message, but I know exactly where it came from. I just can't begin to guess how. When I woke up this morning Ty was exactly where I left him, with my computer screen telling me that the update had been completed. I left him there, bracing the door to my bedroom with furniture to make sure I wouldn't have any surprise visits later today like I had yesterday.

The second message reads, **You need me. I'll make you understand.**

But he's definitely not here at the school. Or if he is, he hasn't found me yet. Where else would he go?

I try responding to the message but nothing goes through.

This is it. I finally have to call Jack and tell him all about the secret synth I keep in my closet. I'm sure that won't hurt our bliss-bubble at all.

I dial his number. No answer. Instead, a new text message pops up on my screen.

You don't need him. Come home, I'll show you.

I run home as fast as my legs will carry me. My kitchen and living room are empty. And yet there's no longer any stuff piled up against the bedroom door. Instead, the door is wide open.

"Hello?" I say, loud enough that anyone nearby would hear me without alerting the neighbors.

Maybe I should alert the neighbors.

"Angie! In here." A voice I've grown to love calls out from the hallway and I run to him. But when I find him, he's not alone.

Jack and Ty are standing across from another on either side of my tiny bedroom. It would almost look like a stalemate if it weren't for the knife sitting in Ty's automated fingers.

"What have you done?" I ask Ty.

"Me? What have you done? What did you try to do? You wanted to erase everything I am, after all that I've done for you." Ty's face holds no trace of emotion. Only stoicism.

"What you've done for me?" I exclaim.

"How do you think you've survived this long, Angie? After all the money you spent. Who do you think has been funding you for all these months? You clearly can't be trusted to make decisions on your own. It led you to this sniveling idiot."

I don't know why, but it's that phrase that shocks me into action. This, this isn't the Ty I knew. Not anymore. It's not even the glitchy synth who decided to date crash because he figured it was in my best interest. I don't know what he is, but I know exactly what he wants. It isn't happily ever after. Not for Jack.

But maybe for me. He is supposed to love me, after all.

18

Without thinking, I lunge for the knife without a plan or even a hope. When I'm within inches of it, Ty lets it fall to the floor with a clatter, grabbing my arm before I can lunge for it myself.

He's impossibly strong. I don't know how I ever thought I'd be able to hold him in this room using only stuff I found around my apartment. I feel it as a bone in my arm snaps, but he won't even let me fall to the floor.

"Stop, Angela. You're hurting yourself." Ty is watching me with something resembling compassion, like he's not the cause of all of this.

"You're the one hurting me. Let me go. Let us go," I plead.

"No, I need to take care of you."

Jack springs into action, and as soon as I see him move forward, I scream for him not to. I doubt that Ty would even hesitate to stab him, and even without the knife it would be far too easy for a synthetic human to permanently damage a genuine one. But I'm too late, Jack's body has collided with Ty's, which doesn't move so much as an inch. In less than a moment, Jack is sprawled on the floor with Ty's foot on his neck.

"No!" I yell. "Please. You'll kill him."

"Yes."

Jack's hands claw at Ty's leg, but he doesn't give so much as an inch. I have to do something.

With my good arm, I grab for the knife. Each second is moving far too slowly. Either Ty doesn't see me, or he doesn't think I can hurt him. And maybe I can't. I run for the closet.

At the base of his charging stand is one of those teeny reset buttons that are impossible to press by accident. But you can do it with a sharp object like the one in my hand.

Jack's not breathing.

I press in as hard as I can and count to three. Before I'm finished, so is Ty.

* * *

"That's it. It's done." Jack raises his hands in surrender as soon as he finishes pushing Ty's shipping crate into the back of the moving van. It took a matter of minutes for his friend Ian to wipe out all of his original programming, leaving Ty—or the synth, he's not really Ty any more—as little more than a good looking shell. Not technically something you're allowed to sell, but what choice did we have. Reset him completely or let him kill Jack. He had already come far too close. There's still a bruise on Jack's throat. Hardly a choice at all. And now the robot that was Ty is a hot commodity for exactly that reason. Not the murderous reason, the other one. Who wouldn't want a blank slate to play around with, especially with all of the mods you can download and install right from the internet?

Well, I wouldn't. And I think at this point, the shiny new toy syndrome that synths held for Jack has probably disappeared as well.

He never did get the full story about where Ty came from or where things went wrong. I'll probably save that for another day. Or year. And still, I don't think he'll be looking to get a robo-assistant of his own any time soon.

Either way, I have some explaining to do. To Jack, to Ty's buyer, to wherever it was that Ty was getting all of his funding. Nothing good has come of this. At least for now Jack is still by my side, holding my hand, promising we'll get passed this. He's far too good for me.

And they all live happily ever after?

The End

Kellie has been in love with stories in all of their forms for as long as she can remember. Admittedly, sometimes that means falling into places like Stars Hollow and Sunnydale, but books have always been her true love.

Kellie spent part of her twenties living in Galway, Ireland and swooning after various lilting accents but is now back home in Ontario, Canada. Her family includes two Glen of Imaal Terriers and an Australian Labradoodle. To learn more, visit:
http://www.KellieSheridan.com

JACLYN AND THE BEANSTALK
A retelling of Jack and the Beanstalk
by M. Clarke

They said the monsters that lived in the mountains had teeth like sharks and eyes as red as blood. They said these monsters drank blood and feasted on the flesh of humans. With skin as white as snow, they moved so fast, human eyes couldn't follow. Unable to go out during the day, they were given their name—night monsters. They were everyone's worst nightmare. Various versions of the night monster tale had been told through the generations to keep the young ones from wandering late into the night and causing mischief. But regardless of the stories, those brave individuals who ventured out to find the truth never made it back home. Did they fall climbing the mountain? Or had they become the monsters' dinner? Nobody knew, but I needed to find out.

"Mom, I'll be back." I placed a cool damp cloth on her forehead and kissed her cheek. "I'm going to find a way to pay for your medicine. You just hang on, okay?" I had to give her hope—something for her to hold on to so that she wouldn't give up. The truth was, if I didn't come back from where I was planning to go, she would be dead. Mom's welfare was my incentive, my motivation to come back home in one piece.

Mom grabbed my wrist, but she could barely hold on. Heat radiated from her touch on my skin, and then became cool again when she dropped her hand. "Where are you going?" Her words were weak and hardly audible.

Unable to tell her the truth, I bit my tongue and forced a lie. "I'm going to find a job. Then I'll buy the medicine that will make you better."

Mom closed her eyes for a second, sighed, then reopened them. "You're so young, and you only have the skills of a farmer."

"I'm nineteen. I can do anything." I removed the cloth from her forehead, dunked it into the bucket that I had placed next to her bed, squeezed out the excess water, and replaced it. "I want you to do what

1

I just did, when you can't feel the coolness from the cloth anymore. Can you please do that for me?"

Mom nodded and said, "The town is dangerous for a young single lady. You shouldn't wander by yourself. Ask my friend's son Jack to take you."

There was no way in hell I was going to ask Jack. Not only was he scrawny, he was an arrogant ass. He would tease me and call me shorty, or call me a tomboy from the way I'd dressed. I didn't think he'd ever seen me wear a dress before. He also brought out the worst in me, making me sassy and mean. Just the thought of him made me angry.

"Don't worry about me, Mom. I can take care of myself. I learned a lot self-defense from Dad."

Dad had wished for a son instead of a daughter, teaching me how to shoot the crossbow, fight with a sword, and every weapon he'd owned. Besides that, he made sure I knew how to tend our farm.

"I know," Mom said, somberly. "You're all grown up, and I'm so proud of you. You had to take all the burden when your…" she paused to take a deep breath, and her eyes told me she was hurting inside, but she remained strong for me, "when your father left us."

"He didn't leave us, Mom," I snapped. I bit my bottom lip, feeling sorry for sounding so harsh with her, but I couldn't help it. I knew for certain that my father traveled with a group called Monstra Slayers. He'd told me he was going hunting, but I knew better. Mom had no idea. She would have forbidden my dad to go if she'd been aware of the reason why he had taken off.

They were on a hunt for the cave. For the monsters' domain possessed diamonds, gold, and treasure beyond fathom that could save us all. I had overheard him talking to his friends at our house one night. But because my father had been gone for several weeks, I needed to find a way to help my mom. She needed medication, and we had no money saved to pay for it. Times were rough during the months when the weather was dry.

"If he didn't leave us, where is he?" Mom inhaled a deep breath and held it longer than usual.

I placed my hand on her shoulder. "No more talking, Mom. It's making you weaker. Stop thinking about Dad. He's doing something to get you medication. You have to trust him. Have some faith. He loves you."

Mom placed her hand over her mouth, trying to stop herself from crying but couldn't stifle the sobs that escaped her. "I'm sorry. It's been rough without your dad."

"I know." I cupped her hand in mine. "It's going to be okay." I said those words more for me than her.

If going to town was dangerous, it meant that I was practically going on a suicide mission, traveling through the woods and to Mount Cain by myself. Even though it was hard to swallow, I did consider asking Jack, after Mom had suggested it, but I didn't want to risk his life too, and also, I was being selfish. I didn't want to share any treasures I would find. Besides, I didn't think Jack could keep up with me. He would most likely be in my way instead of actually helping. I imagined I'd end up having to protect him instead of the other way around.

"Please be careful," Mom moaned. It took so much effort for her to speak.

Placing her hand down to her side I said, "I made you some fresh bread and there's water on the table within your reach. Please try to eat something. I promise to bring you some meat when I come home." It was a weak promise, but it was one I was going to try my best to keep. Smelling the aroma of the fresh bread was making my stomach churn. How badly I wanted to eat another piece, but I had to pace myself.

Mom's eyes were already closed. Watching her chest rise and fall with the beat of my own, I knew she was asleep, and for now she was stable. Grabbing a sack full of bread and my canteen from the kitchen, I closed the door softly behind me. Looking up at the sky as I stepped out onto the pebbled ground, an eerie feeling rose in me. It didn't help that the clouds were ominous—thick and dark. It would really suck traveling with rain pouring down on me.

From the back of the stable, I hitched my white horse to a small wagon and guided her outside. The nervousness of traveling alone crept up on me as I secured her harness. Caressing the side of my horse's face I asked, "You ready to go on an adventure with me, Angel? I'm sorry to take you along, but I have no choice. My mom is sick and we need to move quickly. I wish I had super speed. It would really come in handy right now." I snorted at the ridiculous thought, and at the idea of what I must look like talking to a horse.

After placing my daggers, sword, crossbow, and other necessities in the wagon, I hopped up onto its seat and grabbed the reins. I gave

Angel a good smack, sending her off like a shot. The air whipped at my face, tossing my long ash-brown hair. Looking over my shoulder, I was filled with guilt for leaving my mom. But it had to be done.

I rode on for miles and miles as I watched the sun guide me, setting lower and lower with each passing minute. It was getting darker and Angel and I needed to rest. Hearing a stream up ahead, a place where I'd been before, I got off the wagon, untied Angel from it, and guided her to the water.

"Drink, Angel," I said, stroking her neck.

After she'd enough, I weaved around the tall trees back to the wagon. Glancing around, I looked for a spot to rest for the night. I needed to find a good hiding place that could conceal the wagon, Angel, and myself. Taking out my canteen, I took a sip, then whipped around to the sound behind me, as I reached for the dagger I'd stashed at my belt.

"Hello," an old man greeted, taking off his hat in a gentlemanly fashion. He was dressed in dark brown from head to toe. His long-sleeve shirt was torn and grungy, and his pants and long tailored jacket were smudged with dirt. Holding onto the reins of his donkey, he flashed a warm smile.

His kind eyes and gentle demeanor had me lowering my hand, though I stayed guarded and alert. Releasing my dagger, I placed my canteen back in its holder, and shoved my sack of bread aside. "Hello," I greeted back. "What brings you here to this neck of the woods?"

"Fishing. But I had no luck today. How about you?" He placed his dirty hat back on his head. "Pretty girl such as yourself shouldn't be traveling alone."

"Don't worry about me. I can take care of myself. But thank you for your kindness." I tipped my head in respect.

The stranger took several steps toward me. When I backed away, he stopped. "I don't mean to scare you, but is that a knife at your waist?"

Instinctively, I placed my hand back on my belt, making sure it was still there. I didn't know why, but I had the need to touch it. It was like a security blanket for me, as was the smaller dagger hitched inside my boot. "Yes," I answered. The sunlight hit the precise spot, making its reflection shine in the old man's eyes.

"That's a special dagger," he said.

He was right. Daggers didn't usually light up like that, but this one did. My dad told me it could kill anything. I assumed he was trying to let me know "anything" included monsters. Since we had two and one of them was missing, I presumed he had taken it with him to Mount Cain.

The old man backed away. "I thought you could help me catch a fish or something to eat. If you do, I'll cook it for you and be your company tonight. Looks like you could use some. I'm sure you're pretty hungry from your travels."

My survival lessons told me to deny his request, but again his kind eyes and soft tender voice had me trusting him. Perhaps it was that he reminded me of my grandfather that had passed away years ago, or perhaps it was the prospect of not being alone. Either way, I followed my gut and agreed.

Shivering from the sudden wind, I put on the black cape my mom had made for me and headed back to Angel with the old man. "I'm Jaclyn," I said.

"I'm Edmond." He smiled, striding along beside me. "My companion's name is Monte." He patted Monte, but the donkey seemed reluctant to follow him.

"Where are you from?" I asked.

"I'm a wanderer," he answered. "I don't stay anywhere. I move from town to town."

"Oh," I said. "How interesting." I pointed to my left. "This is my horse, Angel." She was just beyond my reach. Standing there, as the sunlight dimly glowed down on her, making it's last stretch for the day, she looked glorious, majestic, especially being all white. She really looked like an angel, but a horse angel, if there ever was such a thing. All she needed was a horn and a pair of wings. Now, that would have been marvelous, especially since she'd be able to fly me to Mount Cain.

"She's a beauty," he complimented. "Almost as beautiful as my donkey." Hearing him chuckle at his own words, it was contagious. I laughed beside him.

"Obviously, I don't ride him. He travels with me for the companionship, but he's slower than me."

5

After we made sure my wagon and Angel were safely tucked away, I caught not one or two, but four fish, and then we made a small fire. With my knife, Edmond scaled the fish and fired them up with a long skinny, thin branch. Recalling my sack of bread, I went to retrieve it from my wagon.

"Here," I offered. "I baked them this morning. I can only offer you a small piece, though. I have a long journey ahead so I'm going to have to save as much as I can."

"Thank you. That's very kind." He took it from my hand and savored the first bite. "Delicious. Did you say you baked them yourself?"

Being that my mouth was full of fish, I swallowed and nodded 'Yes.'

"May I ask you where you're going?" Edmond asked.

He must have seen the somber look on my face. I took several sips of water, trying to avoid his question. It was none of his business. When I didn't respond, he took another bite of bread. I continued to drink from my canteen, and now it was almost empty. Knowing I could fill it up at the stream, I took in as much as I could.

"I think I know where you're heading. This road only leads to one place. But why would you go there?"

"I..." I didn't know why I felt embarrassed. He had no idea what my life was like. "Yes. I'm going to Mount Cain," I finally admitted when he just kept staring at me. "I have to. I have no other choice. My dad is missing and my mom needs medicine. The drought dried out our farm and we have no crops to sell."

Edmond sucked on the bone of the fish to get every last bit of meat. "I see. You are searching for the treasure. Then let me tell you a story of how the night monsters were created. But before I begin, do you know the story of Adam and Eve?"

"Yes, of course. Everyone knows the Bible. It's not a story."

Edmond licked his fingers and wiped them on his coat. Leaning back against the trunk of the tree to rest, he began. "Adam and Eve had two children, Cain and Abel. Cain murdered his brother, Abel, out of pure jealousy because God preferred Abel's gift over Cain's. As his punishment, he was transformed into a demon. In addition, he was given a mark on his hand as a reminder of what he had done and also for others to remember . . . thou shall not kill. We called it the mark of Cain."

"What did it look like?"

Edmond picked up a small branch and drew on a patch of dirt. It looked like a number seven with two small lines, never touching and heading east.

Edmond continued. "He was cursed to walk the earth alone, night after night, for all eternity. Burned by the daytime sun, he was forced to have no contact with civilization. Also, he could not consume his daily food. The only thing that could satisfy his hunger was blood, so he would come out at night to hunt the mortals."

My hand flew to my mouth as I gasped, my heart thumping fast in my chest. "He drank—" I couldn't say the word.

Edmond nodded, understanding, and continued. "Soon after, Cain met a powerful witch named Lilith. Lilith, also called the Goddess of Night, was a demon, the bearer of disease, illness, and death. She showed Cain how to use his own blood for magic and evoke unknown mystical powers. From Lilith, Cain learned how to create others of his kind."

"How?"

"A mortal must be bitten by a night monster. The venom in their saliva, combined with a few drops of the night monster's own blood begins the transformation. This can only happen as long as the mortal is not drained of too much blood."

"That's crazy," I breathed, unable to grasp the idea. I poked the fire with a long shiny branch to keep it burning.

"Some changes that the new night monsters go through include their skin developing a strange pallor and becoming cold to the touch. They become feather light on their feet and have extreme photosensitivity. Their increased senses include super hearing and sight, sense of smell, taste, and touch. The night monsters exude sex appeal and a heightened release of pheromones. This helps to attract the mortals. Cain became lonely and created his own family. The mortals began to fight back after the night monsters wiped out a whole town. They would drag the monsters one by one from their lairs to burn in the sun. Rumor has it that the remaining night monsters hide on Mount Cain. Thus began the great myth of the night monsters, or vampires. So . . . you think you can win?"

His question threw me off, and his tale had me scared shitless. "There's no proof of your story." Those words were more for me than him. I didn't want to be afraid. My courage was based on my mom being ill. She needed me. I was her only hope. Anger brewed inside me. *How dare he try to dissuade me!* Maybe he was on his way to the cave and wanted to keep the treasure for himself, I thought. Then I rationalized, he was probably too old to climb the mountain.

Edmond lifted the corner of his lips. "Perhaps no one made it out alive to tell."

"Maybe the person who made it out didn't want to brag about it, because he's the one with lots of treasure," I challenged.

"I hope for your sake you're right." He sounded sincere yet worried. "You should get some sleep." He stretched his arms to the sky and yawned. "I need to get some rest too."

"Thanks for the dinner," I said, standing up.

"Why don't you sleep in your wagon and I'll sleep here by the fire. I'll keep watch."

It took me a few seconds to respond. I knew I was safe with him, but I wasn't sure if he could fight off any intruders. Feeling drained, I nodded in agreement. "Thank you. I could use a good night's sleep."

"Before you go, I want you to have these." He reached into his pocket and brought his hand out, opening his fingers one by one. In his palm were three beans. "They're magic beans. They will help you reach your destination."

Wow! If only he could hear himself. Maybe he was becoming delusional from traveling alone and having a donkey as his companion. "Thank you for your kindness, but no, thank you." I sounded rude but I wasn't going to pretend.

Edmond's brows scrunched together. He extended his hand with a frown. "Take them, silly girl. You don't know how much these are worth. Men have died in search of these beans."

I shook my head, took them and shoved them into my pants pocket. "Thanks. " I caressed Angel's face to say goodnight and hopped aboard the wagon. Using my cape as a blanket, I made sure it covered the length of my body and then closed my eyes.

<hr />

Stretching and yawning, I awoke with an ache in my back and a soft breeze caressing my cheeks. My eyes shot open to the sunrise in the east, and I knew it was just the peak of dawn. Recalling the events of my journey and Edmond, I climbed down from my wagon. He was nowhere to be found and the fire had been put out. When I checked to see if my weapons, sack of bread, and water canteen were still there, my heart found its steady beat. Not wanting to waste any more precious time, I led Angel and the wagon onto the dirt road and ventured out.

I made short stops to take care of my necessities and even ate a piece of bread. Back on the road again, I hastened Angel's pace as much as I could. I needed to make it to the mountain before it became dark so I could see where I was climbing. And if the stories were true, the monster came out during the night, and I didn't want to be around for that.

When I reached my destination, I hid the wagon and Angel again, enclosing them amongst an area of high vegetation. Tapping about my body, I checked where my weapons were tucked: my hip, both of my boots, the long sword and crossbow behind my back, a bottle of holy water hanging as a necklace around my neck, and a long rope. I wasn't sure if the holy water would cause any harm, but I had enough blades around my body to reach any angle if needed.

Standing in front of the wall of the mountain, I tilted my head way back to see the grandness of it. Yup, I wanted to puke. Looking far up, I could see the opening of the cave. It could possibly take me days to climb up there. As I released a long, disappointed sigh, I thought about my sick mother in bed. I wondered if she was doing as I had instructed.

"For my mother," I grunted as I tossed up the rope. When it swung around the nearby small tree, I wrapped the other end around my waist and started to climb. Planting my feet on the rock or anything that jutted out that I could use as an anchor, I hoisted myself up. This was a lot harder than I'd thought it would be, but I couldn't think about that now. I had no time for fear or doubts.

Pulling on the rope, I walked up the wall to the tree it was fastened to. After loosening it from there, I tossed it up to the next tree. Thank goodness the mountain hadn't been created from rocks alone. However, after a few tree swings, there were no more trees, so I wrapped the rope around my body. Then I took out the two small daggers from my boots, punctured through the mountain wall cracks as hard as I could, and wedged my feet anywhere I could secure them. *This was worse!* It didn't help that the higher I climbed, the colder it was.

My cape danced about in the wind, and the cool breeze slapped at my hands and face. If only I could slingshot myself up there, or if my cape could turn magical and carry me where I needed to be. Thinking about crazy things like that kept my mind occupied. One thing was apparent about using the dagger and the rope, my arm muscles were working overtime, and I didn't know how long I could keep it up.

My whole body burned from being overworked and my legs were wobbly. I had not prepared for this amount of strenuous exertion. *What was I thinking?* Reaching into my pocket, I pulled out the three beans Edmond had given me. He had told me these were magic beans, and that I could use them to help me. For a moment, I almost whispered into my palm like it was a genie in a bottle, then shook my head. Beans weren't magic. There was no magic in reality. It only existed in fairy tales. We were both crazy. Come to think of it, I wasn't crazy—I was insane.

Just then the wind whooshed by so fast that it knocked the beans out of my hand. I managed to retrieve two back, but the third plummeted to the ground. *Ugh!* Releasing an irate sigh, I placed the remaining beans back into my pocket. With an even longer sigh, I took another stride up. At that moment, the knife in the crack slipped. My heart leapt out of my chest as I clung for my life. I tried to hug the mountain with every inch of my body, but it was no use.

I was dropping fast. Pain ripped through the palms of my hands as I tried to grip anything that I could hold on to. Images of my parents flashed before my eyes. I was too young to die. I had my whole life ahead of me. As desperation and the will to live roared through me, I fought even harder as my body continued to fall, slamming against the rock. Then there was nothing I could do. Death was inevitable.

Coming to terms with the last moment of my life, the beautiful gray clouds were my final view. *Sorry, Mom. I failed you.* Those were my last thoughts as my body floated like I was flying. Closing my eyes and accepting my fate, I hit the ground. Only . . . I wasn't dead. My body ached like I had crashed onto something hard and my eyes shot open. Next thing I knew, my body was being elevated. *Was I ascending to Heaven?*

Cold air brushed against my body as I went up and up. Getting to my knees, I got a better view of what was happening. *Holy shit!* I was standing on a giant leaf. It looked like a beanstalk. Although it seemed impossible, I was grateful. *It saved me! Edmond and his beans saved me!* He wasn't crazy after all. Either I was dreaming, or I really had died and this was my Heaven or my Hell. A spark of hope gushed through me, and I was beyond elated to be alive.

Seeing the entrance to the cave at eye level just as the beanstalk stopped growing, I jumped off. Assessing my injuries, I noted that my cape was miraculously intact, not even a scratch or a tear. My pants and shirt were smudged with dirt, and the palms of my hands were covered with small open wounds. I was thankful that they weren't gushing with blood; however, they would need to be attended to. But right now, I had no choice but to ignore them.

Untying my cape, I hid it behind a tree, figuring it would only get in the way. Drawing my sword from its sheath on my back, I tiptoed cautiously towards the opening of the cave. The sun had set, but I had no choice but to enter. It was a decision I couldn't debate. After all, this was my second chance. I was meant to be here. I just hoped I wasn't walking into a death trap.

⁓ ⚭ ⁓

The sound of my footsteps echoed softly through the cave. I moved forward with my sword ready to strike anything that might attack. I had imagined I would have to walk in complete darkness, but the dim lanterns that hung every few feet made it bearable. Seeing my breath mist in the air, I knew it was cold but didn't feel the chill. Full of adrenaline and scared out of my mind, my body moved with unfamiliarity. Every muscle in me stiffened, and I had never felt my heart thump so fast in my entire existence.

After making it through the narrow passageway, what I saw before me was unfathomable. The cave had opened up to a cavern and a beautiful, yet sinister looking dark castle appeared in my line of vision. The castle looked almost identical to the one in our hometown, the one that belonged to our king. However, I could feel a dark and evil element oozing from the surroundings. So far I hadn't seen any kind of monster, but it did feel as if someone was watching me from all angles. Goose bumps trickled along my arms and then across my body.

Stepping onto a bridge, I expected to have an army of monsters attacking me, but nothing happened. I was thankful for the lanterns along it so I could clearly see what was ahead. It seemed as though this place had been deserted. Walking further, I listened for any sound—mainly footsteps, and then searched for anything in the air, but still, there were no monsters. My eyes flickered to either side of the bridge.

The murky river was still and dark. I could imagine figures popping out from it so I kept my eyes straight ahead.

Two giant wooden doors were already opened in front of me. I took one step onto the polished marble floor. A crystal chandelier hung from the center of the high ceiling. Every few feet there was a white marble post. And at the far end of the wall, items made from gemstones were displayed in a glass case. I couldn't tell what exactly the items were, but the lights inside highlighted them. They sparkled like diamonds. And in the front of the glass case was a massive caldron filled with gold coins. Purposely enticing the intruders.

This was too easy, I thought. It must be a trap. Cautiously, I moved forward, and when I was almost to the center, that was when I felt it. The eerie skin-crawling danger signals, traveling through every vein in my body. At that moment, shadows came out of the darkness, and I became immobile and speechless, as my heart pounded mercilessly against my chest. Trembling, I tugged on the necklace that held the bottle of holy water.

God help me. Countless men hissed at me. Though they looked as if they were normal human beings, I knew better. Twitching their noses, most likely smelling blood from the cuts on my palms, their eyes marked me as I stood in place. I had become their prey.

The one nearest to me came forward. I got a good look at his razor-sharp teeth when he growled at me. One thing I noted was that they were each wearing a different type of clothing—from that of a farmer, to a high-class socialite. But all their clothes were bloody and torn. I assumed that they didn't change, nor take baths, since their stench was horrific. I shook my head at these messed-up thoughts. What was I doing? *Run!* I told myself, but I couldn't move. *Which way?* By the time I got my muscles moving again, they had surrounded me.

Growls and hisses echoed in my ears. As I waited for them to attack, I realized they were toying with me, coming closer, and then moving away to give me room. I wondered if they could smell the holy water. Every time I pointed it at them, threatening to use it, they would back away.

One brave one came face to face with me. His eyes glowed red and fierce. Ready to attack me, he raised his sharp nails and opened his mouth to prepare to take a bite. He roared, and heat sizzled from his face when I threw holy water at him. I was beyond grateful that it worked. A part of me felt powerful, but at the same time, I was deadly

12

afraid. I guess I had pissed off his family because that's when they all came at me at once.

It was a matter of life and death, and there was no way in hell it was going to be mine. The monsters cried out in pain when I sprayed the holy water at them again. This only temporary disabled them, but it gave me a few seconds to swing my sword, beheading the one on my right. There were three ways to kill a vampire: drench them in holy water, behead them, or stake them in the heart with a silver blade. I was going to do all three.

Continuing to wield my long sword, I decapitated the ones that came at me from the right and used the smaller dagger to stab through the heart of the one on the left. The ones that were beheaded died instantly, while others had their bodies sizzle and then burn. Instantly, they all turned to black ashes on the ground. Knowing there were some behind me, I ducked, then swung my leg across to knock them down. I splashed holy water on them, moving sideways to block a blow, then I kicked a monster hard in the stomach. It caused a ripple effect and I was able to knock down several at once.

As I whipped around to make sure I was covering all aspects of my body, I was killing like a pro hit man—or in my case, a hit woman. Never had I imagined being able to kill the monsters through a single slice or jab. With regards to the measure of my ability, I was also quite surprised by my strength and endurance.

By the time I was exhausted and out of breath, they were all dead. *Unbelievable!* How in the world had I accomplished that? Stunned, I took a moment to assess. Black ashes floated around me the way snowflakes would fall, only these were disgusting remnants of the monsters I'd just killed. Grimacing, I dusted them off wherever they landed on my body.

Eyeing the gold coins, I took a few careful steps, and stopped. I exhaled a long sigh, knowing there were some more crawling on the ceiling when I saw shadows on the ground. It looked like they had the same thought and were heading for the gold coins. When the timing was right, running as fast as I could, I drew out my crossbow from my back and slide across the floor on my knees. With my back practically touching the floor and the crossbow pointing straight up at them, I shot one in the head, one in the heart, and the last one in the gut.

I shielded myself with my arms the best I could when black ashes rained down on me. When I stood up, I was right in front of the cauldron. After putting my weapons away, I glanced around, wondering if picking up the coin pieces would make something pop up from it or trip an alarm. What was the point of coming this far without taking anything back? I went against my instincts and stashed as many coins as possible in my pockets. Then there it was—I should have listened to my gut.

"Welcome," a low seductive voice greeted, coming out of the darkness. It was one simple word, but it was enough to give me quivers that I couldn't explain.

I expected to see a man, but six women appeared instead, gliding across the floor. They seemed like they floated from their graceful steps and the way their beautiful long white dresses draped and trailed behind them. And just like the monsters, they had pale skin and long sharp nails. Hissing softly, they came toward me with a smile I wasn't sure was friendly.

Having a clear view, I pulled out my weapon again. Although they were beautiful, the sight of their teeth told me they were dangerous. When I opened up the bottle of holy water, they backed away with an angry moan. Looking beyond them, a man caught my attention. Dressed in rich-looking fabrics suited for a king and wearing all black, he was stunning, taking my breath away. He was too beautiful to be a monster. *Was he?* Although he had the same pale skin, his looked silky to touch.

I knew he was, in fact, a monster when he closed the gap between us in a split second. He moved much faster than any of the others I'd killed. Feeling his closeness made me dizzy. Somehow he had an effect on me as his steel-black mysterious and mesmerizing eyes pierced through mine. There was some kind of connection—a pull. I couldn't understand why it was happening, but I had no control over it.

"I've been waiting for you," he breathed, his lips almost touching mine. Feeling his air exchanging with mine increased my heart rate, not to mention my lust rate. My heart hammered faster, but it wasn't from fear. His breath was warm and sweet, and I wanted to lick his lips. *What was wrong with me?* I had to snap out of it.

Frozen in place, I couldn't move. When he backed away, whatever spell he held me under was gone. I blinked and gasped.

"You are as beautiful as I had imagined you'd be." He walked in circles around me. I could feel his eyes undressing me, either that or he was checking out his dinner.

Chills pricked through me from his words, but I managed to ask, "Do I know you?"

He stopped and stood behind me. My muscles tightened when his chest pressed against my back, and his hands tenderly gripped my shoulders. It got worse when his lips brushed against the tip of my ear and his hot breath seeped against my neck as he said, "No, but you will soon."

"Who are you?" I whimpered, feeling weak in the knees. My emotions were playing tug-of-war, loving the way he was making me feel—erotic and desired—and hating that such a monster could make me lust for him.

The monster moved my hair to one side. With his long finger, he stroked along the vein in my neck. "Your dream come true. With me, your life will change. With me, I will give you more power than you can imagine."

"What if I don't want it?" I asked hesitantly.

He whipped me around to face him. "Have you heard of Mary Magdalene?"

Recalling the Bible, Mary was a dedicated follower with a pure heart. She washed Jesus' feet with her hair. "Yes."

"Some people say that we were friends. Some people say that she was a healer. These stories are all true. I've been waiting for Mary Magdalene's descendant to help me bring my people back to the light."

"How?" I was shaken by what he was saying. Scared out of my mind but still with the thought of my mom, I begged, "I'm not Mary Magdalene's descendant. You have the wrong person. *Please,* I need to help my mom. She's very sick. All I need is just one coin. I'll do anything for you in return." As long as it wasn't being his meal or killing humans, I thought.

He craned his head, studying my face as his fingernails ran down my neck. I jerked when I felt a sting. He had scratched me, causing a wound to open. A few drops of blood seeped down my neck. I could feel the wetness from them. Bringing the nail up he had just pricked me with, he licked it with his tongue. Closing his eyes, he inhaled deeply, and then exhaled with a low growl. It was the hottest thing, yet the most fearful I'd ever seen. The way he moaned in pleasure, one would think he was having an orgasm.

Opening his eyes with an appealing grin, he said, "You are her descendant."

When I took several steps back, the group of women hissed and clawed at me in warning.

"How do you know?" I said a bit louder than I had intended, stepping away from them.

In an instant, one arm was wrapped around my waist while his other hand caressed my hair. Hypnotized by his eyes, all I could do was stare. "I could taste it in your sweet blood. I can't wait to taste more," he cooed like a lover.

"No," I whispered. Fighting for the will to move with everything I had, made no difference. I didn't understand how he had a hold on me. Standing frozen and unable to move left me so vulnerable that I shed a single teardrop. "Please, let me go." My words were soft and hardly audible.

Instead of answering me, he watched that pearl-like drop trail down my face and slip down my neck. Leaning closer to me, he pressed his tongue on the teardrop and glided it up to my face while one of his hands cupped my breast. Another soft sensual growl escaped him. With a yank, he ripped my shirt open and glided his tongue to the tip of my breast as he kneaded them playfully.

A tingling sensation blazed between my legs, and I felt a burning, yearning sensation I had never felt before. I wanted him. I wanted him to rip off the rest of my clothes so I could feel his naked body against mine. But what was I thinking? *What the hell?* I had to snap out of it, but it was difficult when he pressed his body to mine and conquered my lips.

He was kissing me in the most heated passionate way, one I never knew could exist. I parted my lips, allowing the penetration of his tongue to glide in and out of my mouth. *Holy Shit!* I was screwed. My body had a mind of its own, and I wanted him inside me. *Stop!* I told myself. This was so wrong, so demented. But it got worse when he lifted me up effortlessly and pressed me to one of the pillars. His hardness was rubbing between my legs while he was sucking my neck. Was he drinking my blood? I didn't feel a bite. He must be sucking on the scratch. *Oh, please stop.* I couldn't take it anymore.

After feeling wetness on my face and my hands, I knew the women monsters were licking and kissing them while the monster was still kissing me. My body suddenly felt lighter. I panicked when I realized they had taken my weapons away, even the bottle of holy water. Somehow I managed to snap out of it and said, "Stop it. No." I had no idea, beside the words I spat out, why he released me.

"Can we taste her, Master?" one of the female monsters asked in a sheepish tone.

"No." He glanced at all of the women. "You are not to harm her or touch her. Do you understand?" His tone was stern, but I could tell they would obey him by their gestures. The women bent low with submission and cowardly took steps backward. Then he turned to me. "You don't say no to me. Do you know who I am?"

I shook my head. "You're a monster!" I huffed. "I will never submit to you. You can't keep me. Either kill me or let me go."

The Master bored his eyes into mine. "I am Cain. You will do as I say. As you have seen, I can make you do whatever I want."

The one and only Cain? The one that killed his brother? Shifting my eyes to his hands, I could see the mark. Casting the thought aside, I said boldly and stupidly, "No, I stopped you. I said no and you backed away. My blood holds power over you, or is *no* just a magic word for me?"

He did not like what I had to say. Flashing an evil eye at me, he looked mad as hell.

"Take her," he commanded without answering me again. Then, he was out of my sight within a blink of an eye.

I shivered from what would come next. Before I had a chance to protest, the six women lifted me up in a reclining position over their heads.

I didn't know where they were taking me, but I never guessed it would be a massive bedroom. I got up as quickly as possible and pushed off the bed. I must have been under some kind of spell and knocked out to not remember how I got there or when they had changed my clothes. I was now wearing a seductive red dress that showed more of my cleavage than I would ever allow.

Glancing around, I marveled at the expensive furniture, from the black velvet curtains to what looked like a mahogany handcrafted dresser and table. On the table were countless lit candles, giving off a sweet aroma as well as lighting the room.

As I backed away, getting a clear view of the room, I bumped into the bed. Feeling the softness of the comforter, I admired all the beauty and the quality of the fine things in life I never had. I jerked and turned to the sound of the door opening. Cain entered.

"Please make yourself comfortable. This will be your room," he said with conviction.

"I can't stay here. I told you, my mom is sick. She'll die." Though my tone was calm, there was urgency in it.

Cain narrowed his eyes at me, as if he was debating my dilemma, but I knew better. Monsters didn't give a shit about anyone but themselves. "Then . . . let her die."

I didn't know what possessed me, but I was overwhelmed with emotions I couldn't control. Without any weapons or thought, I ran to him. Cain grabbed my two wrists before I had a chance to punch him. He twisted me around so that my back was pressed to his chest. While one hand gripped my neck, the other hand was wrapped around my waist. My breath quickened as my chest rose and fell from the adrenaline and from being deathly scared. I was insane! *What was I thinking?* What good could come of this? I could only hope he wouldn't kill me.

"Jaclyn. I don't want to hurt you," he said. "But I will if you do that again. Don't ever defy me. Don't ever underestimate me. And don't ever think that I won't kill your loved ones. I have your father and I know where you live."

"How do you know my name?" I whimpered, shivering. "Where's my dad?"

"The whereabouts of your father are none of your concern. As I've said before, you are the descendant of Mary Magdalene. Your blood can heal us. Once I re-carve my mark with your fresh blood during the red moon, my family will be able to walk in the daylight. The mark will be gone, and I've waited so long for that to happen."

"I can't stay that long. Please, let my dad go so he can help my mom, then I promise to stay," I begged.

"It doesn't matter, Jaclyn." His eyes became darker. "You'll all be dead anyway. I'm going to make you my wife, and together we'll rule the world. Mary turned me down, but I can guarantee you won't."

Before I could say anything, he was out of my room. No way in hell was he going to use me. Now was a good time to plan my escape and find my dad—*but how?* I opened the curtains to see if I could break the window, but to my surprise, there was none.

I ran to the door, even though I knew it was locked, and knowing I wouldn't be able to break it down. Giving up on the door, I looked for a way out, hoping there was a secret passageway, but it wasn't likely that I'd be able to find one. After all, what good was a secret passageway if it was easy to detect? Just when I was about to give up, the sound of the doorknob turning had me on alert. Cain was coming back for me.

To my surprise, a handsome stranger entered in a hurry and closed the door. Geared up like he was in a battle, his eyes raked over me from head to toe. It looked as though he was enjoying the view. For a moment, we were stuck, staring at each other.

"Jaclyn, let's go," he ordered. "I know you like what you see, but I need you to snap out of your lustful stare and follow me."

He had not just said that to me! I narrowed my eyes at him in anger. "Who the hell are you?"

His eyebrows furrowed and he looked at me like I was an idiot. "I'm offering to help you escape, and the first thing you ask is who I am? Don't you recognize me? It's me, Jack," he said it as if I should have known.

My mind reeled to the past as I recalled Jack being tall, skinny, and arrogant. I could see that image clearly in my mind. However, after he'd said his name, I knew it was him for sure. But this Jack was muscular, a bit taller, good looking, yummier—I couldn't believe I just thought that—but definitely still arrogant. It wasn't my fault that he looked different. I could already tell we were going to bump heads.

"Jack?" I crossed my arms and gaped at him. "Well, well, well . . . looks like you finally grew a dick."

Surprisingly, his lips curled into a hint of a smile he tried to hide. "You mean it got even bigger."

I raised my eyebrows in disbelief. "You wish." Then I changed the subject. "How did you find me? How did you know I was here?" I was beyond happy to see him with an overwhelming gratitude, but he needed to get rid of that cockiness.

"Edmond told me to help you. But right now, we need to get out of here."

"Edmond?" I repeated as Jack used a key to open the door then led me out of the room.

"How do you know him?"

"I'll tell you later," he answered, and handed me a sword. "Just in case."

I snapped out of my stupor and realized our nightmare had just begun. Keeping our steps as quiet as we could, we ran down the long hallway and exited through a door.

"Wait." I yanked my arm away from his grasp. "My dad is here. We need to find him." I also wanted to find my weapons, especial the shiny dagger, but I knew we didn't have time.

"We need to get you out of here first. What good is it if we get caught? We'll come back and save him, I promise."

As much as I wanted to find my dad, I knew he was right. We went down a dimly lit winding staircase that seemed endless, making me dizzy. It was difficult to walk in this puffy dress, but since our lives were at stake, I found a way to make do.

As if Jack knew how I was feeling he said, "We're almost there."

The harsh wind would have knocked me down, had Jack not saved me. It felt so strange to be in his strong arms. We were out of the castle, but we still had to climb down to the base of the mountain. I didn't know how long I had been knocked out in bed, but seeing the sunrise, I could estimate.

"Here," Jack said, pointing to the beanstalk that had saved me earlier. "Go first. We have to hurry." After he had tied a rope around my waist, he did his. "Place your hands on the stalk as if you were climbing down a pole. Don't think about it too much. Just fall."

After I anchored myself, I nodded. The next thing I knew, I was pushed. I couldn't believe he had done that. I screamed with all the air in my lungs. That asshole tricked me. Obviously, he thought I couldn't do it. My stomach dropped as I fell faster, and I felt the impact of the leaf stem that slapped me on the way down.

Jack managed to lessen the pull of gravity, so by the time I landed on the ground, the fall was bearable. But I still fell flat on my ass. That freakin' hurt. It got awkward when Jack fell on top of me. We were face-to-face, staring into each other's eyes as time stood still . . . until it looked like he was going to kiss me. No way was I going to allow him to make a move on me, so I shoved him off.

"What the hell was that for?" he gasped.

I was thinking how he pushed me off the cliff and all the times he made fun of me when we were young. Yeah…I was holding a grudge when I should have been more thankful. "You could have warned me," I snapped, standing up.

Jack shrugged his shoulders. "I don't know what you're talking about."

Frowning, I said, "I need to get my horse and wagon." Before I could take a step in the direction I had hid them, Jack gripped my arm.

"They're not there. Edmond has them."

"What? Did he follow me?" I was fuming mad. "How the hell are we supposed to get home?"

"With my horse." Jack pointed to the direction of a nearby tree, and then took out his sword that was strapped to his back. I couldn't see a horse from where I stood, but assumed he wasn't lying about it. "Edmond was worried about you. He told me to help you."

"Who *exactly* is he?"

"He's one of the original members of the group called Monstra Slayers," Jack stated as he started hacking at the beanstalk with his sword. "He's retired now, but he's full of knowledge."

"How do you know him?"

"I'm one of them. There are many of us. We're a secret organization."

"You're one of them?" I gasped. "I'm pretty sure my dad is part of the group, too."

"There are many of us. I didn't know he was."

Then it suddenly hit me that he was trying to chop down the beanstalk. "What are you doing?" I asked in a state of panic. "You promised we would go back and save my dad."

Jack stopped mid-swing and looked at me. "Sweetheart. We've got to chop this down or his slaves will climb down during the night and invade the town."

I rolled my eyes. "They're monsters. Can't they just fly or jump down?"

"No. They can't, but Cain can. They would have to climb down the mountain so chopping this beanstalk buys us time if they decide to pay us a visit. By the time they could make it down the mountain and to our town, it would be daylight. So, sweetheart, step aside and let me do my job."

"Fine. But don't call me sweetheart," I said, moving behind him.

Jack whacked at the stalk in a way one would use an axe to chop down a tree. He looked sexy as hell doing it too, but I would never let him know that. Something about the way his muscles flexed and the way sweat beaded on his forehead and dripped down his face was deliciously alluring. I would have never imagined the strength he possessed, as I watched him use all his might. I was enjoying the view but was getting antsy and needed to get to my mom.

"Hurry up, Jack. Can't you chop any faster?"

He stopped and raised a brow. "I'm doing the best I can. What's so urgent? 'Cause I know it's not about the monsters. The sun is already starting to rise."

"My mom is sick. I need to buy her medication," I explained.

"Don't worry. Edmond is with her now. He was able to bribe a local doctor to see your mom. By the time you return home, she'll be good as new."

Tears pooled in my eyes. Edmond was wonderful. I'd told him that my mom was sick and he made an effort to help me out. I needed to thank him for being such a caring being. Jack went back to what he was doing so I started to whack the beanstalk next to him with my sword.

"What are you doing?" He stopped.

I rolled my eyes. "I'm making bean soup. What does it look like I'm doing? Maybe with my help we can actually chop it down before the sun sets again."

Jack chuckled. "Sweetheart, you'll just get in my way. Step aside."

"Hell, no," I said, and used all my strength to give it a good whack.

We both worked silently toward one goal, and a few hours later, it was nearly done. The stalk teetered and swayed, almost ready to fall.

"Watch out!" Jack warned, yanking me toward him.

When the stalk hit the earth, I felt the power of its entity. My body leapt off the ground even with Jack holding me. Our bodies separated. That is when I saw his black horse. It was absolutely stunning.

"What's his name?" I asked, caressing the side of his face.

"Devil," he said, hopping on, and then gave me his hand to help me up.

"Hmm...interesting," I commented, wondering how he got his name. Instead of wrapping my arms around his waist to secure myself, I took a fistful of his shirt.

"It's okay to put your arms around me. I won't bite," Jack said against the wind as we rode fast into the open land.

The vision of Jack chopping down the stalk came to mind. He was sexy as hell. Brushing off the thought I said, "Oh, I'm not afraid of you, Jack. You're sweaty and you stink." His chest vibrated from the rhythm of his chuckle. His laugh was contagious as we rode for miles and miles on end.

The sun had set long before we pulled into a small town, and not only was my stomach grumbling, but my throat felt like it was on fire. Being that it was late into the night, not a soul was present. Some houses had a candle lit in the window, but other than that, it was pretty dark. After we got off Devil, Jack tied him up, and then we entered a small pub.

It looked like they were about to close. Jack and I were the only customers.

"Good evening, folks," a man greeted us from behind the bar. "I'm getting ready to close, but it looks like both of you need a drink. Have a seat at the bar. What will it be?"

Jack sat on the stool next to mine. "Whisky for me and a glass of water for her."

I raised my brows in discontent. "No. Whisky for me too."

"Have you ever had one before?" Jack asked.

"Many times." I bit my bottom lip and lied as I watched the barkeeper pour our drinks and slide them in front of us. After what I'd been through, I needed something strong.

Jack lifted his mug toward me. "Cheers, for making it out alive— until next time."

I clanked my glass against his. "Thanks for coming after me."

"You can thank Edmond for letting me know you were up there alone." He twitched his brows. "Also, I can think of a few things you can do to thank me." I wasn't sure what he meant by that until he said, "They have spare rooms upstairs."

"In your dreams, jackass," I spat and took a gulp of the whisky. *Holy shit, that burned.* Turning away from him so he couldn't see my expression, I waited for the sensation to go away. Hearing Jack chuckle, my face turned red from embarrassment.

"Would you like more?" Jack asked, trying not to laugh.

I got off the stool and narrowed my eyes at him. "No. I've had enough. I would like to leave now." Reaching into my pocket, I pulled out a gold coin and placed it in front of the barkeeper. "This is for you. Thank you for serving us."

"Where did you get that?" Jack and the barkeeper practically yelled at me in accord.

Astounded by their reaction, I remained silent.

Jack's eyes grew heated and fierce. "You took them? How could you?"

"I-I—it's for my mom." It was hard to get the words out when they were staring at me like I had committed a horrible crime. "There were so many. What's the big deal if they miss three...or five?" I shrugged my shoulders.

"Howww many?" Jack asked slowly, looking pissed and worried.

"Enough?" I said softly.

The barkeeper slid it back to me, unable to look my way. "That gold coin is like a beacon. They follow the coin. My life is not worth one gold coin. They will come for you." His tone was calm, yet full of warning.

According to Cain, the fact that I had Mary's blood meant he was coming for me anyway, so it didn't matter. I was going to rescue my dad. "Then let them come."

The barkeeper gripped my hand. "Let them come?" he seethed. His eyes were filled with anger. "Do you know what they will do to us? How dare you even suggest that? Who do you think you are?"

I yanked my hand back. Who did he think he was, talking to me like that? "I'm Jaclyn the vampire slayer," I said with conviction. I had no idea what possessed me to say that, besides, I wasn't a part of Monstra Slayer like Jack. "And my friend," I pointed to Jack, "he's—" It wasn't a laughing matter, but I couldn't help myself. Snorting and recalling how hot he looked chopping down the stalk, I said, "You can call him—Jack and the beanstalk."

They said these monsters that lived in the mountains had teeth like sharks and eyes as red as blood. They said these monsters drank blood and feasted on the flesh of humans. They said the story was just a tale to keep the young ones from getting into trouble at night, but they were wrong. These monsters were real. I'd seen them. I'd killed them. Now, they were coming for me. I say, let them come. I'll be waiting!

The End

International Bestselling, award winning, Author Mary Ting/M. Clarke resides in Southern California with her husband and two children. She enjoys oil painting and making jewelry. Writing her first novel, Crossroads Saga, happened by chance. It was a way to grieve the death of her beloved grandmother, and inspired by a dream she once had as a young girl. When she started reading new adult novels, she fell in love with the genre. It was the reason she had to write one-Something Great. Why the pen name, M Clarke? She tours with Magic Johnson Foundation to promote literacy and her children's chapter book-No Bullies Allowed. To find out more, visit: http://www.m-clarke.com